PENGUIN BOOKS

THE FURTHER ADVENTURES OF
SHERLOCK HOLMES

Richard Lancelyn Green is the son of the writer Roger Lancelyn Green. He has edited the 1901 burlesque of William Gillette's play, *Sheerluck Jones*, and Penguin's *The Uncollected Sherlock Holmes* and *Letters to Sherlock Holmes*. He and J. M. Gibson are the authors of the Soho Series Bibliography of Sir Arthur Conan Doyle and they have also edited three volumes of his lesser-known work: *Essays on Photography*, *Uncollected Stories* and *Letters to the Press*.

THE FURTHER ADVENTURES OF SHERLOCK HOLMES

AFTER SIR ARTHUR CONAN DOYLE

COLLECTED AND INTRODUCED BY
RICHARD LANCELYN GREEN

PENGUIN BOOKS

PENGUIN BOOKS

Published by the Penguin Group
Penguin Books Ltd, 80 Strand, London WC2R 0RL, England
Penguin Putnam Inc., 375 Hudson Street, New York, New York 10014, USA
Penguin Books Australia Ltd, 250 Camberwell Road, Camberwell, Victoria 3124, Australia
Penguin Books Canada Ltd, 10 Alcorn Avenue, Toronto, Ontario, Canada M4V 3B2
Penguin Books India (P) Ltd, 11 Community Centre, Panchsheel Park, New Delhi – 110 017, India
Penguin Books (NZ) Ltd, Cnr Rosedale and Airborne Roads, Albany, Auckland, New Zealand
Penguin Books (South Africa) (Pty) Ltd, 24 Sturdee Avenue, Rosebank 2196, South Africa

Penguin Books Ltd, Registered Offices: 80 Strand, London WC2R 0RL, England

www.penguin.com

This selection first published by Penguin Books 1985
17

Selection and Introduction copyright © Richard Lancelyn Green, 1985
All rights reserved

The Acknowledgements on Pages 7 and 8 constitute an extension of this copyright page

Printed in England by Clays Ltd, St Ives plc
Filmset in 10/12 pt Monophoto Bembo

CONTENTS

6   *Contents*

ACKNOWLEDGEMENTS

'The Adventure of the First-Class Carriage' (*Strand Magazine*, February 1947) copyright 1947 by Ronald A. Knox.

'The Adventure of the Sheffield Banker' (written 1911) published as 'The Case of the Man who was Wanted' (*Cosmopolitan*, August 1948); copyright 1948 by Arthur Whitaker.

'The Adventure of the Unique *Hamlet*' (privately printed, 1920) copyright 1920 by Vincent Starrett.

'The Adventure of the Marked Man' (*Ellery Queen's Mystery Magazine*, July 1944) copyright 1944 by Stuart Palmer, renewed 1972.

'The Adventure of the Megatherium Thefts' privately printed as 'The Strange Case of the Megatherium Thefts', 1945; copyright 1945 by S. C. Roberts.

'The Adventure of the Trained Cormorant' published as 'Holmes in Scotland' (*Blackwood's Magazine*, September 1953); copyright 1953 by W. R. Duncan Macmillan.

'The Adventure of Arnsworth Castle' published as 'The Adventure of the Red Widow' (in *The Exploits of Sherlock Holmes*, 1954); copyright 1954 by Adrian Conan Doyle.

'The Adventure of the Tired Captain' (*Sherlock Holmes Journal*, Winter 1958, Spring 1959) copyright © Alan Wilson, 1958, 1959.

'The Adventure of the Green Empress' published as 'The Adventure of the Second Stain' (Johannesburg *Sunday Times*, 3 December 1967; copyright © F. P. Cillié, 1967.

'The Adventure of the Purple Hand' (privately printed, 1982) copyright © D. O. Smith, 1982.

'The Adventure of Hillerman Hall' published as 'How a Hermit was Disturbed in His Retirement' (in *The Great Detectives*, 1981); copyright © Julian Symons, 1981.

The editor wishes to thank the following authors, executors, agents, and publishers for permission to include the stories in this book: Denis O. Smith, Julian Symons, Alan Wilson; the Earl of Oxford and Asquith; Messrs A. P. Watt & Son; Rayne Rowe; Michael Murphy (Literary Executor, Vincent Starrett); the Scott Meredith Literary Agency, Inc.; the Oxford University Press; and John Murray.

Thanks are also due to W. R. Duncan Macmillan and F. P. Cillié; to Blackwood Pillans and Wilson (publishers of *Blackwood's Magazine*) the proprietors of the Johannesburg *Sunday Times*, the editors of the *Sherlock Holmes Journal*, and last but not least to Marvin P. Epstein of New Jersey to whom this book is dedicated.

At the time of their original publication, the authors of the stories collected here gratefully acknowledged their debt to Sir Arthur Conan Doyle and his estate for the inspiration and for permission to use characters and settings created by him. On their behalf and on his own the editor wishes to do likewise.

INTRODUCTION

The *Strand Magazine* for December 1893 revealed that Sherlock Holmes and Professor Moriarty had perished at the Reichenbach Falls. That at least was the belief of Dr Watson and of his creator. 'Holmes died in the Xmas number,' said Conan Doyle, 'so there's an end to his adventures.' He had failed to see how potent was the spirit he had conjured up or how indestructible was the myth to which he had given birth. The public would not accept the demise of such a popular character and many people were anxious to see the vacuum filled.

'Suppose someone imagining himself to be "on the same intellectual plane" as Mr Conan Doyle should drag Sherlock Holmes to life again. What would be Mr Doyle's remedy?' asked the *St James's Gazette*, pointing to stories which used characters created by Dickens, to Walter Besant's sequel to Ibsen, *The Doll's House and After*, and to the sham *Don Quixote* by Avellaneda. The truth was that there was no remedy, for Holmes had already assumed an independent existence.

Few authors could resist the temptation of writing a Sherlock Holmes parody, or of interviewing him, or of composing memorial verses in his honour. They haunted the Reichenbach Falls in their attempt to resuscitate the great detective or they summoned up his ghost. They welcomed him into their books and they called him by other names. Sherlock Holmes was popular wherever he went. New stories were already appearing in Germany, Spain, and Russia which bore his name; he was soon pitting his wits against France's foremost gentleman-cambrioleur; and, as his brother Mycroft said, he was to be heard of everywhere.

Scholars began to unravel the confused chronology and to search for answers to some of the biographical problems. It seemed that readers would never be content, for they could not know enough about Sherlock Holmes. Doyle's hand was forced and forced again, and he would go down to the vaults of Cox and Co., at Charing Cross, to retrieve further stories, but still the public wished for more. And so it was that experts of the highest calibre one of whom according to Doyle knew more about the subject than he did himself, took up the pen for Dr Watson and helped him to chronicle a number of the previously unrecorded cases.

THE ADVENTURE OF
THE FIRST-CLASS CARRIAGE

Ronald Knox is one of the most learned authorities on Sherlock Holmes and the person who first showed how the methods of 'Higher Criticism' and classical scholarship might be applied to the stories. He was born in 1888, the youngest son of an Anglican bishop, and he died in 1957 having been for forty years a convert to the Catholic faith. Like his brother, E. V. Knox, he became an early and ardent admirer of Sherlock Holmes through reading the stories in the *Strand Magazine*. It was one of the few secular periodicals allowed in the Knox household and the first to which the children had access. 'Quotations from the epistles of Dr Watson,' his brother said later, 'were considered proper by myself and my brothers on all suitable and unsuitable occasions.'

A family magazine provided them with the opportunity to write an essay on the inconsistencies found in the stories and this in turn served as the basis for the famous paper, 'Studies in the Literature of Sherlock Holmes', which Ronald read to the Gryphon Club in Oxford in 1911. Both essays were sent to

Conan Doyle, who, if he failed to give his opinion of the first, at least found much to amuse him in the second. He read it in the Oxford *Blue Book* where it was first published in July 1912. It then became one of Ronald Knox's most popular talks and gained widespread acclaim in 1928 when it was included in his *Essays in Satire*.

Knox's other Sherlockian writings include his first book, *Juxta Salices* of 1910, in which Holmes forms a member of the symposium, and *Memories of the Future* of 1923, where Lady Opal describes the great statue of the detective in Baker Street; there were also reviews, leading articles, letters to the Press, and an essay on 'Mycroft and Moriarty' in H. W. Bell's 1934 anthology, *Baker Street Studies*. Knox was a close friend of G. K. Chesterton and a member of the Detection Club. He edited *The Best Detective Stories of the Year 1928*, giving in the introduction his famous decalogue or list of rules to be adhered to by mystery writers, and he was the author of six detective novels, most of which it must be said feature the rather characterless and unmemorable amateur sleuth, Miles Bredon.

For a time Knox became disenchanted with the Sherlockian world. 'I can't *bear* books about Sherlock Holmes,' he told an editor who had asked him to review one. 'It is so depressing that my one permanent achievement is to have started a bad joke. If I did start it.' But his old enthusiasm was revived after the war and it was then that he agreed to write 'The Adventure of the First-Class Carriage' for the *Strand Magazine*.

Many people felt that Sherlock Holmes was the only person who could restore the magazine's flagging fortunes. The editors were finding it more and more difficult to compete with the newer and brasher pocket magazines which their own by then resembled. Richard Usborne, in a review of *The Annotated Sherlock Holmes* in 1967, explained what the problems were. He said that he was sorry that the compiler had not included any of the articles which E. V. Knox had written for *Punch*:

I'd also like to have seen again that complete Holmes story that we got Ronald Knox to write for the dying (dear old) *Strand* in 1947, 'The Adventure of the First-Class Carriage'. I say 'we', I was assistant to Macdonald Hastings, who edited the *Strand* in its last three years. We were ourselves as hag-ridden by the Holmes legend in those days as the magazine's readers (not very many) appeared to be. The *Strand* had meant Holmes to us as boys, and the Holmes/Paget face scowled in at the window as we wondered how to make the pocket-size (paper shortage) *Strand* profitable again. Half the time we wanted to kill its crippling name and start on a new formula, with nudes and shorties to rival the money-making *Lilliput* and *Men Only*. The other half of the time we wanted to recall Doyle, Kipling, Jacobs, and Wodehouse and go back complete to gaslight, assegais, and hansom cabs. When the *Strand* finally folded in 1950, my old sixth-form master wrote to me regretfully: 'I loved the dear old *Strand*. To tell you the truth, I have not opened a copy of it in this century.' Perhaps he was the typical reader we were up against.

Knox's story appeared in the February 1947 issue and an attempt was made to re-create the original atmosphere. 'Do you remember this?' asked the editorial over a photograph of the opening page of 'The Adventure of Shoscombe Old Place': 'It was the last of the Sherlock Holmes stories, published in the *Strand Magazine* in 1927. In this issue, Monsignor Ronald Knox, faithfully imitating the style of the great master, recalls Holmes and Watson to the pages of the *Strand* again. To the immortal memory of Sir Arthur Conan Doyle, we offer the first Apocryphal Adventure of Sherlock Holmes.' A *Strand Magazine* heading by Garth Jones (the artist who designed the covers for *The Hound of the Baskervilles*), dating from before the First World War, and illustrations by Tom Purvis, 'In loving memory of Sidney Paget', completed the effect. It bore as a main title, 'The Apocryphal Sherlock Holmes', and was intended to be the first of a series, but in the event it was the only one published.

The story is original and is not one of those mentioned by Dr Watson, but it is firmly in the tradition and has many touches which are highly evocative and convincing. Even if it is not based on actual fact the case of the disappearance of Mr Nathaniel Swithinbank would easily pass as the work of the deutero-Watson who, according to Knox's earlier thesis, had himself written pastiches after the demise of his friend.

Spurious Dr Watsons have been the curse of scholars ever since the real one first put pen to paper. Two in particular have had undue attention paid to their work as it was discovered among Conan Doyle's own papers. One is the plot outline for a story involving the use of stilts, and the other is a complete story.

THE ADVENTURE OF
THE SHEFFIELD BANKER

The 'Star Man's Diary' of 13 June 1942 announced a 'Sherlock Holmes "Find"'. It was nothing less than the 'manuscript of an unpublished adventure of the greatest of all fiction detectives', and news of its discovery had been given by 'the author's son', Adrian Conan Doyle, who had come across it when going through his father's papers in search of material for a biography being written by Hesketh Pearson. 'Unfortunately,' the Diary continued, 'our inevitable curiosity is not to be satisfied; there is no likelihood of the story being published.' No reason was given, but the writer of the piece was left in no doubt that it was indeed in Doyle's own handwriting. 'Every line of my father's stories, from the earliest days, was in his own neat writing,' Adrian told him, and then, quoting a remark first made in 1914 by a proof-reader of the *Strand Magazine*, he added: 'It was so meticulously clear that the publishers always referred to him as the "Printer's Friend".'

Word of the discovery soon reached America and William King, the London representative of the Associated Press, was asked to find out more about it. In his dispatch, dated 12 September 1942, he reported that the story had been in a chest with other family documents and that the envelope containing it had a note by Doyle's widow which explained that her

husband had refrained from publishing it because he felt it was
not up to his usual standard. Both Adrian Conan Doyle and
Hesketh Pearson agreed that the standard was lower than usual,
but neither appeared to doubt its authenticity; indeed, rather the
reverse, for King ended by saying: 'The story was written
several years before Sir Arthur died, but the state of the paper
would indicate, his son said, that it was not among the last of
his Sherlock Holmes stories. It is in the same neat handwriting
which characterized all his manuscripts.'

No one was more eager for the work to be published than
Edgar W. Smith of the Baker Street Irregulars. He said in a letter
to the *Saturday Review of Literature* on 10 October 1942 that its
discovery was of 'cosmic importance', and no matter how
inferior the story was, no argument designed to justify its
suppression would have any validity. 'The world is too eager,
too insistent, for *more* – no matter *what* – of Sherlock Holmes!'

The first opportunity for the public to judge for themselves
came in August 1943 when the *Strand Magazine* published the
chapter from Pearson's biography containing extracts from it.
But the full story was still withheld. An offer of $20,000 from
an American magazine was declined, and Adrian Conan Doyle
also refused to cable the story to the president of the Baker Street
Irregulars so that it might be read out at the annual dinner after
the guests had been sworn to secrecy.

Nothing more was heard of it until 1947 when a further batch
of Conan Doyle manuscripts came to light in a bank vault at
Crowborough, including the essay called 'Some Personalia
about Mr Sherlock Holmes' which was written in 1917. This
came to the attention of the editor of Hearst's *Cosmopolitan* and
he asked if he might publish it, but as it had already been
published in the *Strand Magazine* and in Doyle's autobiography,
he was offered instead 'The Man who was Wanted' and gladly
accepted it. He was under the impression that it had also been
found in the bank vault and that it was in manuscript form.
'Found!' said the cover of the August 1948 issue, 'The Last
Adventure of Sherlock Holmes. A hitherto unpublished story

by Sir Arthur Conan Doyle.' It was, as those who had seen it had warned, somewhat below the usual standard. 'We are aware,' the editor admitted, 'that there are several inconsistencies in this story. We have not tried to correct them. The story is published as it was found except for minor changes in spelling and punctuation.'

In England, the story was offered to the *Strand Magazine* but the editors turned it down as they could not afford the fee, and it was still available when the editor of the *Sunday Dispatch* contacted Denis Conan Doyle on 12 August 1948. Negotiations dragged on until December when a price of £250 was agreed, and the new literary agents, Pearn, Pollinger, and Higham, who had replaced A. P. Watt & Son, then arranged very advantageous terms for the sale of foreign rights. The first part of the story appeared in the paper on 2 January and the rest followed on 9 and 16 January. Once again there was a warning about the inconsistencies and, to forestall further criticism, the editor added a statement by Denis Conan Doyle which said: 'My father apparently withheld publication of "The Case of the Man who was Wanted" because he did not consider it to be up to his usual standard. His family took the same view and for that reason have withheld publication until now, but public interest in this story has been so great that we have finally yielded to pressure and decided to allow it to be published in the *Sunday Dispatch*.'

When news of the story was first given, many people urged that it should be published and, in the words of Edgar Smith, called for 'the immediate subsumption of this new Revelation into the full canon of the Sacred Writings'; but when this was done they were less kind. 'Some notable Sherlockians are pretty severe,' Vincent Starrett admitted in his 'Books Alive' column in the *Chicago Tribune* on 19 September 1948:

Joseph Henry Jackson thinks the story 'falls flat on its face'. Russell McLauchlin inclines to the belief that it was written, a few years ago, by Adrian Conan Doyle, son of that Sir Arthur who was, as we all know, Dr Watson's literary agent. H. B. Williams thinks the two Doyle

boys, Adrian and Denis, may have found the tale in fragmentary form
among their father's papers, and have completed it as best they could.
Jeremiah Buckley declares the work to be a forgery and its perpetrator
an American. Prof. Finlay Christ also hints at forgery, and so the game
goes on.

In fact, as Starrett was soon to learn, it was not by Conan
Doyle and nor was it a forgery. The true author was Arthur
Whitaker. He was born in 1882 and married in 1909, and was
an architect by profession. Shortly after his marriage, he found
that he had time on his hands and, having always been a great
admirer of Sherlock Holmes, he worked out some half-dozen
plots. One of these, the story in question, he wrote out in full
and sent to Conan Doyle suggesting that they might collab-
orate. Doyle replied on 7 March 1911, saying:

Dear Sir,

I read your story. It is not bad and I don't see why you should not
change the names, and try to get it published yourself. Of course you
could not use the names of my characters.

It is impossible for me to join with another in any case for the result
would be that my price would at once be pushed down 75 per cent by
Editors.

Sometimes I am open to purchase ideas which I lay aside and use at
my own time in my own way. I did this once before and gave 10
guineas for the idea, working it on my own lines. If you wished I would
do this for you, but I could not guarantee to use it, and you could get
no personal credit from it. On the whole you would be wiser to use
it yourself.

Yours faithfully,

Arthur Conan Doyle

Whitaker decided he would accept the offer and a cheque for
ten guineas was sent to him on 14 March 1911. Then, inspired
with new literary enthusiasm, he wrote four or five of the other
stories, one of which, 'The Missing Bales', featuring a private
detective called Harold Quest, was published in *Novel Magazine*
in April 1913. But the remainder were set to one side. Through-

out his life his abiding interest was natural history. Before writing the Holmes story he had had an article on bats published in the *Naturalist*, and others were to follow, while his collection grew to be one of the finest in the country (the bird notes and diaries are now divided between the Edward Grey Institute in Oxford and the British Trust for Ornithology in Tring, while the birds' eggs, butterflies, and moths went to the Sheffield City Museum). His interest in ornithology tended to take precedence over his work as an architect, but he did design at least one cinema and a number of town houses in his home town of Sheffield. His name was also occasionally to be seen in the correspondence columns of the local papers where he would often write in verse – as he did on his hand-drawn Christmas cards and in letters to his friends.

Whitaker retained a carbon copy of the story, and this was read by his brother and sister (to whom he gave the Doyle letter), and by other friends (including one to whom he gave the inscribed visiting-card from Doyle which had accompanied the cheque), but he had almost forgotten about it when in September 1945 he chanced to read Hesketh Pearson's biography and came across the incorrect attribution. On 24 September 1945, he wrote to Pearson, pointing out that he was the author. 'My pride,' he said, 'is not unduly hurt by your remark that "The Man who was Wanted" is certainly not up to scratch for the sting is much mitigated by your going on to remark that it carries the authentic trade-mark! This, I feel, is a great compliment to my one and only effort at plagiarism.'

Pearson acknowledged the letter on 26 September, saying that the opening of the story was certainly good enough for him to have claimed it as authentic and suggesting that he would add a note to all future editions, to read as follows:

Two years after the publication of this book I heard from Mr Arthur Whitaker of Sheffield that he had written the unpublished story entitled 'The Man who was Wanted' about thirty-five years before. He had sent it to Doyle suggesting a collaboration. Doyle replied that the story should be rewritten, but added that he was prepared to give

£10.10 for it, as he was open to purchase ideas for plots to be used how, when and if he liked. Mr Whitaker accepted the offer, and Doyle filed the story among his papers. Owing to its characteristic opening, I believed it to be his own, and there was nothing in writing to suggest that it was not.

Although a new edition did appear in 1946, under the Guild Books imprint, it did not contain the note as the proofs were not sent to the author in time.

On 31 October 1948, Pearson again wrote to Whitaker, having just received press-cuttings from America which made it clear that the story had been published under Doyle's name. He was thinking of writing an article about it, but by December, after he had contacted Vincent Starrett and received a copy of the *Cosmopolitan*, he decided that he would do nothing further, mainly because of the animosity previously shown towards him by Doyle's sons. 'Whatever I do or say in the matter of this story,' he explained, 'they will probably regard as malicious, which is the reason I have decided to keep out of the business as far as possible, let Starrett have the main facts, and leave the matter entirely in his hands.' He and Whitaker each wrote to Starrett but, with the publication of the story in the *Sunday Dispatch*, Whitaker felt that he should in all fairness disclose the truth to Denis Conan Doyle without further delay. This he did on 12 January 1949. The letter was then forwarded to Adrian Conan Doyle in Tangier. He replied on 21 January and angrily demanded evidence of Whitaker's authorship. 'Unless such proof is forthcoming to satisfy our lawyers, we give you fair warning that we will at once bring action for damages in the event that any person casts any aspersion, without solid proof, against our MS.'

Whitaker was astonished at the tone of the letter and pointed out that he had the original carbon copy and could produce a score of witnesses who had seen and read the story long before Doyle's death. But the matter was already in the hands of Vertue, Son & Churcher, the solicitors for the Conan Doyle estate. Whitaker therefore turned to his own solicitors, Lapage

Norris Sons and Saleby. On 3 February 1949 he was able to produce the original letter from Conan Doyle, and on 15 February the affair was brought to a satisfactory conclusion. The Doyles acknowledged that the story was indeed by Arthur Whitaker and, though he expected no remuneration, they agreed to pay him part of the proceeds (£150 in all, of which £21 went on legal expenses). The press had meanwhile been kept at a distance, but once the matter was resolved, the *Sunday Dispatch* carried an article by John Bingham setting the record straight and explaining how the confusion had arisen. Whitaker had little time to savour his new-found fame, as he died suddenly on 10 July 1949.

The curious history entitles the story to a place in this collection and, though it was criticized at the time when thought to be Conan Doyle's own because of the disconcerting double time-scale, erratic dating, and impossible references to Mary Morstan (who was dead by 1895), it is nevertheless of a high standard, and, as it deceived Doyle's widow, his sons, and two biographers, both Hesketh Pearson and John Dickson Carr, it will always have a very special place in the Sherlock Holmes apocrypha.

THE ADVENTURE OF
THE UNIQUE *HAMLET*

Vincent Starrett, who, as has been seen, was one of the first to learn the truth about Arthur Whitaker, and who had also been one of the first in America to mention the story of 'The Man who was Wanted', as he had done so in the *Chicago Tribune* on 12 September 1942, was born in Toronto in 1886 and began his 'career of Conan Doyle idolatry' when he was ten years old. In 1918 he wrote his first article, 'In Praise of Sherlock Holmes', for *Reedy's Mirror*; it was a 'paean of gratitude' following the publication of *His Last Bow*, and a copy was sent to Conan Doyle. It was to be the inspiration for a series of articles which were collected in 1933 as *The Private Life of Sherlock Holmes*. But

before then he had made his second contribution to the 'literature of the legend'. This was 'The Adventure of the Unique
Hamlet', which was written in 1920 and privately printed by
Walter Hill for distribution at Christmas among their friends
(one of whom was Conan Doyle). It is described as a 'hitherto
unchronicled adventure of Mr Sherlock Holmes', but the author
also hoped that it would be read as a 'genial satire on book
collecting and Shakespearean commentators'.

Starrett was a man of many parts, a noted critic, essayist,
journalist, anthologist, poet, biographer, and book collector,
but he will be best remembered as a 'Sherlockophile'. In 1934
he was a founding member of the Baker Street Irregulars; in
1940 he edited an anthology of Sherlockiana (which included
his pastiche); and thereafter he produced a stream of poems,
articles, and introductions. 'The fact is,' he admitted later, 'I can
scarcely write a paragraph on any subject now, without bringing Holmes into the argument.' Under Conan Doyle's influence
he wrote a fictional account of the Oscar Slater case, *Too Many
Sleuths*, and his detective novels were indebted to Sherlock
Holmes. One of them, *The Casebook of Jimmie Lavender*, was
actually dedicated to 'Dr John H. Watson, formerly of Baker
Street, London, who wrote the original prescription'. Although
not a great crime writer, Starrett had by the time of his death
in 1974 established himself as one of America's greatest book-
men and the doyen of the Sherlockians.

As well as appearing in his own anthology, *221B*, 'The
Adventure of the Unique *Hamlet*' was also included in Ellery
Queen's *Misadventures of Sherlock Holmes* of 1944, and in the
revised edition of *The Private Life of Sherlock Holmes* published
in 1960. It was Starrett's only pastiche, though he once said that
he might do something similar by creating a 'synthetic' story.
He explained his reason for wanting to do so in a letter to Ellery
Queen:

I've always wanted to do a synthetic Sherlock – the beginning of one
story, the middle of another, and the conclusion of a third; or perhaps
six or eight of the adventures merged into a perfect Holmes tale. I may

yet do it. The reason would be to produce a Holmes adventure that I could completely admire, and which would contain everything I like – the opening at the breakfast table, with a page or two of deduction; the appearance of Mrs Hudson, followed instantly by the troubled client, who would fall over the threshold in a faint; the hansom in the fog, and so on. I think it could be done. I find when I think of the Holmes stories that almost instinctively I think of just such a yarn, wonder which one it is, then realize it's a cento existing only in my mind.

Two other writers of Sherlockian pastiche may be mentioned in connection with Starrett; they are Harry Bedford-Jones and August Derleth.

Shortly after the publication of *The Private Life of Sherlock Holmes*, Starrett learnt from Dr Logan Clendenning that a series of unpublished Sherlock Holmes stories had come to light; they had been sent to Alexander Woollcott by a Mr H. E. Twinells, of Palm Springs, with an ingenious explanation of how they came to be in his custody. Starrett was greatly intrigued and soon Clendenning obtained copies for him. 'Although obviously pastiches,' Starrett said later, 'the tales were extremely clever. I knew at once, however, that they were not by Conan Doyle and shortly, by a series of deductions, worthy of the master himself, I was certain that they *were* by my old friend Bedford-Jones.' As with Hosmer Angel, Mr Twinells was betrayed by his typewriter and paper for they were identical to those used by Bedford-Jones.

There were at least three of these stories, each based on a title given by Dr Watson. One concerned the Atkinson brothers of Trinconmalee; another dealt with the fate of the barque, *Matilda Briggs*; and a third contained an account of the case of the Aluminium Crutch. The last was published as a Sherlock Holmes pastiche in the *Palm Springs News* in January and February 1936 (and later in the *Baker Street Journal*), but the other two had the names changed and were made into ordinary detective stories.

The pastiches by August Derleth were on a more ambitious

scale and eventually developed into a parallel saga, complete
with its own Higher Criticism and a Society. Derleth was born
in Sauk City, Wisconsin, in 1909 and became one of America's
most prolific writers, as well as being an editor and publisher
of note. He died in 1971 with over a hundred and thirty books
to his name.

He became fond of Sherlock Holmes when he was a boy, and
his first pastiche was written in the autumn of 1928 when he was
in his junior year at the University of Wisconsin. His intention
was to produce a new series of Sherlock Holmes stories. Their
form, he said later, was not to be the 'ridiculing imitation
designed for laughter', but the 'fond and admiring one less
widely known as pastiche'. Doyle, however, refused to allow
him to use the names of Sherlock Holmes and Dr Watson, so
he settled instead on 'Solar Pons', which was syllabically similar
and implied a 'bridge of light'; the companion became Dr
Lyndon Parker and they had lodgings in Praed Street. The first
story, 'The Adventure of the Black Narcissus', was published in
Dragnet in February 1929. Ten more stories followed in rapid
succession, with three being written during a single day, and
Pons was then consigned to limbo. There he would have stayed
but for the interest of Ellery Queen, who included 'The Adventure of the Norcross Riddle' in *The Misadventures of Sherlock
Holmes* and thereby made the name of Solar Pons known to a
wider audience. Derleth was then persuaded to revise the earlier
stories and to publish them in book form. This had the title *In
Re: Sherlock Holmes*, which was the entry which Derleth had
placed in his diary before writing the first story; there was an
introduction by Vincent Starrett; and a specially created
imprint, Mycroft and Moran. Many more adventures followed
in the years ahead, including long stories and a novel.

Solar Pons evolved out of Sherlock Holmes but became a
distinct character, a distinction which was highlighted when the
editor of the *Baker Street Journal* published 'The Adventure of
the Circular Room' using the names of Holmes and Watson.
As a Pons story, it is a success; but as a Sherlock Holmes pastiche,

it has serious shortcomings. As Starrett said, Pons was an 'ecto-plasmic emanation of his great prototype', a clever impersona-tor, and a brilliant pupil, but he was very definitely not Sherlock Holmes. He was more in the tradition of the Picklock Holes stories of R. C. Lehmann which first appeared in *Punch* in 1893, and a precursor of the Schlock Homes stories by Robert L. Fish.

THE ADVENTURE OF
THE MARKED MAN

The original Schlock Homes story was published in the 'Depart-ment of "First Stories"' in *Ellery Queen's Mystery Magazine* in 1960, and it proved so popular that the author, a consulting engineer, was persuaded to write more. He continued to do so from time to time until his death in 1981.

Fred Dannay and Manfred B. Lee, who were the two halves of 'Ellery Queen', played a very significant role in the fostering of detective literature. Their memories were long, their tastes catholic, and their patronage widespread, and they were directly responsible for many stories and sequels which might otherwise never have been written. They had a virtual monopoly of the Schlock Homes stories; they also encouraged Barry Perowne to continue his sequels to Raffles which he had begun in the 1930s, and from Michael Harrison (whose theories on the origin of Sherlock Holmes they published) they got a series of new Dupin tales. All the great mystery writers, living and dead, have been represented in the pages of their magazine and there has been a steady flow of Sherlockian parody and pastiche. One of the earliest of these was 'The Adventure of the Marked Man', which appeared in the July 1944 issue. It was one of two Sherlock Holmes stories written specially for them by Stuart Palmer, the other being 'The Adventure of the Remarkable Worm', which was published in *The Misadventures of Sherlock Holmes*.

Palmer was born in 1905 and died in 1968. He came across the name of Sherlock Holmes for the first time at the age of twelve when he read *The Pursuit of the House-Boat* by John

Kendrick Bangs. Within a few years he knew all the original stories by heart and had even taken the trouble to write a letter of appreciation to Sherlock Holmes at his Baker Street address. He made his début as a detective story writer in 1931, but it was his second book, *The Penguin Pool Murders*, which established his reputation and that of his heroine, the schoolteacher turned sleuth, Miss Hildegarde Withers. 'She could never have existed at all,' he said later, 'if it had not been for her illustrious predecessor.' Her love of the abstruse, her curiosity, and her habit of withholding information until the denouement owed their origin to Sherlock Holmes.

The two pastiches, one serious and one comic, were written while Palmer was marooned at an army post in Oklahoma, where he was serving as an instructor, and both, he said, were 'patterned in the great tradition and yet conceived in all humbleness and respect'. They were the only two he wrote, though his interest in Sherlock Holmes and in the unrecorded cases mentioned by Dr Watson never diminished. The fate of the Dutch steamship *Friesland*, the singular adventures of the Grice Patersons in the Island of Uffa and the other 'lost delightful stories' would, he insisted, always be more precious to him than the missing songs of Sappho.

THE ADVENTURE OF
THE MEGATHERIUM THEFTS

For S. C. Roberts, later to become one of the leading authorities on the life of Dr Johnson, it was the first six volumes of the *Strand Magazine* which served as his introduction to Sherlock Holmes. He was born in 1887 and was a scholar, then fellow, and finally Master of Pembroke College, Cambridge. He was Secretary to the University Press between 1922 and 1948, and Vice-Chancellor of the university from 1949 to 1951.

Although he met Conan Doyle in 1911, his first contribution to the literature of Sherlock Holmes (which was afterwards

privately printed) was 'A Note on the Watson Problem' in the
Cambridge Review of 25 January 1929, this being a commentary
on the studies by Ronald Knox which had appeared in *Essays
in Satire*. It was followed by an essay on the early career of Dr
Watson, a 'prolegomena to the study of a biographical problem', which was published in *Life and Letters* in February 1930,
and in an *Essays of the Year* anthology, and was then made into
one of Faber and Faber's Criterion Miscellanies, where it was
extended to include details of Watson's later years. This became,
as *The Times* said, the 'standard life' of Dr Watson and it placed
Roberts in the forefront of the new scholarship, scholarship
which reached its climax in 1932 with the publication of a 'really
authoritative biography' of Sherlock Holmes by T. S. Blakeney,
and of a 'textbook for advanced students' by H. W. Bell, giving
the chronology of the stories. Both books were reviewed by
Roberts in the *Observer*. He also became a member of the first
Sherlock Holmes Society of London and was a contributor to
Bell's *Baker Street Studies*.

Of his four Sherlockian pastiches, the first was a short play
called *Christmas Eve*, which was privately printed in 1936 for
distribution at Christmas. Then in 1945, following the theft of
some books from the Athenaeum library, he published 'The
Strange Case of the Megatherium Thefts'. Later, in July 1951,
to coincide with the Sherlock Holmes Exhibition in Baker
Street and under the auspices of the National Book League, he
gave a public lecture at the Victoria and Albert Museum on 'The
Personality of Sherlock Holmes' which included a few tantaliz-
ing extracts from Dr Watson's account of 'The Death of
Cardinal Tosca'. At the same time, he was made Life President
of the new Sherlock Holmes Society, and it was in that capacity
(and as a Trustee of Shakespeare's birthplace) that in 1963 he
revealed his discovery of the unpublished manuscript by Dr
Watson of 'The Case of the Missing Quarto', a counterpart to
the earlier story by Vincent Starrett. All his early articles, essays,
and pastiches, including the introduction to the World's Classics
edition of Sherlock Holmes stories, were collected in 1953 as

Holmes and Watson: A Miscellany, and he remained an active Sherlockian until his death in 1966.

THE ADVENTURE OF
THE TRAINED CORMORANT

W. R. Duncan Macmillan's story, originally called 'Holmes in Scotland', provides an account of perhaps the most intriguing of the unrecorded cases, the one referred to in 'The Veiled Lodger' concerning the trained cormorant, the politician, and the lighthouse keeper.

The origin of the title would appear to date back to Conan Doyle's days in Edinburgh when he visited the Isle of May in the Firth of Forth. The island had little to recommend it but it did have a lighthouse, cormorants, and solan geese, and Doyle used it twice in the early 1880s, first in a semi-autobiographical sketch, 'After Cormorants with a Camera', which was published in the *British Journal of Photography* in 1881, and again in 'John Barrington Cowles', which appeared in *Cassell's Saturday Journal* in 1884. It is appropriate therefore that the story should have been written by a Scotsman, that it should have a Scottish setting, and that it should have first appeared in an Edinburgh magazine. And it is also appropriate that it should have been *Blackwood's Magazine* as this was a periodical in which during his early years Doyle was most anxious to have a story published. Unlike *Chambers's Journal*, which accepted his first story in 1879, *Blackwood's* rejected many manuscripts which he offered them, including two which have been claimed as prototypes of the Sherlock Holmes stories, 'The Haunted Grange of Goresthorpe' and 'Uncle Jeremy's Household'. The first was sent to them in about 1880 and never returned, while the second reached them in 1884 and was eventually published in the *Boy's Own Paper*.

Duncan Macmillan's story was published in *Blackwood's* in September 1953 and was originally prefaced by a short account of its origin. The author said that he seemed to be walking with

Dr Watson in the Shades. He asked if Sherlock Holmes had ever been guilty of egotism or boastfulness, but Watson denied it. He then asked if the claims which Holmes had made about his earlier cases were justified, and, on being pressed to give an example, mentioned the case involving the trained cormorant. Watson immediately felt at ease and when they had seated themselves in a convenient bower he gave an account of the case. When it was over, his listener asked him if it was indeed the true story of the statesman, the lighthouse keeper, and the trained cormorant. 'Yes, my dear sir,' said the doctor in a voice both placid and content, 'it is indeed.'

THE ADVENTURE OF
ARNSWORTH CASTLE

The stories which make up *The Exploits of Sherlock Holmes* were almost contemporary with 'Holmes in Scotland'. They were based on the titles mentioned by Dr Watson and were written by Adrian Conan Doyle and John Dickson Carr.

Adrian was the youngest son of Sir Arthur Conan Doyle and was born in 1910. His whole life was to be dedicated to the memory of his father. As a boy, he accompanied him on lecture tours to Australia, America, South Africa, and Scandinavia, where he witnessed both the fulsome praise given to the creator of Sherlock Holmes and the sometimes harsh criticism directed against the 'apostle of spiritualism'. His formal education was limited to a few years at a crammer and thereafter he devoted most of his time to his hobbies of motor racing, painting, and zoology. He was married in 1938 and soon afterwards visited the Cameroons on a reptile-hunting expedition. Too head-strong to submit to the discipline of the Armed Forces, he spent the war years in virtual retirement at Bignell Wood, in the New Forest, where he was surrounded by a collection of armour, old keys, and family papers.

The running of the literary estate was initially left to his brother, Denis, but in 1943 Adrian entered the fray by accusing

Hesketh Pearson of having written a fraudulent biography which did not do justice to his father, and in 1945 produced his own panegyric in pamphlet form called *The True Conan Doyle*. A year or two later, John Dickson Carr was chosen as the official biographer and the two men became friends. Both shared the belief that England was in decline and that, under the new Labour government, it was no longer a fit place in which to live. Carr, having completed his biography, returned to America, while Adrian went into a self-imposed exile, settling first in Tangier, later in Portugal, and finally in Switzerland. The two men met in New York in 1952 when Adrian was there to supervise the opening of his Sherlock Holmes Exhibition, which included the reconstruction of the sitting-room at 221B which he had purchased from the Marylebone Council. They had on earlier occasions discussed the possibility of reviving Sherlock Holmes, but now a firm decision to do so was taken.

Carr already had some experience in this field as he had written two humorous sketches for the Mystery Writers of America. The first, 'The Adventure of the Conk-Singleton Papers', was performed in April 1948, and the other, 'The Adventure of the Paradol Chamber', a year later. In one Queen Victoria was accused of having attempted to poison Gladstone, while the other had the French ambassador removing his trousers in her presence. Despite being in poor taste, Carr insisted that he meant no disrespect to Sherlock Holmes.

The first of the *Exploits*, 'The Adventure of the Seven Clocks', was a full-scale collaboration based on an idea provided by Carr. 'Some of it is written line by line alternately,' said Adrian at the time of its publication. 'We cannot tell, nor can anyone else, who wrote which phrase. When we write, our brains are each a half, forming a whole.' Another two were written in the same way but the collaboration was not easy. Carr found it hard to write in a style other than his own and did not always feel that the stories were improved by the emendations made by Adrian. He wrote three more on his own and then 'fell ill', leaving Adrian to complete the series. In America, the first story was taken by *Life* and the rest by *Collier's*, while in England they appeared in the London *Evening Standard* and other regional newspapers.

The reaction from the readers was mixed and Sherlockians were divided among themselves. Some allowed their judgement to be clouded by the resentment which they felt for Adrian, while others welcomed his change of attitude as he was now giving his blessing to a literary form which he and his brother had previously tried to suppress. He said, for example, in a letter to the *Irish Times*:

> By trying to carry on with the unwritten cases of Sherlock Holmes referred to by Dr Watson in the original tales, and by painstakingly preserving the original style and setting of the stories, I am doing exactly what my father would have wished, i.e. to give a little more of the Baker Street secrets from a Conan Doyle pen for the pleasure and amusement of the old friends of Mr Sherlock Holmes and Dr Watson.

It was not only what his father might have wished, it was also in many ways what his father had done, for the later stories were pastiches of his own earlier style. But they were authentic in a way which Adrian's could never be. The fact that he was Conan Doyle's son or that he was able to handle his father's magnifying glass or write on his father's desk was no guarantee of his ability as a writer and such things could not by themselves create plots or provide examples of logical reasoning. This did however come with practice and while some of the earlier stories in the series are derivative, and even cumbersome, with clumsy manipulations of plot, the later ones have a certain elegance of their own. The last story, which is included here, is undoubtedly the most memorable.

After the publication of *The Exploits of Sherlock Holmes* in 1954 and the death of his brother a year later, Adrian became more closely involved with his father's estate. There were various court cases and controversies: one was the attempt to get unpaid royalties from Russia, another was the argument with

Irving Wallace over whether Dr Joseph Bell or Doyle himself was the 'original' of Sherlock Holmes. In 1959 Adrian edited and paid for a large scrapbook to commemorate his father's centenary, and in 1963 he helped to found Sir Nigel Films which, in association with another film company, produced the Sherlock Holmes film, *Fog*, or *A Study in Terror*, and which later was responsible for a disastrous film based on the Brigadier Gerard stories.

His other major concern was with his share of the family archives. In 1955 he had promised them to Dublin; in 1962 he gave them to the City of Geneva, and in 1965, with the help of the Swiss government, he purchased the Château de Lucens and opened it to the public the following year as the Sir Arthur Conan Doyle Foundation. It was intended as a permanent memorial to his father, but under financial pressure he tried to sell part of the collection to an American university and suffered the indignity of being 'exposed' by the *Sunday Times* in April 1969. He died on 2 June 1970. The château was sold and the papers which remained were transferred to a local library.

Adrian Conan Doyle made a significant contribution to the literature of Sherlock Holmes and one which will outlive any damage which he may unwittingly have done to his father's reputation by his somewhat excessive zeal.

THE ADVENTURE OF
THE TIRED CAPTAIN

The *Sherlock Holmes Journal* is the source of the next story. The Sherlock Holmes Society's magazine was first issued in 1952 and from 1956 was edited by Lord Donegall. Unlike its older rival, the *Baker Street Journal*, which has published a flood of parodies and pastiches of varying merit, the *Journal* has included only a few. Pastiches, the editor explained later, were anathema to him unless they were exceptionally brilliant, and only three ever came into this category, one by A. Lloyd Taylor and two by Alan Wilson. Taylor's concerned Vamberry, the wine merchant (which was appropriate as he had been responsible for the decorations in the Sherlock Holmes Public House), and Alan Wilson's were 'The Adventure of the Tired Captain' and 'The Adventure of the Paradol Chamber'.

Wilson was born in 1923 and was introduced to the Sherlock Holmes stories by his father. By the age of twelve he had read them all many times with the exception of 'The Solitary Cyclist', which for some reason escaped his notice. It was this story which helped to revive his earlier enthusiasm when he came across it after the war.

Lord Donegall felt that 'The Adventure of the Tired Captain' had 'achieved perfection' and was 'a hundred per cent Watson', and it was with this that Alan Wilson first made his mark in 1958. 'The Adventure of the Paradol Chamber', which described Señor Paradol's connection with Vigor, the Hammersmith Wonder, followed in 1961. There were also articles on the date of *The Valley of Fear* (he opted for 1891); on Watson's integrity as an author; on the location of the opium den mentioned in 'The Man with the Twisted Lip'; and on 'Holmes the Histrionic'. The last of these put forward the thesis that Holmes had trained for the stage and had only left the profession when passed over in favour of Henry Irving. It was a subject on which Wilson spoke with authority as he had been to drama school and was himself an actor.

Wilson was also a member of the Milvertonians of Hampstead, a branch society founded by Humphrey Morton and Peter Richard which became active in 1958 with the publication of its own Christmas card. Its aim was to further the study of Milvertoniana and to this end the society published a series of well-researched papers. It was most active between 1958 and 1963, though it continued in existence until Morton's death in 1969. 'Son of Escott', an article which dealt with Holmes's flirtation with the maid of Charles Augustus Milverton and its unexpected sequel, was Wilson's major 'Milverton story'. It was like 'The Giant Rat of Sumatra', a story for which the world was not prepared – indeed for which the world would never be prepared – and it appeared in the *Baker Street Journal*.

In addition, Alan Wilson adapted 'Black Peter' for the radio and was the winner of the Sherlock Holmes Society Photographic Competition of 1963. He also compiled an encyclopedia, listing all the characters and places mentioned in the stories. *Give Me Data* was ready for publication in the early 1960s but was set to one side when another book appeared covering much of the same ground. His Sherlockian activity ceased in 1963 when he left England to become a staff director for the New Zealand Drama Council.

THE ADVENTURE OF
THE GREEN EMPRESS

It is appropriate that 'The Adventure of the Second Stain' ('The Adventure of the Green Empress') should follow 'The Adventure of the Tired Captain', as both took place at the same period. At the start of 'The Adventure of the Naval Treaty', Watson says:

> The July which immediately succeeded my marriage was made memorable by three cases of interest in which I had the privilege of being associated with Sherlock Holmes and of studying his methods. I find them recorded in my notes under the headings of 'The Adventure of the Second Stain', 'The Adventure of the Naval Treaty', and 'The Adventure of the Tired Captain'.

He was not then at liberty to describe the first because it implicated so many of the first families in the kingdom and he feared that the new century would have come before the facts could be made public. It had, however, provided an excellent example of Holmes's methods and the detective's handling of the case had impressed all those associated with it. 'I still retain,' Watson added, 'an almost verbatim report of the interview in which he demonstrated the true facts of the case to Monsieur Dubuque of the Paris police, and Fritz von Waldbaum, the well-known specialist of Danzig, both of whom had wasted their energies upon what proved to be side-issues.'

In 1903, when the public first heard of Holmes's return, many people were curious to learn about the 'second stain', and the editors of the New York *Bookman* were particularly anxious to see it published as it had always intrigued them. 'The mere title of the story shows genius of a high order,' they said, 'and rouses the most intense expectation.' Indeed, it was so important to their peace of mind that the junior editor was dispatched to Paris to discuss the matter with Monsieur Dubuque and on the same tour met Conan Doyle and asked him to do everything in his power to ensure that the story was written. Doyle immediately obliged, but 'The Adventure of the Second Stain' as published did not contain any references to Monsieur Dubuque or to Fritz von Waldbaum. Sherlockian scholars realized that there must have been three cases bearing the same name, the one mentioned in 'The Adventure of the Naval Treaty', another referred to in 'The Adventure of the Yellow Face', and the one which Doyle had written. It was left to the *Sunday Times* of Johannesburg to discover details of the first.

On 18 June 1967, the paper announced an 'Intriguing Contest for Our Readers', saying that as part of its duty to encourage good writing, it would be offering a prize of 200 rand for a Sherlock Holmes story based on the description of 'The Adventure of the Second Stain' given in 'The Adventure of the Naval Treaty'. The closing date was 30 September 1967 and the length was to be between 5,000 and 7,000 words. The paper later said that the other reference to the case and the one bearing its name were to be ignored.

Ninety-five separate versions were received by the closing date and on 27 November, after two months of deliberation, the joint-winners were announced. They were F. P. Cillié and Miles Masters. The first had chosen a suitably aristocratic setting and the other had used the Jack the Ripper mystery. The runners-up had chosen a wide range of subjects, including national and international politics, espionage, domestic scandals, the Boer War, and the gold mines.

François Paulus Cillié, whose entry was published in the

Johannesburg *Sunday Times* on 3 December 1967, was educated
in Port Elizabeth and took an honours degree in economics at
Stellenbosch University. An addict of the Sherlock Holmes
stories since his boyhood, he was only twenty-four at the time
of the competition. His story was written in the evenings and
at night while his fiancée was doing night duty at a hospital; and
by day he was working as an economist on the staff of a
commercial bank.

THE ADVENTURE OF
THE PURPLE HAND

Many people of all ages have turned their hand to Sherlockian
pastiche and examples of their work are to be found in many
small publications such as a booklet issued in 1976 called *The
Non-Canonical Sherlock Holmes*. But few can compare with those
written by D. O. Smith, whose stories have been appearing
annually since 1982 under the imprint of Diogenes Publications. 'The Adventure of the Purple Hand' was the first and has
been followed by 'The Unseen Traveller' and 'The Zodiac
Plate'; it is the author's intention to produce a full volume in the
course of time.

Denis Smith was born in 1948 and, as with so many other
authors represented here, became interested in Sherlock Holmes
at the age of twelve. He tried his hand at a variety of jobs before
going to York University where he read philosophy. That and
his other interests, which include logic, literature, the railways
of Britain, and maps (which he sometimes 'reads' for hours on
end), added to his detailed knowledge of the Sherlock Holmes
stories which he has analysed from every conceivable angle, will
help to explain why he is so proficient in this field. He is a regular
contributor to the *Sherlock Holmes Journal* and hopes one day to
produce the definitive chronology of the stories.

THE ADVENTURE OF
HILLERMAN HALL

All the stories in this volume, with the exception of the last, date from the years when Holmes was at the height of his activities, but 'The Adventure of Hillerman Hall' by Julian Symons is set in the 1920s during his retirement.

Julian Symons was born in 1912 and first made his mark in the 1930s as the editor of *Twentieth-Century Verse*, then as a biographer, social historian, and critic. He turned to crime writing in a light-hearted way before the war and soon afterwards established himself as a leading exponent of it, though his use of irony to show the violence behind the respectable masks of society place many of his books on the level of the orthodox novel. He is an authority on detective fiction and has written a standard history of it, as well as books about Edgar Allan Poe and Conan Doyle.

'The Adventure of Hillerman Hall' comes from *The Great Detectives*. The book was originally to have been a series of 'biographies', but the author decided that as too much was known about some and too little about others, he would vary the technique in each case. 'The story should suggest the master,' he reflected, 'without ever attempting to enter into competition with him.' Parody would be avoided and, although the book was to have excellent coloured illustrations by Tom Adams, the text was to be independent of them. Of the first story, originally called 'How a Hermit was Disturbed in His Retirement', he said: 'The Sherlock Holmes story relies very little upon biographical detail, chiefly because there is no shortage of biographies and biographical essays in the form of full-length books, which may easily be consulted. What is offered here is Sherlock in retirement, and a narrative which has a tease, if not exactly a twist, in the tail.'

It is one of a number of works which demonstrate the fascination which Symons has always felt for the myth of Sherlock Holmes. In 1974 he wrote *A Three Pipe Problem*, concerning a television actor, Sheridan Haynes, who wears the mask of Sherlock Holmes and assumes his character. The book neatly reversed the usual theme of the criminal behind the mask by having a rather commonplace man wearing the mask of the great detective.

Julian Symons was the guest of honour at the annual dinner of the Sherlock Holmes Society in 1975 but, despite being in some ways the literary heir of Dorothy L. Sayers, he has never indulged as she did in Sherlockian scholarship, preferring instead to concentrate on the character of Conan Doyle and on those writers who influenced him or were influenced by him.

THE UNTOLD TALES
OF DR JOHN H. WATSON

Dr Watson provides the names of some forty cases other than those which he described. His yearbooks covering the period when Holmes was in active practice filled a shelf and there were a number of dispatch-cases crammed with notes. It is therefore not surprising that further details should from time to time be made public, but it is remarkable that the new adventures and misadventures should now exceed the number of the originals. For the curious or insatiable reader there is a wide choice. He may opt for further stories from the pen of Dr Watson, such as 'The Adventure of the Purple Maculas' by James C. Iraldi concerning Henry Staunton, whom Holmes had helped to hang. Or there is 'The Darkwater Hall Mystery' by Kingsley Amis, in which Watson describes his own attempt at deduction and at seduction. Or there are reminiscences by those who knew the great detective, such as J. C. Masterman's 'The Case of the Gifted Amateur', which is told by Inspector Lestrade. Or there are the novels which have cross-fertilized fact and fiction so that Edwin Drood, Raffles, Dracula, Tarzan, and their ilk seek the detective's advice in the company of such distinguished personages as Sigmund Freud, Oscar Wilde, Queen Victoria, the Tsar, and Theodore Roosevelt. Or there are those in which

Holmes or his children, or his children's children, investigate a more recent mystery, or in which Moriarty or his brother try in vain to clear their family name. The list it seems is endless and continues to grow with each succeeding year.

Apocryphal Sherlock Holmes stories are not designed to compete with the originals, as that may be left to the many rivals who have followed in his wake, their intention is rather to reflect and enhance the achievements of Mr Holmes. If the stories in this book can kindle afresh the fire in the rooms in Baker Street, or echo the noise of the hansom cabs, or catch the sound of a foot upon the stair, then they will have achieved their end.

RICHARD LANCELYN GREEN

I

THE ADVENTURE OF
THE FIRST-CLASS CARRIAGE

Ronald A. Knox

❧✦❧

The general encouragement extended to my efforts by the public is my excuse, if excuse were needed, for continuing to act as chronicler of my friend Sherlock Holmes. But even if I confine myself to those cases in which I have had the honour of being personally associated with him, I find it difficult to make a selection among the large amount of matter at my disposal.

As I turn over my records, I find that some of them deal with events of national or even international importance; but the time has not yet come when it would be safe to disclose (for instance) the true facts about the recent change of government in Paraguay. Others (like the case of the Missing Omnibus) would do more to gratify the modern craving for sensation; but I am well aware that my friend himself is the first to deplore it when I indulge what is, in his own view, a weakness.

My preference is for recording incidents whose bizarre features gave special opportunity for the exercise of that analytical talent which he possessed in such a marked degree. Of these, the case of the Tattooed Nurseryman and that of the Luminous Cigar-Box naturally suggest themselves to the mind. But perhaps my friend's gifts were even more signally displayed when he had occasion to investigate the disappearance of Mr Nathaniel Swithinbank, which provoked so much speculation in the early days of September, five years back.

Mr Sherlock Holmes was, of all men, the least influenced by

what are called class distinctions. To him the rank was but the guinea stamp; a client was a client. And it did not surprise me, one evening when I was sitting over the familiar fire in Baker Street – the days were sunny but the evenings were already falling chill – to be told that he was expecting a visit from a domestic servant, a woman who 'did' for a well-to-do, childless couple in the southern Midlands. 'My last visit,' he explained, 'was from a countess. Her mind was uninteresting, and she had no great regard for the truth; the problem she brought was quite elementary. I fancy Mrs John Hennessy will have something more important to communicate.'

'You have met her already, then?'

'No, I have not had the privilege. But anyone who is in the habit of receiving letters from strangers will tell you the same – handwriting is often a better form of introduction than hand-shaking. You will find Mrs Hennessy's letter on the mantelpiece; and if you care to look at her j's and her w's, in particular, I think you will agree that it is no ordinary woman we have to deal with. Dear me, there is the bell ringing already; in a moment or two, if I mistake not, we shall know what Mrs Hennessy, of the Cottage, Guiseborough St Martin, wants of Sherlock Holmes.'

There was nothing in the appearance of the old dame who was shown up, a few minutes later, by the faithful Mrs Hudson to justify Holmes's estimate. To the outward view she was a typical representative of her class; from the bugles on her bonnet to her elastic-sided boots everything suggested the old-fashioned caretaker such as you may see polishing the front doorsteps of a hundred office buildings any spring morning in the city of London. Her voice, when she spoke, was articulated with unnecessary care, as that of the respectable working-class woman is apt to be. But there was something precise and businesslike about the statement of her case which made you feel that this was a mind which could easily have profited by greater educational advantages.

'I have read of you, Mr Holmes,' she began, 'and when things

began to go wrong up at the Hall it wasn't long before I thought
to myself, if there's one man in England who will be able to see
light here, it's Mr Sherlock Holmes. My husband was in good
employment, till lately, on the railway at Chester; but the time
came when the rheumatism got hold of him, and after that
nothing seemed to go well with us until he had thrown up his
job, and we went to live in a country village not far from
Banbury, looking out for any odd work that might come our
way.

'We had only been living there a week when a Mr Swithinbank and his wife took the old Hall, that had long been standing
empty. They were newcomers to the district, and their needs
were not great, having neither chick nor child to fend for; so
they engaged me and Mr Hennessy to come and live in the
lodge, close by the house, and do all the work of it for them.
The pay was good and the duties light, so we were glad enough
to get the billet.'

'One moment!' said Holmes. 'Did they advertise, or were
you indebted to some private recommendation for the appointment?'

· 'They came at short notice, Mr Holmes, and were directed
to us for temporary help. But they soon saw that our ways suited
them, and they kept us on. They were people who kept very
much to themselves, and perhaps they did not want a set of
maids who would have followers, and spread gossip in the
village.'

'That is suggestive. You state your case with admirable clear-
ness. Pray proceed.'

'All this was no longer ago than last July. Since then they have
once been away in London, but for the most part they have lived
at Guiseborough, seeing very little of the folk round about.
Parson called, but he is not a man to put his nose in where he
is not wanted, and I think they must have made it clear they
would sooner have his room than his company. So there was
more guessing than gossiping about them in the countryside.
But, sir, you can't be in domestic employment without finding

out a good deal about how the land lies; and it wasn't long before my husband and I were certain of two things. One was that Mr and Mrs Swithinbank were deep in debt. And the other was that they got on badly together.'

'Debts have a way of reflecting themselves in a man's correspondence,' said Holmes, 'and whoever has the clearing of his waste-paper basket will necessarily be conscious of them. But the relations between man and wife? Surely they must have gone very wrong indeed before there is quarrelling in public.'

'That's as may be, Mr Holmes, but quarrel in public they did. Why, it was only last week I came in with the blancmange, and he was saying, *The fact is, no one would be better pleased than you to see me in my coffin.* To be sure, he held his tongue after that, and looked a bit confused; and she tried to put a brave face on it. But I've lived long enough, Mr Holmes, to know when a woman's been crying. Then last Monday, when I'd been in drawing the curtains, he burst out just before I'd closed the door behind me, *The world isn't big enough for both of us.* That was all I heard, and right glad I'd have been to hear less. But I've not come round here just to repeat servants'-hall gossip.

'Today, when I was cleaning out the waste-paper basket, I came across a scrap of a letter that tells the same story, in his own handwriting. Cast your eye over that, Mr Holmes, and tell me whether a Christian woman has the right to sit by and do nothing about it.'

She had dived her hand into a capacious reticule and brought out, with a triumphant flourish, her documentary evidence. Holmes knitted his brow over it, and then passed it on to me. It ran: 'Being of sound mind, whatever the numskulls on the jury may say of it.'

'Can you identify the writing?' my friend said.

'It was my master's,' replied Mrs Hennessy. 'I know it well enough; the bank, I am sure, will tell you the same.'

'Mrs Hennessy, let us make no bones about it. Curiosity is a well-marked instinct of the human species. Your eye having lighted on this document, no doubt inadvertently, I will wager you took a look round the basket for any other fragments it might contain.'

'That I did, sir; my husband and I went through it carefully together, for who knew but the life of a fellow-creature might depend on it? But only one other piece could we find written by the same hand, and on the same note-paper. Here it is.' And she smoothed out on her knee a second fragment, to all appearances part of the same sheet, yet strangely different in its tenor. It seemed to have been torn away from the middle of a sentence; nothing survived but the words 'in the reeds by the lake, taking a bearing at the point where the old tower hides both the middle first-floor windows'.

'Come,' I said, 'this at least gives us something to go upon. Mrs Hennessy will surely be able to tell us whether there are any landmarks in Guiseborough answering to this description.'

'Indeed there are, sir; the directions are plain as a pikestaff. There is an old ruined building which juts out upon the little lake at the bottom of the garden, and it would be easy enough to hit on the place mentioned. I daresay you gentlemen are wondering why we haven't been down to the lake-side ourselves to see what we could find there. Well, the plain fact is, we were scared. My master is a quiet-spoken man enough at ordinary times, but there's a wild look in his eye when he's roused, and I for one should be sorry to cross him. So I thought I'd come to you, Mr Holmes, and put the whole thing in your hands.'

'I shall be interested to look into your little difficulty. To speak frankly, Mrs Hennessy, the story you have told me runs on such familiar lines that I should have been tempted to dismiss the whole case from my mind. Dr Watson here will tell you that I am a busy man, and the affairs of the Bank of Mauritius urgently require my presence in London. But this last detail about the reeds by the lake-side is piquant, decidedly piquant, and the whole matter shall be gone into. The only difficulty is a practical one. How are we to explain my presence at Guiseborough without betraying to your employers the fact that you and your husband have been intruding on their family affairs?'

'I have thought of that, sir,' replied the old dame, 'and I think we can find a way out. I slipped away today easily enough because my mistress is going abroad to visit her aunt, near Dieppe, and Mr Swithinbank has come up to Town with her to see her off. I must go back by the evening train, and had half thought of asking you to accompany me. But no, he would get to hear of it if a stranger visited the place in his absence. It would be better if you came down by the quarter-past ten train tomorrow, and passed yourself off for a stranger who was coming to look at the house. They have taken it on a short lease, and plenty of folks come to see it without troubling to obtain an order-to-view.'

'Will your employer be back so early?'

'That is the very train he means to take; and to speak truth, sir, I should be the better for knowing that he was being watched. This wicked talk of making away with himself is enough to make anyone anxious about him. You cannot mistake him, Mr Holmes,' she went on; 'what chiefly marks him out is a scar on the left-hand side of his chin, where a dog bit him when he was a youngster.'

'Excellent, Mrs Hennessy; you have thought of everything. Tomorrow, then, on the quarter-past ten for Banbury without fail. You will oblige me by ordering the station fly to be in readiness. Country walks may be good for health, but time is more precious. I will drive straight to your cottage, and you or your husband shall escort me on my visit to this desirable country residence and its mysterious tenant.' With a wave of his hand, he cut short her protestations of gratitude.

'Well, Watson, what did you make of her?' asked my companion when the door had closed on our visitor.

'She seemed typical of that noble army of women whose hard scrubbing makes life easy for the leisured classes. I could not see her well because she sat between us and the window, and her veil was lowered over her eyes. But her manner was enough to convince me that she was telling us the truth, and that she is sincere in her anxiety to avert what may be an appalling tragedy.

As to its nature, I confess I am in the dark. Like yourself, I was particularly struck by the reference to the reeds by the lake-side. What can it mean? An assignation?'

'Hardly, my dear Watson. At this time of the year a man runs enough risk of cold without standing about in a reed-bed. A hiding-place, more probably, but for what? And why should a man take the trouble to hide something, and then obligingly litter his waste-paper basket with clues to its whereabouts? No, these are deep waters, Watson, and we must have more data before we begin to theorize. You will come with me?'

'Certainly, if I may. Shall I bring my revolver?'

'I do not apprehend any danger, but perhaps it is as well to be on the safe side. Mr Swithinbank seems to strike his neighbours as a formidable person. And now, if you will be good enough to hand me the more peaceful instrument which hangs beside you, I will try out that air of Scarlatti's, and leave the affairs of Guiseborough St Martin to look after themselves.'

I often had occasion to deprecate Sherlock Holmes's habit of catching trains with just half a minute to spare. But on the morning after our interview with Mrs Hennessy we arrived at Paddington station no later than ten o'clock – to find a stranger, with a pronounced scar on the left side of his chin, gazing out at us languidly from the window of a first-class carriage.

'Do you mean to travel with him?' I asked, when we were out of earshot.

'Scarcely feasible, I think. If he is the man I take him for, he has secured solitude all the way to Banbury by the simple process of slipping half a crown into the guard's hand.' And, sure enough, a few minutes later we saw that functionary shepherd a fussy-looking gentleman, who had been vigorously assaulting the locked door, to a compartment farther on. For ourselves, we took up our post in the carriage next but one behind Mr Swithinbank. This, like the other first-class compartments, was duly locked when we had entered it; behind us the less fortunate passengers accommodated themselves in seconds.

'The case is not without its interest,' observed Holmes, laying down his paper as we steamed through Burnham Beeches. 'It presents features which recall the affairs of James Phillimore, whose disappearance (though your loyalty may tempt you to forget it) we investigated without success. But this Swithinbank mystery, if I mistake not, cuts even deeper. Why, for example, is the man so anxious to parade his intention of suicide, or fictitious suicide, in the presence of his domestic staff? It can hardly fail to strike you that he chose the moment when the good Mrs Hennessy was just entering the room, or just leaving it, to make those remarkable confidences to his wife. Not content with that, he must leave evidence of his intentions lying about in the waste-paper basket. And yet this involved the risk of having his plans foiled by good-natured interference. Time enough for his disappearance to become public when it became effective! And why, in the name of fortune, does he hide something only to tell us where he has hidden it?'

Amid a maze of railway-tracks, we came to a standstill at Reading. Holmes craned his neck out of the window, but reported that all the doors had been left locked. We were not destined to learn anything about our elusive travelling-companion until, just as we were passing the pretty hamlet of Tilehurst, a little shower of paper fragments fluttered past the window on the right-hand side of the compartment, and two of them actually sailed in through the space we had dedicated to ventilation on that bright morning of autumn. It may easily be guessed with what avidity we pounced on them.

The messages were in the same handwriting with which Mrs Hennessy's find had made us familiar; they ran, respectively, 'Mean to make an end of it all' and 'This is the only way out.' Holmes sat over them with knitted brows, till I fairly danced with impatience.

'Should we not pull the communication-cord?' I asked.

'Hardly,' answered my companion, 'unless five-pound notes are more plentiful with you than they used to be. I will even anticipate your next suggestion, which is that we should look out of the windows on either side of the carriage. Either we have

a lunatic two doors off, in which case there is no use in trying
to foresee his next move, or he intends suicide, in which case he
will not be deterred by the presence of spectators, or he is a man
with a scheming brain who is sending us these messages in order
to make us behave in a particular way. Quite possibly, he wants
to make us lean out of the windows, which seems to me an
excellent reason for not leaning out of the windows. At Oxford
we shall be able to read the guard a lesson on the danger of
locking passengers in.'

So indeed it proved; for when the train stopped at Oxford
there was no passenger to be found in Mr Swithinbank's carriage. His overcoat remained, and his wide-awake hat; his port-
manteau was duly identified in the guard's van. The door on the
right-hand side of the compartment, away from the platform,
had swung open; nor did Holmes's lens bring to light any details
about the way in which the elusive passenger had made his exit.

It was an impatient horse and an injured cabman that awaited
us at Banbury, when we drove through golden woodlands to
the little village of Guiseborough St Martin, nestling under the
shadow of Edge Hill. Mrs Hennessy met us at the door of her
cottage, dropping an old-fashioned curtsy; and it may easily be
imagined what wringing of hands, what wiping of eyes with
her apron, greeted the announcement of her master's disappearance. Mr Hennessy, it seemed, had gone off to a neighbouring
farm upon some errand, and it was the old dame herself who
escorted us up to the Hall.

'There's a gentleman there already, Mr Holmes,' she informed us. 'Arrived early this morning and would take no
denial; and not a word to say what business he came on.'

'That is unfortunate,' said Holmes. 'I particularly wanted a
free field to make some investigations. Let us hope that he will
be good enough to clear off when he is told that there is no
chance of an interview with Mr Swithinbank.'

Guiseborough Hall stands in its own grounds a little way
outside the village, the residence of a squire unmistakably, but
with no airs of baronial grandeur. The old, rough walls have

been refaced with pointed stone, the mullioned windows exchanged for a generous expanse of plate-glass, to suit a more recent taste, and a portico has been thrown out from the front door to welcome the traveller with its shelter. The garden descends at a precipitous slope from the main terrace, and a little lake fringes it at the bottom, dominated by a ruined eminence that serves the modern owner for a gazebo.

Within the house, furniture was of the scantiest, the Swithinbanks having evidently rented it with what fittings it had, and introduced little of their own. As Mrs Hennessy ushered us into the drawing-room, we were not a little surprised to be greeted by the wiry figure and melancholy features of our old rival, Inspector Lestrade.

'I knew you were quick off the mark, Mr Holmes,' he said, 'but it beats me how you ever heard of Mr Swithinbank's little goings-on; let alone that I didn't think you took much stock in cases of common fraud like this.'

'Common fraud?' repeated my companion. 'Why, what has he been up to?'

'Drawing cheques, and big ones, Mr Holmes, when he knew that his bank wouldn't honour them; only little things of that sort. But if you're on his track I don't suppose he's far off, and I'll be grateful for any help you can give me to lay my hands on him.'

'My dear Lestrade, if you follow out your usual systematic methods, you will have to patrol the Great Western line all the way from Reading to Oxford. I trust you have brought a dragnet with you, for the line crossed the river no less than four times in the course of the journey.' And he regaled the astonished inspector with a brief summary of our investigations.

Our information worked like a charm on the little detective. He was off in a moment to find the nearest telegraph office and put himself in touch with Scotland Yard, with the Great Western Railway authorities, with the Thames Conservancy. He promised, however, a speedy return, and I fancy Holmes cursed himself for not having dismissed the jarvey who had brought us from the station, an undeserved windfall for our rival.

'Now, Watson!' he cried, as the sound of the wheels faded away into the distance.

'Our way lies to the lake-side, I presume.'

'How often am I to remind you that the place where the criminal tells you to look is the place not to look? No, the clue to the mystery lies, somehow, in the house, and we must hurry up if we are to find it.'

Quick as a thought, he began turning out shelves, cupboards, escritoires, while I, at his direction, went through the various rooms of the house to ascertain whether all was in order, and whether anything suggested the anticipation of a hasty flight. By the time I returned to him, having found nothing amiss, he was seated in the most comfortable of the drawing-room arm-chairs, reading a book he had picked out of the shelves – it dealt, if I remember right, with the aborigines of Borneo.

'The mystery, Holmes!' I cried.

'I have solved it. If you will look on the bureau yonder, you will find the household books which Mrs Swithinbank has obligingly left behind. Extraordinary how these people always make some elementary mistake. You are a man of the world, Watson; take a look at them and tell me what strikes you as curious.'

It was not long before the salient feature occurred to me. 'Why, Holmes,' I exclaimed, 'there is no record of the Hennessys being paid any wages at all!'

'Bravo, Watson! And if you will go into the figures a little more closely, you will find that the Hennessys apparently lived on air. So now the whole facts of the story are plain to you.'

'I confess,' I replied, somewhat crestfallen, 'that the whole case is as dark to me as ever.'

'Why, then, take a look at that newspaper I have left on the occasional table; I have marked the important paragraph in blue pencil.'

It was a copy of an Australian paper, issued some weeks

previously. The paragraph to which Holmes had drawn my attention ran thus:

ROMANCE OF RICH MAN'S WILL

The recent lamented death of Mr John Macready, the well-known sheep-farming magnate, has had an unexpected sequel in the circumstance that the dead man, apparently, left no will. His son, Mr Alexander Macready, left for England some years back, owing to a misunderstanding with his father – it was said – because he announced his intention of marrying a lady from the stage. The young man has completely disappeared, and energetic steps are being taken by the lawyers to trace his whereabouts. It is estimated that the fortunate heirs, whoever they be, will be the richer by not far short of a hundred thousand pounds sterling.

Horse-hoofs echoed under the archway, and in another minute Lestrade was again of our party. Seldom have I seen the little detective looking so baffled and ill at ease. 'They'll have the laugh of me at the Yard over this,' he said. 'We had word that Swithinbank was in London, but I made sure it was only a feint, and I came racing up here by the early train, instead of catching the quarter-past ten and my man in it. He's a slippery devil, and he may be half-way to the Continent by this time.'

'Don't be down-hearted about it, Lestrade. Come and interview Mr and Mrs Hennessy, at the lodge; we may get news of your man down there.'

A coarse-looking fellow in a bushy red beard sat sharing his tea with our friend of the evening before. His greasy waistcoat and corduroy trousers proclaimed him a manual worker. He rose to meet us with something of a defiant air; his wife was all affability.

'Have you heard any news of the poor gentleman?' she asked.

'We may have some before long,' answered Holmes. 'Lestrade, you might arrest John Hennessy for stealing that porter's cap you see on the dresser, the property of the Great Western Railway Company. Or, if you prefer an alternative charge, you might arrest him as Alexander Macready, *alias* Nathaniel Swithinbank.' And while we stood there literally thunderstruck, he tore off the red beard from a chin marked with a scar on the left-hand side.

'The case was difficult,' he said to me afterwards, 'only because we had no clue to the motive. Swithinbank's debts would almost have swallowed up Macready's legacy; it was necessary for the couple to disappear, and take up the claim under a fresh *alias*. This meant a duplication of personalities, but it was not really difficult. She had been an actress; he had really been a railway porter in his hard-up days. When he got out at Reading, and passed along the six-foot way to take his place in a third-class carriage, nobody marked the circumstance, because on the way from London he had changed into a porter's clothes; he had the cap, no doubt, in his pocket. On the sill of the door he left open, he had made a little pile of suicide-messages, hoping that when it swung open these would be shaken out and flutter into the carriages behind.'

'But why the visit to London? And, above all, why the visit to Baker Street?'

'That is the most amusing part of the story; we should have seen through it at once. He wanted Nathaniel Swithinbank to disappear finally, beyond all hope of tracing him. And who would hope to trace him, when Mr Sherlock Holmes, who was travelling only two carriages behind, had given up the attempt? Their only fear was that I should find the case uninteresting; hence the random reference to a hiding-place among the reeds, which so intrigued you. Come to think of it, they nearly had Inspector Lestrade in the same train as well. I hear he has won golden opinions with his superiors by cornering his man so neatly. *Sic vos non vobis*, as Virgil said of the bees; only they tell us nowadays the lines are not by Virgil.'

II

THE ADVENTURE OF
THE SHEFFIELD BANKER

Arthur Whitaker

꧁꧂

During the late autumn of 'ninety-five a fortunate chance enabled me to take some part in another of my friend Sherlock Holmes's fascinating cases.

My wife not having been well for some time, I had at last persuaded her to take a holiday in Switzerland in the company of her old school friend Kate Whitney, whose name may be remembered in connection with the strange case I have already chronicled under the title of 'The Man with the Twisted Lip'. My practice had grown much, and I had been working very hard for many months and never felt in more need myself of a rest and a holiday. Unfortunately I dared not absent myself for a long enough period to warrant a visit to the Alps. I promised my wife, however, that I would get a week or ten days' holiday in somehow, and it was only on this understanding that she consented to the Swiss tour I was so anxious for her to take. One of my best patients was in a very critical state at the time, and it was not until August was gone that he passed the crisis and began to recover. Feeling then that I could leave my practice with a good conscience in the hands of a *locum tenens*, I began to wonder where and how I should best find the rest and change I needed.

Almost at once the idea came to my mind that I would hunt up my old friend Sherlock Holmes, of whom I had seen nothing for several months. If he had no important inquiry in hand, I would do my uttermost to persuade him to join me.

Within half an hour of coming to this resolution I was standing in the doorway of the familiar old room in Baker Street.

Holmes was stretched upon the couch with his back towards me, the familiar dressing-gown and old brier pipe as much in evidence as of yore.

'Come in, Watson,' he cried, without glancing round. 'Come in and tell me what good wind blows you here?'

'What an ear you have, Holmes,' I said. 'I don't think that I could have recognized your tread so easily.'

'Nor I yours,' said he, 'if you hadn't come up my badly lighted staircase taking the steps two at a time with all the familiarity of an old fellow lodger; even then I might not have been sure who it was, but when you stumbled over the new mat outside the door which has been there for nearly three months, you needed no further announcement.'

Holmes pulled out two or three of the cushions from the pile he was lying on and threw them across into the armchair. 'Sit down, Watson, and make yourself comfortable; you'll find cigarettes in a box behind the clock.'

As I proceeded to comply, Holmes glanced whimsically across at me. 'I'm afraid I shall have to disappoint you, my boy,' he said. 'I had a wire only half an hour ago which will prevent me from joining in any little trip you may have been about to propose.'

'Really, Holmes,' I said, 'don't you think this is going a little *too* far? I begin to fear you are a fraud and pretend to discover things by observation, when all the time you really do it by pure out-and-out clairvoyance!'

Holmes chuckled. 'Knowing you as I do it's absurdly simple,' said he. 'Your surgery hours are from five to seven, yet at six o'clock you walk smiling into my rooms. Therefore you must have a *locum* in. You are looking well, though tired, so the obvious reason is that you are having, or about to have, a holiday. The clinical thermometer, peeping out of your pocket, proclaims that you have been on your rounds today, hence it's pretty evident that your real holiday begins tomorrow. When, under these circumstances, you come hurrying into my rooms – which, by the way, Watson, you haven't visited for nearly three months – with a new Bradshaw and a timetable of excursion bookings bulging out of your coat pocket, then it's more than probable you have come with the idea of suggesting some joint expedition.'

'It's all perfectly true,' I said, and explained to him, in a few words, my plans. 'And I'm more disappointed than I can tell you,' I concluded, 'that you are not able to fall in with my little scheme.'

Holmes picked up a telegram from the table and looked at it thoughtfully. 'If only the inquiry this refers to promised to be of anything like the interest of some we have gone into together, nothing would have delighted me more than to have persuaded you to throw your lot in with mine for a time; but really I'm afraid to do so, for it sounds a particularly commonplace affair,' and he crumpled the paper into a ball and tossed it over to me.

I smoothed it out and read: 'To Holmes, 221B Baker Street, London, S.W. Please come to Sheffield at once to inquire into case of forgery. Jervis, Manager British Consolidated Bank.'

'I've wired back to say I shall go up to Sheffield by the one-thirty a.m. express from St Pancras,' said Holmes. 'I can't go sooner as I have an interesting little appointment to fulfil tonight down in the East End, which should give me the last information I need to trace home a daring robbery from the British Museum to its instigator – who possesses one of the oldest titles and finest houses in the country, along with a most insatiable greed, almost mania, for collecting ancient documents. Before discussing the Sheffield affair any further, however, we had perhaps better see what the evening paper has to say about it,' continued Holmes, as his boy entered with the *Evening News*, *Standard*, *Globe* and *Star*. 'Ah, this must be it,' he said, pointing to a paragraph headed: Daring Forger's Remarkable Exploits in Sheffield.

Whilst going to press we have been informed that a series of most cleverly forged cheques have been successfully used to swindle the Sheffield banks out of a sum which cannot be less than six thousand pounds. The full extent of the fraud has not yet been ascertained, and the managers of the different banks concerned, who have been interviewed by our Sheffield correspondent, are very reticent.

It appears that a gentleman named Mr Jabez Booth, who resides at Broomhill, Sheffield, and has been an employee since January 1881 at the British Consolidated Bank in Sheffield, yesterday succeeded in cashing quite a number of cleverly forged cheques at twelve of the principal banks in the city and absconding with the proceeds.

The crime appears to have been a strikingly deliberate and well-thought-out one. Mr Booth had, of course, in his position in one of the principal banks in Sheffield, excellent opportunities of studying the various signatures which he forged, and he greatly facilitated his chances of easily and successfully obtaining cash for the cheques by opening banking accounts last year at each of the twelve banks at which he presented the forged cheques and by this means becoming personally known at each.

He still further disarmed suspicion by crossing each of the forged cheques and paying them into his account, while, at the same time, he drew and cashed a cheque of his own for about half the amount of the forged cheque paid in.

It was not until early this morning, Thursday, that the fraud was discovered, which means that the rascal has had some twenty hours in which to make good his escape. In spite of this we have little doubt but that he will soon be laid by the heels, for we are informed that the finest detectives from Scotland Yard are already upon his track, and it is also whispered that Mr Sherlock Holmes, the well-known and almost world-famous criminal expert of Baker Street, has been asked to assist in hunting down this daring forger.

'Then there follows a lengthy description of the fellow, which I needn't read but will keep for future use,' said Holmes, folding the paper and looking across at me. 'It seems to have been a pretty smart affair. This Booth may not be easily caught for, though he hasn't had a long time in which to make his escape, we mustn't lose sight of the fact that he's had twelve months in which to plan how he would do the vanishing trick when the time came. Well! What do you say, Watson? Some of the little problems we have gone into in the past should at least have taught us that the most interesting cases do not always present the most bizarre features at the outset.'

'"So far from it, on the contrary, quite the reverse," to quote Sam Weller,' I replied. 'Personally nothing would be more to my taste than to join you.'

'Then we'll consider it settled,' said my friend. 'And now I must go and attend to that other little matter of business I spoke to you about. Remember,' he said, as we parted, 'one-thirty at St Pancras.'

I was on the platform in good time, but it was not until the hands of the great station clock indicated the very moment due for our departure, and the porters were beginning to slam the carriage doors noisily, that I caught the familiar sight of Holmes's tall figure.

'Ah! here you are Watson,' he cried cheerily. 'I fear you must have thought I was going to be too late. I've had a very busy evening and no time to waste; however, I've succeeded in putting into practice Phileas Fogg's theory that "a well-used minimum suffices for everything", and here I am.'

'About the last thing I should expect of you,' I said as we settled down into two opposite corners of an otherwise empty first-class carriage, 'would be that you should do such an un-methodical thing as to miss a train. The only thing which would surprise me more, in fact, would be to see you at the station ten minutes before time.'

'I should consider that the greatest evil of the two,' said Holmes sententiously. 'But now we must sleep; we have every prospect of a heavy day.'

It was one of Holmes's characteristics that he could command sleep at will; unfortunately he could resist it at will also, and often and often have I had to remonstrate with him on the harm he must be doing himself, when, deeply engrossed in one of his strange or baffling problems, he would go for several consecutive days and nights without one wink of sleep.

He put the shades over the lamps, leaned back in his corner, and in less than two minutes his regular breathing told me he was fast asleep. Not being blessed with the same gift myself, I lay back in my corner for some time, nodding to the rhythmical throb of the express as it hurled itself forward through the darkness. Now and again as we shot through some brilliantly illuminated station or past a line of flaming furnaces, I caught for an instant a glimpse of Holmes's figure coiled up snugly in the far corner with his head sunk upon his breast.

It was not until after we had passed Nottingham that I really fell asleep and, when a more than usually violent lurch of the train over some points woke me again, it was broad daylight, and Holmes was sitting up, busy with a Bradshaw and boat timetable. As I moved, he glanced across at me.

'If I'm not mistaken, Watson, that was the Dore and Totley tunnel through which we have just come, and if so we shall be in Sheffield in a few minutes. As you see I've not been wasting my time altogether, but studying my Bradshaw, which, by the way, Watson, is the most useful book published, without exception, to anyone of my calling.'

'How can it possibly help you now?' I asked in some surprise.

'Well, it may or it may not,' said Holmes thoughtfully. 'But in any case it's well to have at one's finger tips all knowledge which may be of use. It's quite probable that this Jabez Booth may have decided to leave the country and, if this supposition is correct, he would undoubtedly time his little escapade in conformity with information contained in this useful volume. Now I learn from this *Sheffield Telegraph* which I obtained at Leicester, by the way, when you were fast asleep, that Mr Booth cashed the last of his forged cheques at the North British Bank in Saville Street at precisely two-fifteen p.m. on Wednesday last. He made the round of the various banks he visited in a hansom, and it would take him about three minutes only to get from this bank to the G.C. station. From what I gather of the order in which the different banks were visited, he made a circuit, finishing at the nearest point to the G.C. station, at which he could arrive at about two-eighteen. Now I find that at two twenty-two a boat express would leave Sheffield G.C., due in Liverpool at four-twenty, and in connection with it the White Star liner *Empress Queen* should have sailed from Liverpool docks at six-thirty for New York. Or again at two forty-five a boat train would leave Sheffield for Hull, at which town it was due at four-thirty in time to make a connection with the Holland steam packet, *Comet*, sailing at six-thirty for Amsterdam.

'Here we are provided with two not unlikely means of escape, the former being the most probable; but both worth bearing in mind.'

Holmes had scarcely finished speaking when the train drew up.

'Nearly five past four,' I remarked.

'Yes,' said Holmes, 'we are exactly one and a half minutes behind time. And now I propose a good breakfast and a cup of strong coffee, for we have at least a couple of hours to spare.'

After breakfast we visited first the police station where we learned that no further developments had taken place in the matter we had come to investigate. Mr Lestrade of Scotland Yard had arrived the previous evening and had taken the case in hand officially.

We obtained the address of Mr Jervis, the manager of the bank at which Booth had been an employee, and also that of his landlady at Broomhill.

A hansom landed us at Mr Jervis's house at Fulwood at seven-thirty. Holmes insisted upon my accompanying him, and we were both shown into a spacious drawing-room and asked to wait until the banker could see us.

Mr Jervis, a stout, florid gentleman of about fifty, came puffing into the room in a very short time. An atmosphere of prosperity seemed to envelop, if not actually to emanate from him.

'Pardon me for keeping you waiting, gentlemen,' he said, 'but the hour is an early one.'

'Indeed, Mr Jervis,' said Holmes, 'no apology is needed unless it be on our part. It is, however, necessary that I should ask you a few questions concerning this affair of Mr Booth, before I can proceed in the matter, and that must be our excuse for paying you such an untimely visit.'

'I shall be most happy to answer your questions as far as it lies in my power to do so,' said the banker, his fat fingers playing with a bunch of seals at the end of his massive gold watch chain.

'When did Mr Booth first enter your bank?' said Holmes.

'In January 1881.'

'Do you know where he lived when he first came to Sheffield?'

'He took lodgings at Ashgate Road, and has, I believe, lived there ever since.'

'Do you know anything of his history or life before he came to you?'

'Very little I fear; beyond that his parents were both dead, and that he came to us with the best testimonials from one of the Leeds branches of our bank, I know nothing.'

'Did you find him quick and reliable?'

'He was one of the best and smartest men I have ever had in my employ.'

'Do you know whether he was conversant with any other language besides English?'

'I feel pretty sure he wasn't. We have one clerk who attends to any foreign correspondence we may have, and I know that Booth has repeatedly passed letters and papers on to him.'

'With your experience of banking matters, Mr Jervis, how long a time do you think he might reasonably have calculated would elapse between the presentation of the forged cheques and their detection?'

'Well, that would depend very largely upon circumstances,' said Mr Jervis. 'In the case of a single cheque it might be a week or two, unless the amounts were so large as to call for special inquiry, in which case it would probably never be cashed at all until such inquiry had been made. In the present case, when there were a dozen forged cheques it was most unlikely that some one of them should not be detected within twenty-four hours and so lead to the discovery of the fraud. No sane person would dare to presume upon the crime remaining undetected for a longer period than that.'

'Thanks,' said Holmes, rising. 'Those were the chief points I wished to speak to you about. I will communicate to you any news of importance I may have.'

'I am deeply obliged to you, Mr Holmes. The case is naturally causing us great anxiety. We leave it entirely to your discretion to take whatever steps you may consider best. Oh, by the way, I sent instructions to Booth's landlady to disturb nothing in his rooms until you had had an opportunity of examining them.'

'That was a very wise thing to do,' said Holmes, 'and may be the means of helping us materially.'

'I am also instructed by my company,' said the banker, as he bowed us politely out, 'to ask you to make a note of any expenses incurred, which they will of course immediately defray.'

A few moments later we were ringing the bell of the house in Ashgate Road, Broomhill, at which Mr Booth had been a lodger for over seven years. It was answered by a maid who informed us that Mrs Purnell was engaged with a gentleman upstairs. When we explained our errand she showed us at once up to Mr Booth's rooms, on the first floor, where we found Mrs Purnell, a plump, voluble, little lady of about forty, in conversation with Mr Lestrade, who appeared to be just concluding his examination of the rooms.

'Good morning, Holmes,' said the detective, with a very self-satisfied air. 'You arrive on the scene a little too late; I fancy I have already got all the information needed to catch our man!'

'I'm delighted to hear it,' said Holmes dryly, 'and must indeed congratulate you, if this is actually the case. Perhaps after I've made a little tour of inspection we can compare notes.'

'Just as you please,' said Lestrade, with the air of one who can afford to be gracious. 'Candidly I think you will be wasting time, and so would you if you knew what I've discovered.'

'Still I must ask you to humour my little whim,' said Holmes, leaning against the mantelpiece and whistling softly as he looked round the room.

After a moment he turned to Mrs Purnell. 'The furniture of this room belongs, of course, to you?'

Mrs Purnell assented.

'The picture that was taken down from over the mantelpiece last Wednesday morning,' continued Holmes, 'that belonged to Mr Booth, I presume?'

I followed Holmes's glance across to where an unfaded patch on the wallpaper clearly indicated that a picture had recently been hanging. Well as I knew my friend's methods of reasoning, however, I did not realize for a moment that the little bits of spiderweb which had been behind the picture, and were still clinging to the wall, had told him that the picture could only have been taken down immediately before Mrs Purnell had received orders to disturb nothing in the room; otherwise her brush, evidently busy enough elsewhere, would not have spared them.

The good lady stared at Sherlock Holmes in open-mouthed astonishment. 'Mr Booth took it down himself on Wednesday morning,' she said. 'It was a picture he had painted himself, and he thought no end of it. He wrapped it up and took it out with him, remarking that he was going to give it to a friend. I was very much surprised at the time, for I knew he valued it very much; in fact he once told me that he wouldn't part with it for anything. Of course, it's easy to see now why he got rid of it.'

'Yes,' said Holmes. 'It wasn't a large picture, I see. Was it a water colour?'

'Yes, a painting of a stretch of moorland, with three or four large rocks arranged like a big table on a bare hilltop. Druidicals, Mr Booth called them, or something like that.'

'Did Mr Booth do much painting, then?' inquired Holmes.

'None, whilst he's been here, sir. He has told me he used to do a good deal as a lad, but he had given it up.'

Holmes's eyes were glancing round the room again, and an exclamation of surprise escaped him as they encountered a photo standing on the piano.

'Surely that's a photograph of Mr Booth,' he said. 'It exactly resembles the description I have of him.'

'Yes,' said Mrs Purnell, 'and a very good one it is too.'

'How long has it been taken?' said Holmes, picking it up.

'Oh, only a few weeks, sir. I was here when the boy from the photographer's brought them up. Mr Booth opened the packet whilst I was in the room. There were only two photos, that one and another which he gave to me.'

'You interest me exceedingly,' said Holmes. 'This striped lounge suit he is wearing. Is it the same that he had on when he left Wednesday morning?'

'Yes, he was dressed just like that, as far as I can remember.'

'Do you recollect anything of importance that Mr Booth said to you last Wednesday before he went out?'

'Not very much, I'm afraid, sir. When I took his cup of chocolate up to his bedroom, he said — '

'One moment,' interrupted Holmes. 'Did Mr Booth usually have a cup of chocolate in the morning?'

'Oh, yes, sir, summer and winter alike. He was very particular about it and would ring for it as soon as ever he waked. I believe he'd rather have gone without his breakfast almost than have missed his cup of chocolate. Well, as I was saying, sir, I took it up to him myself on Wednesday morning, and he made some remark about the weather and then, just as I was leaving the room, he said, "Oh, by the way, Mrs Purnell, I shall be going away tonight for a couple of weeks. I've packed my bag and will call for it this afternoon."'

'No doubt you were very much surprised at this sudden announcement?' queried Holmes.

'Not very much, sir. Ever since he's had this auditing work to do for the branch banks, there's been no knowing when he would be away. Of course, he'd never been off for two weeks at a stretch, except at holiday times, but he had so often been away for a few days at a time that I had got used to his popping off with hardly a moment's notice.'

'Let me see, how long has he had this extra work at the bank – several months, hasn't he?'

'More. It was about last Christmas, I believe, when they gave it to him.'

'Oh, yes, of course,' said Holmes carelessly, 'and this work naturally took him from home a good deal?'

'Yes, indeed, and it seemed to quite tire him, so much evening and night work too, you see, sir. It was enough to knock him out, for he was always such a very quiet, retiring gentleman and hardly ever used to go out in the evenings before.'

'Has Mr Booth left many of his possessions behind him?' asked Holmes.

'Very few, indeed, and what he has are mostly old useless things. But he's a most honest thief, sir,' said Mrs Purnell paradoxically, 'and paid me his rent, before he went out on Wednesday morning, right up to next Saturday, because he wouldn't be back by then.'

'That was good of him,' said Holmes, smiling thoughtfully. 'By the way, do you happen to know if he gave away any other treasures before he left?'

'Well, not *just* before, but during the last few months he's taken away most of his books and sold them I think, a few at a time. He had rather a fancy for old books and has told me that some editions he had were worth quite a lot.'

During this conversation, Lestrade had been sitting drumming his fingers impatiently on the table. Now he got up. 'Really, I fear I shall have to leave you to this gossip,' he said. 'I must go and wire instructions for the arrest of Mr Booth. If only you would have looked before at this old blotter, which I found in the wastebasket, you would have saved yourself a good deal of unnecessary trouble, Mr Holmes,' and he triumphantly slapped down a sheet of well-used blotting paper on the table.

Holmes picked it up and held it in front of a mirror over the sideboard. Looking over his shoulder I could plainly read the reflected impression of a note written in Mr Booth's hand-writing, of which Holmes had procured samples.

It was to a booking agency in Liverpool, giving instructions to them to book a first-class private cabin and passage on board the *Empress Queen* from Liverpool to New York. Parts of the note were slightly obliterated by other impressions, but it went on to say that a cheque was enclosed to pay for tickets, etc., and it was signed J. Booth.

Holmes stood silently scrutinizing the paper for several minutes.

It was a well-used sheet, but fortunately the impression of the note was well in the centre, and hardly obliterated at all by the other marks and blots, which were all round the outer circumference of the paper. In one corner the address of the Liverpool booking agency was plainly decipherable, the paper evidently having been used to blot the envelope with also.

'My dear Lestrade, you have indeed been more fortunate than I had imagined,' said Holmes at length, handing the paper back to him. 'May I ask what steps you propose to take next?'

'I shall cable at once to the New York police to arrest the fellow as soon as he arrives,' said Lestrade, 'but first I must make quite certain the boat doesn't touch at Queenstown or anywhere and give him a chance of slipping through our fingers.'

'It doesn't,' said Holmes quietly. 'I had already looked to see as I thought it not unlikely, at first, that Mr Booth might have intended to sail by the *Empress Queen*.'

Lestrade gave me a wink for which I would dearly have liked to have knocked him down, for I could see that he disbelieved my friend. I felt a keen pang of disappointment that Holmes's foresight should have been eclipsed in this way by what, after all, was mere good luck on Lestrade's part.

Holmes had turned to Mrs Purnell and was thanking her.

'Don't mention it, sir,' she said. 'Mr Booth deserves to be caught, though I must say he's always been a gentleman to me. I only wish I could have given you some more useful information.'

'On the contrary,' said Holmes, 'I can assure you that what you have told us has been of the utmost importance and will very materially help us. It's just occurred to me, by the way, to wonder if you could possibly put up my friend Dr Watson and myself for a few days, until we have had time to look into this little matter?'

'Certainly, sir, I shall be most happy.'

'Good,' said Holmes. 'Then you may expect us back to dinner about seven.'

When we got outside, Lestrade at once announced his intention of going to the police office and arranging for the necessary orders for Booth's detention and arrest to be cabled to the head of the New York police; Holmes retained an enigmatical silence as to what he purposed to do but expressed his determination to remain at Broomhill and make a few further inquiries. He insisted, however, upon going alone.

'Remember, Watson, you are here for a rest and holiday and I can assure you that if you did remain with me you would only find my programme a dull one. Therefore, I insist upon your finding some more entertaining way of spending the remainder of the day.'

Past experience told me that it was quite useless to remonstrate or argue with Holmes when once his mind was made up, so I consented with the best grace I could, and leaving Holmes, drove off in the hansom, which he assured me he would not require further.

I passed a few hours in the art gallery and museum and then, after lunch, had a brisk walk out on the Manchester Road and

enjoyed the fresh air and moorland scenery, returning to Ashgate Road at seven with better appetite than I had been blessed
with for months.

Holmes had not returned, and it was nearly half past seven
before he came in. I could see at once that he was in one of his
most reticent moods, and all my inquiries failed to elicit any
particulars of how he had passed his time or what he thought
about the case.

The whole evening he remained coiled up in an easy chair
puffing at his pipe and hardly a word could I get from him.

His inscrutable countenance and persistent silence gave me no
clue whatever as to his thought on the inquiry he had in hand,
although I could see his whole mind was concentrated upon it.

Next morning, just as we had finished breakfast, the maid
entered with a note. 'From Mr Jervis, sir; there's no answer,' she
said.

Holmes tore open the envelope and scanned the note hurriedly and, as he did so, I noticed a flush of annoyance spread
over his usually pale face.

'Confound his impudence,' he muttered. 'Read that, Watson.
I don't ever remember to have been treated so badly in a case
before.'

The note was a brief one:

The Cedars, Fulwood
September sixth
Mr Jervis, on behalf of the directors of the British Consolidated Bank,
begs to thank Mr Sherlock Holmes for his prompt attention and valued
services in the matter concerning the fraud and disappearance of their
ex-employee, Mr Jabez Booth.

Mr Lestrade, of Scotland Yard, informs us that he has succeeded in
tracking the individual in question who will be arrested shortly. Under
these circumstances they feel it unnecessary to take up any more of Mr
Holmes's valuable time.

'Rather cool, eh, Watson? I'm much mistaken if they don't
have cause to regret their action when it's too late. After this I

shall certainly refuse to act for them any further in the case, even if they ask me to do so. In a way I'm sorry because the matter presented some distinctly interesting features and is by no means the simple affair our friend Lestrade thinks.'

'Why, don't you think he is on the right scent?' I exclaimed.

'Wait and see, Watson,' said Holmes mysteriously. 'Mr Booth hasn't been caught yet, remember.' And that was all that I could get out of him.

One result of the summary way in which the banker had dispensed with my friend's services was that Holmes and I spent a most useful and enjoyable week in the small village of Hathersage, on the edge of the Derbyshire moors, and returned to London feeling better for our long moorland rambles.

Holmes having very little work in hand at the time, and my wife not yet having returned from her Swiss holiday, I prevailed upon him, though not without considerable difficulty, to pass the next few weeks with me instead of returning to his rooms at Baker Street.

Of course, we watched the development of the Sheffield forgery case with the keenest interest. Somehow the particulars of Lestrade's discoveries got into the papers, and the day after we left Sheffield they were full of the exciting chase of Mr Booth, the man wanted for the Sheffield bank frauds.

They spoke of 'the guilty man restlessly pacing the deck of the *Empress Queen*, as she ploughed her way majestically across the solitary wastes of the Atlantic, all unconscious that the inexorable hand of justice could stretch over the ocean and was already waiting to seize him on his arrival in the New World'. And Holmes after reading these sensational paragraphs would always lay down the paper with one of his enigmatical smiles.

At last the day on which the *Empress Queen* was due at New York arrived, and I could not help but notice that even Holmes's usually inscrutable face wore a look of suppressed excitement as he unfolded the evening paper. But our surprise was doomed to be prolonged still further. There was a brief paragraph to say that the *Empress Queen* had arrived off Long Island at six a.m.

after a good passage. There was, however, a case of cholera on board, and the New York authorities had consequently been compelled to put the boat in quarantine, and none of the passengers or crew would be allowed to leave her for a period of twelve days.

Two days later there was a full column in the papers stating that it had been definitely ascertained that Mr Booth was really on board the *Empress Queen*. He had been identified and spoken to by one of the sanitary inspectors who had had to visit the boat. He was being kept under close observation, and there was no possible chance of his escaping. Mr Lestrade of Scotland Yard, by whom Booth had been so cleverly tracked down and his escape forestalled, had taken passage on the *Oceania*, due in New York on the tenth, and would personally arrest Mr Booth when he was allowed to land.

Never before or since have I seen my friend Holmes so astonished as when he had finished reading this announcement. I could see that he was thoroughly mystified, though why he should be so was quite a puzzle to me. All day he sat coiled up in an easy chair, with his brows drawn down into two hard lines and his eyes half closed as he puffed away at his oldest brier in silence.

'Watson,' he said once, glancing across at me. 'It's perhaps a good thing that I was asked to drop that Sheffield case. As things are turning out I fancy I should only have made a fool of myself.'

'Why?' I asked.

'Because I began by assuming that somebody else wasn't one – and now it looks as though I had been mistaken.'

For the next few days Holmes seemed quite depressed, for nothing annoyed him more than to feel that he had made any mistake in his deductions or got on to a false line of reasoning.

At last the fatal tenth of September, the day on which Booth was to be arrested, arrived. Eagerly but in vain we scanned the evening papers. The morning of the eleventh came and still brought no news of the arrest, but in the evening papers of that day there was a short paragraph hinting that the criminal had escaped again.

For several days the papers were full of the most conflicting rumours and conjectures as to what had actually taken place, but all were agreed in affirming that Mr Lestrade was on his way home alone and would be back in Liverpool on the seventeenth or eighteenth.

On the evening of the last named day Holmes and I sat smoking in his Baker Street rooms, when his boy came in to announce that Mr Lestrade of Scotland Yard was below and would like the favour of a few minutes' conversation.

'Show him up, show him up,' said Holmes, rubbing his hands together with an excitement quite unusual to him.

Lestrade entered the room and sat down in the seat to which Holmes waved him, with a most dejected air.

'It's not often I'm at fault, Mr Holmes,' he began, 'but in this Sheffield business I've been beaten hollow.'

'Dear me,' said Holmes pleasantly, 'you surely don't mean to tell me that you haven't got your man yet.'

'I do,' said Lestrade. 'What's more, I don't think he ever will be caught!'

'Don't despair so soon,' said Holmes encouragingly. 'After you have told us all that's already happened, it's just within the bounds of possibility that I may be able to help you with some little suggestions.'

Thus encouraged Lestrade began his strange story to which we both listened with breathless interest.

'It's quite unnecessary for me to dwell upon incidents which are already familiar,' he said. 'You know of the discovery I made in Sheffield which, of course, convinced me that the man I wanted had sailed for New York on the *Empress Queen*. I was in a fever of impatience for his arrest, and when I heard that the boat he had taken passage on had been placed in quarantine, I set off at once in order that I might actually lay hands upon him myself. Never have five days seemed so long.

'We reached New York on the evening of the ninth, and I rushed off at once to the head of the New York police and from him learned that there was no doubt whatever that Mr Jabez Booth was indeed on board the *Empress Queen*. One of the sanitary inspectors who had had to visit the boat had not only seen but actually spoken to him. The man exactly answered the description of Booth which had appeared in the papers. One of the New York detectives had been sent on board to make a few inquiries and to inform the captain privately of the pending arrest. He found that Mr Jabez Booth had actually had the audacity to book his passage and travel under his real name without even attempting to disguise himself in any way. He had a private first-class cabin, and the purser declared that he had been suspicious of the man from the first. He had kept himself shut up in his cabin nearly all the time, posing as an eccentric semi-invalid person who must not be disturbed on any account. Most of his meals had been sent down to his cabin, and he had been seen on deck but seldom and hardly ever dined with the rest of the passengers. It was quite evident that he had been trying to keep out of sight, and to attract as little attention as possible. The stewards and some of the passengers who were approached on the subject later were all agreed that this was the case.

'It was decided that during the time the boat was in quarantine nothing should be said to Booth to arouse his suspicions but that the purser, steward and captain, who were the only persons in the secret, should between them keep him under observation until the tenth, the day on which passengers would be allowed to leave the boat. On that day he should be arrested.'

Here we were interrupted by Holmes's boy who came in with a telegram. Holmes glanced at it with a faint smile.

'No answer,' he said, slipping it in his waistcoat pocket. 'Pray continue your very interesting story, Lestrade.'

'Well, on the afternoon of the tenth, accompanied by the New York chief inspector of police and detective Forsyth,' resumed Lestrade, 'I went on board the *Empress Queen* half an hour before she was due to come up to the landing stage to allow passengers to disembark.

'The purser informed us that Mr Booth had been on deck and

that he had been in conversation with him about fifteen minutes before our arrival. He had then gone down to his cabin and the purser, making some excuse to go down also, had actually seen him enter it. He had been standing near the top of the companionway since then and was sure Booth had not come up on deck again since.

'"At last," I muttered to myself, as we all went down below, led by the purser who took us straight to Booth's cabin. We knocked but, getting no answer, tried the door and found it locked. The purser assured us, however, that this was nothing unusual. Mr Booth had had his cabin door locked a good deal and, often, even his meals had been left on a tray outside. We held a hurried consultation and, as time was short, decided to force the door. Two good blows with a heavy hammer broke it from the hinges, and we all rushed in. You can picture our astonishment when we found the cabin empty. We searched it thoroughly, and Booth was certainly not there.'

'One moment,' interrupted Holmes. 'The key of the door – was it on the inside of the lock or not?'

'It was nowhere to be seen,' said Lestrade. 'I was getting frantic for, by this time, I could feel the vibration of the engines and hear the first churning sound of the screw as the great boat began to slide slowly down towards the landing stage.

'We were at our wits' end; Mr Booth must be hiding somewhere on board, but there was now no time to make a proper search for him, and in a very few minutes passengers would be leaving the boat. At last the captain promised us that, under the circumstances, only one landing gangway should be run out and, in company with the purser and stewards, I should stand by it with a complete list of passengers ticking off each one as he or she left. By this means it would be quite impossible for Booth to escape us even if he attempted some disguise, for no person whatever would be allowed to cross the gangway until identified by the purser or one of the stewards.

'I was delighted with the arrangement, for there was now no way by which Booth could give me the slip.

'One by one the passengers crossed the gangway and joined the jostling crowd on the landing stage and each one was identified and his or her name crossed off my list. There were one hundred and ninety-three first-class passengers on board the *Empress Queen*, including Booth, and, when one hundred and ninety-two had disembarked, his was the only name which remained!

'You can scarcely realize what a fever of impatience we were in,' said Lestrade, mopping his brow at the very recollection, 'nor how interminable the time seemed as we slowly but carefully ticked off one by one the whole of the three hundred and twenty-four second-class passengers and the three hundred and ten steerage from my list. Every passenger except Mr Booth crossed that gangway, but he certainly did not do so. There was no possible room for doubt on that point.

'He must therefore be still on the boat, we agreed, but I was getting panic-stricken and wondered if there were any possibility of his getting smuggled off in some of the luggage which the great cranes were now beginning to swing up on to the pier.

'I hinted my fear to detective Forsyth, and he at once arranged that every trunk or box in which there was any chance for a man to hide should be opened and examined by the customs officers.

'It was a tedious business, but they didn't shirk it, and at the end of two hours were able to assure us that by no possibility could Booth have been smuggled off the boat in this way.

'This left only one possible solution to the mystery. He *must* be still in hiding somewhere on board. We had had the boat kept under the closest observation ever since she came up to the landing stage, and now the superintendent of police lent us a staff of twenty men and, with the consent of the captain and the assistance of the pursers and stewards, etc., the *Empress Queen* was searched and re-searched from stem to stern. We didn't leave unexamined a place in which a cat could have hidden, but the missing man wasn't there. Of that I'm certain – and there you have the whole mystery in a nutshell, Mr Holmes. Mr Booth certainly *was* on board the *Empress Queen* up to, and at, eleven o'clock on the morning of the tenth, and although he could not by any possibility have left it, we are nevertheless face to face with the fact that he wasn't there at five o'clock in the afternoon.'

Lestrade's face, as he concluded his curious and mysterious narrative, bore a look of the most hopeless bewilderment I ever saw, and I fancy my own must have pretty well matched it, but Holmes threw himself back in his easy chair, with his long thin legs stuck straight out in front of him, his whole frame literally shaking with silent laughter. 'What conclusion have you come to?' he gasped at length. 'What steps do you propose to take next?'

'I've no idea. Who could know what to do? The whole thing is impossible, perfectly impossible; it's an insoluble mystery. I came to you to see if you could, by any chance, suggest some entirely fresh line of inquiry upon which I might begin to work.'

'Well,' said Holmes, cocking his eye mischievously at the bewildered Lestrade, 'I can give you Booth's present address, if it will be of any use to you?'

'His what!' cried Lestrade.

'His present address,' repeated Holmes quietly. 'But before I do so, my dear Lestrade, I must make one stipulation. Mr Jervis has treated me very shabbily in the matter, and I don't desire that my name shall be associated with it any further. Whatever you do you must not hint the source from which any information I may give you has come. You promise?'

'Yes,' murmured Lestrade, who was in a state of bewildered excitement.

Holmes tore a leaf from his pocket book and scribbled on it: Mr A. Winter, c/o Mrs Thackaray, Glossop Road, Broomhill, Sheffield.

'You will find there the present name and address of the man you are in search of,' he said, handing the paper across to Lestrade. 'I should strongly advise you to lose no time in getting hold of him, for though the wire I received a short time ago — which unfortunately interrupted your most interesting narrative — was to tell me that Mr Winter had arrived back home again after a temporary absence, still it's more than probable that he will leave there, for good, at an early date. I can't say how soon — not for a few days I should think.'

Lestrade rose. 'Mr Holmes, you're a brick,' he said, with more real feeling than I have ever seen him show before. 'You've saved my reputation in this job just when I was beginning to look like a perfect fool, and now you're forcing me to take all the credit, when I don't deserve one atom. As to how you have found this out, it's as great a mystery to me as Booth's disappearance was.'

'Well, as to that,' said Holmes airily, 'I can't be sure of all the facts myself, for of course I've never looked properly into the case. But they are pretty easy to conjecture, and I shall be most happy to give you my idea of Booth's trip to New York on some future occasion when you have more time to spare.

'By the way,' called out Holmes, as Lestrade was leaving the room, 'I shouldn't be surprised if you find Mr Jabez Booth, alias Mr Archibald Winter, a slight acquaintance of yours, for he would undoubtedly be a fellow passenger of yours, on your homeward journey from America. He reached Sheffield a few hours before you arrived in London and, as he has certainly just returned from New York, like yourself, it's evident you must have crossed on the same boat. He would be wearing smoked glasses and have a heavy dark moustache.'

'Ah!' said Lestrade, 'there *was* a man called Winter on board who answered to that description. I believe it must have been he, and I'll lose no more time,' and Lestrade hurried off.

'Well, Watson, my boy, you look nearly as bewildered as our friend Lestrade,' said Holmes, leaning back in his chair and looking roguishly across at me, as he lighted his old brier pipe.

'I must confess that none of the problems you have had to solve in the past seemed more inexplicable to me than

Lestrade's account of Booth's disappearance from the *Empress Queen*.'

'Yes, that part of the story is decidedly neat,' chuckled Holmes, 'but I'll tell you how I got at the solution of the mystery. I see you are ready to listen.

'The first thing to do in any case is to gauge the intelligence and cunning of the criminal. Now, Mr Booth was undoubtedly a clever man. Mr Jervis himself, you remember, assured us as much. The fact that he opened banking accounts in preparation for the crime twelve months before he committed it proves it to have been a long-premeditated one. I began the case, therefore, with the knowledge that I had a clever man to catch, who had had twelve months in which to plan his escape.

'My first real clues came from Mrs Purnell,' said Holmes. 'Most important were her remarks about Booth's auditing work which kept him from home so many days and nights, often consecutively. I felt certain at once, and inquiry confirmed, that Mr Booth had had no such extra work at all. Why then had he invented lies to explain these absences to his landlady? Probably because they were in some way connected, either with the crime, or with his plans for escaping after he had committed it. It was inconceivable that so much mysterious outdoor occupation could be directly connected with the forgery, and I at once deduced that this time had been spent by Booth in paving the way for his escape.

'Almost at once the idea that he had been living a double life occurred to me, his intention doubtless being to quietly drop one individuality after committing the crime and permanently take up the other – a far safer and less clumsy expedient than the usual one of assuming a new disguise just at the very moment when everybody is expecting and looking for you to do so.

'Then there were the interesting facts relating to Booth's picture and books. I tried to put myself in his place. He valued these possessions highly; they were light and portable, and there was really no reason whatever why he should part with them. Doubtless, then, he had taken them away by degrees and put them someplace where he could lay hands on them again. If I could find out where this place was, I felt sure there would be every chance I could catch him when he attempted to recover them.

'The picture couldn't have gone far for he had taken it out with him on the very day of the crime . . . I needn't bore you with details . . . I was two hours making inquiries before I found the house at which he had called and left it – which was none other than Mrs Thackary's in Glossop Road.

'I made a pretext for calling there and found Mrs T. one of the most easy mortals in the world to pump. In less than half an hour I knew that she had a boarder named Winter, that he professed to be a commercial traveller and was from home most of the time. His description resembled Booth's save that he had a moustache and wore glasses.

'As I've often tried to impress upon you before, Watson, details are the most important things of all, and it gave me a real thrill of pleasure to learn that Mr Winter had a cup of chocolate brought up to his bedroom every morning. A gentleman called on the Wednesday morning and left a parcel, saying it was a picture he had promised for Mr Winter, and asking Mrs Thackary to give it to Winter when he returned. Mr Winter had taken the rooms the previous December. He had a good many books which he had brought in from time to time. All these facts taken in conjunction made me certain that I was on the right scent. Winter and Booth were one and the same person, and as soon as Booth had put all his pursuers off the track he would return, as Winter, and repossess his treasures.

'The newly taken photo and the old blotter with its telltale note were too obviously intentional means of drawing the police on to Booth's track. The blotter, I could see almost at once, was a fraud, for not only would it be almost impossible to use one in the ordinary way so much without the central part becoming undecipherable, but I could see where it had been touched up.

'I concluded therefore that Booth, alias Winter, never actually intended to sail on the *Empress Queen*, but in that I

underestimated his ingenuity. Evidently he booked *two* berths
on the boat, one in his real, and one in his assumed name, and
managed very cleverly to successfully keep up the two characters throughout the voyage, appearing first as one individual and
then as the other. Most of the time he posed as Winter, and for
this purpose Booth became the eccentric semi-invalid passenger
who remained locked up in his cabin for such a large part of his
time. This, of course, would answer his purpose well; his eccentricity would only draw attention to his presence on board and
so make him one of the best-known passengers on the boat,
although he showed so little of himself.

'I had left instructions with Mrs Thackary to send me a wire
as soon as Winter returned. When Booth had led his pursuers
to New York, and there thrown them off the scent, he had
nothing more to do but to take the first boat back. Very
naturally it chanced to be the same as that on which our friend
Lestrade returned, and that was how Mrs Thackary's wire
arrived at the opportune moment it did.'

III

THE ADVENTURE OF
THE UNIQUE *HAMLET*

Vincent Starrett

❦

'Holmes,' said I one morning, as I stood in our bay window, looking idly into the street, 'surely here comes a madman. Someone has incautiously left the door open and the poor fellow has slipped out. What a pity!'

It was a glorious morning in the spring, with a fresh breeze and inviting sunlight, but as it was early few persons were as yet astir. Birds twittered under the neighbouring eaves, and from the far end of the thoroughfare came faintly the droning cry of an umbrella repairman; a lean cat slunk across the cobbles and disappeared into a courtway; but for the most part the street was deserted, save for the eccentric individual who had called forth my exclamation.

Sherlock Holmes rose lazily from the chair in which he had been lounging and came to my side, standing with long legs spread and hands in the pockets of his dressing-gown. He smiled as he saw the singular personage coming along; and a personage the man seemed to be, despite his curious actions, for he was tall and portly, with elderly whiskers of the variety called mutton-chop, and eminently respectable. He was loping curiously, like a tired hound, lifting his knees high as he ran, and a heavy double watch chain bounced against and rebounded from the plump line of his figured waistcoat. With one hand he clutched despairingly at his tall silk hat, while with the other he made strange gestures in the air, in a state of emotion bordering on distraction. We could almost see the spasmodic workings of his countenance.

'What in the world can ail him?' I cried. 'See how he glances at the houses as he passes.'

'He is looking at the numbers,' responded Sherlock Holmes with dancing eyes, 'and I fancy it is ours that will give him the greatest happiness. His profession, of course, is obvious.'

'A banker, I should imagine, or at least a person of affluence,' I ventured, wondering what curious detail had betrayed the man's vocation to my remarkable companion in a single glance.

'Affluent, yes,' said Holmes with a mischievous twinkle, 'but not exactly a banker, Watson. Notice the sagging pockets, despite the excellence of his clothing, and the rather exaggerated madness of his eye. He is a collector, or I am very much mistaken.'

'My dear fellow!' I exclaimed. 'At his age and in his station! And why should he be seeking us? When we settled that last bill – '

'Of books,' said my friend severely. 'He is a book collector. His line is Caxtons, Elzevirs and Gutenberg Bibles, not the sordid reminders of unpaid grocery accounts. See, he is turning in, as I expected, and in a moment he will stand upon our hearthrug and tell the harrowing tale of a unique volume and its extraordinary disappearance.'

His eyes gleamed and he rubbed his hands together in satisfaction. I could not but hope that his conjecture was correct, for he had had little recently to occupy his mind, and I lived in constant fear that he would seek that stimulation his active brain required in the long-tabooed cocaine bottle.

As Holmes finished speaking, the doorbell echoed through the house; then hurried feet were sounding on the stairs, while the wailing voice of Mrs Hudson, raised in protest, could only have been occasioned by frustration of her coveted privilege of bearing up our caller's card. Then the door burst violently inwards and the object of our analysis staggered to the centre of the room and pitched headforemost upon our centre rug. There he lay, a magnificent ruin, with his head on the fringed border and his feet in the coal scuttle; and sealed within his motionless lips was the amazing story he had come to tell – for that it was amazing we could not doubt in the light of our client's extraordinary behaviour.

Sherlock Holmes ran quickly for the brandy, while I knelt beside the stricken man and loosened his wilted neckband. He was not dead, and when we had forced the flask beneath his teeth he sat up in groggy fashion, passing a dazed hand across his eyes. Then he scrambled to his feet with an embarrassed apology for his weakness, and fell into the chair which Holmes invitingly held towards him.

'That is right, Mr Harrington Edwards,' said my companion soothingly. 'Be quite calm, my dear sir, and when you have recovered your composure you will find us ready to listen.'

'You know me then?' cried our visitor. There was pride in his voice and he lifted his eyebrows in surprise.

'I had never heard of you until this moment; but if you wish to conceal your identity it would be well,' said Sherlock Holmes, 'for you to leave your bookplates at home.' As Holmes spoke he returned a little package of folded paper slips, which he had picked from the floor. 'They fell from your hat when you had the misfortune to collapse,' he added whimsically.

'Yes, yes,' cried the collector, a deep blush spreading across his features. 'I remember now; my hat was a little large and I folded a number of them and placed them beneath the sweatband. I had forgotten.'

'Rather shabby usage for a handsome etched plate,' smiled my companion; 'but that is your affair. And now, sir, if you are quite at ease, let us hear what it is that has brought you, a collector of books, from Poke Stogis Manor – the name is on the plate – to the office of Sherlock Holmes, consulting expert in crime. Surely nothing but the theft of Mahomet's own copy of the Koran can have affected you so strongly.'

Mr Harrington Edwards smiled feebly at the jest, then sighed. 'Alas,' he murmured, 'if that were all! But I shall begin at the beginning.

'You must know, then, that I am the greatest Shakespearean

commentator in the world. My collection of *ana* is unrivalled and much of the world's collection (and consequently its knowledge of the veritable Shakespeare) has emanated from my pen. One book I did not possess: it was unique, in the correct sense of that abused word, the greatest Shakespeare rarity in the world. Few knew that it existed, for its existence was kept a profound secret among a chosen few. Had it become known that this book was in England – anywhere, indeed – its owner would have been hounded to his grave by wealthy Americans.

'It was in the possession of my friend – I tell you this in strictest confidence – of my friend, Sir Nathaniel Brooke-Bannerman, whose place at Walton-on-Walton is next to my own. A scant two hundred yards separate our dwellings; so intimate has been our friendship that a few years ago the fence between our estates was removed, and each of us roamed or loitered at will in the other's preserves.

'For some years, now, I have been at work upon my greatest book – my magnum opus. It was to be my last book also embodying the results of a lifetime of study and research. Sir, I know Elizabethan London better than any man alive; better than any man who ever lived, I think –' He burst suddenly into tears.

'There, there,' said Sherlock Holmes gently. 'Do not be distressed. Pray continue with your interesting narrative. What was this book – which, I take it, in some manner has disappeared? You borrowed it from your friend?'

'That is what I am coming to,' said Mr Harrington Edwards, drying his tears, 'but as for help, Mr Holmes, I fear that is beyond even you. As you surmise, I needed this book. Knowing its value, which could not be fixed, for the book is priceless, and knowing Sir Nathaniel's idolatry of it, I hesitated before asking for the loan of it. But I had to have it, for without it my work could not have been completed, and at length I made my request. I suggested that I visit him and go through the volume under his eyes, he sitting at my side throughout my entire examination, and servants stationed at every door and window, with fowling pieces in their hands.

'You can imagine my astonishment when Sir Nathaniel laughed at my precautions. "My dear Edwards," he said, "that would be all very well were you Arthur Rambridge or Sir Homer Nantes (mentioning the two great men of the British Museum), or were you Mr Henry Hutterson, the American railway magnate; but you are my friend Harrington Edwards, and you shall take the book home with you for as long as you like." I protested vigorously, I can assure you; but he would have it so, and as I was touched by this mark of his esteem, at length I permitted him to have his way. My God! If I had remained adamant! If I had only –'

He broke off and for a moment stared blindly into space. His eyes were directed at the Persian slipper on the wall, in the toe of which Holmes kept his tobacco, but we could see that his thoughts were far away.

'Come, Mr Edwards,' said Holmes firmly. 'You are agitating yourself unduly. And you are unreasonably prolonging our curiosity. You have not yet told us what this book is.'

Mr Harrington Edwards gripped the arm of the chair in which he sat. Then he spoke, and his voice was low and thrilling.

'The book was a *Hamlet* quarto, dated 1602, presented by Shakespeare to his friend Drayton, with an inscription four lines in length, written and signed by the Master, himself!'

'My dear sir!' I exclaimed. Holmes blew a long, slow whistle of astonishment.

'It is true,' cried the collector. 'That is the book I borrowed, and that is the book I lost! The long-sought quarto of 1602, actually inscribed in Shakespeare's own hand! His greatest drama, in an edition dated a year earlier than any that is known; a perfect copy, and with four lines in his own handwriting! Unique! Extraordinary! Amazing! Astounding! Colossal! Incredible! Un—'

He seemed wound up to continue indefinitely; but Holmes, who had sat quite still at first, shocked by the importance of the loss, interrupted the flow of adjectives.

'I appreciate your emotion, Mr Edwards,' he said, 'and the

book is indeed all that you say it is. Indeed, it is so important that we must at once attack the problem of rediscovering it. The book, I take it, is readily identifiable?'

'Mr Holmes,' said our client, earnestly, 'it would be impossible to hide it. It is so important a volume that, upon coming into its possession, Sir Nathaniel Brooke-Bannerman called a consultation of the great binders of the Empire, at which were present Mr Riviere, Messrs Sangorski and Sutcliffe, Mr Zaehnsdorf and certain others. They and myself, with two others, alone know of the book's existence. When I tell you that it is bound in brown levant morocco, with leather joints and brown levant doublures and flyleaves, the whole elaborately gold-tooled, inlaid with seven hundred and fifty separate pieces of various coloured leathers, and enriched by the insertion of eighty-seven precious stones, I need not add that it is a design that never will be duplicated, and I mention only a few of its glories. The binding was personally done by Messrs Riviere, Sangorski, Sutcliffe and Zaehnsdorf, working alternately, and is a work of such enchantment that any man might gladly die a thousand deaths for the privilege of owning it for twenty minutes.'

'Dear me,' quoth Sherlock Holmes, 'it must indeed be a handsome volume, and from your description, together with a realization of its importance by reason of its association, I gather that it is something beyond what might be termed a valuable book.'

'Priceless!' cried Mr Harrington Edwards. 'The combined wealth of India, Mexico and Wall Street would be all too little for its purchase.'

'You are anxious to recover this book?' asked Sherlock Holmes, looking at him keenly.

'My God!' shrieked the collector, rolling up his eyes and clawing at the air with his hands. 'Do you suppose – ?'

'Tut, tut!' Holmes interrupted. 'I was only teasing you. It is a book that might move even you, Mr Harrington Edwards, to theft – but we may put aside that notion. Your emotion is too sincere, and besides you know too well the difficulties of hiding such a volume as you describe. Indeed, only a very daring man would purloin it and keep it long in his possession. Pray tell us how you came to lose it.'

Mr Harrington Edwards seized the brandy flask, which stood at his elbow, and drained it at a gulp. With the renewed strength thus obtained, he continued his story:

'As I have said, Sir Nathaniel forced me to accept the loan of the book, much against my wishes. On the evening that I called for it, he told me that two of his servants, heavily armed, would accompany me across the grounds to my home. "There is no danger," he said, "but you will feel better"; and I heartily agreed with him. How shall I tell you what happened? Mr Holmes, it was those very servants who assailed me and robbed me of my priceless borrowing!'

Sherlock Holmes rubbed his lean hands with satisfaction. 'Splendid!' he murmured. 'This is a case after my own heart. Watson, these are deep waters in which we are adventuring. But you are rather lengthy about this, Mr Edwards. Perhaps it will help matters if I ask you a few questions. By what road did you go to your home?'

'By the main road, a good highway which lies in front of our estates. I preferred it to the shadows of the wood.'

'And there were some two hundred yards between your doors. At what point did the assault occur?'

'Almost midway between the two entrance drives, I should say.'

'There was no light?'

'That of the moon only.'

'Did you know these servants who accompanied you?'

'One I knew slightly; the other I had not seen before.'

'Describe them to me, please.'

'The man who is known to me is called Miles. He is clean-shaven, short and powerful, although somewhat elderly. He was known, I believe, as Sir Nathaniel's most trusted servant; he had been with Sir Nathaniel for years. I cannot describe him minutely for, of course, I never paid much attention to him.

The other was tall and thickset, and wore a heavy beard. He was a silent fellow; I do not believe that he spoke a word during the journey.'

'Miles was more communicative?'

'Oh yes – even garrulous, perhaps. He talked about the weather and the moon, and I forget what else.'

'Never about books?'

'There was no mention of books between any of us.'

'Just how did the attack occur?'

'It was very sudden. We had reached, as I say, about the half-way point, when the big man seized me by the throat – to prevent outcry, I suppose – and on the instant, Miles snatched the volume from my grasp and was off. In a moment his companion followed him. I had been half throttled and could not immediately cry out; but when I could articulate, I made the countryside ring with my cries. I ran after them, but failed even to catch another sight of them. They had disappeared completely.'

'Did you all leave the house together?'

'Miles and I left together; the second man joined us at the porter's lodge. He had been attending to some of his duties.'

'And Sir Nathaniel – where was he?'

'He said good-night on the threshold.'

'What has he had to say about all this?'

'I have not told him.'

'You have not told him?' echoed Sherlock Holmes, in astonishment.

'I have not dared,' confessed our client miserably. 'It will kill him. That book was the breath of his life.'

'When did all this occur?' I put in, with a glance at Holmes.

'Excellent, Watson,' said my friend, answering my glance. 'I was just about to ask the same question.'

'Just last night,' was Mr Harrington Edwards's reply. 'I was crazy most of the night, and didn't sleep a wink. I came to you the first thing this morning. Indeed, I tried to raise you on the telephone, last night, but could not establish a connection.'

'Yes,' said Holmes, reminiscently, 'we were attending Mme Trentini's first night. We dined later at Albani's.'

'Oh, Mr Holmes, do you think you can help me?' cried the abject collector.

'I trust so,' answered my friend, cheerfully. 'Indeed, I am certain I can. Such a book, as you remark, is not easily hidden. What say you, Watson, to a run down to Walton-on-Walton?'

'There is a train in half an hour,' said Mr Harrington Edwards, looking at his watch. 'Will you return with me?'

'No, no,' laughed Holmes, 'that would never do. We must not be seen together just yet, Mr Edwards. Go back yourself on the first train, by all means, unless you have further business in London. My friend and I will go together. There is another train this morning?'

'An hour later.'

'Excellent. Until we meet, then!'

We took the train from Paddington Station an hour later, as we had promised, and began our journey to Walton-on-Walton, a pleasant, aristocratic little village and the scene of the curious accident to our friend of Poke Stogis Manor. Sherlock Holmes, lying back in his seat, blew earnest smoke rings at the ceiling of our compartment, which fortunately was empty, while I devoted myself to the morning paper. After a bit I tired of this occupation and turned to Holmes to find him looking out of the window, wreathed in smiles, and quoting Horace softly under his breath.

'You have a theory?' I asked, in surprise.

'It is a capital mistake to theorize in advance of the evidence,' he replied. 'Still, I have given some thought to the interesting problem of our friend, Mr Harrington Edwards, and there are several indications which can point to only one conclusion.'

'And whom do you believe to be the thief?'

'My dear fellow,' said Sherlock Holmes, 'you forget we

already know the thief. Edwards has testified quite clearly that it was Miles who snatched the volume.'

'True,' I admitted, abashed. 'I had forgotten. All we must do then, is to find Miles.'

'And a motive,' added my friend, chuckling. 'What would you say, Watson, was the motive in this case?'

'Jealousy,' I replied.

'You surprise me!'

'Miles had been bribed by a rival collector, who in some manner had learned about this remarkable volume. You remember Edwards told us this second man joined them at the lodge. That would give an excellent opportunity for the substitution of a man other than the servant intended by Sir Nathaniel. Is not that good reasoning?'

'You surpass yourself, my dear Watson,' murmured Holmes. 'It is excellently reasoned, and as you justly observe, the opportunity for a substitution was perfect.'

'Do you not agree with me?'

'Hardly, Watson. A rival collector, in order to accomplish this remarkable coup, first would have to have known of the volume, as you suggest, but also he must have known upon what night Mr Harrington Edwards would go to Sir Nathaniel's to get it, which would point to collaboration on the part of our client. As a matter of fact, however, Mr Edwards's decision to accept the loan was, I believe, sudden and without previous determination.'

'I do not recall his saying so.'

'He did not say so, but it is a simple deduction. A book collector is mad enough to begin with, Watson; but tempt him with some such bait as this Shakespeare quarto and he is bereft of all sanity. Mr Edwards would not have been able to wait. It was just the night before that Sir Nathaniel promised him the book, and it was just last night that he flew to accept the offer – flying, incidentally, to disaster also. The miracle is that he was able to wait an entire day.'

'Wonderful!' I cried.

'Elementary,' said Holmes. 'If you are interested, you will do well to read Harley Graham on *Transcendental Emotion*; while I have myself been guilty of a small brochure in which I catalogue some twelve hundred professions and the emotional effect upon their members of unusual tidings, good and bad.'

We were the only passengers to alight at Walton-on-Walton, but rapid inquiry developed that Mr Harrington Edwards had returned on the previous train. Holmes, who had disguised himself before leaving the coach, did all the talking. He wore his cap peak backwards, carried a pencil behind his ear, and had turned up the bottoms of his trousers; while from one pocket dangled the end of a linen tape measure. He was a municipal surveyor to the life, and I could not but think that, meeting him suddenly in the highway I should not myself have known him. At his suggestion, I dented the crown of my hat and turned my jacket inside out. Then he gave me an end of the tape measure, while he, carrying the other, went on ahead. In this fashion, stopping from time to time to kneel in the dust and ostensibly to measure sections of the roadway, we proceeded towards Poke Stogis Manor. The occasional villagers whom we encountered on their way to the station paid us no more attention than if we had been rabbits.

Shortly we came in sight of our friend's dwelling, a picturesque and rambling abode, sitting far back in its own grounds and bordered by a square of sentinel oaks. A gravel pathway led from the roadway to the house entrance and, as we passed, the sunlight struck fire from an antique brass knocker on the door. The whole picture, with its background of gleaming countryside, was one of rural calm and comfort; we could with difficulty believe it the scene of the curious problem we had come to investigate.

'We shall not enter yet,' said Sherlock Holmes, passing the gate leading into our client's acreage; 'but we shall endeavour to be back in time for luncheon.'

From this point the road progressed downward in a gentle decline and the vegetation grew more thickly on either side of the road. Sherlock Holmes kept his eyes stolidly on the path before us, and when we had covered about a hundred yards he stopped. 'Here,' he said, pointing, 'the assault occurred.'

I looked closely at the earth, but could see no sign of struggle.

'You recall it was midway between the two houses that it happened,' he continued. 'No, there are few signs; there was no violent tussle. Fortunately, however, we had our proverbial fall of rain last evening and the earth has retained impressions nicely.' He indicated the faint imprint of a foot, then another, and still another. Kneeling down, I was able to see that, indeed, many feet had passed along the road.

Holmes flung himself at full length in the dirt and wriggled swiftly about, his nose to the earth, muttering rapidly in French. Then he whipped out a glass, the better to examine something that had caught his eye; but in a moment he shook his head in disappointment and continued with his exploration. I was irresistibly reminded of a noble hound, at fault, sniffing in circles in an effort to re-establish a lost scent. In a moment, however, he had it, for with a little cry of pleasure he rose to his feet, zigzagged curiously across the road and paused before a bridge, a lean finger pointing accusingly at a break in the thicket.

'No wonder they disappeared,' he smiled as I came up. 'Edwards thought they continued up the road, but here is where they broke through.' Then stepping back a little distance, he ran forward lightly and cleared the hedge at a bound.

'Follow me carefully,' he warned, 'for we must not allow our own footprints to confuse us.' I fell more heavily than my companion, but in a moment he had me up and helped me to steady myself. 'See,' he cried, examining the earth; and deep in the mud and grass I saw the prints of two pairs of feet.

'The small man broke through,' said Sherlock Holmes, exultantly, 'but the larger rascal leaped over the hedge. See how deeply his prints are marked; he landed heavily here in the soft ooze. It is significant, Watson, that they came this way. Does it suggest nothing to you?'

'That they were men who knew Edwards's grounds as well

as the Brooke-Bannerman estate,' I answered; and thrilled with pleasure at my friend's nod of approbation.

He flung himself upon the ground without further conversation, and for some moments we both crawled painfully across the grass. Then a shocking thought occurred to me.

'Holmes,' I whispered in dismay, 'do you see where these footprints tend? They are directed towards the home of our client, Mr Harrington Edwards!'

He nodded his head slowly, and his lips were tight and thin. The double line of impressions ended abruptly at the back door of Poke Stogis Manor!

Sherlock Holmes rose to his feet and looked at his watch.

'We are just in time for luncheon,' he announced, and brushed off his garments. Then, deliberately, he knocked upon the door. In a few moments we were in the presence of our client.

'We have been roaming about in the neighbourhood,' apologized the detective, 'and took the liberty of coming to your rear door.'

'You have a clue?' asked Mr Harrington Edwards eagerly.

A queer smile of triumph sat upon Holmes's lips.

'Indeed,' he said quietly, 'I believe I have solved your little problem, Mr Harrington Edwards.'

'My dear Holmes!' I cried, and 'My dear sir!' cried our client.

'I have yet to establish a motive,' confessed my friend; 'but as to the main facts there can be no question.'

Mr Harrington Edwards fell into a chair; he was white and shaking.

'The book,' he croaked. 'Tell me.'

'Patience, my good sir,' counselled Holmes kindly. 'We have had nothing to eat since sun-up, and we are famished. All in good time. Let us first have luncheon and then all shall be made clear. Meanwhile, I should like to telephone to Sir Nathaniel Brooke-Bannerman, for I wish him also to hear what I have to say.'

Our client's pleas were in vain. Holmes would have his little joke and his luncheon. In the end, Mr Harrington Edwards staggered away to the kitchen to order a repast, and Sherlock Holmes talked rapidly and unintelligibly into the telephone and came back with a smile on his face. But I asked no questions; in good time this extraordinary man would tell his story in his own way. I had heard all that he had heard, and had seen all that he had seen; yet I was completely at sea. Still, our host's ghastly smile hung heavily in my mind, and come what would I felt sorry for him. In a little time we were seated at table. Our client, haggard and nervous, ate slowly and with apparent discomfort; his eyes were never long absent from Holmes's inscrutable face. I was little better off, but Sherlock Holmes ate with gusto, relating meanwhile a number of his earlier adventures – which I may some day give to the world, if I am able to read my illegible notes made on the occasion.

When the dreary meal had been concluded we went into the library, where Sherlock Holmes took possession of the easiest chair with an air of proprietorship that would have been amusing in other circumstances. He screwed together his long pipe and lighted it with almost malicious lack of haste, while Mr Harrington Edwards perspired against the mantel in an agony of apprehension.

'Why must you keep us waiting, Mr Holmes?' he whispered. 'Tell us, at once, please, who – who –' His voice trailed off into a moan.

'The criminal,' said Sherlock Holmes smoothly, 'is –'

'Sir Nathaniel Brooke-Bannerman!' said a maid, suddenly putting her head in at the door; and on the heels of her announcement stalked the handsome baronet, whose priceless volume had caused all this commotion and unhappiness.

Sir Nathaniel was white, and he appeared ill. He burst at once into talk.

'I have been much upset by your call,' he said, looking meanwhile at our client. 'You say you have something to tell me about the quarto. Don't say – that – anything – has happened – to it!' He clutched nervously at the wall to steady himself and I felt deep pity for the unhappy man.

Mr Harrington Edwards looked at Sherlock Holmes. 'Oh, Mr Holmes,' he cried pathetically, 'why did you send for him?'

'Because,' said my friend, 'I wish him to hear the truth about the Shakespeare quarto. Sir Nathaniel, I believe you have not been told as yet that Mr Edwards was robbed, last night, of your precious volume – robbed by the trusted servants whom you sent with him to protect it.'

'What!' screamed the titled collector. He staggered and fumbled madly at his heart, then collapsed into a chair. 'My God!' he muttered, and then again: 'My God!'

'I should have thought you would have been suspicious of evil when your servants did not return,' pursued the detective.

'I have not seen them,' whispered Sir Nathaniel. 'I do not mingle with my servants. I did not know they had failed to return. Tell me – tell me all!'

'Mr Edwards,' said Sherlock Holmes, turning to our client, 'will you repeat your story, please?'

Mr Harrington Edwards, thus adjured, told the unhappy tale again, ending with a heartbroken cry, of 'Oh, Nathaniel, can you ever forgive me?'

'I do not know that it was entirely your fault,' observed Holmes cheerfully. 'Sir Nathaniel's own servants are the guilty ones, and surely he sent them with you.'

'But you said you had solved the case, Mr Holmes,' cried our client, in a frenzy of despair.

'Yes,' agreed Holmes, 'it is solved. You have had the clue in your own hands ever since the occurrence, but you did not know how to use it. It all turns upon the curious actions of the taller servant, prior to the assault.'

'The actions of – ?' stammered Mr Harrington Edwards. 'Why, he did nothing – said nothing!'

'That is the curious circumstance,' said Sherlock Holmes. Sir Nathaniel got to his feet with difficulty.

'Mr Holmes,' he said, 'this has upset me more than I can tell you. Spare no pains to recover the book and to bring to justice the scoundrels who stole it. But I must go away and think – think –'

'Stay,' said my friend. 'I have already caught one of them.'

'What! Where?' cried the two collectors together.

'Here,' said Sherlock Holmes, and stepping forward he laid a hand on the baronet's shoulder. 'You, Sir Nathaniel, were the taller servant, you were one of the thieves who throttled Mr Harrington Edwards and took from him your own book. And now, sir, will you tell us why you did it?'

Sir Nathaniel Brooke-Bannerman staggered and would have fallen had not I rushed forward and supported him. I placed him in a chair. As we looked at him we saw confession in his eyes; guilt was written in his haggard face.

'Come, come,' said Holmes impatiently. 'Or will it make it easier for you if I tell the story as it occurred? Let it be so, then. You parted with Mr Harrington Edwards on your doorstep, Sir Nathaniel, bidding your best friend good-night with a smile on your lips and evil in your heart. And as soon as you had crossed the door, you slipped into an enveloping raincoat, turned up your collar, and hastened by a shorter road to the porter's lodge, where you joined Mr Edwards and Miles as one of your own servants. You spoke no word at any time, because you feared to speak. You were afraid Mr Edwards would recognize your voice, while your beard, hastily assumed, protected your face and in the darkness your figure passed unnoticed.

'Having struggled and robbed your best friend, then, of your own book, you and your scoundrelly assistant fled across Mr Edwards's fields to his own back door, thinking that, if investigation followed, I would be called in, and would trace those footprints and fix the crime upon Mr Harrington Edwards – as part of a criminal plan, prearranged with your rascally servants, who would be supposed to be in the pay of Mr Edwards and the ringleaders in a counterfeit assault upon his person. Your mistake, sir, was in ending your trail abruptly at Mr Edwards's back door. Had you left another trail, then, leading back to your own domicile, I should unhesitatingly have arrested Mr Harrington Edwards for the theft.

'Surely you must know that in criminal cases handled by me, it is never the obvious solution that is the correct one. The mere fact that the finger of suspicion is made to point at a certain individual is sufficient to absolve that individual from guilt. Had you read the little works of my friend and colleague, Dr Watson, you would not have made such a mistake. Yet you claim to be a bookman!'

A low moan from the unhappy baronet was his only answer.

'To continue, however; there at Mr Edwards's own back door you ended your trail, entering his house – his own house – and spending the night under his roof, while his cries and ravings over his loss filled the night and brought joy to your unspeakable soul. And in the morning, when he had gone forth to consult me, you quietly left – you and Miles – and returned to your own place by the beaten highway.'

'Mercy!' cried the defeated wretch, cowering in his chair. 'If it is made public, I am ruined. I was driven to it. I could not let Mr Edwards examine the book, for that way exposure would follow; yet I could not refuse him – my best friend – when he asked its loan.'

'Your words tell me all that I did not know,' said Sherlock Holmes sternly. 'The motive now is only too plain. The work, sir, was a forgery, and knowing that your erudite friend would discover it, you chose to blacken his name to save your own. Was the book insured?'

'Insured for £100,000, he told me,' interrupted Mr Harrington Edwards excitedly.

'So that he planned at once to dispose of this dangerous and dubious item, and to reap a golden reward,' commented Holmes. 'Come, sir, tell us about it. How much of it was forgery? Merely the inscription?'

'I will tell you,' said the baronet suddenly, 'and throw myself upon the mercy of my friend, Mr Edwards. The whole book, in effect, was a forgery. It was originally made up of two imperfect copies of the 1604 quarto. Out of the pair I made one perfect volume, and a skilful workman, now dead, changed the date for me so cleverly that only an expert of the first water could have detected it. Such an expert, however, is Mr Harrington Edwards – the one man in the world who could have unmasked me.'

'Thank you, Nathaniel,' said Mr Harrington Edwards gratefully.

'The inscription, of course, also was forged,' continued the baronet. 'You may as well know everything.'

'And the book?' asked Holmes. 'Where did you destroy it?'

A grim smile settled on Sir Nathaniel's features. 'It is even now burning in Mr Edwards's own furnace,' he said.

'Then it cannot yet be consumed,' cried Holmes, and dashed into the cellar, to emerge some moment later, in high spirits, carrying a charred leaf of paper in his hand.

'It is a pity,' he cried, 'a pity! In spite of its questionable authenticity, it was a noble specimen. It is only half consumed; but let it burn away. I have preserved one leaf as a souvenir of the occasion.' He folded it carefully and placed it in his wallet. 'Mr Harrington Edwards, I fancy the decision in this matter is for you to announce. Sir Nathaniel, of course, must make no effort to collect the insurance.'

'Let us forget it, then,' said Mr Harrington Edwards, with a sigh. 'Let it be a sealed chapter in the history of bibliomania.' He looked at Sir Nathaniel Brooke-Bannerman for a long moment, then held out his hand. 'I forgive you, Nathaniel,' he said simply.

Their hands met; tears stood in the baronet's eyes. Powerfully moved, Holmes and I turned from the affecting scene and crept to the door unnoticed. In a moment the free air was blowing on our temples, and we were coughing the dust of the library from our lungs.

'They are a strange people, these book collectors,' mused Sherlock Holmes as we rattled back to town.

'My only regret is that I shall be unable to publish my notes on this interesting case,' I responded.

'Wait a bit, my dear Doctor,' counselled Holmes, 'and it will be possible. In time both of them will come to look upon it as a hugely diverting episode, and will tell it upon themselves. Then your notes shall be brought forth and the history of another of Mr Sherlock Holmes's little problems shall be given to the world.'

'It will always be a reflection upon Sir Nathaniel,' I demurred.

'He will glory in it,' prophesied Sherlock Holmes. 'He will go down in bookish circles with Chatterton, and Ireland, and Payne Collier. Mark my words, he is not blind even now to the chance this gives him for a sinister immortality. He will be the first to tell it.'

'But why did you preserve the leaf from *Hamlet*?' I inquired. 'Why not a jewel from the binding?'

Sherlock Holmes laughed heartily. Then he slowly unfolded the leaf in question, and directed a humorous finger to a spot upon the page.

'A fancy,' he responded, 'to preserve so accurate a characterization of either of our friends. The line is a real jewel. See, the good Polonius says: "That he is mad, 'tis true; 'tis pittie; and pittie 'tis 'tis true." There is as much sense in Master Will as in Hafiz or Confucius, and a greater felicity of expression . . . Here is London, and now, my dear Watson, if we hasten we shall be just in time for Zabriski's matinée!'

IV

THE ADVENTURE OF
THE MARKED MAN

Stuart Palmer

It was on a blustery afternoon late in April of the year 'ninety-five, and I had just returned to our Baker Street lodgings to find Sherlock Holmes as I had left him at noon, stretched out on the sofa with his eyes half-closed, the fumes of black shag tobacco rising to the ceiling.

Busy with my own thoughts, I removed the litter of chemical apparatus which had overflowed into the easy chair, and settled back with a perturbed sigh. Without realizing it, I must have fallen into a brown study. Suddenly Holmes's voice brought me back to myself with a start.

'So you have decided, Watson,' said he, 'that not even this difference should be a real barrier to your future happiness?'

'Exactly,' I retorted. 'After all, we cannot –' I stopped short. 'My dear fellow!' I cried, 'this is not at all like you!'

'Come, come, Watson. You know my methods.'

'I had not known,' I said stiffly, 'that they embraced having your spies and eavesdroppers dog the footsteps of an old friend, simply because he chose a brisk spring afternoon for a walk with a certain lady.'

'A thousand apologies! I had not realized that my little demonstration of a mental exercise might cause you pain,' murmured Holmes in a deprecating voice. He sat up, smiling. 'Of course, my dear fellow, I should have allowed for the temporary mental aberration known as falling in love.'

'Really, Holmes!' I retorted sharply. 'You should be the last person to speak of psycho-pathology – a man who is practically a walking case history of manic-depressive tendencies –'

He bowed. 'A touch, a distinct touch! But Watson, in one respect you do me an injustice. I was aware of your plans to meet a lady only because of the excessive pains you took with your toilet before going out. The lovely Emilia, was it not? I shall always remember her courage in the affair of the Gorgiano murder in Mrs Warren's otherwise respectable rooming-house. And indeed, why not romance? There has been a very decent interval since the passing of your late wife, and the widow Lucca is a most captivating person.'

'That is still beside the point. I do not see –'

'None so blind, Watson, none so blind,' retorted Holmes, stuffing navy-cut into his cherrywood pipe, a sure sign that he was in one of his most argumentative moods. 'It is really most simple, my dear fellow. It was not difficult for me to deduce that your appointment, on an afternoon as pleasantly gusty as this, was in the park. The remnants of peanut shell upon your best waistcoat speak all too plainly of the fact that you have been amusing yourself by feeding the monkeys. And your return at such an early hour, obviously having failed to ask the lady to dine with you, indicates most clearly that you have had some sort of disagreement while observing the antics of the hairy primates.'

'Granted, Holmes, for the moment. But pray continue.'

'With pleasure. As a good medical man, you cannot fail to have certain deep convictions as to the truth contained in the recent controversial publications of Mr Charles Darwin. What is more likely than that in the warmth of Indian Summer romance you were unwise enough to start a discussion of Darwin's theories with the Signora Lucca, who like most of her countrywomen is no doubt deeply religious? Of course she prefers the Garden of Eden account of humanity's beginning. Hence your first quarrel and your hasty return home, where you threw yourself into a chair and permitted your pipe to go out while you threshed through the entire situation in your mind.'

'That is simple enough, now that you explain it,' I admitted grudgingly. 'But how could you possibly know the conclusion which I had just reached?'

'Elementary, Watson, most elementary. You returned with your normally placid face contorted into a pout, the lower lip protruding most angrily. Your glance turned to the mantelpiece where lies a copy of *The Origin of Species*, and you looked even more belligerent than before. But then after a moment the flickering flames of the fireplace caught your eye, and I could not fail to see how that domestic symbol reminded you of the connubial felicity which you once enjoyed. You pictured yourself and the lovely Italian seated before such a fire, and your expression softened. A distinctly fatuous smile crossed your face, and I knew that you had decided that no theory should be permitted to come between you and the lady you plan to make the second Mrs Watson.' He tapped out the cherrywood pipe into the grate. 'Can you deny that my deductions are substantially correct?'

'Of course not,' I retorted, somewhat abashed. 'But Holmes, in a less enlightened reign than this our Victoria's, you would be in grave danger of being burned as a witch.'

'A wizard, pray,' he corrected. 'But enough of mental exercises. Unless I am mistaken, the persistent ringing of the doorbell presages a client. If so, it is a serious case and one which may absorb all my faculties. Nothing trivial would bring out an Englishman during the hour sacred to afternoon tea.'

There was barely time for Holmes to turn the reading lamp so that it fell upon the empty chair, and then there were quick steps on the stair and an impatient knocking at the door. 'Come in!' cried Holmes.

The man who entered was still young, some eight and thirty at the outside, well-groomed and neatly if not fashionably attired, with something of professional dignity in his bearing. He put his bowler and his sturdy malacca stick on the table, and then turned towards us, looking questioningly from one to the other. I could see that his normally ruddy complexion was of an unhealthy pallor. Obviously our caller was close to the breaking point.

'My name is Allen Pendarvis,' he blurted forth, accepting the chair to which Holmes was pointing. 'I must apologize for bursting in upon you like this.'

'Not in the least,' said Holmes. 'Pray help yourself to tobacco, which is there in the Persian slipper. You have just come up from Cornwall, I see.'

'Yes, from Mousehole, near Penzance. But how – ?'

'Apart from your name – "By the prefix Tre-, Pol-, Pen- ye shall know the Cornishmen" – you are wearing a raincoat, and angry storm clouds have filled the south-west sky most of the day. I see also that you are in great haste, as the Royal Cornishman pulled into Paddington but a few moments ago, and you have lost no time in coming here.'

'*You*, then, are Mr Holmes!' decided Pendarvis. 'I appeal to you, sir. No other man can give me the help I require.'

'Help is not easy to refuse, and not always easy to give,' Holmes replied. 'But pray continue. This is Dr Watson. You may speak freely in his presence, as he has been my collaborator on some of my most difficult cases.'

'No one of your cases,' cried Pendarvis, 'can be more difficult than mine! I am about to be murdered, Mr Holmes. And yet – and yet I have not an enemy in the world! Not one person, living or dead, could have a reason to wish me in my coffin. All the same, my life has been thrice threatened, and once attempted, in the last fortnight!'

'Most interesting,' said Holmes calmly. 'And have you any idea of the identity of your enemy?'

'None whatever. I shall begin at the beginning, and hold nothing back. You see, gentlemen, my home is in a little fishing village which has not changed materially in hundreds of years. As a matter of fact, the harbour quay of Mousehole, which lies just beyond my windows, was laid down by the Phoenicians in the time of Uther Pendragon, the father of King Arthur, when they came trading for Cornish tin . . .'

'I think in this matter we must look closer home than the Phoenicians,' said Holmes drily.

'Of course. You see, Mr Holmes, I live a very quiet life. A small income left to me by a deceased aunt makes it possible for me to devote my time to the avocation of bird photography.' Pendarvis smiled with modest pride. 'A few of my photographs of terns on the nest have been printed in ornithology magazines. Only the other day –'

'Nor do I suspect the terns,' Holmes interrupted. 'And yet someone seeks your life, or your death. By the way, Mr Pendarvis, does your wife inherit your estate in the unhappy event of your demise?'

Pendarvis looked blank. 'Sir? But I have never married. I live alone with my brother Donal. Bit of a gay dog, Donal. Romantic enough for us both. All of the scented missives in the morning mail are addressed to him.'

'Ah,' said Holmes. 'We need not apply the old rule of *cherchez la femme*, then? That eliminates a great deal. You say that your brother is your heir?'

'I suppose so. There is not much to inherit, really. The income stops at my death, and who would want my ornithological specimens?'

'That puts a different light on it, most certainly. But let us set aside the problem of *cui bono*, at least for the moment. What was the first intimation that someone had designs upon your life?'

'The first threat was in the form of a note, roughly printed upon brown butcher's-paper and shoved beneath the door last Thursday week. It read: "Mr Allen Pendarvis, you have but a short while to live".'

'You have that note?'

'Unfortunately, no, I destroyed it, thinking it to be but the work of a stupid practical joker.' Pendarvis sighed. 'Three days later came the second.'

'Which you kept, and brought with you?'

Pendarvis smiled wryly. 'That would be impossible. It was chalked upon the garden wall, repeating the first warning. And the third was marked in the mud of the harbour outside my bedroom window, visible on last Sunday morning at low tide, but speedily erased. It said "Ready to die yet, Mr Allen Pendarvis?"'

'These warnings were of course reported to the police?'

'Of course. But they did not take them seriously.'

Holmes gave me a look, and nodded. 'We understand that official attitude, do we not, Watson?'

'Then you can also understand, Mr Sherlock Holmes, why I have come to you. I am not used to being pooh-poohed by a local sub-inspector! And so, when it finally happened last night –' Pendarvis shuddered.

'Now,' interrupted Holmes, as he applied the flame of a wax vesta to his clay pipe, 'we progress. Just what did happen?'

'It was late,' the ornithologist began. 'Almost midnight, as a matter of fact, when I was awakened by the persistent ringing of the doorbell. My housekeeper, poor soul, is hard of hearing, and so I arose and answered the door myself. Imagine my surprise to find no one there. Without all was Stygian blackness, the intense gloomy stillness of a Cornish village at that late hour. I stood there for a moment, shivering, holding my candle and peering into the darkness. And then a bullet screamed past me, missing my heart by a narrow margin and extinguishing the candle in my hand!'

Holmes clasped his lean hands together, smiling. 'Really! A pretty problem, eh, Watson! What do you make of it?'

'Mr Pendarvis is lucky in that his assailant is such a poor shot,' I replied. 'He must have presented a very clear target, holding a light in the doorway.'

'A clear target indeed,' Holmes agreed. 'And why, Mr Pendarvis, did not your brother answer the door?'

'Donal was in Penzance,' Pendarvis answered. 'For years it has been his invariable custom to attend the Friday night boxing matches there. Afterwards he usually joins some of his cronies at the Capstan and Anchor.'

'Returning in the wee sma' hours? Of course, of course. And

now, Mr Pendarvis, I believe I have all that I need. Return to your home. You shall hear from us shortly.' Holmes waved a languid hand at the door. 'A very good evening to you, sir.'

Pendarvis caught up his hat and stick, and stood dubiously in the doorway. 'I must confess, Mr Holmes, that I had been led to expect more of you.'

'More?' said Holmes. 'Oh, yes. My little bill. It shall be mailed to you on the first of the month. Good-night, sir.'

The door closed upon our dissatisfied client, and Holmes, who had been leaning back on the sofa in what appeared to be the depths of dejection, abruptly rose and turned towards me. 'Well, Watson, the solution seems disappointingly easy, does it not?'

'Perhaps so,' I said stiffly. 'But you are skating upon rather thin ice, are you not? You may have sent that poor man to his death.'

'To his death? No, my dear Watson. I give you my word on that. Excuse me, I must write a note to our friend Gregson of the Yard. It is most important that an arrest be made at once.'

'An arrest? But of whom?'

'Who else but Mr Donal Pendarvis? A telegram to the authorities of Penzance should suffice.'

'The brother?' I cried. 'Then you believe that he was not actually attending the boxing matches at the time of the attempted murder of our client?'

'I am positive,' said Sherlock Holmes, 'that he was engaged in quite other activities.' I waited, but evidently he preferred not to take me further into his confidence. Holmes took quill and paper, and did not look up again until he had finished his note and dispatched it by messenger. 'That,' he said, 'should take care of the situation for the time being.' Whereupon he rang for Mrs Hudson, requesting a copious dinner.

My friend maintained his uncommunicative silence during the meal, and devoted the rest of the evening to his violin. It was not until we were at the breakfast table next morning that there was any reference whatever to the case of the Cornish ornithologist.

The doorbell rang sharply, and Holmes brightened. 'Ah, at last!' he cried. 'An answer from Gregson. No, it is the man himself, and in a hurry, too.' The steps on the stairs came to our door, and in a moment Tobias Gregson, tall, pale, flaxen-haired as ever, entered.

Smartest and sharpest of the Scotland Yard Inspectors, Holmes had always called him. But Gregson was in a bad frame of mind at the moment.

'You have had us for fair, Mr Holmes,' he began. 'I felt in my bones that I should not have obeyed your unusual request, but remembering the assistance you have given us in the past, I followed out your suggestion. Bad business, Mr Holmes, bad business!'

'Really?' said Holmes.

'Quite. It's this man Pendarvis, Donal Pendarvis, that you wanted arrested.'

'No confession?'

'Certainly not. And moreover, the fellow is no doubt instituting a suit at law this very minute, for false arrest.'

Holmes almost dropped his cup. 'You mean that he is no longer in custody?'

'I mean exactly that. He was arrested last night and held in Penzance gaol, but he made such a fuss about it that Owens, the sub-inspector, was forced to let him go free.'

Sherlock Holmes drew himself up to his full height, throwing aside his napkin. 'I agree, sir. Bad business it is.' He stood in deep thought for a moment. 'And the other request I made? Have they located a man of that description?'

'No, Mr Holmes. Sub-inspector Owens has lived in Penzance all his life, and he swears that no such person exists.'

'Impossible, quite impossible,' said Holmes. 'He must be mistaken!'

Gregson rose. 'We all have our successes and our failures,' he said comfortingly. 'Good morning, Mr Holmes. Good morning, doctor.'

As the door closed behind him, Holmes turned suddenly to

me. 'And why, Watson, are you not already packing? Do you not choose to accompany me to Cornwall?'

'To Cornwall? But I understood . . .'

'You have heard everything, and understood nothing. I shall have to demonstrate to you, and to the sub-inspector, on the scene. But enough of this. The game is afoot. You had best bring your service revolver and a stout ash, for there may be rough work before this little problem is solved.' He consulted his watch. 'Ah, we have just half an hour to catch the ten o'clock train from Paddington.'

We boarded it with but a moment or two to spare, and when we were rolling south-west through the outskirts of London my friend began a dissertation upon hereditary tendencies in finger-print groupings, a subject upon which he was planning a mono-graph. I kept my impatience to myself as long as I could, and finally interrupted him. 'I have but one question, Holmes. Why are we going to Cornwall?'

'The spring flowers, Watson, are at the height of their season. The perfume will be pleasant after the fogs of London. Mean-while, I intend to have a nap. You might occupy yourself with considering the unusual nature of the warning notes received by Mr Allen Pendarvis.'

'Unusual? But they seemed clear enough to me. They were definitely intended to let Mr Pendarvis know that he was a marked man.'

'Brilliantly put, Watson!' said Sherlock Holmes, and placidly settled down to sleep.

He did not awaken until we were past Plymouth, and the expanse of Mount's Bay was outside our window. There were whitecaps rolling in from the sea, and a gusty wind. 'I fancy there will be more rain by dusk,' said Holmes pleasantly. 'An excellent night for the type of hunting we expect to engage in.'

We had hardly alighted at Penzance when a broad man in a heavy tweed ulster approached us. He must have stood fifteen stone of solid brawn and muscle, and his face was grave. An apple-cheeked young police constable followed him.

'Mr Holmes?' said the elder man. 'I am Sub-inspector Owens. We were advised that you might be coming down. And high time it is. A sorry muddle you have got us into.'

'Indeed?' said Holmes coolly. 'It has happened, then?'

'It has,' replied Sub-inspector Owens seriously. 'At two o'clock this afternoon.' The constable nodded in affirmation, very grave.

'I trust,' Holmes said, 'that you have not moved the body?'

'The body?' The two local policemen looked at each other, and the constable guffawed. 'I was referring,' Owens went on, 'to the suit for false arrest. A writ was served upon me in my office.'

My companion hesitated only a moment. 'I should not, if I were you, lose any sleep over the forthcoming trial of the case. And now before going any farther, Dr Watson and I have just had a long train journey and are in need of sustenance. Can you direct us to the Capstan and Anchor, inspector?'

Owens scowled, then turned to his assistant. 'Tredennis, will you be good enough to show these gentlemen to the place?' He turned back to Holmes. 'I shall expect you at the police station in an hour, sir. This affair is not yet settled to my satisfaction.'

'Nor to mine, sir,' said Holmes, and we set off after the constable. That strapping young man led us at a fast pace to the sign of the Capstan and Anchor. 'Into the saloon bar with you, Watson,' my companion said to me in a low voice. He lingered a moment at the door, and then turned and joined me. 'Just as I thought. Constable Tredennis has taken up his post in a doorway across the street. We are not trusted by the local authorities.'

He ordered a plate of kidneys and bacon, but left them to cool while he chatted with the barmaid, a singularly ordinary young woman from all that was apparent to me. But Holmes returned to the table smiling. 'She confesses to knowing Mr Donal Pendarvis, at least to the point of giggling when his name is mentioned. But she says that he has not been frequenting the public house in recent weeks. By the way, Watson, suppose I asked you for a description of our antagonist? What sort of game are we hunting, should you say?'

'Mr Donal Pendarvis?'

Holmes frowned. 'That gentleman resembles his extraordinarily dull brother, from best accounts. No, Watson, dig deeper than that. Look back upon the history of the case, the warning messages –'

'Very well,' said I. 'The intended murderer is a poor shot with a rifle. He is a person who holds a grudge a long time – even a fancied grudge, for Mr Allen Pendarvis does not even have an idea of the identity of his assailant. He is a man of primitive mentality, or else he would not have stooped to the savagery of torturing his intended victim with warning messages. He is a newcomer to the town, a stranger . . .'

'Hold, Watson!' interrupted Holmes, with an odd smile. 'You have reasoned amazingly. Yet I hear the patter of rain against the panes, and we must not keep our constable waiting in the doorway.'

A brisk walk uphill, with the rain in our faces, brought us at last to the steps of the police station, but there I found that the way was barred, at least to me. Sub-inspector Owens, it appeared, wished to speak to Mr Holmes alone.

'And so it shall be,' replied Holmes pleasantly, to the burly constable in the door. He turned to me. 'Watson, I stand in need of your help. Would you be good enough to occupy the next hour or so in a call on one or two of your local colleagues? You might represent yourself as in search of a casual patient whose name has escaped you. But you have, of course, some important reason for locating him. A wrong prescription, I fancy . . .'

'Really, Holmes!'

'Be as vague as you can about age and appearance, Watson, but specify that the man you seek is a crack shot, he is very conversant with the locality, of unimpeachable respectability and – most important of all – he has a young and beautiful wife.'

'But Holmes! You imply that is the description of our murderer? It is the exact opposite of what I had imagined.'

'The reverse of the coin, Watson. But you must excuse me. Be good enough to meet me here in – shall we say – two hours? Off with you now, I must not keep the sub-inspector cooling his heels.'

He passed on inside and I turned away into the rain-swept street, shaking my head dubiously. How I wished, at the moment, for the warmth and comfort of my fireside, any fireside! But well I knew that Holmes had some method in his madness. With difficulty I managed to secure a hansom cab, and for a long time rattled about the steep streets of the ancient town of Penzance, in search of the ruby lamp outside the door which would signify the residence of a medical man.

My heart was not in the task, and it was no surprise to me that, in spite of the professional courtesy with which I was greeted by my medical colleagues, they were unable to help me by so much as one iota. Owens, for all his pomposity, had been correct when he reported that of all the citizenry of Penzance, no such person as Holmes sought had ever existed. Or if he had, he was not among their patients.

I returned to the police station to find Holmes waiting for me. 'Aha, Watson!' he cried genially. 'What luck? Very little, I suppose, else you should not wear the hangdog look of a retriever who has failed to locate the fallen bird. No matter. If we cannot go to our man, he shall come to us. I have to some extent regained the confidence of the sub-inspector, Watson. You see, I have given my word that before noon tomorrow Mr Donal Pendarvis shall have withdrawn his suit for false arrest. In return we are to have the support of a stalwart P.C. for this night's work.'

In a few moments there appeared down the street the figure of a uniformed man astride a bicycle. It turned out to be our friend Tredennis, who apologized for his delay. This was to have been his evening off duty, and it had been necessary to hurry home and explain matters to his better half.

'Maudie she worries if I'm not reporting in by nine o'clock,' he said, his pink cheeks pinker than ever with the exertion of his ride. 'But I told her that any man would be glad to volunteer for a tour of duty with Mister Holmes, the celebrated detective from England.'

'From *England*?' I put in wonderingly. 'And where are we now?'

'In Cornwall,' said Holmes, nudging me gently with his elbow. 'Ah, Watson, I see that your hansom has been kept waiting. Any moment now and we shall be setting our trap, somewhere near the home of Mr Pendarvis.'

'It's a good three miles, sir,' said Constable Tredennis. 'By the road, that is. Along the shore it's a good bit less, but it's coming high tide and no easy going at any season.'

'We shall take the road,' Holmes decided. Soon we were rattling along a cobbled street that wound up and down dale, past looming ranks of fishermen's houses, with the wind blowing ever wet and fresh against our cheeks. 'A land to make a man cherish his hearth, eh, Watson?'

We rode on in silence for some time, and then the constable stopped the cab at the head of a steep sloping street that wound down towards the shore. There was a strong odour of herring about the place, mingled with that of tar and salt seaweed. I observed that as we went down the sloping street Holmes gave a most searching glance right and left, and that at every subsequent street corner he took the utmost pains to see that we were not followed.

Frankly, I knew not what near-human game we were hoping to entrap in this rain-swept, forgotten corner of a forgotten seaside town, but I was well assured, from the manner in which Holmes held himself, that the adventure was a grave one, and nearing its climax. I felt the reassuring weight of the revolver in my coat pocket, and then suddenly the constable caught my arm.

'In here,' he whispered. We turned into a narrow passage near the foot of the street, passed through what appeared to be in the dimness a network of mews and stables, and came at last to a narrow door in the wall, which Holmes unlocked with a key affixed to a block of wood. We entered it together, and closed it behind us.

The place was black as ink, but I felt that it was an empty house. The planking beneath my feet was old and bare, and my outstretched hand touched a stone wall wet with slime. Then we came to an empty window with a broken shutter, through which the dank night air came chilly.

'We are in what was the Grey Mouse Inn,' whispered the young constable. 'Yonder, Mr Holmes, is the house.'

We peered across a narrow street and through the open, unshaded window panes of a library, brilliantly lighted by two oil lamps. I could see a line of bookcases, a table, and a mantelpiece in the background. For a long while there was nothing more to see except the dark street, the darker doorway of the house, and that one lighted window.

'There is no other entrance?' demanded Holmes in a whisper.

'None,' said the constable. 'The other windows give out on to the harbour, and at this hour the tide is passing high.'

'Good,' said Holmes. 'If our man comes, he must come this way. And we shall be ready for him.'

'More than ready,' said young Tredennis stoutly. He hesitated. 'Mr Holmes, I wonder if you would be willing to give a younger man a word of advice. What, do you think, are the opportunities for an ambitious policeman up London way? I have often thought of trying to better myself . . .'

'Listen!' cried Holmes sharply. There had come a sharp screaming sound, like the shriek of a rusty gate. It came again, and I recognized it as the cry of a gull.

The silence crept back again. From far away came the barking of a dog, suddenly silenced. Then suddenly appeared in the room across the way, a man in a wine-coloured dressing-gown who entered the library, turned down the lamps, and blew them out. It could be none other than our client, Mr Allen Pendarvis.

'As usual he keeps early hours,' said Holmes drily. We waited until one might have counted a hundred, and then another light showed in the room. The man returned, bearing a lamp – but mysteriously, in the few minutes that had passed, he had changed his apparel. Mr Pendarvis now wore a dinner coat with the collar and tie askew. He crossed to the bookcase, removed a volume, and from the recess took out a small flask, which he placed in his pocket. Then he put back the book and left the room.

'A lightning-change artist!' I cried.

Holmes, gripping my arm, said, 'Not quite, Watson. That is the brother. They are very alike, from this distance.'

We waited in silence, for what seemed an interminable length of time. But no light reappeared. Finally Holmes turned to me. 'Watson,' he said, 'we have drawn another blank. I should have sworn that the murderer would have struck tonight. I dislike to turn back . . .'

'My orders, sir, are to remain here until sunrise,' put in the constable. 'If you wish to return to the town, rest assured that I shall keep my eyes open.'

'I am sure of it,' said Holmes. 'Come, Watson. The game is too wary. We have no more to do here.'

He led me back across the sagging floor, through the door into the mews, and finally brought me out into the street again. But once there, instead of heading up the slope towards where our hansom was waiting, he suddenly drew me into the shadows of an alleyway. I would have spoken, but I felt his bony fingers across my lips. 'Shh, Watson. Wait here – and never take your eyes off that doorway.'

We waited, for what seemed an eternity. I stared with all my might at the doorway of the Pendarvis house. But I saw nothing, not even when Holmes gripped my arm.

'Now! Watson,' he whispered, and started out in that direction, I tardily at his heels.

As we came closer I saw that a man was standing with his finger pressed against the Pendarvis doorbell. Holmes and I flung ourselves upon him, but he was a wiry customer, and we for all our superior strength and numbers were flung back and forth like hounds attacking a bear. And then the door was

opened suddenly from within, and we all tumbled into a hallway lighted only by a candle held aloft in the hand of the
surprised householder.

Our captive suddenly ceased his struggles, and Holmes and
I drew back to see that we had succeeded in overcoming none
other than Constable Tredennis himself. He held in his right
hand an extremely businesslike revolver, which fell to the carpet
with a dull thump.

'Mr Pendarvis,' said Holmes, 'Mr Donal Pendarvis, permit
me to introduce you to your intended murderer.'

No one spoke. But the apple-cheeked constable now had a
face the colour of the under side of a flounder. All thought of
resistance was gone. 'You are uncanny, Mr Holmes,' the young
man muttered. 'How could you know?'

'How could I fail to know?' said Holmes, arranging his
dishevelled clothing. 'It was fairly evident that since there was
no citizen in Penzance who possessed both an ability as a marks-
man, a knowledge of the tides, and an attractive young wife,
our man must be a member of the profession where marksman-
ship is encouraged.' He turned towards the man who still held
the candle, though with trembling fingers. 'It was also evident
that your brother, who still sleeps soundly upstairs, was never
intended as a victim at all. Else the murderer would hardly have
bothered with warning messages. It was you, Mr Donal Pendarvis, who was the bull's-eye of the target.'

'I – I do not understand,' said the man with the candle,
backing away. I kept a close grip upon the unresisting form of
the prisoner, and watched Holmes as he quietly produced his
cherrywood pipe and lighted it.

'There was an excellent motive for Constable Tredennis to
murder you, sir,' said Holmes to our unwilling host. 'No man
cares to have his garden plucked by a stranger. Your death
would have begun an inquiry which would have led straight to
the husband of the lady you see on Friday nights . . .'

'That is a black lie!' shouted Tredennis, and then subsided.

'Unless,' Holmes continued quietly, 'it was obvious to all the world that Donal Pendarvis was killed by accident, that he met his death at the hands of a madman with an unexplained grudge against his brother Allen. That is why the warning notes so unnecessarily stressed the name of *Allen* Pendarvis. That is why the murderer-to-be carefully missed his supposed victim and shot out the candle. I did my best, Mr Pendarvis, to assure your safety by having you taken into custody. That subterfuge failed, and so I was forced to this extreme means.'

Tredennis twisted out of my grasp. 'Very well, make an end of it!' he cried. 'I admit it all, Mr Holmes, and shall gladly leave it to a jury of my peers –'

'You had best leave it to me, at the moment,' advised Holmes. 'Mr Pendarvis, you do not know me, but I have saved your life. May I ask a favour in return?'

Donal Pendarvis hesitated. 'I am listening,' he said. 'You understand, I admit nothing . . .'

'Of course. I venture to suggest that, instead of remaining here in the household of your brother and amusing yourself with dangerous dalliance, you betake yourself to fields which offer a greater opportunity for the use of your time and energy. The wheat fields of Canada, perhaps, or the veldt of South Africa . . .'

'And if I refuse?'

'The alternative,' said Holmes, 'is an exceedingly unpleasant scandal, involving a lady's name. Your lawsuit for false arrest will present the yellow press with unusual opportunities, will it not, when they learn that it all arose from an honest attempt upon my part to save your neck from a just punishment?'

Mr Donal Pendarvis lowered the candle, and a slow smile spread across his handsome face. 'I give you my word, Mr Holmes. I shall leave by the first packet.'

He extended his hand, and Holmes grasped it. And then we turned back into the night, our prisoner between us. We went up the cobbled street in silence, the young constable striding forward as to the gallows.

We found the hansom still waiting, and set off at once for

Penzance. But it was Holmes who called on the driver to stop as we pulled into the outskirts of the town.

'Can we drop you off at your dwelling, constable?' he asked.

The young man looked up, his eyes haunted. 'Do not make sport of me, Mr Holmes. You copped me for fair and I am ready to –'

Holmes half-shoved him out of the hansom. 'Be off with you, my young friend. You must leave it to me to satisfy your sub-inspector with a story which Doctor Watson and I shall contrive out of moonbeams. For your part, you must make up your own mind as to your tactics in dealing with your Maudie. After all, the immediate problem is removed, and if you wish to transfer to some other duty with less night work, here is my card. I shall be glad to say a word in your behalf to the powers at Scotland Yard.'

The hansom, at Holmes's signal, rolled onward again, cutting short the incoherent thanks of the chastened young constable.

'I am quite aware of what is in your mind,' said Holmes to me as we approached our destination. 'But you are wrong. The ends of justice will be better served by sending our young culprit back to his Maudie instead of by publicly disgracing him . . .'

'It is of no use, Holmes,' said I firmly. 'Nothing that you can say will change my decision. Upon our return to London I shall ask Emilia to become my wife.'

Sherlock Holmes let his hand fall on my shoulder, in a comradely gesture. 'So be it. Marry her and keep her. One of these days I shall return to the country and the keeping of bees. We shall see who suffers the sharpest stings.'

V

THE ADVENTURE OF
THE MEGATHERIUM THEFTS

S. C. Roberts

I have already had occasion, in the course of these reminiscences of my friend Sherlock Holmes, to refer to his liking for the Diogenes Club, the club which contained the most unsociable men in London and forbade talking save in the Strangers' Room. So far as I am aware, this was the only club to which Holmes was attracted, and it struck me as not a little curious that he should have been called upon to solve the extraordinary mystery of the Megatherium Thefts.

It was a dull afternoon in November and Holmes, turning wearily from the cross-indexing of some old newspaper-cuttings, drew his chair near to mine and took out his watch.

'How slow life has become, my dear Watson,' he said, 'since the successful conclusion of that little episode in a lonely west-country village. Here we are back amongst London's millions and nobody wants us.'

He crossed to the window, opened it a little, and peered through the November gloom into Baker Street.

'No, Watson, I'm wrong. I believe we are to have a visitor.'

'Is there someone at the door?'

'Not yet. But a hansom has stopped opposite to it. The passenger has alighted and there is a heated discussion in progress concerning the fare. I cannot hear the argument in detail, but it is a lively one.'

A few minutes later the visitor was shown into the sitting-room – a tall, stooping figure with a straggling white beard, shabbily dressed and generally unkempt. He spoke with a slight stutter.

'M–Mr Sherlock Holmes?' he inquired.

'That is my name,' replied Holmes, 'and this is my friend, Dr Watson.'

The visitor bowed jerkily and Holmes continued: 'And whom have I the honour of addressing?'

'My n–name is Wiskerton – Professor Wiskerton – and I have ventured to call upon you in connection with a most remarkable and puzzling affair.'

'We are familiar with puzzles in this room, Professor.'

'Ah, but not with any like this one. You see, apart from my p–professional standing, I am one of the oldest members of –'

'The Megatherium?'

'My dear sir, how did you know?'

'Oh, there was no puzzle about that. I happened to hear some reference in your talk with the cabman to your journey having begun at Waterloo Place. Clearly you had travelled from one of two clubs and somehow I should not associate you with the United Services.'

'You're p–perfectly right, of course. The driver of that cab was a rapacious scoundrel. It's s–scandalous that –'

'But you have not come to consult me about an extortionate cab–driver?'

'No, no. Of course not. It's about –'

'The Megatherium?'

'Exactly. You see, I am one of the oldest m–members and have been on the Committee for some years. I need hardly tell you the kind of standing which the Megatherium has in the world of learning, Mr Holmes.'

'Dr Watson, I have no doubt, regards the institution with veneration. For myself, I prefer the soothing atmosphere of the Diogenes.'

'The w–what?'

'The Diogenes Club.'

'N–never heard of it.'

'Precisely. It is a club of which people are not meant to hear — but I beg your pardon for this digression. You were going to say?'

'I was g-going to say that the most distressing thing has happened. I should explain in the first place that in addition to the n-noble collection of books in the Megatherium library, a collection which is one of our most valuable assets, we have available at any one time a number of books from one of the circulating libraries and —'

'And you are losing them?'

'Well — yes, in fact we are. But how did you know?'

'I didn't know — I merely made a deduction. When a client begins to describe his possessions to me, it is generally because some misfortune has occurred in connection with them.'

'But this is m-more than a m-misfortune, Mr Holmes. It is a disgrace, an outrage, a —'

'But what, in fact, has happened?'

'Ah, I was c-coming to that. But perhaps it would be simpler if I showed you this document and let it speak for itself. P-personally, I think it was a mistake to circulate it, but the Committee overruled me and now the story will be all over London and we shall still be no nearer a solution.'

Professor Wiskerton fumbled in his pocket and produced a printed document marked *Private and Confidential* in bold red type.

'What do you m-make of it, Mr Holmes? Isn't it extra-ordinary? Here is a club whose members are selected from among the most distinguished representatives of the arts and sciences and this is the way they treat the c-club property.'

Holmes paid no attention to the Professor's rambling commentary and continued his reading of the document.

'You have brought me quite an interesting case, Professor', he said, at length.

'But it is more than interesting, Mr Holmes. It is astonishing. It is inexplicable.'

'If it were capable of easy explanation, it would cease to be interesting and, furthermore, you would not have spent the money on a cab-fare to visit me.'

'That, I suppose, is true. But what do you advise, Mr Holmes?'

'You must give me a little time, Professor. Perhaps you will be good enough to answer one or two questions first?'

'Willingly.'

'This document states that your Committee is satisfied that no member of the staff is implicated. You are satisfied yourself on that point?'

'I am not s-satisfied about anything, Mr Holmes. As one who has s-spent a great part of his life amongst books and libraries, the whole subject of the maltreatment of books is repugnant to me. Books are my life-blood, Mr Holmes. But perhaps I have not your s-sympathy?'

'On the contrary, Professor, I have a genuine interest in such matters. For myself, however, I travel in those byways of bibliophily which are associated with my own profession.'

Holmes moved across to a shelf and took out a volume with which I had long been familiar.

'Here, Professor,' he continued, 'if I may rid myself of false modesty for the moment, is a little monograph of mine *Upon the Distinction Between the Ashes of the Various Tobaccos.*'

'Ah, most interesting, Mr Holmes. Not being a smoker myself, I cannot pretend to appraise your work from the point of view of scholarship, but as a bibliophile and especially as a c-collector of out-of-the-way monographs, may I ask whether the work is still available?'

'That is a spare copy, Professor; you are welcome to it.'

The Professor's eyes gleamed with voracious pleasure.

'But, Mr Holmes, this is m-most generous of you. May I b-beg that you will inscribe it? I derive a special delight from what are called "association copies".'

'Certainly,' said Holmes, with a smile, as he moved to the writing-table.

'Thank you, thank you,' murmured the Professor, 'but I fear I have distracted you from the main issue.'

'Not at all.'

'But what is your p-plan, Mr Holmes? Perhaps you would like to have a look around the Megatherium? Would you care, for instance, to have luncheon tomorrow — but no, I fear I am engaged at that time. What about a c-cup of tea at four o'clock?'

'With pleasure. I trust I may bring Dr Watson, whose co-operation in such cases has frequently been of great value?'

'Oh-er-yes, certainly.'

But it did not seem to me that there was much cordiality in his assent.

'Very well, then,' said Holmes. 'The document which you have left with me gives the facts and I will study them with great care.'

'Thank you, thank you, Tomorrow, then, at four o'clock,' said the Professor, as he shook hands, 'and I shall t-treasure this volume, Mr Holmes.'

He slipped the monograph into a pocket and left us.

'Well, Watson,' said Holmes, as he filled his pipe, 'What do you make of this curious little case?'

'Very little, at present. I haven't had a chance to examine the *data*.'

'Quite right, Watson. I will reveal them to you.' Holmes took up the sheet which the Professor had left.

'This is a confidential letter circulated to members of the Megatherium and dated November 1889. I'll read you a few extracts:

"In a recent report the Committee drew attention to the serious loss and inconvenience caused by the removal from the Club of books from the circulating library. The practice has continued . . . At the end of June, the Club paid for no less than 22 missing volumes. By the end of September 15 more were missing . . . The Committee were disposed to ascribe these malpractices to some undetected individual member, but they have regretfully come to the conclusion that more members than one are involved. They are fully satisfied that no member of the staff is in any way implicated . . . If the offenders can be identified, the Committee will not hesitate to apply the Rule which empowers expulsion."

'There, Watson, what do you think of that?'

'Most extraordinary, Holmes – at the Megatherium, of all clubs.'

'*Corruptio optimi pessima*, my dear Watson.'

'D'you think the Committee is right about the servants?'

'I'm not interested in the Committee's opinions, Watson, even though they be the opinions of Bishops and Judges and Fellows of the Royal Society. I am concerned only with the facts.'

'But the facts are simple, Holmes. Books are being stolen in considerable quantities from the club and the thief, or thieves, have not been traced.'

'Admirably succinct, my dear Watson. And the motive?'

'The thief's usual motive, I suppose – the lure of illicit gain.'

'But what gain, Watson? If you took half a dozen books, with the mark of a circulating library on them, to a second-hand bookseller, how much would you expect to get for them?'

'Very little, certainly, Holmes.'

'Yes, and that is why the Committee is probably right in ruling out the servants – not that I believe in ruling out anybody or anything on *a priori* grounds. But the motive of gain won't do. You must try again, Watson.'

'Well, of course, people are careless about books, especially when they belong to someone else. Isn't it possible that members take these books away from the club, intending to return them, and then leave them in the train or mislay them at home?'

'Not bad, my dear Watson, and a perfectly reasonable solution if we were dealing with a loss of three or four volumes. In that event our Professor would probably not have troubled to enlist my humble services. But look at the figures, Watson – twenty-two books missing in June, fifteen more in September. There's something more than casual forgetfulness in that.'

'Thats true, Holmes, and I suppose we can't discover much before we keep our appointment at the Megatherium tomorrow.'

'On the contrary, my dear Watson, I hope to pursue a little independent investigation this evening.'

'I should be delighted to accompany you, Holmes.'

'I am sure you would, Watson, but if you will forgive me for saying so, the little inquiry I have to make is of a personal nature and I think it might be more fruitful if I were alone.'

'Oh, very well,' I replied, a little nettled at Holmes's superior manner, 'I can employ myself very profitably in reading this new work on surgical technique which has just come to hand.'

I saw little of Holmes on the following morning. He made no reference to the Megatherium case at breakfast and disappeared shortly afterwards. At luncheon he was in high spirits. There was a gleam in his eye which showed me that he was happily on the trail.

'Holmes,' I said, 'you have discovered something.'

'My dear Watson,' he replied, 'your acuteness does you credit. I have discovered that after an active morning I am extremely hungry.'

But I was not to be put off.

'Come, Holmes, I am too old a campaigner to be bluffed in that way. How far have you penetrated into the Megatherium mystery?'

'Far enough to make me look forward to our tea-party with a lively interest.'

Being familiar with my friend's bantering manner, I recognized that it was no good pressing him with further questions for the moment.

Shortly after four o'clock Holmes and I presented ourselves at the portals of the Megatherium. The head porter received us very courteously and seemed, I thought, almost to recognize Sherlock Holmes. He conducted us to a seat in the entrance-hall and, as soon as our host appeared, we made our way up the noble staircase to the long drawing-room on the first floor.

'Now let me order some tea,' said the Professor. 'Do you like anything to eat with it, Mr Holmes?'

'Just a biscuit for me, Professor, but my friend Watson has an enormous appetite.'

'Really, Holmes –' I began.

'No, no. Just a little pleasantry of mine,' said Holmes, quickly. I thought I observed an expression of relief on the Professor's face.

'Well, now, about our p-problem, Mr Holmes. Is there any further information that I can give you?'

'I should like to have a list of the titles of the books which have most recently disappeared.'

'Certainly, Mr Holmes, I can get that for you at once.'

The Professor left us for a few minutes and returned with a paper in his hand. I looked over Holmes's shoulder while he read and recognized several well-known books that had been recently published, such as *Robbery under Arms*, *Troy Town*, *The Economic Interpretation of History*, *The Wrong Box*, and *Three Men in a Boat*.

'Do you make any particular deductions from the titles, Mr Holmes?' the Professor asked.

'I think not,' Holmes replied; 'there are, of course, certain very popular works of fiction, some other books of more general interest and a few titles of minor importance. I do not think one could draw any conclusion about the culprit's special sphere of interest.'

'You think not? Well, I agree, Mr Holmes. It is all very b-baffling.'

'Ah,' said Holmes suddenly, 'this title reminds me of something.'

'What is that, Mr Holmes?'

'I see that one of the missing books is *Plain Tales from the Hills*. It happens that I saw an exceptionally interesting copy of that book not long ago. It was an advance copy, specially bound and inscribed for presentation to the author's godson who was sailing for India before the date of publication.'

'Really, Mr Holmes, really? That is of the greatest interest to me.'

'Your own collection, Professor, is, I suspect, rich in items of such a kind?'

'Well, well, it is not for me to b-boast, Mr Holmes, but I certainly have one or two volumes of unique association value on my shelves. I am a poor man and do not aspire to first folios, but the p-pride of my collection is that it could not have been assembled through the ordinary channels of trade ... But to return to our problem, is there anything else in the Club which you would like to investigate?'

'I think not,' said Holmes, 'but I must confess that the description of your collection has whetted my own bibliographical appetite.'

The Professor flushed with pride.

'Well, Mr Holmes, if you and your friend would really care to see my few t-treasures, I should be honoured. My rooms are not f-far from here.'

'Then let us go,' said Holmes, with decision.

I confess that I was somewhat puzzled by my friend's behaviour. He seemed to have forgotten the misfortunes of the Megatherium and to be taking a wholly disproportionate interest in the eccentricities of the Wiskerton collection.

When we reached the Professor's rooms I had a further surprise. I had expected not luxury, of course, but at least some measure of elegance and comfort. Instead, the chairs and tables, the carpets and curtains, everything, in fact, seemed to be of the cheapest quality; even the bookshelves were of plain deal and roughly put together. The books themselves were another matter. They were classified like no other library I had ever seen. In one section were presentation copies from authors; in another were proof-copies bound in what is known as 'binder's cloth'; in another were review copies; in another were pamphlets, monographs, and off-prints of all kinds.

'There you are, Mr Holmes,' said the Professor, with all the pride of ownership. 'You may think it is a c-collection of oddities, but for me every one of these volumes has a p-personal and s-separate association – including the item which came into my hands yesterday afternoon.'

'Quite so,' said Holmes, thoughtfully, 'and yet they all have a common characteristic.'

'I don't understand you.'

'No? But I am waiting to see the remainder of your collection, Professor. When I have seen the whole of your library, I shall perhaps be able to explain myself more clearly.'

The Professor flushed with annoyance.

'Really, Mr Holmes, I had been warned of some of your p-peculiarities of manner; but I am entirely at a loss to know what you are d-driving at.'

'In that case, Professor, I will thank you for your hospitality and will beg leave to return to the Megatherium for consultation with the Secretary.'

'To tell him that you can't f-find the missing books?'

Sherlock Holmes said nothing for a moment. Then he looked straight into the Professor's face and said, very slowly:

'On the contrary, Professor Wiskerton, I shall tell the Secretary that I can direct him to the precise address at which the books may be found.'

There was silence. Then an extraordinary thing happened.

The Professor turned away and literally crumpled into a chair; then he looked up at Holmes with the expression of a terrified child:

'Don't do it, Mr Holmes. Don't do it, I b-b-beseech you. I'll t-tell you everything.'

'Where are the books?' asked Holmes, sternly.

'Come with me and I'll show you.'

The Professor shuffled out and led us into a dismal bedroom. With a trembling hand he felt in his pocket for his keys and opened a cupboard alongside the wall. Several rows of books were revealed and I quickly recognized one or two titles that I had seen on the Megatherium list.

'Oh, what m-must you think of me, Mr Holmes?' the Professor began, whimpering.

'My opinion is irrelevant,' said Sherlock Holmes, sharply. 'Have you any packing-cases?'

'No, but I d-daresay my landlord might be able to find some.'

'Send for him.'

In a few minutes the landlord appeared. Yes, he thought he

could find a sufficient number of cases to take the books in the cupboard.

'Professor Wiskerton,' said Holmes, 'is anxious to have all these books packed at once and sent to the Megatherium, Pall Mall. The matter is urgent.'

'Very good, sir. Any letter or message to go with them?'

'No,' said Holmes, curtly, 'but yes – stop a minute.'

He took a pencil and a visiting-card from his pocket and wrote 'With the compliments of' above the name.

'See that this card is firmly attached to the first of the packing-cases. Is that clear?'

'Quite correct, sir, if that's what the Professor wants.'

'That is what the Professor most particularly wants. Is it not, Professor?' said Holmes, with great emphasis.

'Yes, yes, I suppose so. But c-come back with me into the other room and l-let me explain.'

We returned to the sitting-room and the Professor began:

'Doubtless I seem to you either ridiculous or despicable or both. I have had two p-passions in my life – a passion for s-saving money and a passion for acquiring b-books. As a result of an unfortunate dispute with the Dean of my faculty at the University, I retired at a c-comparatively early age and on a very small p-pension. I was determined to amass a collection of books; I was equally determined not to s-spend my precious savings on them. The idea came to me that my library should be unique, in that all the books in it should be acquired by some means other than p-purchase. I had friends amongst authors, printers, and publishers, and I did pretty well, but there were many recently published books that I wanted and saw no m-means of getting until – well, until I absent-mindedly brought home one of the circulating library books from the Mega-therium. I meant to return it, of course. But I didn't. Instead, I b-brought home another one ...'

'*Facilis descensus* ...' murmured Holmes.

'Exactly, Mr Holmes, exactly. Then, when the Committee began to notice that books were disappearing, I was in a quandary. But I remembered hearing someone say in another connection that the b-best defence was attack and I thought that if I were the first to go to you, I should be the last to be s-suspected.'

'I see,' said Holmes. 'Thank you, Professor Wiskerton.'

'And now what are you going to do?'

'First,' replied Holmes, 'I am going to make certain that your landlord has those cases ready for dispatch. After that, Dr Watson and I have an engagement at St James's Hall.'

'A trivial little case, Watson, but not wholly without interest,' said Holmes, when we returned from the concert hall to Baker Street.

'A most contemptible case, in my opinion. Did you guess from the first that Wiskerton himself was the thief?'

'Not quite, Watson. I never guess. I endeavour to observe. And the first thing I observed about Professor Wiskerton was that he was a miser – the altercation with the cabman, the shabby clothes, the unwillingness to invite us to lunch. That he was an enthusiastic bibliophile was, of course, obvious. At first I was not quite certain how to fit these two characteristics properly together, but after yesterday's interview I remembered that the head porter of the Megatherium had been a useful ally of mine in his earlier days as a Commissionaire and I thought a private talk with him might be useful. His brief characterization put me on the right track at once – "Always here reading", he said, "but never takes a square meal in the club." After that, and after a little hasty research this morning into the Professor's academic career, I had little doubt.'

'But don't you still think it extraordinary, in spite of what he said, that he should have taken the risk of coming to consult you?'

'Of course it's extraordinary, Watson. Wiskerton's an extra-ordinary man. If, as I hope, he has the decency to resign from the Megatherium, I shall suggest to Mycroft that he puts him up for the Diogenes.'

VI

THE ADVENTURE OF
THE TRAINED CORMORANT

W. R. Duncan Macmillan

It started one August morning, I remember, about the turn of the century. Holmes and I were cooped up together. My wife was on a visit to her aunt's, and, for a few days, I was a dweller once more in my old quarters in Baker Street. Holmes was in the doldrums, with nothing whatsoever to do. A heavy silence filled the room. There was also the smell of our untasted bacon and eggs and the knowledge, which we both shared, that I had removed the needle from his hypodermic syringe and locked away all my own instruments.

I think we were both rather surprised that I had, at last, summoned up the courage to do so, but it was a matter to which neither of us was inclined to refer.

I sat by the open window whence were contributed the additional effluvia of asphalt and horse-dung, which arose from the street below. Mrs Hudson came in to clear away the breakfast table, but on seeing how the things were disposed, made as if to withdraw.

Holmes roused himself sufficiently to say, 'Just leave us the coffee, if you would, Mrs Hudson, but take everything else. Neither the Doctor nor I has much appetite this morning.'

When the good woman had gone, I helped myself to a cup of coffee and returned to my seat at the window.

'A breath of fresh air would do us both a world of good,' I remarked platitudinously.

'Yes,' he replied, with some show of animation. 'A nice case, with a large fee and a long sea voyage, would be very tempting. Where would you like to go, Watson? Madeira, the Mediterranean or the isles of Greece?'

I was beginning to quote, again without any great originality, 'Where burning Sappho ...', when we heard a knock at the door and Mrs Hudson came in once more. This time she carried a telegram which she offered to Holmes on a salver.

I watched him tear open the envelope and was pleased to see his face light up with interest as he read the message.

'No answer, just for the moment,' he remarked. 'I'll attend to it later.'

When we were alone, he sprang up and brought the telegram over for me to read. 'There you are, Watson. An answer to our prayers. Not quite so romantic or so far away as the isles of Greece – but this might well entail a visit to the Western Isles.'

'Where Johnson's Bozzy reached and retched,' I thought to myself with a much lighter heart.

'May I see what it says?' I asked aloud.

I read 'Come at once. Must have your assistance. Expense no matter. Ivy Scott-Burns.'

I also took time to note that the message had been dispatched from Oban.

'Is this lady known to you?' I inquired.

'Oh! yes,' replied Holmes. 'Her father was one of our wealthiest brewers. She inherited his fortune some years ago and more recently married a rather pushful politician – of the kind that has been described as "a Scotsman on the make". She's really a likeable, if simple sort of woman. When I made her acquaintance my task was to extricate her from an affair with an out-and-out adventurer. She indicated to me then, in somewhat overwhelming terms, that she was most grateful for my poor services. It was a straightforward affair, but lucrative. I can only hope that history will repeat itself. It often does, especially, I'm thankful to say, in our line of business.'

'Then you are going to help her?'

'My dear Watson, of course I am – and what's more you're

coming too. Get that neighbour of yours to take over your practice for the next ten days, tell your wife to stay where she is, and off we go.'

I protested, but feebly. My friend soon succeeded in over-ruling my excuses and fell to organizing our departure.

In a couple of hours or so, when I returned from making the necessary arrangements for the supervision of my patients, I found him making a final note of certain particulars which he had been abstracting from Bradshaw.

I put down the packed bag which I carried and waited until he had finished.

'Watson, my dear fellow, we travel tonight to Glasgow by train,' he said. 'Tomorrow we take a ship belonging to a certain Mr David MacBrayne and sail down the Firth of Clyde, through some narrows called the Kyles of Bute to a place named Ardrishaig. Thereafter we pass through the Crinan Canal and take another vessel to Oban. I believe we could do the whole journey by train, but in this weather I have elected to follow the longer and airier route.'

'That, if I may say so, is very wise and considerate of you.'

Holmes inclined his head in a mock bow and, smiling, blandly for him, went on: 'It is by no means the end of my consideration for your welfare. Had we elected to travel all the way by train, we should have been carried through Glenogle, which, according to the Journals of Our Gracious Queen, she found comparable to the Khyber Pass. I thought, perhaps, that you would rather not be reminded of any part of the North-West Frontier.'

'I am obliged to you, Holmes,' I assured him. 'There is no point in stirring up unhappy memories, even although, as in my case, they are now old and overlaid by happier events of more recent date.'

Later that evening we made our way in good time to Euston, where we were lucky enough to get a first-class compartment to ourselves, so that we could take a side each, stretch out and sleep in some degree of comfort.

The next morning we were advised at Glasgow to shave and wash quickly before catching an early train to Greenock. There we boarded a broad-beamed and well-appointed paddle-steamer named *Columba*, in which we were provided with an excellent breakfast. We did such full justice to it that I remarked to Holmes, 'A somewhat different performance from that of yesterday morning.'

It was perhaps thoughtless or inconsiderate on my part. In any event, he disdained to answer.

Thereafter we sat on deck in the sunshine and enjoyed some of the finest scenery that either of us had ever seen, at home or abroad. As our ship beat her way sturdily along the route so happily chosen by Holmes, the islands, hills and sea lochs with their shore-side villages all contributed to provide us with an ever-changing and entrancing panorama.

Rested, refreshed, at peace with each other and with life in general, we sailed into the beautiful bay of Oban that same evening.

When we had disembarked, we were accosted on the pier by a professional gentleman of somewhat startling appearance. He wore the conventional top-hat, wide-pointed collar, cravat and frock-coat of these days, and so I immediately assumed that he belonged to one of the learned professions.

The unusual items were his trousers and his immense size. His lower limbs were clad in the gayest pair of shepherd-tartan trousers that I have ever seen, and when one raised one's eyes from their fascination in order to study the rest of the man, his head appeared to be in the skies. He must have been well over six feet in his stocking soles and some seventeen stones in weight.

'Mr Sherlock Holmes?' he inquired with outstretched hand. 'My name is MacKelvie.' Holmes admitted his identity, shook hands and introduced me.

'Gentlemen,' said Mr MacKelvie, 'let me inform you at the outset that I practise the Law in this town and have the honour to act for Mrs Scott-Burns. There are certain instructions which I have to give you on her behalf. For that purpose, since the matter involved is, in my humble opinion, bound to take some time and consideration, I have booked rooms for you in an hotel, just along there on the sea-front.'

'Nice and airy,' murmured Holmes, adding more audibly, 'I'm sure we are much obliged to you, sir.'

'I suggest then,' went on MacKelvie, 'that you let the porter here relieve you of your luggage and that we walk along to the hotel. It's but a step or two.'

We signified our assent, handed over our bags, and set off, one on either side of our outsized adviser. 'I have chosen a couple of bedrooms for you which overlook the Bay, and I have also thought it prudent to reserve for your use a private sitting-room. The point is,' he went on to amplify, 'I think that this evening after you have had a wash, a rest and some dinner, we might have a consultation. That is, of course, if you are not too tired.'

Once more Holmes assented to the proposal and added some expression of our appreciation for the arrangements made for our comfort.

About nine o'clock that night Mr MacKelvie rejoined us. I think that he had perhaps consumed a little something to loosen his tongue, but his wits were all about him and he lost no time in presenting to us a clear outline of the problem which Holmes was called upon to solve.

'I believe that you are aware, sir, of the personal circumstances of our client, Mrs Scott-Burns.'

Holmes nodded his assent. He was in one of his favourite attitudes, leaning well back in a comfortable armchair and, passing his pipe from hand to mouth, contentedly puffing smoke from time to time towards the ceiling.

'Very well then,' MacKelvie continued, 'I shall now proceed to tell you what I know of the antecedent career of her husband. I shall say at once it has not been without incident or success. He came from a decent, lower middle-class home. His father was farm-manager and factor on a small estate in this county. It belonged to a wealthy industrialist of what is known as the *nouveau riche* type. The boy Burns, as he was then known – the hyphenation being, as you will guess, of fairly recent origin – was a brilliant scholar. His father's employer became his patron. The lad won a bursary to one of our best known public schools in Edinburgh, went on to the University there and was further encouraged to join the Scottish Bar. He must have been given an allowance for his first year or two, but very quickly he found his feet and began to pick up a practice.

'His next step took him into politics. The young man's patron was an enthusiastic Liberal. He was persuaded to back Burns in standing for one of the more fashionable divisions in Glasgow, where I am told he put up a very good fight but was defeated, although he reduced his opponent's majority. The Liberals, however, gained the day, with the result that we had a new Lord Advocate who belonged to that party and who promptly appointed Master Burns to be one of his assistants in the administration of the Criminal Law of this country. He thus became what we call an Advocate–depute. Shortly after this – I do hope you do not find me tedious?'

We assured Mr MacKelvie on this point and pressed him to proceed.

'Shortly after receiving this appointment, young Burns, still under forty years of age, took Silk. I take it you know the phrase? He became a Q.C.'

Once more we nodded our assent.

'Very well then. The next thing was that he was appointed to be Sheriff of Argyll, which was a rare honour for a native of these parts. Now,' said MacKelvie, with a show of reluctance, 'I am afraid I must weary you with some slight account of certain duties attaching to that high office. The Sheriff of a County in Scotland has administrative duties to perform, especially on the occasion of a Parliamentary Election, or other and perhaps rarer forms of civil commotion, such as an out-and-out riot. He also hears appeals from the judgements in civil cases of the Sheriff-substitutes in his district. I need not give you any further details of these two aspects of his function, since they

do not touch upon the matter in hand. There is, however, a third
field of action and this, I think, is not without interest to us.

'The Sheriffs, along with certain other dignitaries, fulfil in
Scotland the functions performed in England by the Masters
of Trinity House. We call them the Commissioners of
Northern Lights and they are responsible for the efficient main-
tenance of all the lighthouses round our stormy and treacherous
coasts.

'For their services the Commissioners receive no remuneration, but each summer every lighthouse is inspected, and the
tour of inspection is made in a well-appointed yacht, wherein
the catering provided is on a generous scale.'

'You mean,' said Holmes with a smile, 'that instead of being
paid for the work they do in relation to lighthouses, these
gentlemen are given annually this rather special sea-trip?'

'Exactly so,' Mr MacKelvie agreed, going on hastily to add,
'I suspect you think I am being irrelevant, so I shall press on and
make my point at once. It is simply this: most of the Commissioners, being elderly, get nothing much out of these trips but
a good time and the seeds of gout, whereas the effect of them
on Mr Scott-Burns was quite different. In him they developed
a passion for the kind of yachting which may be enjoyed
without danger or discomfort in and round these Western Isles.'

'In other words, a most expensive pastime?' queried Holmes.

Once more Mr MacKelvie remarked, 'Exactly so.' After a
moment's pause he continued: 'Of course, there are ways and
means of arranging these things, as you may well imagine. Let
me just say that we soon began to notice that nearly every time
a large steam-yacht came into the Bay, Scott-Burns was a guest
aboard her.'

'You need say no more,' remarked Holmes, smiling once
again.

'Now I am nearly finished with what I have called the
antecedent history,' said MacKelvie. 'On one of those cruises he
met the lady who is now his wife and our client. There was, I
believe, a whirlwind courtship and thereafter a fashionable

wedding in London. The next step was taken just before the last
General Election which, as we all remember, resulted in a not
unexpected defeat for the Liberals. Scott-Burns resigned his
Sheriffdom, joined the Tories and was given one of the safest
seats in the country. What his wife's contribution to Party Funds
must have been I cannot even guess. But,' went on MacKelvie,
'it must have been something very considerable.' He paused
again before adding, 'Now, as you know, he has achieved office.
He is Secretary for Scotland.'

'And,' remarked Holmes, with a smile, 'unless I am mistaken
we are very nearly posted up to date?'

'Yes,' agreed MacKelvie, 'I think that is the case.'

'Then Watson,' said Holmes, turning to me, 'I think you
might summon some slight refreshment. I arranged with the
head waiter at dinner-time that if we rang the bell he would
bring up a tray.'

I attended to these matters, and for the next ten minutes or
so we fortified the inner man with a little sustenance of one kind
and another, and chatted idly as we admired what could still be
seen of the superb view out towards Mull in the shadows of the
fading light.

We were brought back to the topic in hand when Holmes
asked, 'What had this man's patron to say to the sudden change
of political front?'

'Oh,' answered MacKelvie, 'he's dead now. He may have
turned in his grave, but, had he been alive, he would doubtless
have taken the matter as a personal insult.'

'One could hardly have blamed him,' said Holmes. 'Let us sit
down again and hear the rest of your story. I imagine you will
now be prepared to tell us why we have been summoned.'

'Yes, I think so,' agreed MacKelvie as we settled down and
he took up once more the thread of his tale. 'Mrs Scott-Burns
was promptly persuaded to charter the finest steam-yacht ever
seen in these waters. She and her husband spend much of their
time cruising in the Hebrides, and also, last Easter, he alone used
the yacht when he went to investigate one of the usual com-

plaints which are made from time to time about the necessity for new piers and safe harbours for the fishing fleet.'

'I take it that Mr and Mrs Scott-Burns are in these parts just now, even although I saw no large yacht in the Bay?' The inflexion of Holmes's voice made it clear that this was not only a question, but something in the nature of a goad.

'It depends what you mean by "these parts",' said MacKelvie imperturbably. 'They must be about a hundred and fifty miles away. After I had heard what Mrs Scott-Burns had to say yesterday morning, I advised them to go and have a look at St Kilda.'

'What on earth made you do a thing like that?' I demanded, aghast.

'All in good time, Watson.' said Holmes; 'I think I have inadvertently tempted our good friend here to put the cart before the horse; or, in other words, to depart from the chosen sequence of his narrative. Pray, sir,' he went on, with a slight inclination towards Mr MacKelvie, 'forgive me and do, please, continue with the same admirable clarity.'

'Thank you, sir,' replied MacKelvie, with a smile, 'although it is perhaps I who should apologize. In filling in the background for you, I fear I have been intolerably long-winded. However, now, in the words of the famous showman, we can cut the cackle and come to the horses.'

'My dear sir,' said Holmes, with a wave of his hand, 'take it in your own time and in your own way.'

'Very well, then,' replied MacKelvie, 'let me start off again with what happened yesterday morning, before I advised our client to be off to St Kilda.'

Our informant, sitting at ease, continued. 'Yesterday morning, about half past seven, I was looking out of my bedroom window, which commands a fine view of the Bay. I saw one of our local lobster-fishermen rowing out to lift his pots. I then saw someone waving a handkerchief on board Mrs Scott-Burns's yacht, which had apparently come in during the night and lay out there at anchor. The fisherman rowed over to the yacht, backed in to a companionway that hung over the side and took a lady on board. They then rowed in towards the shore and, to my astonishment, made for the little slip or jetty which runs out directly opposite my house. Very shortly I was able to see that the lady was Mrs Scott-Burns and, somehow or other, I guessed that she was coming to see me.

'I dressed hurriedly and went to meet her. She told me that she was much relieved to find me up and about at such an hour, and begged me to help her, assuring me repeatedly that the matter was both urgent and important.

'Of course I agreed to do what I could, and brought her into my dining-room, gave her some tea and listened to her tale of woe. Now, please bear with me if I keep you just a little longer in suspense. After I had heard what she had to say, I launched my own little rowing-boat and took her back to her yacht, which shortly afterwards up-anchored and sailed out of the Bay.'

At this point I saw Holmes's eyebrows rise up in his forehead, but he made no comment.

'Now, at last,' said MacKelvie, 'I come to the crux of the matter. This is what our client had to tell me.

'A couple of days ago, in the early morning, Mr and Mrs Scott-Burns were aboard the yacht, which was cruising somewhere off the west coast of Mull. They had no guests with them, but the crew numbers about sixteen. On several previous occasions our client's husband had told her about a man he knew, one of the lighthouse-keepers stationed on the lonely rock known as Dubh Heartach. There, presumably to pass the time and also to vary a monotonous diet, he has trained a pair of cormorants to fish for him, after the fashion of the Chinese.'

'Very little training is required, I should imagine,' said Holmes. 'The birds are released on a string and hauled in by their owner every time they dive and come up with a fish. Thereafter they are made to disgorge their catch. A somewhat cruel and crude business, to my way of thinking.'

'I quite agree,' remarked MacKelvie; 'but all the same, I must confess I should like to witness it. In any event, our client was deeply interested and expressed a strong desire to see the birds at work.

'On the morning in question, her husband woke her at an unusually early hour, informed her that conditions were perfect for the purpose and, bidding her arise and dress, had the Captain of the yacht steam for the lighthouse.

'Shortly afterwards he came again to her cabin and urged her to hasten, as the Captain was of the opinion that the weather was deteriorating and there was no time to spare.

'Mrs Scott-Burns completed her toilet and went on deck as fast as she could. There was the usual Atlantic swell, but in addition to that she could see that the wind was rising from the west. However, as they neared the lighthouse, the Captain undertook to stand close in to it by slowly reversing his engines and so counteracting the drifting of the vessel.

'Then, I gather, no sooner had the yacht been manoeuvred into position, than the keeper appeared on the rock with his two birds.'

'Yes,' remarked Holmes, 'I suppose he would need to keep them in captivity so as to have them hungry and keen for the job.'

'That would not be difficult,' I interposed, 'they are ravenous brutes at any time.'

Mr MacKelvie, noting that our comments were over, sailed on, so to speak, on even keel.

'The next thing, it would seem, was that owing either to the weather or the churning-up of the sea by the yacht, the first two or three attempts by the cormorants to catch fish were of no avail. They dived, but without success, so that it looked as if the outing were to be a failure. But at this point Scott-Burns excused himself from the deck, and, going below to the galley, obtained some fresh herrings with which to tempt the birds.

'Appearing at a hatchway below deck level, he proceeded to feed these herrings to the birds until the exhibition was proclaimed a huge success, and the Captain, because of the weather, thankfully took his yacht clear of the rock.'

'You did say,' remarked Holmes without apparent relevance, 'that the herrings were fresh?'

Mr MacKelvie regarded him with some surprise and then answered, 'Yes. At least I think so. I seem to remember that our client told me that the birds swallowed them head-first.'

'Thank you,' said Holmes, 'now do please continue and tell us what was the next thing to happen.'

'How do you know that anything happened?' asked Mac-Kelvie playfully.

'We would hardly be here if it hadn't,' Holmes replied drily.

'Very well,' continued MacKelvie, this time with a little more emphasis than he had employed up to date, 'when Mrs Scott-Burns returned to her cabin, she found that a valuable pearl and diamond brooch had disappeared from her dressing-table – where she is convinced it lay before she went on deck a few minutes previously.'

'What immediate steps did she take?' Holmes asked the question without intensity of interest, as if the information were no news to him.

'She made a thorough search of her cabin and then reported matters to her husband and the Captain, who happened at the time to be together on the bridge.'

'What course of action did they propose to adopt?'

'After some discussion, with the idea of giving the thief a chance to repent and to restore the brooch without detection, it was agreed to announce that Mr Scott-Burns had lost an 1837 sovereign which he wore on his watch-chain, that the finder would receive a reward of ten pounds, and that anyone finding any other article of value which might have been mislaid would also be handsomely rewarded.'

'That scheme, I imagine,' remarked Holmes, 'originated from our client.'

'Quite so,' MacKelvie agreed. 'She is a very kind-hearted woman.'

'Nothing came of it, of course?' Holmes queried.

'No,' replied MacKelvie, 'I think we can take it that the yacht was searched from stem to stern and that the brooch is still amissing.'

After a moment's reflection Holmes inquired, 'And in the course of your interview with our client she authorized you to send me this telegram?'

Mr MacKelvie examined the message which Holmes produced from his pocket.

'Yes,' he said, 'she dictated that to me. These are her own words.'

'Very well, then,' Holmes went on, 'thank you very much indeed. You have drawn us a very clear picture, but I think we have done all we can tonight. When the yacht returns from St Kilda I should like to look over her and to meet our client once again.

'There is just one other matter,' he added; 'would you be so good as to find out when the man from the lighthouse is due to be relieved and where he is due to be brought ashore. I should like to be there to welcome him home. We might even provide him with a little entertainment after his long and lonely vigil.'

I could not refrain from asking, 'Do you remember Sam Weller's simile? "Anything for a quiet life, as the man said when he applied for a sitivation on a lighthouse." He may not be of a very social or convivial turn of mind.'

'We shall see,' answered Holmes placidly, 'we can but do our best.'

After a little more desultory conversation, our meeting broke up and we went gratefully to bed.

The following morning, as we were strolling along the esplanade in a state of happy but companionable silence, Holmes suddenly halted and said to me: 'You know, Watson, I've been thinking things over. I shall change our plan. I shall go at once to MacKelvie's office and ask him to meet the lighthouse-keeper. My impression of the people here is that they do not open up too easily to strangers and, not only that, they are more friendly after what is called in these parts a dram. MacKelvie can meet the man and bring him along to us at our hotel once he has overcome his natural diffidence.'

Without waiting for any comment I might have had to make, Holmes left me. However, after he had gone a few yards, he turned to call back, 'I'll see you at the hotel for luncheon.'

I continued my stroll and returned to the hotel about half-past twelve. When I entered the hall, Holmes rose from a chair to greet me with the words, 'Splendid, my dear Watson. You could not have timed it better. The keeper is due back at any minute now. He is to be met at the pier here by MacKelvie, who will bring him up to our room immediately after luncheon. Let us go in now and be ready for them in good time.'

I remember clearly that we had a very pleasant luncheon and that Holmes seemed to be in no hurry over it, but I assumed that he had left a message so that we would be summoned just as soon as our visitors arrived. As things turned out, there was no need to hurry. Having finished our meal, we waited a good half-hour upstairs in our sitting-room before anything else happened.

Then there was a knock at the door, and before Holmes or I had time to answer it, Mr MacKelvie entered, looking as cool as a cucumber and carrying over his shoulder the inert body of a man.

'Bless my soul! what has happened?' I cried. 'Is this man ill, has he had an accident?'

MacKelvie lowered his burden without apparent effort and laid him on a sofa.

I hurried over to the recumbent figure and made a swift examination.

'Holmes,' I announced, 'this man is suffering from alcoholic poisoning. I must use a stomach-pump and administer hot coffee to him immediately.'

Instead of answering me, Holmes turned to MacKelvie, who had gone into peals of laughter on hearing my diagnosis, and said to him angrily: 'Sir, you have by far exceeded your instructions.'

The enormous MacKelvie wiped tears from his eyes and managed to gasp out, 'I like that. Dammit, man, your last words to me were, "Remember, my dear sir, expense is of no matter."' Then, pulling himself together so that he appeared to be as sober as any judge, he continued: 'However, you need not be frightened, Doctor. He's not poisoned. He's just had two or three glasses of good whisky on an empty stomach, after some months of complete abstinence. He'll be as right as rain in a couple of hours: sooner, if you care to pour coffee into him.'

Holmes stood thoughtful for a minute or two, then he directed me to fetch a rug from his room and cover up the lighthouse-keeper. As I left to fulfil this request, I heard Holmes ask MacKelvie to go down to the head waiter and obtain a large jug of coffee, hot, strong and black.

When I returned with the rug, Holmes was standing by the window, once more deep in meditation. He said nothing until MacKelvie reappeared saying that the coffee would be up in ten minutes. Then, once more addressing MacKelvie, he said: 'I think we shall cancel that order. It is clear to me that this man will be of no further use to us as a witness today. It is also within the scope of my knowledge that he will have no recollection of being brought here. He may remember meeting a kind gentleman who treated him to a number of drinks. He will not remember any more than that. I think that if we can find some small, deserted room, we will carry him there stealthily and abandon him. When he comes to himself again, he will doubtless find his own way home. If he is discovered before then, his condition will account for any questions which any person may feel inclined to ask.'

Holmes spoke with such quiet authority that neither of us offered any criticism of his plan.

MacKelvie went out to cancel the coffee and to scout for suitable accommodation. Then he returned and gave me a nod. Together we lifted the unconscious lighthouse-keeper, carried him a short distance along a deserted corridor, and laid him on a sofa in a shabby little cubby-hole, apparently designed to let such commercial travellers as were willing to dispense with comfort write up their books in peace. This time he lay breathing stertorously.

'What about the rug,' I whispered.

'Better to let him have all the air he can get,' answered MacKelvie, not unkindly. 'Poor chap, he'll have a shocking headache when he wakes up. Besides, Mr Holmes does not want to be connected with him.'

When we returned to our sitting-room, Holmes was once more standing by the window. Pointing towards the Bay, he asked, 'Would that, by any chance, be our client's yacht?'

MacKelvie took one look and answered, 'Yes. By Jove, it is.'

'Very well,' remarked Holmes, 'as it has turned out, nothing could have been better timed or better arranged. We shall go aboard her as soon as she is safely anchored and, what is more, we shall take a plumber with us.'

'A plumber?' echoed MacKelvie, as if he could not believe his ears.

'Exactly so,' replied Holmes; 'a decent, discreet and competent plumber.'

Knowing better than to question Holmes's inscrutable ways at such a stage as this, all I said was, 'I'm sure Mr MacKelvie will know of just the right type of man.'

Shortly afterwards, perhaps after the lapse of about an hour, we were all rowed out to the yacht, where we were most graciously received by Mrs Scott-Burns. Our companion was left on deck with his bag of tools. The rest of us were escorted to a large dining-saloon, where we were entertained to polite conversation and tea by our client.

Her husband, I regretted to note, sat glowering at us. He had nothing to say for himself and struck me as being both sulky and conceited.

Our client, on the other hand, could not have been more charming, and I never knew Holmes to be in more gallant mood than he was then with her.

When the two stewards who had been waiting on us removed

the tea-things and withdrew, she told us all that had happened at Dubh Heartach, but since her account tallied in all particulars with that which we had received from Mr MacKelvie, I need not repeat it.

Holmes asked one or two questions to clear up small points, but nothing new came out of them. The only thing was that the lady was insistent that the brooch had been on her dressing-table, while Holmes seemed to be pressing her to say that it might have been left elsewhere.

At the close of her narrative, Holmes obtained permission to search her cabin, saying something rather airy about 'Another pair of eyes'. In a moment or two he, MacKelvie and I were escorted to the scene of the occurrence and left to our own devices. No sooner had the door of the cabin shut out our client, than Holmes turned to me and said, 'Nip up on deck and fetch our friend the plumber.'

I did so immediately, and when we returned to the cabin Holmes at once drew his attention to the fitted wash-hand basin. 'Do you see this waste-pipe?' he demanded.

'Yes, sir,' said the man very civilly.

'Do you notice that there is a bend in it?'

'Yes, sir,' agreed the plumber once more.

'Things could stick in it?' insisted Holmes.

'I suppose they could. That is,' qualified the plumber, 'if they were small enough to go through the grill over which the plug is placed.'

'And the pipe is made of lead?' Holmes went on, as if no reference had been made to the grill.

'Yes, sir,' said the plumber once more.

'Then please be so good as to cut through it at floor level.'

The plumber gave one protesting look at the imperious Holmes, then took a saw from his tool-kit, fell on his knees and set to work.

When he had sawn through the bottom of the pipe, Holmes ordered him to disconnect the top of it from the basin.

'I can't,' cried the plumber, who appeared to be almost in

tears, 'I could not do such a thing without breaking the beautiful basin – and what would my lady say then?'

Holmes, who appeared to be quite unmoved by this outburst, merely said, quietly and firmly, 'Smash it. I suggest you use a hammer.'

The plumber was clearly about to protest further, but Holmes silenced him by pointing out that he would very probably get the order for replacing the basin, and sent him off to borrow the largest weapon he could find.

We stood in silence while the plumber was away. I noticed that Holmes looked round the cabin with some interest, but he made no attempt to search it.

When the plumber returned he carried, not a hammer, but a heavy iron crowbar. 'Just the thing,' cried Holmes, and, snatching it out of his grasp, he lifted it high in the air and smashed the basin to smithereens.

Then, dropping to his knees, with his back to us, he seemed to brush aside the broken portions of porcelain and lift up the waste-pipe which he had so rudely disconnected. I happened to notice that the grill had come off the top of it.

Holding the pipe by both ends and shaking it this way and that, he cried, 'Just as I thought. Here we are.'

When he extended a hand, held palm-upwards, we saw to our astonishment and delight that it contained the missing brooch.

'How the devil did you know it was there?' demanded Mac-Kelvie, quite flabbergasted. Holmes forbore to answer, but led the way back to the saloon, where he restored the missing property to its rightful amd most grateful owner.

'I just can't believe that I can have been so forgetful,' she complained. 'But, of course, one does wash one's jewellery from time to time.'

'All's well that ends well, my dear lady,' Holmes purred cat-like. 'Do please employ my poor services as often as you like. It is a pleasure to help you and,' he added, with a twinkle, 'very little strain upon the imagination.'

Her husband maintained his sulky silence. I took it that he regarded the whole affair as much ado about nothing.

Shortly afterwards, when we had been almost overwhelmed by the expressions of our client's wonder and admiration, we were rowed ashore.

As we climbed up the steps at the side of the pier and were once more on terra firma, MacKelvie turned to Holmes and said rather sadly, 'Well, that is the end of that. But I don't believe a word of it. I'll stake my professional reputation there was something fishy going on there. And,' he added with a laugh, 'I don't mean the herrings.'

'Well, you should,' countered Holmes, with a broad smile. 'However, I'll make you an offer. Come to dinner with us tonight and afterwards I'll tell you all about it.'

Later that evening, as we sat at our ease before the opened window of our sitting-room, once more looking out over the Bay to the Hills of Mull, Holmes gave us this *résumé* of the facts as he had perceived and pieced them together.

'It began, of course,' he said, 'with the wealthy wife and the not-so-wealthy husband.

'When they were first married, she was able to finance his political aspirations. Later, when he persuaded her to take up yachting, she chartered a vessel, instead of buying one. That suggested to me that she had not full control of her father's fortune, but was instead merely a liferentrix. From that it follows that the income from her father's estate is paid to her and that she has full control over it. Owing to the passage of the Married Women's Property Acts, the husband cannot touch it. Accordingly, if he were in need of a substantial sum at any time, he would have to ask her for it and, it is to be assumed, tell her why he wanted it.

'Now I can imagine without any difficulty that a man of his type might well have to make a parting present to a former lady friend. Ladies of that kind are rapacious, and wives do not regard even ante-marital alliances with any degree of favour or enthusiasm.'

MacKelvie's vast bulk began to heave with laughter until I thought he would shake his chair asunder. 'I think I see it now,' he gasped; 'but how did you spot it?'

'It was all very simple,' replied Holmes. 'Scott-Burns knew the lighthouse-keeper. He had been up in these parts by himself at Easter-time. I have no doubt but that he arranged the whole thing then, most probably assuring the keeper that he was about to play a practical joke on his wife, saying that she was culpably careless with her jewellery. Remember that it was he who chose the time for the exhibition: when the conditions were all against a *bona fide* performance by the birds. In addition to that I was satisfied that after the brooch was missed the yacht was subjected to the most minute search and that the brooch was not on board.'

'But, Holmes, we saw you . . .' I started to say. He waved me to keep quiet and proceeded: 'No, no. The brooch left the yacht and there was only one way in which it could have done so – inside a cormorant. Nobody, except our client, left the ship either before or after the incident.

'Remember too that it was Scott-Burns who left the others on deck and went below to feed the birds. He had an opportunity of slipping into his wife's cabin and stealing the brooch, and he was the only person who could have stuffed it well down the gullet of a herring and fed it to one of the cormorants.

'That, we know, must have been done, because we know, or at least I do, that it reached the lighthouse-keeper.'

'How do you know that?' I cried in amazement.

'Because I removed it from his person when he lay drunk on that sofa here in this room while you two were engaged on other business.'

'You picked his pocket?' I exclaimed in surprise.

'Yes,' Holmes admitted very calmly. 'Put it that way if you like. On the other hand, please remember I had been engaged to recover the brooch for its owner.'

'And having done that,' said MacKelvie, 'what made you decide to carry on as you did?'

'A sense of decency, I suppose,' answered Holmes modestly. 'To avoid a scandal. You see, the lighthouse-keeper will hold his tongue, because he will remember having the brooch and is almost bound to assume that he lost it when he was drunk. Scott-Burns will also keep quiet. He knows for certain that the brooch was never in the pipe of the basin, but dare not say a word to us or to anyone else. She, I think, is so glad to have it back that she has accepted the explanation which I did my best to force upon her. It was all I could do to keep my face straight when I told her, quite unnecessarily, to have a smaller grill fitted to the new basin.'

'Why unnecessarily?' I said.

'Because the former grill was quite small enough for the purpose. That is why I had to burst up the basin and further confound the confusion of the issue.'

'What happened to the grill? Won't somebody find it and notice the discrepancy?'

'No. I put it in my pocket and, when we were being rowed ashore this evening, dropped it into the sea,' replied Holmes once more very flatly.

'And so the brooch was never in the pipe?' MacKelvie repeated reflectively.

'Not until I put it there,' answered Holmes, with a happy smile.

VII

THE ADVENTURE OF
ARNSWORTH CASTLE

Adrian Conan Doyle

❧

'Your conclusions are perfectly correct, my dear Watson,' remarked Sherlock Holmes. 'Squalor and poverty are the natural matrix for crimes of violence.'

'Precisely so,' I agreed. 'Indeed, I was just thinking –' I broke off to stare at him in amazement. 'Good heavens, Holmes,' I cried, 'this is too much. How could you possibly know my innermost thoughts!'

My friend leant back in his chair and, placing his fingertips together, surveyed me from under his heavy drooping eyelids. 'I would do better justice to my limited powers, perhaps, by refusing to answer your question,' he said, with a dry chuckle. 'You have a certain flair, Watson, for concealing your failure to perceive the obvious by the cavalier manner in which you invariably accept the explanation of a sequence of simple but logical reasoning.'

'I do not see how logical reasoning can enable you to follow the course of my mental processes,' I retorted, a trifle nettled by his superior manner.

'There was no great difficulty. I have been watching you for the last few minutes. The expression on your face was quite vacant until, as your eyes roved around the room, they fell on the bookcase and came to rest on Hugo's *Les Misérables* which made so deep an impression upon you when you read it last year. You became thoughtful, your eyes narrowed, it was obvious that your mind was drifting again into that tremendous saga of

human suffering; at length your gaze lifted to the window with
its aspect of snowflakes and grey sky and bleak frozen roofs, and
then, moving slowly on to the mantelpiece, settled on the jack-
knife with which I skewer my unanswered correspondence. The
frown darkened on your face and unconsciously you shook your
head despondently. It was an association of ideas. Hugo's terrible
sub-third strata, the winter cold of poverty in the slums and,
above the warm glow of our own modest fire, the bare knife-
blade. Your expression deepened into one of sadness, the melancholy that comes with an understanding of cause and effect in
the unchanging human tragedy. It was then that I ventured to
agree with you.'

'Well, I must confess that you followed my thoughts with
extraordinary accuracy,' I admitted. 'A remarkable piece of
reasoning, Holmes.'

'Elementary, my dear Watson.'

The year 1887 was moving to its end. The iron grip of the
great blizzards that commenced in the last week of December
had closed on the land, and beyond the windows of Holmes's
lodgings in Baker Street lay a gloomy vista of grey lowering
sky and white-capped tiles dimly discernible through a curtain
of snowflakes.

Though it had been a memorable year for my friend, it had
been of yet greater importance to me, for it was but two months
since that Miss Mary Marston had paid me the signal honour
of joining her destiny to mine. The change from my bachelor
existence as a half-pay ex-Army surgeon into the state of
wedded bliss had not been accomplished without some uncalled-
for and ironic comments from Sherlock Holmes but, as my wife
and I could thank him for the fact that we had found each other,
we could afford to accept his cynical attitude with tolerance and
even understanding.

I had dropped in to our old lodgings on this afternoon, to be
precise December 30th, to pass a few hours with my friend and
inquire whether any new case of interest had come his way since
my previous visit. I had found him pale and listless, his dressing-

gown drawn around his shoulders and the room reeking with the smoke of his favourite black shag, through which the fire in the grate gleamed like a brazier in a fog.

'Nothing, save a few routine inquiries, Watson,' he had replied in a voice shrill with complaint. 'Creative art in crime seems to have become atrophied since I disposed of the late-lamented Bert Stevens.' Then, lapsing into silence, he curled himself up morosely in his armchair and not another word passed between us until my thoughts were suddenly interrupted by the observation that commenced this narrative.

As I rose to go, he looked at me critically.

'I perceive, Watson,' said he, 'that you are already paying the price. The slovenly state of your left jawbone bears regrettable testimony that somebody has changed the position of your shaving mirror. Furthermore, you are indulging in extravagances.'

'You do me a gross injustice.'

'What, at the winter price of fivepence a blossom! Your buttonhole tells me that you were sporting a flower not later than yesterday.'

'This is the first time I have known you penurious, Holmes,' I retorted with some bitterness.

He broke into a hearty laugh. 'My dear fellow, you must forgive me!' he cried. 'It is most unfair that I should penalize you because a surfeit of unexpended mental energy tends to play upon my nerves. But hullo, what's this!'

A heavy step was mounting the stairs. My friend waved me back into my chair.

'Stay a moment, Watson,' said he. 'It is Gregson, and the old game may be afoot once more.'

'Gregson?'

'There is no mistaking that regulation tread. Too heavy for Lestrade's and yet known to Mrs Hudson or she would accompany him. It is Gregson.'

As he finished speaking, there came a knock on the door and a figure muffled to the ears in a heavy cape entered the room.

Our visitor tossed his bowler on the nearest chair and, unwinding the scarf wrapped around the lower part of his face, disclosed the flaxen hair and long pale features of the Scotland Yard detective.

'Ah, Gregson,' greeted Holmes, with a sly glance in my direction. 'It must be urgent business that brings you out in this inclement weather. But throw off your cape, man, and come over to the fire.'

The police agent shook his head. 'There is not a moment to lose,' he replied, consulting a large silver turnip watch. 'The train to Derbyshire leaves in half an hour and I have a hansom waiting below. Though the case should present no difficulties for an officer of my experience, nevertheless I shall be glad of your company.'

'Something of interest?'

'Murder, Mr Holmes,' snapped Gregson curtly, 'and a singular one at that to judge from the telegram from the local police. It appears that Lord Jocelyn Cope, the Deputy-Lieutenant of the County, has been found butchered at Arnsworth Castle. The Yard is quite capable of solving crimes of this nature, but in view of the curious terms contained in the police telegram, it occurred to me that you might wish to accompany me. Will you come?'

Holmes leant forward, emptied the Persian slipper into his tobacco pouch and sprang to his feet.

'Give me a moment to pack a clean collar and toothbrush,' he cried. 'I have a spare one for you, Watson. No, my dear fellow, not a word. Where would I be without your assistance? Scribble a note to your wife, and Mrs Hudson will have it delivered. We should be back tomorrow. Now, Gregson, I'm your man and you can fill in the details during our journey.'

The guard's flag was already waving as we rushed up the platform at St Pancras and tore open the door of the first empty smoker. Holmes had brought three travelling rugs with him and as the train roared its way through the fading winter daylight we made ourselves comfortable enough in our respective corners.

'Well, Gregson, I shall be interested to hear the details,' remarked Holmes, his thin eager face framed in the ear-flaps of his deerstalker and a spiral of blue smoke rising from his pipe.

'I know nothing beyond what I have already told you.'

'And yet you used the word "singular" and referred to the telegram from the county police as "curious". Kindly explain.'

'I used both terms for the same reason. The wire from the local inspector advised that the officer from Scotland Yard should read the *Derbyshire County Guide* and the *Gazetteer*. A most extraordinary suggestion!'

'I should say a wise one. What have you done about it?'

'The *Gazetteer* states merely that Lord Jocelyn Cope is a Deputy-Lieutenant and county magnate, married, childless and noted for his bequests to local archaeological societies. As for the *Guide*, I have it here.' He drew a pamphlet from his pocket and thumbed over the pages. 'Here we are,' he continued. 'Arnsworth Castle. Built reign of Edward III. Fifteenth-century stained-glass window to celebrate Battle of Agincourt. Cope family penalized for suspected Catholic leaning by Royal Visitation, 1574. Museum open to public once a year. Contains large collection of martial and other relics, including small guillotine built originally in Nîmes during French Revolution for execution of a maternal ancestor of the present owner. Never used owing to escape of intended victim and later purchased as relic by family after Napoleonic wars and brought to Arnsworth. Pshaw! That local inspector must be out of his senses, Mr Holmes. There is nothing to help us here.'

'Let us reserve judgement. The man would not have made such a suggestion without reason. In the meantime, I would recommend to your attention the dusk now falling over the landscape. Every material object has become vague and indistinct and yet their solid existence remains, though almost hidden from our visual sense. There is much to be learned from the twilight.'

'Quite so, Mr Holmes,' grinned Gregson, with a wink at me. 'Very poetical, I am sure. Well, I'm for a short nap.'

It was some three hours later that we alighted at a small wayside station. The snow had ceased and beyond the roofs of the hamlet the long desolate slopes of the Derbyshire moors, white and glistening under the light of a full moon, rolled away to the skyline. A stocky, bow-legged man swathed in a shepherd's plaid hurried towards us along the platform.

'You're from Scotland Yard, I take it?' He greeted us brusquely. 'I got your wire in reply to mine and I have a carriage waiting outside. Yes, I'm Inspector Dawlish,' he added in response to Gregson's question. 'But who are these gentlemen?'

'I considered that Mr Sherlock Holmes's reputation –' began our companion.

'I've never heard of him,' interposed the local man, looking at us with a gleam of hostility in his dark eyes. 'This is a serious affair and there is no room for amateurs. But it is too cold to stand arguing here and, if London approves his presence, who am I to gainsay him. This way, if you please.'

A closed carriage was standing before the station, and a moment later we had swung out of the yard and were bowling swiftly but silently up the village high street.

'There'll be accommodation for you at the Queen's Head,' grunted Inspector Dawlish. 'But first to the castle.'

'I shall be glad to hear the facts of this case,' stated Gregson, 'and the reason for the most irregular suggestion contained in your telegram.'

'The facts are simple enough,' replied the other, with a grim smile. 'His Lordship has been murdered and we know who did it.'

'Ah!'

'Captain Jasper Lothian, the murdered man's cousin, has disappeared in a hurry. It's common knowledge hereabouts that the man's got a touch of the devil in him, a hard hand with a bottle, a horse or the nearest woman. It's come as a surprise to none of us that Captain Jasper should end by slaughtering his benefactor and the head of his house. Aye, head's a well-chosen word,' he ended softly.

'If you've a clear case, then what's this nonsense about a guide book?'

Inspector Dawlish leant forward, while his voice sank almost to a whisper. 'You've read it?' he said. 'Then it may interest you to know that Lord Jocelyn Cope was put to death in his own ancestral guillotine.'

His words left us in a chilled silence.

'What motive can you suggest for the murder and for the barbarous method employed?' asked Sherlock Holmes at last.

'Probably a ferocious quarrel. Have I not told you already that Captain Jasper had a touch of the devil in him? But there's the castle and a proper place it looks for deeds of violence and darkness.'

We had turned off the country road to enter a gloomy avenue that climbed between banked snowdrifts up a barren moorland slope. On the crest loomed a great building, its walls and turrets stark and grey against the night sky. A few minutes later, our carriage rumbled under the arch of the outer bailey and halted in a courtyard.

At Inspector Dawlish's knock, a tall stooping man in butler's livery opened the massive oaken door and, holding a candle above his head, peered out at us, the light shining on his weary red-rimmed eyes and ill-nourished beard.

'What, four of you!' he cried querulously. 'It b'aint right her Ladyship should be bothered thisways at such a time of grief to us all.'

'That will do, Stephen. Where is her Ladyship?'

The candle flame trembled. 'Still with him,' came the reply, and there was something like a sob in the old voice. 'She hasn't moved. Still sitting there in the big chair and staring at him, as though she had fallen fast asleep with them wonderful eyes wide open.'

'You've touched nothing, of course?'

'Nothing. It's all as it was.'

'Then let us go first to the museum where the crime was committed,' said Dawlish. 'It is on the other side of the courtyard.'

He was moving away towards a cleared path that ran across the cobblestones when Holmes's hand closed upon his arm. 'How is this!' he cried imperiously. 'The museum is on the other side and yet you have allowed a carriage to drive across the courtyard and people to stampede over the ground like a herd of buffalo.'

'What then?'

Holmes flung up his arms appealingly to the moon. 'The snow, man, the snow! You have destroyed your best helpmate.'

'But I tell you the murder was committed in the museum. What has the snow to do with it?'

Holmes gave vent to a most dismal groan and then we all followed the local detective across the yard to an arched door-way.

I have seen many a grim spectacle during my association with Sherlock Holmes, but I can recall none to surpass in horror the sight that met our eyes within that grey Gothic chamber. It was a small room with a groined roof, lit by clusters of tapers in iron sconces. The walls were hung with trophies of armour and medieval weapons and edged by glass-topped cases crammed with ancient parchments, thumb rings, pieces of carved stone-work and yawning mantraps. These details I noticed at a glance and then my whole attention was riveted to the object that occupied a low dais in the centre of the room.

It was a guillotine, painted a faded red and, save for its smaller size, exactly similar to those that I had seen depicted in woodcuts of the French Revolution. Sprawling between the two uprights lay the body of a tall thin man clad in a velvet smoking jacket. His hands were tied behind him and a white cloth, hideously besmirched, concealed his head or rather the place where his head had been.

The light of the tapers, gleaming on a blood-spattered steel blade buried in the lunette, reached beyond to touch as with a halo the red-gold hair of the woman who sat beside that dread-ful headless form. Regardless of our approach, she remained motionless in her high carved chair, her features an ivory mask from which two dark and brilliant eyes stared into the shadows with the unwinking fixity of a basilisk. In an experience of women covering three continents, I have never beheld a colder nor a more perfect face than that of the chatelaine of Castle Arnsworth keeping vigil in that chamber of death.

Dawlish coughed.

'You had best retire, my Lady,' he said bluntly. 'Rest assured that Inspector Gregson here and I will see that justice is done.'

For the first time, she looked at us and so uncertain was the light of the tapers that for an instant it seemed to me that some swift emotion more akin to mockery than grief gleamed and died in those wonderful eyes.

'Stephen is not with you?' she asked incongruously. 'But, of course, he would be in the library. Faithful Stephen.'

'I fear that his Lordship's death —'

She rose abruptly, her bosom heaving and one hand gripping the skirt of her black lace gown.

'His damnation!' she hissed, and then, with a gesture of despair, she turned and glided slowly from the room.

As the door closed, Sherlock Holmes dropped on one knee beside the guillotine and, raising the blood-soaked cloth, peered down at the terrible object beneath. 'Dear me,' he said quietly. 'A blow of this force must have sent the head rolling across the room.'

'Probably.'

'I fail to understand. Surely you know where you found it?'

'I didn't find it. There is no head.'

For a long moment, Holmes remained on his knee, staring up silently at the speaker. 'It seems to me that you are taking a great deal for granted,' he said at length, scrambling to his feet. 'Let me hear your ideas on this singular crime.'

'It's plain enough. Sometime last night, the two men quarrelled and eventually came to blows. The younger overpowered the elder and then killed him by means of this instrument. The evidence that Lord Cope was still alive when placed in the guillotine is shown by the fact that Captain Lothian had to lash his hands. The crime was discovered this morning by the butler

Stephen, and a groom fetched me from the village, whereupon I took the usual steps to identify the body of his Lordship and listed the personal belongings found upon him. If you'd like to know how the murderer escaped, I can tell you that too. On the mare that's missing from the stable.'

'Most instructive,' observed Holmes. 'As I understand your theory, the two men engaged in a ferocious combat, being careful not to disarrange any furniture or smash the glass cases that clutter up the room. Then, having disposed of his opponent, the murderer rides into the night, a suitcase under one arm and his victim's head under the other. A truly remarkable performance.'

An angry flush suffused Dawlish's face. 'It's easy enough to pick holes in other people's ideas, Mr Sherlock Holmes,' he sneered. 'Perhaps you will give us your theory.'

'I have none. I am awaiting my facts. By the way, when was your last snowfall?'

'Yesterday afternoon.'

'Then there is hope yet. But let us see if this room will yield us any information.'

For some ten minutes, we stood and watched him, Gregson and I with interest and Dawlish with an ill-concealed look of contempt on his weather-beaten face, as Holmes crawled slowly about the room on his hands and knees, muttering and mumbling to himself and looking like some gigantic dun-coloured insect. He had drawn his magnifying glass from his cape pocket and I noticed that not only the floor but the contents of the occasional tables were subjected to the closest scrutiny. Then, rising to his feet, he stood wrapped in thought, his back to the candlelight and his gaunt shadow falling across the faded red guillotine.

'It won't do,' he said suddenly. 'The murder was pre-meditated.'

'How do you know?'

'The cranking handle is freshly oiled, and the victim was senseless. A single jerk would have loosed his hands.'

'Then why were they tied?'

'Ah! There is no doubt, however, that the man was brought here unconscious with his hands already bound.'

'You're wrong there!' interposed Dawlish loudly. 'The design on the lashing proves that it is a sash from one of these window curtains.'

Holmes shook his head. 'They are faded through exposure to daylight,' said he, 'and this is not. There can be little doubt that it comes from a door curtain, of which there are none in this room. Well, there is little more to be learnt here.'

The two police agents conferred together and Gregson turned to Holmes. 'As it is after midnight,' said he, 'we had better retire to the village hostelry and tomorrow pursue our inquiries separately. I cannot but agree with Inspector Dawlish that while we are theorizing here the murderer may reach the coast.'

'I wish to be clear on one point, Gregson. Am I officially employed on this case by the police?'

'Impossible, Mr Holmes!'

'Quite so. Then I am free to use my own judgement. But give me five minutes in the courtyard and Dr Watson and I will be with you.'

The bitter cold smote upon us as I slowly followed the gleam of Holmes's dark lantern along the path that, banked with snow, led across the courtyard to the front door. 'Fools!' he cried, stooping over the powdered surface. 'Look at it, Watson! A regiment would have done less damage. Carriage wheels in three places. And here's Dawlish's boots and a pair of hobnails, probably a groom. A woman now, and running. Of course, Lady Cope and the first alarm. Yes, certainly it is her. What was Stephen doing out here? There is no mistaking his square-toed shoes. Doubtless you observed them, Watson, when he opened the door to us. But what have we here?'

The lantern paused and then moved slowly onwards.

'Pumps. Pumps,' he cried eagerly, 'and coming from the front door. See, here he is again. Probably a tall man from the size of his feet and carrying some heavy object. The stride is shortened and the toes more clearly marked than the heels. A burdened man always tends to throw his weight forward. He returns! Ah, just so, just so! Well, I think that we have earned our beds.'

My friend remained silent during our journey back to the village. But, as we separated from Inspector Dawlish at the door of the inn, he laid a hand on his shoulder.

'The man who has done this deed is tall and spare,' said he. 'He is about fifty years of age with a turned-in left foot and strongly addicted to Turkish cigarettes which he smokes from a holder.'

'Captain Lothian!' grunted Dawlish. 'I know nothing about feet or cigarette holders, but the rest of your description is accurate enough. But who told you his appearance?'

'I will set you a question in reply. Were the Copes ever a Catholic family?'

The local inspector glanced significantly at Gregson and tapped his forehead. 'Catholic? Well, now that you mention it, I believe they were in the old times. But what on earth – !'

'Merely that I would recommend you to your own guide book. Good night.'

On the following morning, after dropping my friend and myself at the castle gate, the two police officers drove off to pursue their inquiries further afield. Holmes watched their departure with a twinkle in his eye.

'I fear that I have done you injustice over the years, Watson,' he commented somewhat enigmatically, as we turned away.

The elderly manservant opened the door to us and, as we followed him into the great hall, it was painfully obvious that the honest fellow was still deeply afflicted by his master's death.

'There is naught for you here,' he cried shrilly. 'My God, will you never leave us in peace?'

I have remarked previously on Holmes's gift for putting others at their ease, and by degrees the old man recovered his composure. 'I take it that this is the Agincourt window,' observed Holmes, staring up at a small but exquisitely coloured stained-glass casement through which the winter sunlight threw a pattern of brilliant colours on the ancient stone floor.

'It is, sir. Only two in all England.'

'Doubtless you have served the family for many years,' continued my friend gently.

'Served 'em? Aye, me and mine for nigh two centuries. Ours is the dust that lies upon their funeral palls.'

'I fancy they have an interesting history.'

'They have that, sir.'

'I seem to have heard that this ill-omened guillotine was specially built for some ancestor of your late master?'

'Aye, the Marquis de Rennes. Built by his own tenants, the varmints; hated him, they did, simply because he kept up old customs.'

'Indeed. What custom?'

'Something about women, sir. The book in the library don't explain exactly.'

'*Le droit de Seigneur*, perhaps.'

'Well, I don't speak heathen, but I believe them was the very words.'

'H'm. I should like to see this library.'

The old man's eyes slid to a door at the end of the hall. 'See the library?' he grumbled. 'What do you want there? Nothing but old books, and her Ladyship don't like – oh, very well.'

He led the way ungraciously into a long low room lined to the ceiling with volumes and ending in a magnificent Gothic fireplace. Holmes, after strolling about listlessly, paused to light a cheroot.

'Well, Watson, I think that we'll be getting back,' said he. 'Thank you, Stephen. It is a fine room, though I am surprised to see Indian rugs.'

'Indian!' protested the old man indignantly. 'They're antique Persian.'

'Surely Indian.'

'Persian, I tell you! Them marks are inscriptions, as a gentleman like you should know. Can't see without your spy-glass?

Well, use it then. Now, drat it, if he hasn't spilled his matches!'

As we rose to our feet after gathering up the scattered vestas, I was puzzled to account for the sudden flush of excitement in Holmes's sallow cheeks.

'I was mistaken,' said he. 'They are Persian. Come, Watson, it is high time that we set out for the village and our train back to town.'

A few minutes later, we had left the castle. But to my surprise, on emerging from the outer bailey, Holmes led the way swiftly along a lane leading to the stables.

'You intend to inquire about the missing horse,' I suggested.

'The horse? My dear fellow, I have no doubt that it is safely concealed in one of the home farms, while Gregson rushes all over the county. This is what I am looking for.'

He entered the first loose-box and returned with his arms full of straw. 'Another bundle for you, Watson, and it should be enough for our purpose.'

'But what is our purpose?'

'Principally to reach the front door without being observed,' he chuckled, as he shouldered his burden.

Having retraced our footsteps, Holmes laid his finger on his lips and, cautiously opening the great door, slipped into a nearby closet, full of capes and sticks, where he proceeded to throw both our bundles on the floor.

'It should be safe enough,' he whispered, 'for it is stone-built. Ah! These two mackintoshes will assist admirably. I have no doubt,' he added, as he struck a match and dropped it into the pile, 'that I shall have other occasions to use this modest stratagem.'

As the flames spread through the straw and reached the mackintoshes, thick black wreaths of smoke poured from the cloakroom door into the hall of Arnsworth Castle, accompanied by a hissing and crackling from the burning rubber.

'Good heavens, Holmes,' I gasped, the tears rolling down my face. 'We shall be suffocated!'

His fingers closed on my arm.

'Wait,' he muttered, and even as he spoke, there came a sudden rush of feet and a yell of horror.

'Fire!'

In that despairing wail, I recognized Stephen's voice. 'Fire!' he shrieked again, and we caught the clatter of his footsteps as he fled across the hall.

'Now!' whispered Holmes, and in an instant he was out of the cloakroom and running headlong for the library. The door was half-open, but as we burst in, the man drumming with hysterical hands on the great fireplace did not even turn his head.

'Fire! The house is on fire!' he shrieked. 'Oh, my poor master! My Lord! My Lord!'

Holmes's hand fell upon his shoulder. 'A bucket of water in the cloakroom will meet the case,' he said quietly. 'It would be as well, however, if you would ask his Lordship to join us.'

The old man sprang at him, his eyes blazing and his fingers crooked like the talons of a vulture.

'A trick!' he screamed. 'I've betrayed him through your cursed tricks!'

'Take him, Watson,' said Holmes, holding him at arm's length. 'There, there. You're a faithful fellow.'

'Faithful unto death,' whispered a feeble voice.

I started back involuntarily. The edge of the ancient fireplace had swung open and in the dark aperture thus disclosed there stood a tall thin man, so powdered with dust that for the moment I seemed to be staring not at a human being but at a spectre. He was about fifty years of age, gaunt and high-nosed, with a pair of sombre eyes that waxed and waned feverishly in a face that was the colour of grey paper.

'I fear that the dust is bothering you, Lord Cope,' said Holmes very gently. 'Would you not be better seated?'

The man tottered forward to drop heavily into an armchair. 'You are the police, of course,' he gasped.

'No. I am a private investigator, but acting in the interests of justice.'

A bitter smile parted Lord Cope's lips.

'Too late,' said he.

'You are ill?'

'I am dying.' Opening his fingers, he disclosed a small empty phial. 'There is only a short time left to me.'

'Is there nothing to be done, Watson?'

I laid my fingers upon the sick man's wrist. His face was already livid and the pulse slow and feeble.

'Nothing, Holmes.'

Lord Cope straightened himself painfully. 'Perhaps you will indulge a last curiosity by telling me how you discovered the truth,' said he. 'You must be a man of some perception.'

'I confess that at first there were difficulties,' admitted Holmes, 'though these dissolved themselves later in the light of events. Obviously the whole key to the problem lay in a conjunction of two remarkable circumstances – the use of a guillotine and the disappearance of the murdered man's head.

'Who, I asked myself, would use so clumsy and bizarre an instrument, except one to whom it possessed some strong symbolic significance and, if this were the case, then it was logical to suppose that the clue to that significance must lie in its past history.'

The nobleman nodded.

'His own people built it for Rennes,' he muttered, 'in return for the infamy that their womenfolk had suffered at his hands. But pray proceed, and quickly.'

'So much for the first circumstance,' continued Holmes, ticking off the points on his fingers. 'The second threw a flood of light over the whole problem. This is not New Guinea. Why, then, should a murderer take his victim's head? The obvious answer was that he wished to conceal the dead man's true identity. By the way,' he demanded sternly, 'what have you done with Captain Lothian's head?'

'Stephen and I buried it at midnight in the family vault,' came the feeble reply. 'And that with all reverence.'

'The rest was simple,' went on Holmes. 'As the body was easily identifiable as yours by the clothes and other personal belongings which were listed by the local inspector, it followed naturally that there could have been no point in concealing the head unless the murderer had also changed clothes with the dead man. That the change had been effected before death was shown by the blood-stains. The victim had been incapacitated in advance, probably drugged, for it was plain from certain facts already explained to my friend Watson that there had been no struggle and that he had been carried to the museum from another part of the castle. Assuming my reasoning to be correct, then the murdered man could not be Lord Jocelyn. But was there not another missing, his Lordship's cousin and alleged murderer, Captain Jasper Lothian?'

'How could you give Dawlish a description of the wanted man?' I interposed.

'By looking at the body of the victim, Watson. The two men must have borne a general resemblance to each other or the deception would not have been feasible from the start. An ash tray in the museum contained a cigarette stub, Turkish, comparatively fresh smoked from a holder. None but an addict would have smoked under the terrible circumstances that must have accompanied that insignificant stump. The footmarks in the snow showed that someone had come from the main building carrying a burden and had returned without that burden. I think I have covered the principal points.'

For a while, we sat in silence, broken only by the moan of a rising wind at the casements and the short sharp panting of the dying man's breath.

'I owe you no explanation,' he said at last, 'for it is to my Maker who alone knows the innermost recesses of the human heart that I must answer for my deed. Nevertheless, though my story is one of shame and guilt, I shall tell you enough to enlist perhaps your forbearance in granting me my final request.

'You must know, then, that following the scandal which brought his army career to its close, my cousin Jasper Lothian has lived at Arnsworth. Though penniless and already notorious for his evil living, I welcomed him as a kinsman, affording him not only financial support but, what was perhaps more valuable, the social aegis of my position in the county.

'As I look back now on the years that passed, I blame myself for my own lack of principle in my failure to put an end to his extravagance, his drinking and gaming, and certain less honourable pursuits with which rumour already linked his name. I had thought him wild and injudicious. I was yet to learn that he was a creature so vile and utterly bereft of honour that he would tarnish the name of his own house.

'I had married a woman considerably younger than myself, a woman as remarkable for her beauty as for her romantic yet singular temperament which she had inherited from her Spanish forebears. It was the old story, and when at long last I awoke to the dreadful truth it was also to the knowledge that only one thing remained for me in life – vengeance. Vengeance against this man who had disgraced my name and abused the honour of my house.

'On the night in question, Lothian and I sat late over our wine in this very room. I had contrived to drug his port and before the effects of the narcotic could deaden his senses I told him of my discovery and that death alone could wipe out the score. He sneered back at me that in killing him I would merely put myself on the scaffold and expose my wife's shame to the world. When I explained my plan, the sneer was gone from his face and the terror of death was freezing his black heart. The rest you know. As the drug deprived him of his senses, I changed clothes with him, bound his hands with a sash torn from the door curtain and carried him across the courtyard to the museum, to the virgin guillotine which had been built for another's infamy.

'When it was over, I summoned Stephen and told him the truth. The old man never hesitated in his loyalty to his wretched master. Together we buried the head in the family vault and then, seizing a mare from the stable, he rode it across the moor to convey an impression of flight and finally left it concealed in a lonely farm owned by his sister. All that remained was for me to disappear.

'Arnsworth, like many mansions belonging to families that had been Catholic in the olden times, possessed a Priest's Hole. There I have lain concealed, emerging only at night into the library to lay my final instructions upon my faithful servant.'

'Thereby confirming my suspicion as to your proximity,' interposed Holmes, 'by leaving no fewer than five smears of Turkish tobacco ash upon the rugs. But what was your ultimate intention?'

'In taking vengeance for the greatest wrong which one man can do to another, I had successfully protected our name from the shame of the scaffold. I could rely on Stephen's loyalty. As for my wife, though she knew the truth she could not betray me without announcing to the world her own infidelity. Life held nothing more for me. I determined therefore to allow myself a day or two in which to get my affairs in order and then to die by my own hand. I assure you that your discovery of my hiding-place has advanced the event by only an hour or so. I had left a letter for Stephen, begging him as his final devoir that he would bury my body secretly in the vaults of my ancestors.

'There, gentlemen, is my story. I am the last of the old line and it lies with you whether or not it shall go out in dishonour.'

Sherlock Holmes laid a hand upon his.

'It is perhaps as well that it had been pointed out to us already that my friend Watson and I are here in an entirely private capacity,' said he quietly. 'I am about to summon Stephen, for I cannot help feeling that you would be more comfortable if he carried this chair into the Priest's Hole and closed the sliding panel after you.'

We had to bend our heads to catch Lord Jocelyn's response.

'Then a Higher Tribunal will judge my crime,' he whispered faintly, 'and the tomb shall devour my secret. Farewell, and may a dying man's blessing rest upon you.'

Our journey back to London was both chilly and depressing. With nightfall, the snow had recommenced and Holmes was in his least communicative mood, staring out of the window at the scattered lights of villages and farmhouses that periodically flitted past in the darkness.

'The Old Year is nodding to its fall,' he remarked suddenly, 'and in the hearts of all these kindly simple folk awaiting the midnight chimes dwells the perennial anticipation that what is to come will be better than what has been. Hope, however ingenuous and disproven by past experience, remains the one supreme panacea for all the knocks and bruises which life metes out to us.' He leant back and began to stuff his pipe with shag.

'Should you eventually write an account of this curious affair in Derbyshire,' he went on, 'I would suggest that a suitable title would be the Red Widow.'

'Knowing your unreasonable aversion to women, Holmes, I am surprised that you noticed the colour of her hair.'

'I refer, Watson, to the popular soubriquet for a guillotine in the days of the French Revolution,' he said severely.

The hour was late when, at last, we reached our old lodgings in Baker Street, where Holmes, after poking up the fire, lost not a moment in donning his mouse-coloured dressing-gown.

'It is approaching midnight,' I observed, 'and as I would wish to be with my wife when this year of 1887 draws to its close, I must be on my way. Let me wish you a Happy New Year, my dear fellow.'

'I heartily reciprocate your good wishes, Watson,' he replied. 'Pray bear my greetings to your wife and my apologies for your temporary absence.'

I had reached the deserted street and, pausing for a moment to raise my collar against the swirl of the snowflakes, I was about to set out on my walk when my attention was arrested by the strains of a violin. Involuntarily, I raised my eyes to the window of our old sitting-room and there, sharply outlined against the lamplit blind, was the shadow of Sherlock Holmes. I could see that keen hawklike profile which I knew so well, the slight stoop of his shoulders as he bent over his fiddle, the rise and fall of the bow-tip. But surely this was no dreamy Italian air, no

complicated improvisation of his own creation, that floated
down to me through the stillness of that bleak winter's night.

> Should auld acquaintance be forgot,
>   And never brought to mind?
> Should auld acquaintance be forgot,
>   And auld lang syne!

A snowflake must have drifted into my eyes for, as I turned
away, the gas-lamps glimmering down the desolate expanse of
Baker Street seemed strangely blurred.

VIII

THE ADVENTURE OF
THE TIRED CAPTAIN

Alan Wilson

I have remarked elsewhere, that the July immediately following my marriage was made memorable by three cases in which I was associated with my friend, Sherlock Holmes. Two of these I have already recounted, but the third was a matter of such delicacy that it is only now that I find myself free to bring the full facts to the public attention. I refer to the singular affair of the Tired Captain.

I was returning home from a visit to a colleague when I found myself passing through Baker Street. As I reached the familiar door, where I had passed with Holmes some of the happiest and most stimulating days of my life I felt that I must call in upon him again and discover what problem was then engaging his incisive intellect. I rang and was let in by our old landlady, Mrs Hudson.

'Go up, Dr Watson,' she said, 'he'll be glad to see you, I know. Indeed, he was only saying to me today that he wished you were still with him. He's hardly stirred from his room for days, and a visit from you will do him good.'

I mounted the stairs and had just reached the sitting-room door when: 'Come right in, my dear Watson,' said the well-remembered voice: 'Your chair is ready, as always.'

'Holmes,' I cried, 'are my steps so very familiar that you know me before I enter the room?'

'A trifle lighter, I fancy, Watson, but nevertheless, unmistakable. Married bliss must have had a rejuvenating effect on you. And how is Mrs Watson? I shall always retain a very great respect for her following her conduct in the Sholto case, and I am not an admirer of Woman in general, as you know.'

'No indeed,' I said warmly. 'My wife and I both feel it is the least worthy trait in your character, Holmes.'

'They irk me,' replied Holmes impatiently. 'They are too much swayed by their emotions; without that cool reasoning which I hold to be essential to the perfectly balanced mind. This note which I received this morning does not promise to change my opinion, rather does it support it.'

He tossed across a small piece of blue notepaper on which was written in the most minute handwriting imaginable: 'Dear Mr Holmes, I am so very worried by my father's health and conduct; indeed I sometimes fear for his sanity. Would it be convenient if I called upon you at 3.15 p.m. tomorrow the 28th? Yours faithfully, Rachel Webber.'

'Then you have an inquiry on hand?' I asked, handing back the note; 'Mrs Hudson rather gave me the impression that you were free at the moment.'

'Free!' ejaculated Holmes bitterly. 'My dear fellow, that is an understatement. Life has been utter stagnation since we unravelled that little affair of the Naval Treaty. I begin to think that the English criminal is a very unenterprising fellow. The recent crimes have all been simple affairs, quite within the capacity of the regular Police Force. Lestrade, Gregson and the rest are kept busy, while the expert . . .' He slumped back in his chair and gazed moodily into the fireplace.

'Well, at least,' I murmured, 'you have this letter which may prove to be the herald of better things.'

'I doubt it,' was the answer. 'The affair seems far more likely to come within your province than mine. But tell me, what do you make of it, Watson? Let the light of your intellect beat upon it.'

Ignoring the sarcasm in his tone which obviously sprang from his apathy and boredom, I took the note and examined it again.

'It is written by a young woman.'

'Bravo!' cried Holmes. 'Such perspicacity is amazing. A woman, you say? Of what age? Pray tell me, I shall be interested to know.'

'Really, Holmes,' I said angrily, 'this is unworthy of you; perhaps you had better examine it yourself.'

'I beg your pardon, my dear fellow. You must forgive me. I can be an unsociable creature at times. As for the note, it is self-evident, of course. It was written by a young woman, as you said. She is left-handed, of very precise temperament, probably short-sighted, and has a small dog of which she is inordinately fond. Apart from these obvious facts I can deduce nothing.'

Long familiarity with my friend's methods enabled me to follow his reasoning: the smallness and neatness of the writing, the exact wording of the note, bore out his theory of his correspondent's precise temperament. 'But the left-handedness,' I exclaimed, 'and why on earth the dog?'

Holmes chuckled. 'My dear Watson, when I see writing where in several places the paper is broken, and the ink is spattered I know that the pen has been pushed, a thing that never happens when writing with the right hand. As for the dog, that I admit is a long shot. But if you examine the bottom of the paper, you will notice one or two marks which by their spacing would seem to indicate the pads of a dog's foot. For a woman normally so careful and precise, to allow a dog on her lap when she writes, she must certainly be inordinately fond of it. But here, if I mistake not, is our client, exactly on time.'

The clock was just striking 3.15 as the door opened in reply to Holmes's 'Come in!' and our visitor entered. She was a very tiny, delicate looking little woman in the late twenties, with a freckled face, wearing spectacles and carrying a small Pekinese dog.

Despite my friend's professed dislike of the sex, I had invariably found him extremely courteous to women and this occasion was no exception. 'My dear Miss Webber,' said he. 'Pray take a seat. I hope you have no objection to tobacco? I find it a great aid to concentration. This is my friend and colleague, Dr Watson, before whom you can speak as freely as to myself.'

Our visitor smiled and took the seat Holmes had indicated.

'I know that Dr Watson can be relied upon,' she said. 'In fact it is really through him that I have come to consult you.'

'Through me?' I exclaimed, looking at her in surprise.

Miss Webber nodded, 'I recently read your account of your first meeting with Mr Holmes in the *Study in Scarlet*, and I thought then that he would be the very person to help me in my own trouble.'

Sherlock Holmes flushed with pleasure. 'My dear Watson,' he cried. 'Allow me to retract any little criticisms I may have made of your work in the past. But Miss Webber, we are anxious to hear what this problem is that worries you so much. Please give me the facts from the beginning. Omit nothing, however trivial you may think it.'

The young lady paused, gently stroking the little dog which lay curled on her lap, its eyes gazing fixedly at Holmes who sat opposite in the shadow, the light from the window falling on our visitor's face.

'My name,' she began, 'is Rachel Webber and I am the only child of Captain Joshua Webber of Hexton Manor near Aldershot. My mother died five years ago while father was abroad, and until his return a year ago I lived alone at the Manor, except for Mrs Marchmont, the housekeeper. Hexton Manor is an old, rambling house, built, I believe, in the seventeenth century. I have always thought it far too big for our needs, and in fact, we only use a few rooms, the rest of the house remaining empty.

'About seven weeks ago, to be exact on the 21st of May my father and I were at breakfast and I was reading a letter that had arrived by the morning post, when I heard a slight exclamation and looking up I observed father gazing fixedly at the butter dish. Then, Mr Holmes, to my amazement and horror, he suddenly picked it up, threw it into the empty fireplace and walked out of the room without another word.

'You can imagine that this left a very unpleasant impression on my mind, but by the evening this had to some extent diminished, only to be aroused again in a very strange way.

'That night I was lying in bed trying to find a reason for my father's extraordinary conduct when I heard footsteps outside my room. I listened as they slowly passed my door. Suddenly there was a heavy bump. I meditated calling to see if it was father, but remembering his odd behaviour of the morning, I decided not and carefully opened my bedroom door.

'Mr Holmes, father was sitting on the stairs taking some papers from an old seaman's trunk which he must have dragged along the corridor. The bump must have been caused by it dropping down the top step. I spoke to him but, at the very first word, he slammed the lid of the box and ordered me to bed in a most unpleasant and peremptory manner.'

'One moment,' interposed Holmes, 'had you ever seen this trunk before?'

'Oh yes, father always kept it in his room, beside his bed. It contained, so I understood, relics of his early naval days, although I had never seen it open.'

'Thank you, Miss Webber, please continue your very interesting statement.'

'Next morning,' our visitor went on, 'I made no reference to the matter and neither did he although, once or twice, I caught him looking at me in a singular manner – almost as if he expected me to say something. However, for a few days all went well until one afternoon I heard my father's voice followed by loud sobs; and then, a sound like a pistol shot. Upon running out I found Mrs Marchmont in tears.

'Apparently father had come upon her while she was polishing the woodwork in the hall and had deliberately fired his pistol into the floor at her feet, at the same time hurling abuse at her of the most vile kind. Upon my arrival he ran into his own study which opens off the hall.'

I could not help glancing at Sherlock Holmes as she was speaking, for the affair seemed to me far too trivial to be of any great value to him. But to my surprise he seemed keenly

interested. He lay back in his chair, his fingertips placed together
in his most judicial manner, and the smoke from his pipe curled
in thick spirals over his head.

'Miss Webber,' he asked, 'is it Mrs Marchmont's habit to do
the polishing herself? Are there no servants?'

'No, Mr Holmes, my father would never engage anyone else,
although I have repeatedly asked him to. Mrs Marchmont deals
with everything herself.'

Upon a sign from my friend the young lady proceeded:
'Since then, my father's eccentricities have continued until,
yesterday, they reached the point that finally decided me to seek
your aid. I have said that the greater part of the Manor has
remained empty. That has been so ever since we came here. But
last night I was woken by a loud banging and hammering which
seemed to come from one of the deserted wings. Upon approaching I beheld father, looking very tired and dishevelled
coming from the direction of the east wing. He was carrying
a hammer. When I spoke to him he curtly ordered me to my
room and retired to his study. I found afterwards that he had
nailed up the doors into the wing so that it is now more cut off
from the house than ever. That is how the matter stands at
present, Mr Holmes, and I would very much value your advice.
What is the reason for my father's strange behaviour and what
do you think I should do?'

'Tell me, Miss Webber,' asked my friend, 'what were these
other eccentricities you mentioned? Pray tell me all the facts
however trivial they may seem.'

Our visitor hesitated a second before speaking: 'He has taken,'
she said in a low voice, 'to talking to himself and to singing
snatches of old songs – sometimes until the early hours of the
morning. One afternoon, he drew a knife and slashed a picture
on the wall in the presence of a friend of mine. To make matters
worse, he has a heavy sporting gun with which he seems to take
a fiendish delight in scaring the tradespeople. I believe he is a
very sick man, Mr Holmes. At the time of these outbreaks he
does not seem conscious of his actions, although he has several

times questioned me afterwards. However, I have always been noncommittal.'

'I see. And there was no sign of anything untoward prior to this butter-dish incident?'

'No, although now I come to think of it, he did receive a letter a few days previously which seemed to give him a shock. He told me he had had bad news about an investment; but more, I do not know.'

'Thank you, Miss Webber, for your statement. It has been most interesting. Dr Watson and I will be very happy to look into it. Pray keep me posted as to any further developments; otherwise we will contact you within the next few days.'

With a smile and a handshake our visitor departed. Holmes returned to his seat and closed his eyes, as was his invariable habit when concentrating on a case.

'Well, Watson, what do you make of it? Quite a pretty little problem is it not?'

'It seems perfectly clear to me,' I replied, 'the man is obviously off his head, and the sooner he is packed off to an institution the better.'

Holmes shook his head. 'My dear Watson, among your many admirable qualities I fear we cannot include imagination. You believe this Captain Webber insane. I on the other hand consider him among the sanest men with whom we have had to deal. I am much indebted to our client for drawing my attention to what promises to be a most instructive little problem. If you care to look in tomorrow evening, Watson, I hope to be able to throw some light on what still remains problematical.'

My practice is rarely very exhausting. But the next day a veritable spate of work prevented me from visiting Baker Street until just after eight o'clock. Nevertheless, Holmes was not in, so I settled down in my old chair and immersed myself in one of Captain Marryat's exciting sea stories. It was not long, however, before I heard footsteps on the stairs, and Sherlock Holmes entered.

'Ah, Watson,' he cried as he took off his coat and his earflapped travelling cap, 'my apologies for keeping you waiting, but the fact is that I have had a most instructive day. In fact,' he chuckled, 'I have won some money.'

'My dear fellow,' I replied heartily, 'allow me to congratulate you. But you surprise me. You have always been so averse to any form of gambling.'

'This can hardly be called gambling, Watson, a mere game of darts, nothing more.'

'Darts,' I exclaimed in astonishment, 'I'm afraid I do not understand.'

My friend rubbed his hands. 'You will, my dear Watson, you will. Only allow me to partake of a little refreshment, which I sorely need, and I will do my best to enlighten you.'

He rang the bell as he spoke and in due course Mrs Hudson brought in a tray of eggs, ham and a large pot of tea. Afterwards we lit our pipes and Holmes began to recount his day's adventures.

'After you left last night I thought carefully over our client's statement, with the aid of an ounce of shag. The salient point appeared to me to be this: why should a man who wished to open a trunk not do it in his own room? Why drag it along the landing on to the stairs, making a loud noise into the bargain? If, as one would imagine, the contents of the trunk were of a private nature, one would surely not arouse the household? It seemed to me, Watson, that there was something very singular in all this.'

'But if,' I suggested, 'the man is insane?'

Holmes snorted impatiently. 'We will not suppose him insane,' he replied, 'we will merely suppose that he wishes to be thought insane. Why otherwise, should he take such pains to make sure that his daughter should notice his little eccentricities? Why should he wait to slash a picture until a third party was present; a school friend, you will remember? No, Watson, he needed a witness. Miss Webber, the housekeeper, the school friend, the various tradespeople, could all testify to his singularity, if not actual insanity.'

'But why should any man wish to appear insane?' I asked, 'there seems to be no conceivable reason for such conduct.'

My friend smiled. 'It was to discover that, my dear fellow, that I made a trip to Aldershot today. There is a very comfortable little hostelry near to Hexton Manor called the Bear Inn, where, over a game of darts, the landlord, a Mr Brooks, waxed very eloquent about our friend, Captain Joshua Webber. Not only has he frightened the tradespeople, Watson, but he has even caused trouble in the inn itself. It seems that a couple of days ago he arrived at the Bear, and asked Brooks for a private room in which to meet a friend. This friend duly arrived and was closeted with the captain. But it was not long before the whole inn was aroused by the sound of a furious altercation from the private room. After an interval the captain and his friend emerged, paid the reckoning and disappeared in the direction of Hexton Manor.'

'But,' I ventured, 'he did not go to Hexton Manor, otherwise surely Miss Webber would have mentioned it?'

Holmes paused. 'Certainly,' he admitted, 'Miss Webber would have mentioned it, if she had known. However, I fancy she does not know, nor does Mrs Marchmont. I have already made inquiries. But why?'

He lay back in his chair gazing thoughtfully at the ceiling, nor did I speak for I could see that his acute mind had embarked on a train of thought which it was unwise to interrupt.

Suddenly he sprang to his feet and crossed to the writing desk. 'My dear Watson,' he cried, 'I have every hope that we shall soon be able to clear up this little matter. This telegram that I am about to dispatch should clarify things. We leave for Aldershot tomorrow.'

'We?'

'If you have no objection?'

'I should be delighted.'

'Then say no more and tomorrow I hope to be able to ring down the curtain on a plot which for ingenuity rivals that other affair which you have so ably chronicled as the "Stockbroker's Clerk League".'

Next morning found me in a train bound for Hampshire, with Holmes seated opposite looking keener and thinner than ever. Before we left, he had received an answer to his telegram of the night before and I could see by the flush on his cheeks that he expected a favourable outcome to our day's adventure. He was in one of his most expansive moods and regaled me on the journey with a series of anecdotes concerning some of the notorious criminals he had known: of Slattery the Poisoner, of Whitcombe the Fence and of Ricoletti of the Club Foot, of whom I have already made mention. Never once did he refer to Miss Webber or to the singular train of events which had led us to desert Baker Street on such a strange mission. However, just before we reached our destination, the flow of conversation ceased and he relapsed into a silence which lasted until we were in the cab which was waiting to take us to Hexton Manor.

It was, indeed, a sombre looking edifice despite the brightness of the day. An avenue of noble elms led up to a fine but gloomy house, all overgrown with dark ivy. Only the centre seemed to be occupied; the two deserted wings, with their shuttered windows, stretching forlornly on either side.

A little grey mouse of a woman whom I knew must be the housekeeper, Mrs Marchmont, ushered us into a large, comfortably furnished room on the ground floor.

'I'm afraid the master is still in his room, sir,' she said apologetically, 'and he has left instructions that on no account is he to be disturbed. I will tell Miss Webber that you are here.' She moved towards the door.

'One moment,' interposed Holmes, 'yesterday when I called, I was told that he had not risen. Has he been in his room all the time?'

'Oh no, sir,' she replied quietly, 'yesterday, he got up for his tea, and after that he went out into the garden. I saw him at about ten o'clock coming out of the store shed, and going towards the east wing; though what he could be doing there I cannot imagine, as it has been unoccupied for years. But perhaps it is not to be wondered at. The master has been acting so strangely lately I've told Miss Webber that I think she should go for the doctor.'

'Well, Mrs Marchmont,' said Holmes with a smile, 'my friend here, Dr Watson, may be of some assistance to us. But about this store shed, I imagine that is that building I observed yesterday on the left of the drive?'

'That is correct, sir. We use it to store wood and implements for the grounds, although I cannot say that they are much used.'

Before Sherlock Holmes could reply, the door opened and our client entered, her pet dog in her arms. She came towards us with a smile.

'I must apologize for my father, Mr Holmes,' she said, 'he has complained several times lately of great fatigue, although he never actually retired to his bed until yesterday.'

'Until my arrival, in fact,' muttered Holmes, glancing quickly at me from under his dark eyebrows. 'Did you tell him that you had been to consult me?'

'No, I did not, although he must have heard someone here yesterday and known that inquiries were being made. I do not understand, however, why he should shut himself away like that.'

'I do, Watson, I do,' whispered Holmes, and then, aloud, 'well it cannot be helped. And now Miss Webber, if you will excuse us I would like to show Dr Watson round this magnificent old house. We do not see many like it in London and the grounds will give us a chance of sunshine we do not often get in Baker Street.'

Miss Webber nodded assent and we left the room. As we reached the hallway I received the distinct impression that someone closed the door of the captain's study which lay opposite.

'All right, Watson, I saw it,' said Holmes as I turned to him in some excitement, 'it seems that the captain is not quite as tired as we are led to believe. But come into the fresh air where we are not so likely to be observed.'

Once outside he walked straight to the shed, which lay partly obscured by a small grove of trees.

'Door padlocked,' he observed, 'although I see by the lock that it has been in recent use. What do you suppose the captain keeps in there that he cannot take out until late at night? We are in deep waters, Watson.'

'Could he not be carrying out some alterations in the east wing?' I suggested. 'He may wish to keep it a secret from his daughter until finished. It could be a new boudoir, for instance.'

Holmes burst into a loud peal of laughter, 'No, Watson, it won't do,' he cried, 'why then, the long series of eccentricities, the simulated madness? Perhaps you are suggesting that the man he met at the inn and with whom he had such a quarrel was a builder and decorator? No, my friend, he would not resort to such red herrings, for that is what they are, unless to cover up something far more serious.'

I was a little hurt at the riducule in his tone, although I could not but admit that my suggestion did sound a trifle absurd when repeated by such a man as Holmes. However, before I could reply the laughter in his voice had died and he was trying to peer through the grime-encrusted window of the shed. But I could see that all was dark within. Suddenly he stopped and examined the ground carefully with his lens.

'Do you notice it?' he asked, holding a long finger close to my nose.

'Paraffin?'

'Exactly, paraffin. I fear, Watson, that my arrival on the scene has precipitated him into desperate action which could have unfortunate results for our client.'

'Should we not search the east wing?' I ventured. 'Surely the key to the mystery lies there?'

'My dear fellow,' he retorted with some asperity, 'you surely do not imagine that I came here yesterday and neglected that obvious line of action? You heard Miss Webber say that every entrance to the east wing from inside the house had been sealed. That is true; I have verified it. The inside doors have been not only locked but have had wooden planks nailed across them, whereas this door which we are now approaching, has been quite frequently in use.'

He had left the shed and we were standing before the massive seventeenth-century door of the east wing. I could see that it had, indeed, been in use of late The grass was all trodden down and the huge padlock was black with the traces of fresh oil. The windows of the whole wing were heavily shuttered and helped to give an appearance of utter desolation to the place.

'And now,' said Holmes as he led the way to a nearby grassy bank, 'if you will give me a little of your attention I would like to state my case. The whole of this story is now clear to me; all that remains is to wind the matter up satisfactorily. We cannot do that, however, until the captain sees fit to rise from his bed. I fancy nightfall should bring forth the quarry.'

'You think then that a serious crime is about to take place?'

He paused, produced his old black clay pipe, and slowly filled it from his pouch.

'If I read the matter aright, Watson, it has already taken place. As I have pointed out, it was obvious to me from the start that Captain Webber's extraordinary conduct could only mean one thing. It is based upon the undeniable fact that the best place to conceal something is among its own kind – a pin in a pincushion is an obvious analogy. The captain's peculiarities had become so well known that one more, even if it happened to be a crime, would pass virtually unnoticed. The problem was not so much the thing itself as the reason for it. You will remember that our client stated that her father had received a letter which he accounted for by saying that it contained bad news of an investment? Two days later began the series of events which have brought us down here.'

'Holmes,' I exclaimed, 'I begin to see. If we can only find out from whom that letter was received . . . !' But I got no farther for he gestured impatiently with his pipe and continued with his explanation.

'Next day, during my profitable little game with the landlord of the Bear, I heard about the "friend" whom Captain Webber was expecting and who later mysteriously vanished. I put two and two together – and what do I find?'

'That the letter was from the friend?'

'Exactly, Watson. You excel yourself today. This letter was from the "friend". It said that he would meet the captain at the inn at a certain day and time. Whereupon the gallant captain begins his terrorizing of Mrs Marchmont and the others and thus gains a reputation for eccentricity he is at considerable pains to encourage. In due course, the "friend" arrives at the trysting place, an argument ensues and the two go off to Hexton Manor where the captain promptly murders the other in the east wing.'

'But good heavens, Holmes!'

My friend shook his head gravely: 'I am afraid no other hypothesis will cover the facts. They were seen going towards the Manor but neither our client nor the housekeeper saw them arrive. No, Watson, the unknown gentleman is in that deserted east wing. We don't yet know how he was killed. But afterwards the captain sealed up the doors and in coming away was seen by his daughter who immediately classed the loud hammering that had awoken her with his other strange behaviour.'

It was one of the worst characteristics of Sherlock Holmes that he was impatient of even the slightest criticism, and this occasion was no exception. I ventured to suggest that Captain Webber would surely realize that as soon as the inevitable inquiries were made about the missing man, the people at the inn would remember the quarrel that had taken place and he would immediately be suspect. But Holmes brushed this objection aside in his imperious fashion.

'No, Watson, Captain Webber knew that no inquiries would be made. It was apparent that the key to these events lay in something that had occurred prior to his return to this country a year ago. There is nothing in his life since which could account for this singular train of events. You saw me send off a telegram yesterday and the reply received this morning gives us much useful information about the captain.'

He paused glancing around the sunlit grounds and at the empty east wing which towered above us.

'In 1877,' he explained, 'Captain Joshua Webber was in command of the barque *Maria Christina*. Does the name suggest nothing to you?'

'*Maria Christina*? Surely that is the name of the ship that was involved in the sensational smuggling case of a few years back?'

'It is,' Holmes continued. 'The first officer, Adam Belter, was accused of serious infringements of the laws appertaining to the import of drugs. There was considerable evidence to incriminate the captain himself. But he managed to extricate himself and never came to trial. In the end, and as a direct result of Webber's evidence, the whole onus of the affair fell upon Belter who was given twelve years.'

'Twelve years,' I exclaimed, 'then he is now free?'

'Yes, he was released eight weeks ago, just about the time that the captain received the letter that gave him such a shock. He knew then that Belter was at large once more and that he was seeking vengeance on the man responsible for his imprisonment. As a result, he planned this whole elaborate scheme which, I must admit, is entirely new in my experience, although I fancy there was something similar in Helsinki in '68.'

'My dear Holmes,' I cried in admiration of this extraordinary man, 'your account of this strange case is so obviously correct that I am amazed that I failed to see the true explanation. I was in possession of the same facts as yourself and yet I was completely in the dark. But what are we to do now to bring him to justice?'

Sherlock Holmes rose from the bank on which we had been seated and led the way back to the Manor.

'It is evident that the captain will not stir from his room while we are still upon the scene,' he observed, 'therefore we must let it be thought that we are leaving. We shall not, however, be going very far.'

Our client looked rather surprised and a little disappointed when Holmes told her that we had been called back to town on urgent business. But my friend, with that courtesy and gentleness which characterized all his dealings with the opposite sex, soon put her at her ease and promised that we would return the following day.

We went no farther than the inn where we were greeted by a familiar figure.

'Well, Mr Holmes, I got your wire. What is it all about?'

'If you will join us in a meal, Lestrade,' replied Holmes, 'I shall be very happy to enlighten you. After sampling my friend Mr Brooks's poultry, we shall be better able to face the little ordeal that awaits us. I hope that you may be able to add a sensational murder case to swell your already enviable reputation.'

Inspector Lestrade looked rather dubious when he heard our narrative. But he had already learned not to treat Holmes's remarkable powers with levity.

'I'm with you,' he said grudgingly.

'Good man, and now if we have finished our meal perhaps we had better start. Have you brought your revolver, Watson?'

'I have my Eleys,' I replied, patting my pocket.

'Then let us proceed to what I confidently expect to be the dénouement of this little affair.'

When we arrived back at the house we did not go in. Instead we turned into the small grove of trees that I have already mentioned. From there we could see the whole of the front of the building and the door of the sinister east wing.

'I don't fancy we shall have long to wait,' whispered Holmes, as we seated ourselves among the trees, 'he will only delay until he thinks everything is clear.'

'But what is he going to do?' asked Lestrade.

'The body, Inspector, the body,' was the reply. 'He cannot leave it there indefinitely, although the east wing is not used. What plans he has made for its disposal I don't know. But my arrival has obviously frightened him and he is being pushed into action. That paraffin worries me, however. Surely he cannot be going to ...' His voice died away and he gripped my arm convulsively as the front door of the Manor opened.

We were disappointed. It was not Captain Webber who emerged but his daughter, out for a stroll in the early evening air, her little pet at her heels. She walked a few times round the patch of gravel, just in front of the house, and once passed so close to us that we could have stretched out and touched her. The dog seemed to know that strangers were about for it began barking shrilly in our direction.

'Hush Suki,' we heard her say as she looked in alarm at the small wood in which we lay concealed. Lucky it was for us that she was short-sighted or we would surely have been discovered. The affair had startled her, however, for shortly afterwards she picked the dog up and returned to the house.

'Thank God,' muttered Holmes, with a sigh of relief, 'I thought we were discovered.'

For some time after this all was silent. Dusk began to fall, making the old mansion look even more depressing than it did in the daytime. I was just thinking that we had come upon a fruitless errand when the front door opened once more, and a man stood before us. He could only be the person we had come to seek out.

He was short, with a lion-like head, quite bald except for a fringe of close-cropped white hair. His dark complexion was dried and wrinkled – and pitted with the marks of an active and dangerous life. Nevertheless, I thought I could discern traces of fatigue and worry on his face as he moved past our place of concealment and approached the padlocked door of the ancient east wing. We saw him produce a large key, and with a loud creak, the heavy door swung open.

'Quietly,' whispered Holmes, and I could see that he was taut with excitement, 'let us follow him.' Our quarry must have heard this remark, for suddenly he was gone and the massive door slammed shut, just as we flung ourselves upon it.

'Fool that I am!' cried Holmes bitterly. 'It is impossible to get this open; we shall have to try the windows. But how are we to break down the shutters?'

With a cry he ran off, returning a second later with a large stone with which he launched a furious attack on the nearest window. The glass shattered and we were about to blast the lock of the shutter with our revolvers when he stopped us.

'Do you see it?' he shouted, pointing up to the second floor. As I looked a chill of horror swept over me.

Just above our heads there was another window and from underneath the shutter was creeping a wreath of grey smoke. While we looked, another one sprang into being and, in a very few moments clouds of smoke were pouring from every crack and crevice in the old walls.

In a second we had burst open the window and were into a dark, empty room. I had a glimpse of thick curtains with heavy oak furniture and then, we were through the opposite door. What followed is very confused. I have a vague recollection of following Holmes and Lestrade up a long staircase and of opening several doors at the top, only to be driven back by the dense smoke which soon filled the whole wing. Time and time again, we tried to force a way through. But each time it was impossible and we soon found ourselves once again in the cool evening air while the building behind us was a mass of flame and smoke. My two companions went immediately to rouse Miss Webber and the housekeeper while I hurried away for assistance.

How long had elapsed I have no idea, but when I returned with the firemen, I found the wing ablaze. Even as we arrived, a section of the roof collapsed with a roar that sent up a shower of sparks and flame. I made my way to where Holmes stood with the weeping Miss Webber and Mrs Marchmont.

'No good, Watson,' said he, drawing me aside, 'I'm afraid the poor devil has been hoist with his own petard. Paraffin is a dangerous substance and to light it in an old place like that, where the wood and furnishings are like tinder, was asking for trouble. Lestrade and I tried to break into the wing from the inside but it was hopeless. He probably burned some old clothes and wood with the body hoping that it would be completely consumed without, however, destroying the building.'

But we were destined to have one more glimpse of Captain Joshua Webber. Suddenly, at an upper window we caught a glimpse of a writhing and contorted face amid a mass of flame. In another second, he had flung himself out and crashed to the earth below. We rushed over but it was too late: the fall had killed him instantly.

'Who knows, perhaps it's as well,' said Holmes in a voice betraying emotion. 'With burns like that life would have been unbearable and, this way, at least, there is no suffering.'

There is little more to tell. For another hour the fire raged despite the frenzied efforts of the firemen who did, at least, succeed in preventing the holocaust from spreading to the rest of the house. At the end nothing was left of the east wing but a few blackened ruins. Among them were found a few charred bones; all that remained of the man, Adam Belter.

'An instructive case, Watson,' remarked Sherlock Holmes, as we sped homewards after delivering our weeping client into the care of a friendly neighbour. 'Had the outcome been successful for him the locals would doubtless have found a remarkable improvement in his condition, although I fancy that, in the end, he had so sunk himself in the part he had set himself to play that he was, in truth, insane. I suppose that the blame for his death must lie at my door. It is certain that had I not spurred him into action by my untimely appearance he would not have chosen such a desperate and spectacular method of disposing of the body. He knew, of course, that if I had met him I could have exposed him instantly; hence his retiring to his room until I had, as he thought, left. That disappointed me. Up till then he had displayed considerable ingenuity, but to imagine that he could throw me off with such a pretence was nothing short of childish. Yes, my dear Watson, if you ever feel tempted to lay this case before your public, I feel that you might do worse than entitle it "The Adventure of the Tired Captain".'

IX

THE ADVENTURE OF
THE GREEN EMPRESS

F. P. Cillié

~✴~

I find it recorded in my note-book that it was towards the end of July 1888, that the attention of my friend Mr Sherlock Holmes was first drawn to the singular occurrences concerning the Malton family and the unfortunate circumstances which these events had on many of the foremost families in the Kingdom.

It will be remembered that I had forsaken my lodgings with Sherlock Holmes at 221B Baker Street when, at the end of the year 1887, Miss Mary Morstan had fulfilled my every hope by becoming my wife. After she and I had settled in our new home, I found that, despite Holmes's misgivings about domesticity and the marital state, my time was so fully occupied that I was able to visit Baker Street only three or four times during the winter of '87.

The spring and summer of '88, however, as I have recorded elsewhere, were made memorable by several cases of interest in which I was privileged to be closely associated with Sherlock Holmes and to study his methods. Under this heading I find reference in my notes to the notorious affair of the Naval Treaty, the tragedy of the Tired Captain and the Adventure of the Second Stain. It is with the last of these cases that the present chronicle is concerned.

My note-book recalls that the evening of 23 July 1888, furnished London with a grim illustration of man's inability to anticipate the fickleness of the elements around him and of the necessity for him to regulate his pattern of life according to these vagaries. On the afternoon of that day, a Monday, Holmes and I had proceeded to the East End of the city in connection with the final tidying up of the affair of the Tired Captain, the dark secret of whose colossal schemes Holmes had only the previous week discovered so unexpectedly beneath the murky waters of the Thames. As my friend and I were on the point of separately returning home that evening – he to Baker Street and I to my wife – a sudden and unexpected squall of rain, driven by a fierce south-wester which had sprung up as if by magic, forced us to seek hurried shelter in a nearby public-house.

'Come now, Watson,' Holmes exclaimed impatiently as we stood contemplating the dismal scene through a grimy plate-glass window, 'surely you acknowledge that for the moment the elements take precedence over your anxiety to return to your wife? Accompany me to 221B and wait there until the London weather becomes less inclement; my rooms are far nearer than yours and I can promise you an instructive ninety minutes –'

'But, Holmes,' I interjected, 'my wife –'

'Nonsense, my dear fellow.'

He darted outside and hailed a cab which was fortuitously standing less than twenty paces from the door. The cabbie drove the horse at a brisk pace and within forty minutes we were in the familiar surroundings of Baker Street, beneath the rooms which had witnessed the beginnings of so many strange adventures, some tragic, some possessing features of humour, but none which did not contain that element of the unusual, that touch of the bizarre, which so appealed to my companion's singular nature.

Holmes's voice interrupted my thoughts, and there was no mistaking the sudden eagerness in his manner, the quickening of interest that I knew so well.

'Hullo, Watson, what urgent business can drive someone to seek my counsel on a night such as this?'

As Holmes spoke his lean frame shivered and he drew his coat more tightly about him, for although it was not raining heavily, the night was bitter.

'As our visitor has just left,' he went on, 'Mrs Hudson can perhaps inform us what kept him waiting upstairs for more than thirty minutes.'

'Really, Holmes!' I cried in astonishment, surveying the empty, desolate street, 'I don't see how on earth –'

'Tut, Watson, the rim tracks in the wet ground are those of a four-wheeler which arrived here recently and departed again. The fresh horse droppings provide secondary confirmation, and from the fact that the coachman emptied his pipe no less than three times against the steps as he stood in the doorway – what! you did not notice the tobacco? – it seems obvious that he was kept waiting for some considerable time. The wet prints on the stairs indicate that the visitor himself waited upstairs in the sitting-room.'

As Holmes spoke we entered the sitting-room, and it was immediately apparent that someone had indeed been there a short while previously. Not only were there clear traces of fresh soil particles on the carpet, but lying across a chair was a heavy walking-stick obviously belonging to the recent caller.

'Ha!' Sherlock Holmes exclaimed, 'our visitor has left us something. I know only of pipes and hats which tell us more of their owners than walking-sticks.'

He took the stick, and after examining it minutely for a few minutes, turning it over and over, testing it for weight, peering intently at the wood, rubbing the metal tip with his thumb, sniffing it and tapping it against his chair, he sighed and handed it to me.

'Well, Watson, what do you make of it? You know my methods. Use them.'

I took the stick and examined it carefully, trying to reason along the lines that my friend usually employed. It was made of heavy, dark wood of above average length.

'I would say it belongs to an elderly gentleman who is of average means and probably of well over medium height,' I remarked after some moments. 'Walking-sticks are mostly used by men fairly advanced in years and while this stick is obviously of good quality, I see nothing which points to unusual value or rarity. I estimate the man's height from the length of the stick itself. Do you agree with me, Holmes?'

'On the contrary, Doctor,' Holmes shook his head. 'I fear that you have missed the point entirely. Although I can't deduce as much from it as I should like to, I think we may safely state that the stick belongs to a youngish man of at least considerable personal wealth, who is of short, stocky build and who at the same time probably possesses unusual bodily strength. We may venture to state, too, I think, that he visited Mexico about five years ago and that he has a rather quick temper and an aggressive nature. But further than that the man is possibly left-handed and also married, I can deduce nothing more about him.'

I stared incredulously at Holmes. 'This time you've gone too far, Holmes! I don't see . . .'

'Tut, Watson, you see everything, but fail to observe and deduce.'

'Modest as my talents doubtless are, Holmes, they have not been entirely without value to you in the past,' I said warmly, nettled by his superior manner.

'Upon my soul, Doctor, a distinct touch!' Holmes chuckled. 'But forgive me, my dear fellow, I did not mean to offend you and I'll gladly point out the features of the stick on which my reasoning is based.'

Taking the long-stemmed cherrywood pipe from the rack and a handful of black shag from his old Persian slipper, Holmes lit it and settled with a sigh into his favourite armchair.

'We have here a stick which is not only uncommonly long and heavy, but unusually thick too. My first conclusion was therefore that the owner possesses considerable physical strength – you will agree, Doctor, that no man would carry around with him an extraordinarily weighty object such as this unless he was comfortably able to do so.

'But it was also soon apparent that the man is, in fact, only of less than medium height. You'll notice that nine inches below the grip the wood is worn smooth, whereas above and below this point the stick is virtually unmarked – surely evidence, Watson, that the owner habitually grasps his stick well below the handle? A quick calculation of the distance between this spot and the tip of the stick convinced me that our man is, as I have said, not very large at all.'

Holmes stood up and, holding the stick at the place he had indicated, extended his arm in the fashion of someone using a walking-stick. The point of the stick was fully ten inches above the carpet.

He settled deeply in his chair again and blew a large cloud of obnoxious blue smoke towards the ceiling.

'And the man's wealth, Holmes?'

'He has recapped the tip of his stick in solid elaborately embossed silver. Would a man of insubstantial means spend thirty shillings on – ?'

'What about his age?'

'A glance at the tip confirms the fact that the silver shows few signs of wear despite being more than a year old, as can be seen from its colour. This in turn proves that our client carries his stick more as an instrument of authority than as an object of physical support. An elderly man would make much practical use of a stick like this, in which case the tip would show clear signs of hard usage. Silver, as you know, Watson, is not one of the hardest metals known to man.'

'And the deduction that he was in Mexico five years ago? How the devil – ?'

'The stick is carved from Mexican blackwood. The exceedingly fine grain and exceptionally high polish are quite unmistakable!'

'He might have bought it at, say, Allenby's in Bond Street,' I objected.

'Hardly, Watson. Sticks of this type are virtually unobtainable in London. No, I am sure he bought it in Mexico.'

'But how can you be sure that his visit occurred five years ago, Holmes?'

'Ah, Watson, that I confess is conjecture on my part. However, the condition of the wood points to the probability of the stick being less than six and more than four years old.'

'What about the man's aggressive nature?' I asked, somewhat mollified by my companion's easy manner.

'When a short, powerful man carries an unusually large, heavy stick, Doctor, and wields that stick more as a weapon than as an ordinary walking-stick, I think it is scarcely an exaggeration to conclude that he possesses an incisive and probably aggressive temperament.'

'The fact that he is left-handed, Holmes.'

'If you look closely at this spot, Watson' − he indicated the place − 'you'll observe one or two faint but unmistakable scratches, marks such as would be made by the gold ring on the third finger of a married man's left hand. I concede that some men also wear rings on their right hand, but I am inclined to think that my first deduction will prove to be correct. Furthermore −

'But here, unless I am much mistaken, is our client himself.'

And in the street below, faintly audible above the rain pattering against our window, we heard the jingle of horses' harness and the splashing of wheels through water. Holmes and I were at the window in an instant and, dimly discernible through the slanting rain outside, we saw a heavily cloaked figure alight from a handsome four-wheeled carriage in the street below and approach our doorway.

'So, Watson, the game's afoot again,' Holmes said with relish, rubbing his thin hands together.

Hardly had he spoken when our door was thrust open and a squat figure strode purposefully into the sitting-room.

'Which of you gentlemen is Mr Sherlock Holmes − ?' the stranger began authoritatively, staring with hard, piercing eyes at Holmes and me in turn.

We had both risen, but Holmes spoke first: 'I am Sherlock Holmes,' he said kindly, 'and this is my associate Dr Watson. But I see that you are wet and tired, and our duty must first be to make you more comfortable.'

So saying, my companion took our visitor's hat and streaming waterproof – mute testimony of the severity of the weather
outside – and put them on the dinner-table. The man's tense,
almost rigid manner relaxed visibly and he slowly removed the
thick scarf and heavy cloak wrapped around him.

As our client turned to the armchair indicated by Holmes and
started to introduce himself, the lamp-light fell upon his face for
the first time. I saw Holmes stiffen, and I myself could barely
suppress an exclamation. The man before us was between thirty-
five and forty years of age – thirty-six, to be precise, as I
discovered later – and was quietly yet well dressed in black
frock-coat, brown gaiters and pearl-grey trousers. But it was his
figure and face, his bearing rather than his dress, which commanded our attention. He was small but powerfully built and
his face had that rugged strength of character and grim determination of purpose which unmistakably marks the man of
action and drive. How well was that face known over all
England and Europe! The man before us was none other than
Lord Malton, Secretary for War, the foremost diplomat and
most popular statesman in Great Britain, the man who only the
previous month had successfully negotiated a non-aggression
treaty with the Empire's most implacable enemy when all had
seemed lost.

Holmes and I bowed silently in deference to our distinguished
visitor's reputation. My friend's face was thoughtful and slightly
puzzled.

'To what – ?' he began.

'I see that you know who I am, gentlemen, and I do not intend
to take up more of your time than is unavoidable,' Lord Malton
interrupted him with that incisiveness of speech and forceful
manner for which he was famous. Underlying his flat, even
tone, however, was an edge of tension and mental strain which
I as a medical man instantly recognized.

'Before I go further, I must emphasize that I am here entirely
in a private capacity. This visit has nothing to do with my
official – er – position . . .'

'I see. Please be as clear and succinct as possible when relating the facts of the case, your Lordship,' Holmes said courteously.

Our visitor glanced briefly at my companion and a wry smile passed across his face.

'I have heard something of your unusual powers, Mr Holmes, and I pray to God that they have not been exaggerated. I have come to you as a last resort and should you, too, be unsuccessful in your endeavours, I will have no alternative but to thrust upon not only my own family, but others too, a hideous scandal which would certainly lead to the immediate termination of my public career and possibly wreck many other innocent lives as well.

'I have heard something of – Ah! My stick!' Suddenly catching sight of his walking-stick, the Secretary for War sprang from his chair and picked it up from the table. With the stick across his knees he settled back again and proceeded with his statement.

'The facts of the case, in brief, are these. My wife, Elizabeth and I have, as it is widely known, in our possession a large emerald, which –'

'The "Green Empress"?' Holmes interjected, scribbling something on his cuff.

'Exactly. The "Green Empress", as it is commonly called, is an emerald approximately as large as – let me see – a man's thumb-nail, and is set in a plain gold ring. The gem is of such incredible rarity and perfection that its true value can only be conjectured; the sum of fifty thousand pounds for which it was purchased two hundred years ago is certainly not within one quarter of its current market value. It originally belong—'

'Quite so.'

'Forgive me, Mr Holmes; you'll not have cause to remind me of brevity again.

'Against my better judgement, I confess, the stone is never secured in my safe but is kept in a small ebony jewel-box which is always, without exception, stored in the top left-hand drawer of my wife's dressing-table – the drawer, I might add, in which all her jewellery is kept. Although the box itself has no lock, the drawer is always locked. My wife is meticulously careful about this and the key is invariably in her possession. Do I make myself clear?'

'Admirably so. Pray continue your interesting narrative,' Holmes answered, as he emptied his pipe's contents into the nearest tea-cup.

'My wife wears the emerald on rather exceptional occasions; at the most, I should say, twice or three times a year. She –'

'One moment,' Holmes interrupted him, 'when did your wife last wear the ring?'

Lord Malton considered for a second. 'She wore it at Ascot two weeks ago. Since that time the box has not left the drawer for an instant. She was emphatic about it when I questioned her two days ago.

'On Friday last, that is, three days ago, the ring was stolen from my wife's bedroom. It was . . .'

He hesitated. I could see that only our visitor's iron will and formidable self-control prevented his composure from breaking. His face was as white as a sheet and his hand trembled perceptibly.

'Quick, Watson!'

I hastily poured a measure of whisky into a tumbler and offered it to the War Secretary. He swallowed the liquid in a single gulp and with an obvious effort succeeded in regaining his composure. 'Thank you,' he said quietly, and after a few moments went on in slow measured tones:

'Living in my house at the time of the theft were, firstly, our servants of whom there are five: Johnson, the butler, an elderly man of nearly sixty years; James Morgan, my personal valet and manservant; and three young women named Lucy, Beryl and Cathy. Also staying at Summerdowne – my home – on Friday last were my brother-in-law, the Duke of Lindford, Major Hugo Dashwood of the First Bengal Lancers, and Sir Graham Hylton-Smith.'

Lord Malton paused, and added softly: 'I need hardly inform

you who these persons are. Their names and reputations are household words throughout the Empire and –'

'Sir Graham Hylton-Smith,' Holmes mused, holding his long thin fingers together before his face, 'is possibly the wealthiest man in the whole of England. He is certainly the largest landed property owner in the country and has interests in virtually every British Colonial possession.

'Major Dashwood is one of the Empire's most celebrated soldiers and it is he who, more than any other man, has succeeded in restoring Britain's perilous position on the North-Western Frontier in India.

'The Duke of Lindford, the foremost financier and industrialist in London, the man whose name is synonymous with Threadneedle Street . . . Yes, I see. Please go on, your Lordship.'

'I come now to the facts concerning the theft itself. On the night in question, that is, last Friday night, Sir Graham, the Duke, Major Dashwood and I played a game of whist until, just after eleven o'clock, we decided to retire. Each was in his own room when, at around half past eleven, we were roused by a loud cry from my wife's bedroom. You must know, Mr Holmes, that my wife and I sleep in separate rooms; she has never been able to adjust herself to my heavy snoring. We rushed to Elizabeth's room and there, standing in his shirt-sleeves before the dressing-table, holding the ebony box in his hand, was my brother-in-law, the Duke of Lindford.

'"You've taken it! Oh, my God, what have you done?" my wife sobbed. She was in a state of near hysteria and I was only able to calm her after some minutes.

'The Duke had by this time replaced the box on the dressing-table. His face was as pale as death and after looking strangely at my wife for a moment, he left the room without a word.

'When she had recovered sufficiently, my wife told us what had happened. She had left her room, she said, and was walking along the passage to the adjacent bathroom, as was her custom before retiring every night, when it suddenly occurred to her that she had forgotten her hairbrush in her room.

'Upon returning there she was surprised to find the door open and her brother, the Duke, standing before the table with her jewel-box in his hand. It was when she discovered, with horror, that the box was quite empty, that my wife gave the cry which aroused us.

'Such were the events of that dreadful night. You may imagine, Mr Holmes, what a desperate search ensued the moment we heard the tale. We searched my wife's bedroom, we looked carefully in the passage, we tore the Duke's room apart, we even searched his clothes – but not a trace of the "Green Empress" did we find. An examination of the jewel-box revealed nothing of significance and an inspection of the drawer and table even less.

'The villain had chosen his moment remarkably well, since from the undamaged condition of the lock it was apparent that the theft had been committed on one of the rare occasions when the drawer was not securely locked. I suppose it was largely self-remorse at this fact which caused my wife's breakdown. I myself got to bed after four o'clock the following morning, and since then I've slept less than five hours. I can tell you, Sir, that I am near the end of my strength, and I am not a weak man.'

The Secretary for War fell silent, but after a while continued again:

'I have naturally not officially notified the police yet, and no one has been allowed to enter or leave Summerdowne save two professional criminal investigators whom I have engaged to find the jewel and to prevent the ghastly scandal hanging over our heads. But they, too ...

'Alas, the significant point that has been uncovered strengthens the case against my brother-in-law. We have learnt that he lost a vast amount of money in Mauritius when the infamous "South Sea Development Corporation" collapsed two months ago, and that he is in considerable financial difficulty at present. Only yesterday M. Dubuque of the Paris Police –'

'What!' Sherlock Holmes exclaimed. During most of Lord

Malton's narrative he had remained silent in his chair with a heavy frown on his face. Now he seemed to come alive again.

'Yes, he and Herr Fritz von Waldbaum, the well-known Danzig specialist, are the two investigators I have employed,' the War Secretary said with surprise. 'Does that startle you?'

'No, no,' Holmes replied. 'It is only that … No matter. I think, your Lordship, that Dr Watson and I will be only too happy to look into your problem. The morning will certainly find us at Summerdowne.'

So saying – somewhat abruptly, it appeared to me – Holmes stood up and collected the War Secretary's belongings. We accompanied our client to the door where, before proceeding downstairs as hurriedly as he had entered, he once more earnestly impressed on my companion the urgency of his mission.

'Well, Watson,' Holmes remarked to me as we stood surveying the sitting-room. 'I fear that it is past eleven o'clock and your wife must be getting concerned over your absence. It has stopped raining and if we're quick in getting a cab you should be home before midnight. If you will make arrangements early tomorrow for Dr Greenwood to relieve you of your professional appointments – but not a word, my dear fellow – you can be here at 221B before eight o'clock.'

I bade Holmes a good night and managed to secure a late cab without much difficulty. I was driven home in silence through the dark, sprawling streets of the deserted city; the cold was intense and my thoughts were only a little less grim as I pondered the strange happenings which had been described to us.

The following morning I was detained by a troublesome patient and arrived at Baker Street only after nine o'clock. The unseasonal weather of the previous evening had mellowed somewhat, but it was a bleak day and the skies were low and grey and ominous. I found Holmes, clad in his old mouse-coloured dressing-gown, moodily pacing up and down in the sitting-room.

'There's something wrong, Watson,' he said irritably; 'something's very wrong indeed. And yet ... If ... No, it is fatal to theorize with insufficient data. You will join me in a quick breakfast of bacon and eggs and then we'll proceed to Summerdowne. Although there are one or two features of the case which are new to me, I don't think it will present us with any great difficulties.'

I was surprised at my friend's statement but did not say so. My long association with Sherlock Holmes had taught me not to question him until he should consider it appropriate to inform me of his conclusions.

Half an hour later we were rattling swiftly along in the direction of Oxford Street. Holmes barely spoke a word during the journey and sat hunched in a corner, frowning and muttering to himself. His heavily lidded eyes and fierce, aquiline features made him look for all the world like a huge lean bird of prey about to descend upon an unsuspecting victim.

He seemed almost annoyed when at last the cab ground to a halt outside a large, fashionable mansion standing well back in spacious grounds. Although the garden appeared to be a little neglected, the whole property spoke of elegance and comfort. Our visitor of the previous evening was there to meet us in person. He greeted us warmly but his hard, proud face looked even more drawn and haggard than it had the night before. After escorting us through the garden he showed us into a large, tastefully furnished drawing-room. Three persons, two men and a tall, pale, beautiful woman were sitting in armchairs.

'Mr Sherlock Holmes and Dr Watson,' our host introduced us. He presented us to, in turn, his wife, Lady Elizabeth Malton, Sir Graham Hylton-Smith, a tall, aristocratic-looking man, and Major Dashwood, a square, unmistakably military man. Sir Graham greeted us courteously by hand while the Major bowed stiffly. I saw Holmes appraise the room and its occupants in a single, penetrating glance, and I thought grimly that his look contained a great deal of menace in it. I was only too well aware of Holmes's singular aversion to greed among the very rich.

'When a starving man steals bread to stay alive, it's natural and understandable, Watson, but when a wealthy man cheats at cards and deals dishonestly in business and even steals, the milk of human kindness turns quite sour within me,' he remarked one day at the conclusion of his distasteful investigation of the Nonpareil Club card scandal, the details of which I have recorded elsewhere.

Lady Elizabeth rose and approached my companion, her pale, sensitive face drawn with anxiety and strain.

'Oh, thank God that you've come, Mr Holmes!' she cried; 'at last we'll see an end to this ghastly matter.'

'I have not come here to encourage hope, Madam, but to examine evidence,' my friend replied sternly. Addressing himself to Lord Malton, he went on: 'I wish first to see the room in which the theft occurred. I trust that the essential details have been left undisturbed?'

'They have,' the War Secretary replied, leading the way down a lofty passage; 'I saw to it personally. The room has remained locked and my wife has slept in one of the spare rooms since Friday.'

'Capital,' Holmes observed, and inquired where the Duke of Lindford was. 'And where are your two crime specialists?' he added a trifle cynically.

'The Duke has remained almost constantly in his room during the past four days and declines to talk to anyone except my wife, who refuses to see him. Dubugue and Von Waldbaum are calling on a bank in the city in connection with the state of my brother-in-law's finances. Ah, here we are.'

Lord Malton unlocked a heavy oak door which opened into what was obviously Lady Elizabeth's boudoir. The room was spacious and attractively decorated and everything in it conveyed an impression of femininity. Facing the large four-poster bed was the dressing-table, simply yet elegantly designed, to which our client had made reference the night before. The War Secretary crossed to the table and unlocked a small, sturdy compartment in which lay, amongst two or three leather cases and other containers, the wooden jewel-box which had been described to us.

Holmes showed little interest in these procedures but remained standing in the doorway, shooting swift, keen glances up and down the corridor and into the bed-chamber. He seemed particularly interested in the door itself, peering intently at the hinges, lock and large brass knob. Then he crossed to the dressing-table and inspected it closely. Something seemed to attract his attention for he frowned and dropped to his knees, crawling around on the carpet and sniffing at it like a bloodhound.

Lord Malton appeared somewhat taken aback at my companion's eccentric methods, but the grim, tired mouth remained silent. Holmes next turned his attention to the jewel-box itself and gingerly picked it up from the table. The box was relatively small, but sturdy and magnificently fashioned in ebony and finely wrought silver.

'This is an exceptionally fine piece of craftsmanship,' he commented, handing the gleaming container to me.

'I bought it in Mexico' — Holmes cast a sardonic look in my direction — 'when I visited the Americas six years ago. My wife treasures it greatly.'

Holmes next turned to the drawer containing Lady Elizabeth's jewellery.

'Dear me, what happened here!' he exclaimed in astonishment.

The drawer was not very large, and neatly arranged in it were a few metal and leather boxes of varying shape and size. But it was not these that had attracted my friend's interest. Disfiguring the boxes and the drawer itself was a large, irregularly shaped, black ink-stain which had obviously been caused by a recent mishap of some nature.

Holmes whipped out his lens and proceeded to make a microscopic examination of the drawer and its contents. His findings evidently pleased him, for he hummed softly and his long, nervous fingers drummed a rapid tattoo against the table. Next he carefully inspected Lady Elizabeth's personal belongings, seeming to display a special interest in her clothing. Then he returned to the open drawer and rubbed his forefinger against one of the larger marks, smelling and tasting the point of his finger.

'The stain is relatively fresh,' he observed, 'the ink is certainly not more than five days old. Underneath the surface the wood is still damp and soft.'

'I think it happened on Thursday night, but I don't know –'

'Exactly. I think, Watson, that there is no more to be learnt here. A brief stroll in the garden before luncheon should stimulate both our mental processes and our appetites.

'Tell me, your Lordship,' he went on, turning to the War Secretary, 'how often are Summerdowne's refuse bins emptied and cleaned?'

A little startled by the question, Lord Malton answered after thinking for a moment: 'Once a week. Every Wednesday, to be precise, which means –'

'Excellent,' Holmes observed, and taking me by the arm, he led the way outside, leaving a slightly annoyed and very puzzled Secretary for War staring after us.

I was at a loss to explain Holmes's behaviour. 'Is there any curious feature to which you would like to draw my attention?' I asked him as we walked across the lawns.

'To the curious feature of the second stain!'

'But there's no second stain.'

'Precisely. That is why I draw your attention to it. Ah, Doctor, this is what I am after,' he said suddenly as we rounded a corner of the house and caught sight of three refuse bins standing against the back wall near the tradesman's entrance.

He strode briskly across to the nearest of them and proceeded to rummage deeply in its interior. After a few moments he uttered an exclamation of disgust and crossed to the second of the bins. The contents of this one apparently also did not yield what he was looking for, for with a gesture of chagrin he opened the last of the bins. After a moment he straightened and held triumphantly before my astonished gaze a crumpled lace hand-kerchief almost totally discoloured with black Indian ink.

'What on earth, Holmes! How did you – ? Is this the second stain to which you've just referred?'

'Hardly, Watson. I referred just now to the curious fact that – But hark! Is that not the luncheon bell that I hear? I think that this afternoon's meal will prove to be most interesting,' he re-marked ominously as we started towards the house.

Lord Malton met us at the door leading to the dining-room and introduced us to two taciturn, solemn-looking men standing near the table. They were M. Dubuque and Fritz von Waldbaum, who had apparently just returned from their mission to the City. Both men appeared to be grim and preoccupied and they hardly spoke a word during the entire meal. Indeed, no one of the company around the table was inclined to indulge in desultory conversation. The atmosphere was tense and the heavy silence was broken only once when Holmes casually inquired of Sir Graham Hylton-Smith whether he had visited Ascot recently, a remark which seemed to startle Lady Elizabeth.

At the completion of the meal Holmes motioned Lord Malton aside and informed him that he intended to interview the Duke of Lindford privately in his room. Our host was surprised at the request and, indeed, conveyed his anxiety in no uncertain manner. But then Holmes whispered something in his ear, whereupon they left the room and proceeded together down the passage to a room not far from Lady Elizabeth's own bed-chamber.

Holmes knocked once briefly, and then quietly entered and closed the door again without waiting for acknowledgement from within. I caught a glimpse of a haggard, unshaven face and hard, staring eyes, but what passed within those walls no one save Holmes and the Duke knew. Holmes emerged again some twenty minutes later and accompanied Lord Malton to the drawing-room without so much as a word. That his mission had been successful, however, was apparent from the gleam in his eye and the spring in his walk.

I followed the two men into the drawing-room and, after summoning Dubuque and Fritz von Waldbaum, Holmes immediately locked the door and drew the curtains.

The moment was a dramatic one and the sternness of Sherlock Holmes's face bore ample testimony to the gravity of the proceedings.

'As you know, gentlemen,' he began, 'a despicable crime was committed in this house four days ago. The real crime, however, as will be clear to you shortly was not one of theft but one of fraud and deception. And this stone, gentlemen, was the villain of the piece.' So saying, Holmes produced from an inner pocket a gold ring containing a huge, sparkling emerald.

We all gaped at Holmes. Despite my long acquaintance with Sherlock Holmes and my intimate knowledge of his methods, I was as astonished as the rest of that distinguished company at Holmes's sorcery. I suppose that I shall never become accustomed to the deceptive ease with which my friend is able to perform the seemingly impossible.

Lord Malton uttered an oath and sprang from his chair. M. Dubuque and Fritz von Waldbaum had also risen with exclamations of astonishment, but Holmes waved them back to their chairs.

'And now, gentlemen, this stone will be subjected to the treatment which it merits.' As he spoke, Holmes picked up from the table two heavy brass shell-cases serving as ash-trays. Placing the ring on the base of one of these, he delivered upon it with the other shell-case such a fearsome blow that the gem shattered into a thousand small fragments.

There was a deathly silence. Had Holmes gone mad? Had his genius crossed the thin red line into insanity? Had the exertions of the previous months been too great a strain even for his phenomenal intellect? These, I confess, were the sinister thoughts which crossed my mind as I witnessed Holmes's staggering performance. The others were as horrified as I was. Dubuque and Von Waldbaum were ashen and a strange light shone in the Frenchman's eye. Lord Malton had risen slowly from his chair: his face was contorted with fury and he seemed about to spring upon Holmes.

'What the devil – ?' he began thickly, his voice shaking with anger.

And then Holmes chuckled. The dry, rasping sound cut through the room like a knife.

'Dr Watson will tell you, gentlemen, that I find it difficult to resist these dramatic little touches of mine. But I am sure that all will be forgiven me when I disclose the small object I have here in my hand.' As he finished speaking my friend turned his palm upwards and slowly opened his long, thin fingers.

'Behold, the "Green Empress",' Sherlock Holmes said dramatically.

A dazed hush descended on the room. Displayed in the dark hollow of Holmes's hand, set in a plain gold ring, was a radiantly sparkling green stone of such scintillating brilliance that it twinkled like a light and seemed almost to come alive in his palm.

I was utterly bewildered. Lord Malton seemed overcome and slowly reached out a trembling hand to the ring. The other two men appeared to be in a mental stupor and sat gaping at my companion. Our host was the first to regain a measure of his composure.

'It's a damned miracle, Mr Holmes!' he cried shakily, getting to his feet. 'It's impossible! Incredible! But what in God's name is the meaning – ?'

'Tut, Sir,' Holmes answered calmly, 'your problem was never a very difficult one, and when I have explained one or two of the more obvious features to you, I think that you and these gentlemen' – he turned to the two crime specialists – 'will be struck by the simplicity and logic of my deductions.'

He handed the emerald to the War Secretary and pacing up and down on the thick carpet, his figure tall and gaunt, Holmes described the remarkable process of deduction which had enabled him to solve the mystery, the incredible conclusion of which we had just witnessed.

'From the moment Lord Malton related his narrative at Baker Street last night, I was struck by several singular and suggestive points which, while hardly conclusive in themselves, were sufficient to arouse my deepest suspicions. The obvious explanation – that the Duke of Lindford had stolen the "Green Empress" – was never entirely acceptable or satisfactory. Consider the facts, gentlemen. Here we have a famous financier, a man who is known to possess one of the sharpest and most astute business brains in London, committing an amateurish, almost unbelievably inept crime. He waits till his sister goes down the passage to the bathroom – for perhaps only a moment or two – and sneaks into her room to steal the ring. How can he possibly be sure that the drawer is not locked when he knows that it is always locked, as Lord Malton informed us? Would a man as resourceful as the Duke leave the door of a room standing wide open – as Lady Elizabeth stated – while he steals a valuable ring? If he did take the ring, why had the drawer not been locked? Surely this is an altogether remarkable series of inconsistencies? You yourselves must have been aware of how poorly the generally accepted explanation fitted some of the facts.

'Then again, what would the Duke's motive be for such an apparently incongruous crime? It has been discovered' – Holmes glanced at the two investigators – 'that the Duke is in financial difficulties at present. What well-known financier in history has not lost money on an unsuccessful business venture at some time or another in his career? And what intelligent and able financier – as we know the Duke to be – has not made good his losses soon afterwards?

'Furthermore, if the Duke had really stolen the emerald, why hadn't he said something – anything at all – when confronted with the fact? It seemed quite inexplicable to me that he had refused to say a single word.

'But if the Duke had not taken the ring – and that he should be the thief seemed to me unlikely – then who had stolen it? Had the ring in fact been stolen at all? There could of course be only one answer to the first question – Lady Elizabeth Malton herself.'

Holmes ceased his pacing and looked at Lord Malton. Our host's face was pale and he stared unseeingly at the table in front of him. I think that the unfortunate man had vaguely suspected something of the truth all along, but had not dared to admit his fears.

'But if Lady Elizabeth was indeed the culprit,' Holmes went on, 'what exactly had she done and what had been her motive? You, Sir,' he nodded at Lord Malton, 'mentioned last night that your wife had visited Ascot recently. Alas, my gravest suspicions were confirmed early this morning when, in reply to certain inquiries, I learnt that she started going to Ascot and other race courses nine months ago and that she lost very heavily – information which naturally provided me with a strong motive for the disappearance of the emerald.

'These, then, were the inferences which I had drawn long before Dr Watson and I arrived at Summerdowne this morning. I came here to find confirmation of a theory which I had already formulated, to look for facts which would substantiate my suspicions beyond reasonable doubt. And I was not long in finding proof.

'An examination of Lady Elizabeth's bed-chamber provided me with several clues, the most suggestive of which, as I pointed out to Dr Watson, was a large ink-stain in the drawer in which she kept her jewellery and which discoloured everything inside. The second interesting feature I found was that the heavy oak door of Lady Elizabeth's room moves noiselessly on its hinges and can be pushed open without a sound, and that the lock on the door is broken –'

'But what about the stain, Holmes,' I protested; 'what on earth did you –'

'Surely the significance of the second stain has not escaped you, Watson?' my friend exclaimed impatiently.

'What second –' I began in astonishment, when Holmes cut me short again.

'The stain that should have been on the "Green Empress" ebony box. Everything in the drawer was black, yet you'll recall that the box itself – as I verified with my lens – did not have a single trace of ink on it. We were informed that the mishap with the ink, as I myself had already deduced in any case, had occurred on Thursday night – the night before the theft. Was it not remarkable that this box, which, as Lord Malton specifically told us, was without exception kept locked in the drawer – and which according to his wife did not leave the drawer for a moment during the week before the theft – should not have a mark on it when everything else in the drawer was stained? It strongly suggested to me that the person who had upset the ink-well had done so at a moment when for some unknown and possibly clandestine purpose the "Green Empress" was not in its customary place – an incident which raised several questions of crucial significance to the case in my mind.'

'Brilliant, Holmes!'

'Tut, Doctor. By this time my reasoning had advanced several stages further. Who had spilt the ink, for instance? In the answer to this question, I felt certain, lay part of the key to the mystery. With my lens I detected unmistakable signs in the drawer that the ink had been dried with a cloth of some sort – the liquid had only soaked a little way into the wood and the edges had not run. I searched Lady Elizabeth's room carefully but was unable to locate the object with which the ink had been mopped up. And then the Doctor and I found an ink-stained handkerchief in one of the dustbins outside. By now I was able with near certainty to reconstruct in my mind the scene which I felt sure had taken place on Friday night.

'After retiring at eleven o'clock, the Duke had suddenly had reason to go to his sister's room. What the precise purpose of his visit was we'll probably never know, but I fancy that a brother and sister have innumerable small matters to discuss together from time to time. Not wishing to disturb his host and the other guests, who had already retired, the Duke knocked quietly, opened the door and entered the room – so quietly, I imagine, that Lady Elizabeth did not hear him come in. At that moment he caught sight of her standing in front of the dressing-table, engaged in what he instantly recognized to be an illicit deed, a crime of some sort which caused him to rush to the table in horror and grab the objects which his sister was holding in her hands. Lady Elizabeth's cry of surprise and shock roused the house and within seconds Lord Malton, Sir Graham and Major Dashwood were in the room. During these few seconds, however, the Duke – acting on a lightning impulse to protect his sister – hid the jewels –'

'But where in God's name?' Lord Malton interrupted. 'We searched –'

'In his mouth,' Holmes said calmly. 'That was the reason for his unwillingness – his inability, in fact – to say anything when questioned by you. He then, as you know, returned to his own room where you, Sir Graham and the Major spent fifteen minutes tearing his room apart and even searching the Duke himself.

'You looked everywhere save in the one place where the two rings really were – in the Duke of Lindford's mouth. Later that morning, when the turmoil had abated somewhat, he carefully hid the rings among the books on the bookshelves, almost an unnecessary precaution as you neglected to search his room a second time.

'After that he remained constantly in his room. In his fearful anxiety to prevent a terrible scandal he could think only of attempting to speak to his sister, which desire he conveyed to her the following day. But your wife, as we know, could not bring herself to face her brother and in this way the one peaceful solution to the whole dreadful business was missed.

'Consider the hideous alternatives before the Duke, gentlemen. Should he expose and betray his sister, a woman whom he loves and honours, or should he remain silent and in so doing admit to his own guilt and forfeit his honour, his career, his very name?'

Holmes paused, his face stern. Then he went on quietly:

'I think that the Duke of Lindford acted more nobly than most of us would have done in similar circumstances, and you owe him a great debt, Lord Malton. Although at this time I naturally could not be sure what exactly Lady Elizabeth had intended to do, I was able to venture an inference with fair accuracy. Dr Watson will tell you that cases of the substitution of worthless fakes for rare and priceless gems have not been unknown to us in the past. In any event, I knew enough of the truth to feel sure that a personal confrontation with the Duke was all that remained for me to be able to fill in the last links of the chain. After considerable persuasion, and only when he realized that I knew most of the details, he reluctantly told me what had occurred on Friday night.

'He had, he said, opened the door as I have described to you and was about to call to his sister when he saw her holding in her hands two rings exactly identical in every visual respect. Although he had not immediately realized the significance and implications of his discovery, the expression on his sister's face had been one of such horror and fear that it had caused him to rush to her, resulting, as we already know, in the cry which roused everyone. The chance recollection of his sister's massive gambling debts – of which he alone knew – had suddenly left him with little doubt as to her intentions. Lady Elizabeth, acting on a blind, panic-stricken impulse to save herself, had blamed the Duke for the disappearance of the gem – which, as I have said, he hurriedly stuffed in his mouth with the fake – when her husband and the others arrived on the scene. The rest of the Duke's account exactly resembles my own reconstruction of the events.

'When the Duke had heard all I knew of the facts, he handed me the two rings and asked me to give them to his brother-in-law. The rest, gentlemen, you know as well as I do.

'And now little remains to be done, Lord Malton, but for you to talk alone with your wife for half an hour and to ascertain in what manner the money which she owes may best be raised. After that I have no doubt that, with these gentlemen's assistance, the whole affair can safely be kept from the public's knowledge. Come, Watson.'

As Holmes finished speaking, he collected his hat and coat and moved towards the door.

My friend was silent and preoccupied when I joined him outside, and he seemed almost unaware of my presence as we walked to the gate and waited for a cab in the road.

When at last one arrived he hurried me inside and gave quick, curt instructions to the cabman.

'Although I am not an unchivalrous man, Watson, I fear that I hardly feel disposed to listen to the sentimental outpourings of feminine gratitude,' he said, pointing to the house as the cabby whipped the horse away.

Running down the garden path, her cheeks streaming with tears, was Lady Elizabeth. I sat back against the cushions and looked at Holmes, his face hard and stern. But then the grim features relaxed, and a soft light touched his eyes for an instant as he spoke: 'Man's folly is endless and great, Watson, but his compassion is greater and his forgiveness even more profound. Surely, Doctor, the ultimate hope for the world lies in this fact?

'And now, if we are quick, I think we should be at Covent Garden just in time for the second performance of *Rigoletto*.'

X

THE ADVENTURE OF
THE PURPLE HAND

D. O. Smith

❧

In the year 1890 I saw little of my friend, Sherlock Holmes. From time to time I was able to follow his progress in the columns of the daily press, and he appeared from all accounts to be as busy as a man could wish to be, but I missed that close involvement with his cases which I had enjoyed before my marriage, and which a variety of circumstances, both on his side and on mine, now prevented. In one thing at least, however, I was fortunate: that on each of the few occasions I was able to renew our acquaintance, I gained a new story for my records which was the equal in interest of any which I had entered in my note-book in the days when we shared bachelor chambers in Baker Street. Holmes himself observed with amusement on more than one occasion that I was for him the stormy petrel of adventure; and if Fate had indeed cast me in that role, I was not one to complain of the fact.

It was a gloriously sunny afternoon towards the end of June. I had had a busy day, but having no further calls upon my time I dismissed my cab in Portman Square and walked the short distance to my friend's lodgings. He was not at home, but the landlady expected him back for tea, so I sat down to wait. I was not the only caller he had had that afternoon, I observed, for a card had been left upon the table, bearing the gilt inscription 'Star of Kandy Tea Company, 37A Crutched Friars; Mark Pringle, proprietor'. Across the reverse of the card was printed 'The Company employs only one salesman: His name is

Quality', and beneath that, in pencil, 'Vital to consult you. Will call back later', to which the initials 'M.P.' were appended.

Holmes was not long in arriving, and it was with evident pleasure that he greeted me. He seemed in high spirits, and tossed across to me an old leather-bound volume he had just purchased at a shop in the Strand. It was a black-letter edition of Dante's *Divine Comedy*, its binding cracked and faded with age.

'Printed at Mainz, some time in the sixteenth century,' remarked my friend. 'According to the bookseller, there is a curious error on page 348, where "honey" is for some unfathomable reason rendered as "rags"; but I know the man of old, and there is no more barefaced rogue in the whole of London. He invents these freaks of printing himself, you see, to excuse his exorbitant prices, and in the hope of attracting the custom of those whose only interest is in such oddities, and who are unlikely ever to actually read the books they buy from him. Unfortunately, he himself neither speaks nor reads any language but English, and, like the crow in the fable, is evidently incapable of conceiving that anyone else can do what he cannot, so he was somewhat discomfited when I was able to point out to him that neither word occurs on the page in question. But it really is very good to see you, my dear fellow! Indeed, the arrival of a doctor in my consulting-rooms rather completes my cosmopolitan day, for my morning's visitors, if you would believe it, were a Member of Parliament, a lighterman, a coal-heaver, and a theologian!'

'There is yet another,' I remarked, indicating the card upon the table by the window.

'Hum! Tea-merchant! Smoked a cigar while he was here. Has helped himself to a drink, too, I see! Why soda-water, I wonder? Hum!'

'No doubt a wealthy, comfortable, City type,' I suggested with a chuckle, 'who sells tea from the Orient, but has never been farther east than Ramsgate in his life, and would not recognize a tea-plant if one were growing in his own garden.

It is not difficult to picture him sitting at that table an hour ago, a stout, florid-faced man, with a glass in one hand and a cigar in the other, the very picture of a well-fed, easy life. An impatient and possibly self-important fellow, too,' I added, 'if he could not wait for your return.'

'There *is* such a type,' replied Holmes, smiling, 'but I very much fancy that Mr Pringle is not of it. If you were to dip your finger into this glass of soda-water, Watson, you would taste upon your finger-end the unmistakable bitterness of quinine. What would that suggest to you, as a physician, bearing in mind that the man who has been dosing himself with it includes upon his visiting-card the name of Kandy, in Ceylon?'

'Malaria!'

'Precisely. Now, malaria is not contracted west of Ramsgate with any great frequency, as I'm sure you would agree, and nor are its unfortunate victims generally marked for their stoutness or their florid faces. Mr Pringle has evidently spent some time in Ceylon, where he has picked up this most tenacious of diseases, but whether it be his illness or some less tangible worry which disturbs him so today, we cannot tell.'

'What do you mean?'

'You observed the used matches that he left us?'

'I believe I saw one in the dish, with the remains of his cigar.'

'Not one, Watson, but five; five matches for one cigar, mark you. Now, while there is some truth in the popular notion that the pleasure of a good cigar helps one to forget one's troubles, it is also true that one must already be untroubled to some extent, in order to derive any pleasure from the cigar in the first place. Anyone who can let a cigar go out, not once, but four times, is very evidently not in the appropriate state of mind. He has also been pacing the floor and has dropped cigar-ash in several places, as you no doubt observed, which also indicates a mood of distraction.'

'Perhaps he is just careless,' I suggested.

'I think not, for you can see that where he noticed that he had dropped the ash – just by the corner of the hearthrug – he has made some attempt to pick it up with his fingers. As to the impatience you ascribed to him, we cannot say; but it seems at least possible that he went out chiefly to get a little fresh air into his lungs, one of the unavoidable effects of quinine being, as you are aware, an unpleasant sensation of nausea.

'You must admit, Watson,' continued my friend, seating himself by the window and gazing down into the street below, as he proceeded to fill his pipe, 'that the balance of probability has swung against your snug, rosy-cheeked City man, and in favour of my perturbed and ague-cheeked tea-planter.'

'No doubt you are correct,' I conceded. 'You almost make me regret that ever I opened my mouth! But, come,' I continued, laughing, 'you have constructed so much of the unknown Mr Pringle; surely you can round out the picture a little now. What age, for instance, would you put upon the fellow, and how would you say he is dressed today?'

'He is, I should say, about forty years of age, and wearing a tweed suit.'

'Well I never!' I cried in astonishment. 'How in the name of Heaven can you tell that?'

'Quite simply because I see the fellow standing on the front doorstep at this moment,' replied Holmes drily.

The man who was shown into our room a few moments later accorded in every respect with the inferences my friend had drawn. A tall, handsome, well-built man, he had, nevertheless, an air of weakness and debility about him, as one worn down by a chronic disease. His face was unnaturally lined and leathery for one his age, his cheeks were sunken and of a sickly, yellowish hue, and his hair was quite grey. But his grip as he shook my hand was firm and strong, and there was a spark in his blue eyes which showed that the disease had not broken his spirit, at any rate.

'Are you quite recovered?' asked Holmes in a kindly voice; 'or is there perhaps something we can offer you? I observed that you had been dosing yourself with quinine, and I know how horribly that can affect the stomach.'

Pringle shook his head. 'It is not the nausea so much with me,' he replied, 'as the infernal ringing in the ears that the stuff gives me. But I've walked about a bit, and looked in a few shop-windows to take my mind from it, and I'll be all right now. Don't either of you fellows ever consider yourself unlucky,' he added with a flash of his eyes, 'until you've had what I've got. No man ever had a more implacable enemy than malaria, I can tell you: no matter how many battles it may lose against you, it will never give up the war. But I did not come here to discuss pathology with you, gentlemen, and in any case I have learned recently that there are things which can strike you harder than any disease. I wish your advice, Mr Holmes.'

'I shall be only too pleased to give it, if you will acquaint me with the facts.'

'Well, we'll call them facts for the moment, but what you will make of them, I don't know. A few snatches of conversation here, a trivial incident there – even as I think of these things now, they strike me as amounting to nothing.'

'You had best let me be the judge of that,' said Holmes. 'Pray proceed with your account.'

'I have lived most of my life in Ceylon,' began our visitor after a moment. 'My father had been a successful coffee-planter there, but he lost everything when the crash came – when, in a single season, those infernal spots of mould destroyed both the island's plantations and its prosperity – and, sadly, neither he nor my mother lived to see the success which was later achieved so rapidly with tea. I was fortunate, for I managed to get in on the new business early on, and after a couple of successful seasons, with a planter by the name of Widdowson, I decided to strike out on my own. I went in with two other fellows of like mind, Bob Jarvis, and Donald Hudson, and by working all the hours in the day, and sometimes, it seemed, more than that, we soon made our plantation one of the finest on the island.

'It was just then, when I was successful – and proud of that success, I don't mind admitting – and more wealthy than I could ever have imagined, that this cursed swamp-fever struck me down. It took poor Jarvis clean away in under a week, so, in a way, I suppose I must count myself fortunate; but I cannot pretend to feel it. For weeks my life was despaired of, until eventually the doctor gave it as his opinion that my only hope lay in quitting the island altogether until the fever was beaten. With great reluctance, then, I returned to England, leaving Hudson in charge of the plantation.

'That was three years ago, and things have since gone very well for me in most ways. The attacks of malaria had become so infrequent, until a couple of months ago, that I fondly believed myself fully cured, and I have managed to set up a company to sell our own tea – a long-standing ambition of ours – which has been at least moderately successful. I have also during my stay here met and married Laetitia Wadham, the most delightful woman in the world. We met at Willoughby Hall, near Gloucester, where she was acting as companion to Lady Craxton, and soon discovered that we had much in common. Her father had been for a time a district magistrate in Ceylon, and she had thus spent some years there as a child. It was at Gloucester that we were married, a small, quiet affair, for she was almost as without kin as I was myself. She had no brothers or sisters, and her mother and father were both dead. After a brief holiday at Lyme Regis, we took a fine modern villa, known as Low Meadow, which lies beside the Thames between Staines and Laleham. It has splendid gardens, about sixty yards in length, which sweep down from the house almost to the river itself, from which they are separated by a narrow belt of trees. It is a place where flowers bloom and birds sing, and there is all a man could wish for to complete his domestic bliss. Once more my life seemed upon an even keel; once more it seemed that nothing could come to blight my happiness.'

Our visitor paused, and, taking a handkerchief from his pocket, mopped his brow, which glistened with beads of perspiration.

'Once more,' he continued after a moment, his voice lower and softer than before, 'once more I have been struck low. And if I had thought malaria to be unseen, insidious, intangible, how much more so is the present evil! Thank you, Dr Watson, a glass of water would be most welcome.

'About seven weeks ago I was, quite suddenly and without warning, laid low with the fever. It came quite out of the blue, for I had not had an attack for nearly a year; but it was as if the disease had been storing its energies for one almighty battle, for I had never been so knocked up by it since I left Colombo, and I felt quite at death's door. There I lay, prostrate in my bed, while outside, the sun warmed the garden, and birds sang gaily, and a beautiful English spring day took its course. How much worse did it make me feel, to know that just beyond my bedroom window was such peace and tranquillity! It was then that an odd thing happened, from which I now believe I can date the beginning of the trouble which has beset me.

'It was, I believe, early in the afternoon. I had been lying for some time in a fevered sweat, slipping in and out of delirious dreams, and barely ever fully conscious. From time to time the warm breeze through my window set the curtains fluttering, and I was, I recall, observing this gentle movement when I gradually became aware of voices, speaking softly, in the garden below. I could not tell if they had at that moment begun, or if they had been speaking for some time whilst I had been asleep, but as I listened it seemed to me that one of the voices was that of my wife. Who her companion might be I did not know, nor, in truth, did I much care. That low, hushed whisper might have been a friend or a stranger, a man or a woman, for all I could tell; for the chief part of my mind was concentrated upon the fiery struggle within my own body, and I had little energy left over to eavesdrop upon the conversation of others. By and by, however, I heard a chinking sound, as of a spoon's being stirred in a jug of lemonade, and a few snatches of the low conversation came to my ears.

'"How is he?" came one voice.

'"Bad, very bad", replied the other. "The doctor has practically given him up."

'"How much longer must we endure this torment?" asked the first.

'"A few weeks at the most, so I understand; then all our troubles will be at an end."

'"Good. You do not know how I have prayed for the day it will all be over, and you and I can know happiness once more."

'Whether I drifted back to sleep then, or whether the conversation ceased, I cannot tell, but I heard no more. That night, however, I was sleeping only fitfully, as a result of the fever, when I was rendered suddenly wide awake by a sharp noise outside my bedroom window. The room was in darkness, and I was alone, for my wife slept in another room during the course of my illness. For a few moments I lay still and listened, but no further sound came to my ears. Then I heard it, a soft, rustling sound, as of the wind disturbing the shrubs in the garden below; but I could see from the stillness of my curtains that there was no wind blowing. I left my bed and crept to the window, and drew the curtain quietly aside. The garden appeared at first to be of a uniform blackness, but gradually I was able to make out the dark shapes of the shrubs and trees. Even as I looked, one shadow seemed to detach itself from the larger shadow of a bush, and flit without a sound across the lawn and into the darkness beside an old stone shed. Almost petrified — for the fever had set my nerves jangling quite enough already, before this unwonted visitation — I watched for fully ten minutes, but saw nothing more.'

'One moment,' interrupted Holmes. 'What was the size of this moving shadow?'

'It seemed at the time somewhat smaller than a man, but it could, of course, have been someone crouching low. It was certainly not an animal I saw, if that is what you have in mind.'

'Do you believe, then, that it was in fact a man?'

'So I should judge,' replied Pringle after a moment, 'especially in the light of subsequent events. But, I must say, it was not a man I should care to meet. There was something so horribly skulking and furtive in the way he scuttled across the lawn.'

'Very well. Pray continue with your most interesting narrative.'

'The next day I was feeling a little better, and could not bear the thought of being cooped up in my bedroom again. I dressed, therefore, and took breakfast with my wife downstairs. I described to her the dark apparition I had seen in the night-time, but she was inclined to dismiss it as simply the product of a fevered imagination. I did not agree with her, but it is true enough that my eyes have in the past been affected both by my illness and by the medicines I have been given to alleviate it, so I did not argue the point. In any case, I had myself devised an explanation which satisfied me at the time: there is a footpath which runs along the bank of the river, at the very foot of our garden, which the locals sometimes use; no doubt the figure I saw was some fellow the worse for drink, who had strayed from the path in the darkness, and ended up by trampling through our shrubbery.

'After breakfast I took my stick with the intention of walking to the riverside –'

'Did you not mention to your wife the conversation you had overheard the previous afternoon?' asked Holmes.

'Not at that time, no. You will gain some notion of my state of mind if I tell you that the whole incident had quite passed out of my head. When I left the house that morning I had no other thought than that it would be pleasant to sit beside the river for a while and watch the sunlight catching the ripples on the surface of the water.

'The path to the river runs down the right-hand side of the garden, separated from the boundary fence for the first twenty or thirty yards of its length by a succession of low sheds and storage buildings, in various stages of dilapidation. My way therefore took me past the very spot where I had seen the figure vanish the night before. Imagine my surprise, then, when I saw that upon the whitewashed wall of the shed was the print of a human hand.'

'What sort of print?' said Holmes sharply, sitting forward in his chair with an expression of heightened interest upon his face.

'It had been deliberately done, for it was quite clear and unsmudged. It was of a bright purple colour, and showed the whole of the hand. I thought at first that it was a drawing, but saw when I got closer that it was a true print, for all the lines and finger-joints showed up clearly. I also saw then that there was something most peculiar and horrible about it: there, at one side, as one would expect, was the print of the thumb, but directly above the palm were not four fingers, but *five!*'

'The right or the left hand?' inquired Holmes.

'The right.'

'How high above the ground?'

'I cannot say exactly. About five feet, I suppose.'

'Very good,' said Holmes, refilling his pipe. 'Your case, Mr Pringle, begins to assume the colours of something truly recherché! I am most grateful that you have brought it to my attention, and I will endeavour to return the favour by bringing a little light into your darkness. Pray continue!'

'Over luncheon that day I mentioned to my wife the mark I had seen upon the wall. "There," I said; "you see, there *was* someone in the garden last night."

'"Perhaps," said she, "although why anyone should do such a silly thing I cannot imagine."

'"Well, it has made a confounded mess of the wall, anyway. I shall have to have it re-painted. Incidentally," I added, as something stirred my memory, "did I hear you speaking to someone in the garden yesterday afternoon?"

'"I do not believe so," she answered after a moment, "unless it was the postman. But, wait — you are quite correct, dear: a charming woman called, collecting for some good cause or other. She was very tired with the heat, so I offered her a glass of lemonade and we sat chatting for five or ten minutes. That must have been what you heard."

'"I suppose it must," said I. I did not mention to my wife the words which I had thought had passed between them, for I was convinced now that they were entirely of my own invention.

I had in the past suffered badly with nightmares when the fever was upon me, and had always felt utterly foolish the next day – when my bad dream would strike me as simply absurd and trivial – so that I had learned to keep such things to myself.

'My health picked up rapidly after a few days, thanks to the fine weather, and the good clean air I was breathing, and life continued as before. Some time later – about the twenty-seventh or -eighth of May, if my memory serves me correctly – I returned home, after three or four days of travelling in the North upon business, to find my wife in high spirits.

'"I hope you do not mind, Mark," said she, "but I have taken the initiative while you were away, and employed a gardener."

'"Not at all," I replied. "That is excellent news." We had previously relied on the intermittent services of an old fellow from the nearby village, but he was really past coping with so large a garden as ours now; for although always pretty, and full of colour, it has a tendency to run riot if left to its own devices, and for all my wife's enthusiasm and endeavour it had been deteriorating for some time. "Is he a local man?" I asked.

'"No," said she. "He is from Hampshire, a man by the name of Dobson. He had placed an advertisement in the gardening journal, and I thought such enterprise should be rewarded. His testimonials were first class, and I am sure he will make an excellent gardener. His wife, too, seemed a splendid woman, and she will be able to help Mary about the house. I thought they could have the old cottage near the river, and I have arranged for a firm of builders from Staines to come tomorrow to set it to rights for them."

'"You *have* been busy!" I cried. "And I agree entirely! It would do the old cottage good to have someone living in it again. I was thinking only last week what a pity it was, to have had it standing empty all this time."

'The cottage is an old, low building, which stands just beyond the belt of trees which separates the garden from the river, and has stood upon that spot since long before ever our own house was built. It had become dilapidated over the years, but, within a few days, the men my wife had hired had brightened it up considerably: the broken slates upon the roof had been replaced, the guttering mended, and the whole of the outside given a fresh, bright coat of paint. All was finished by the end of the week, when the gardener and his wife arrived to take up residence.

'They struck me as a pleasant enough couple, although oddly matched, I thought, in both appearance and manner. The husband, John Dobson, a thin, angular sort of fellow, with hair as black as his face was white, was taciturn almost to the point of rudeness, and had the air about him of one who has suffered much. His wife, Helen, on the other hand, was a small, pink cheeked and dainty woman, with hair the colour of sand, and quite the most chirrupy and voluble person I had ever met. Still, it was not for their conversation or appearance that they were employed, and, in truth, I took little notice of them, leaving it to my wife to issue instructions as to the work they were to do.

'A few days later, rising early, as is my habit, I discovered that I had misplaced my cigar-case. Recalling that I had had it with me the previous evening, when I had sat for a while at the bench by the river, I set out to see if I had left it there. The garden seemed bright and fresh in the morning air, and I smiled as I approached the gardener's little whitewashed cottage, nestled so prettily beneath the towering horse-chestnuts, all adorned as they were with their great pink and white candles.

'"What a splendid little house it is!" I said aloud to the morning air. But no sooner were the words past my lips than I saw something which quite stopped me in my tracks and struck the smile from my face. For there, in the very centre of the clean white wall of the cottage, was the print of a human hand.

'It was in every respect the same as the one I had seen four weeks earlier upon the outhouse wall. It was the print of a right hand, a livid purple in colour, and again with that grotesque and horrible extra finger.'

'It had not been there the previous evening?' interrupted Holmes.

'No. If it had, I should have seen it.'

'You are certain upon the point?'

'Absolutely.'

'Very well. Pray continue.'

'Anger rose within me that someone had again crept unin-vited upon my property in the night, and had desecrated this freshly painted wall. A pail of water stood near by, and next to it was a piece of rag with which someone had evidently been cleaning the cottage windows. In my fury I plunged the rag into the water, with the intention of expunging the odious mark from the wall. To my surprise and disgust, the rag emerged from the water as purple as the mark it was intended to erase. I tilted the pail slightly, and watched with horror the sparkling violet stream which poured over the side and splashed about my boots. I felt quite unable to comprehend the meaning of this sinister transformation, but I did not loiter to ponder the matter. I quickly located my cigar-case at the nearby bench, and hurried in a daze of bewilderment to the house. Just once I glanced back at the cottage to reassure myself that that evil-looking mark was really there upon its wall, and that I had not imagined the whole episode, and as I did so it seemed to me that a curtain quivered at one of the windows, as if someone had hurriedly closed it as I turned.'

'The date of this incident?' inquired Holmes.

Pringle took a small diary from his pocket and leafed through it for a moment in silence. 'I believe it must have been the third of June,' he said at last; 'about three weeks ago.'

Holmes scribbled a note upon a scrap of paper, as his client continued his account.

'The days passed, the wall was cleaned, and the incident forgotten; but I began to have serious misgivings about the new gardener. I had soon learned to tolerate his dark, silent manner – indeed, on the one occasion he had overcome his reserve so far as to actually hold a conversation with me, I had found him both amusing and intelligent, if a little cynical – but what I could not tolerate was the fact that he appeared to do nothing whatsoever to justify the wages he was being paid. Each day I arrived home from town expecting to see some improvement in the appearance of the garden, and each day I was disappointed, until eventually I raised the matter with my wife.

'"Dobson does not seem much of a gardener to me," I remarked one evening. "Where are the testimonials he gave you?"

'"I am afraid I have lost them, Mark," she replied in an apologetic tone. "But I do not think you are being entirely just to the man. He has, after all, only recently begun, and there is such a lot to be done in the garden at this time of the year."

'I could see from the expression upon my wife's face that she felt that my remarks were impugning her judgement, so I shrugged my shoulders and let the matter drop. When I chanced later to recall the conversation, however, it seemed to me then that she had been just a little too ready with the information that the testimonials were lost. It was almost as if she had been waiting for me to ask; as if, indeed, she had been expecting it.

'A day or two after this, I arrived home in the afternoon and went straight into the garden, intending to sit for five minutes in the sunshine and finish the newspaper I had been reading in the train. After a few moments, however, I became aware of voices in the distance. From where I was sitting, a double row of elms and rhododendron bushes formed a natural corridor, along which I had a perfect view. Even as I looked, two people appeared round the corner at the far end of this corridor, my wife and the gardener. They were walking close together, very slowly, apparently in deep conversation. I was about to call out to them – for they had evidently not seen me – when I realized with a shock that they were entwined in embrace, he with his arm across her shoulder, and she with her arm around his waist. My greeting froze upon my lips, and at that very moment my wife looked up and met my gaze. Her mouth fell open and her arms dropped to her side, and for several seconds we stared at each other in silence.

'"What is wrong?" I called, without really knowing why I

did so. My wife's face was such a mask of guilt that I could scarcely bring myself to look at it, and, to be frank, it was evident to me that the only thing that was wrong was that I had surprised their little tête-à-tête. But I called out, nevertheless, and thus presented my wife with an exit from her embarrassment. Why one should wish to assist another to lie to one, I do not know, but my wife took the cue and responded with alacrity.

'"He has sprained his ankle," she called back. "I am helping him back to his house."

'I threw down my newspaper and hurried over to where they stood. There seemed little wrong with his ankle so far as I could see, but, without comment, I helped him to the cottage and left him in the care of his wife. Lettie had returned to the house, and when I saw her later she made no reference to the incident. As I had decided that I would certainly not be the first to bring the matter up, it remained therefore unaired, although I twice caught her looking at me in an odd fashion that evening, as though wondering what was passing in my mind. Since that time I have never seen the two of them together so intimately, but I cannot of course speak for the times I am away from home.

'If I thought then that I had cause to resent the gardener, I was soon to find out that his wife's behaviour could be equally uncongenial to me. Lettie began to refer to the woman continually, in a way which gradually began to irritate me intensely. It was always "But dear, Mrs Dobson says this," or "Helen thinks that we ought to do that."

'One afternoon, I returned home from town unusually early, and hearing the sound of female laughter from the garden, I strolled in that direction. As I approached a rose-covered pergola, on the other side of which was a small arbour, I recognized the voices of my wife and Mrs Dobson.

'"I really don't think I can agree with you, Helen," I heard my wife say.

'"But you must, Lettie, you foolish girl. You are simply being stubborn!" retorted the other. There followed a further remark which I did not catch, then peals of laughter. I was surprised to hear my wife indulging in such banter, but I endeavoured not to show it, as I turned into the arbour where they sat.

'"Hello!" I cried. "You sound jolly!" But even as I spoke I saw the smiles vanish from their faces.

'"Yes, dear. We were discussing the garden," replied my wife, attempting unconvincingly to force a smile to her lips.

'"Really? And what were you saying about it that was so amusing?"

'My wife gave some response, but it was not very interesting, and in any case I was not really listening. It was clear that my appearance had as good as thrown a funeral pall over their gaiety.

'Later that evening, when we were alone, I spoke to my wife about the Dobsons.

'"It does not strike me as an altogether good thing for you to encourage Mrs Dobson in such a degree of intimacy," I remarked somewhat stiffly.

'"But we were only talking together!" she retorted. "Is that so great a crime?"

'"I heard you addressing each other by your Christian names —"

'"And I suppose you think she is not good enough for me, being only a gardener's wife!" my wife cried hotly.

'"Not at all," I returned. "You know that I do not have a snobbish bone in my body, and that you may take what friends you please; but in this case you're the woman's employer, and such intimacy can lead to difficulties."

'"I think not," said she simply, "so let us drop the matter."

'I had never heard my wife speak in this way before, and I do not mind admitting that I was cut to the quick. I could raise no specific objection to this Dobson woman, other than that she had often struck me as somewhat over-bold in her manner for one in her position, but this, in any case, was not really the point. I felt that I was being excluded in my own house, by my own beloved wife, and it was this that hurt me so deeply. Lettie perhaps saw this, for after we had sat a while in silence she began to speak to me in a softer tone, but I treated her advances coldly, and left the room.

'I could not begin to tell you all the wild thoughts that coursed then through my seething brain, but outside in the night air my head seemed to clear and my resolve to harden. If I had nothing specific against the gardener's wife, I had a veritable catalogue of complaints against the gardener himself. I returned to inform my wife of my decision.

'"It is no good," I began. "The Dobsons will have to go. You should not look so surprised, Laetitia: Dobson has done scarcely a day's work since he came here. I am sure that no one else would have tolerated the fellow as long as I have. Apart from anything else, his gardening skills seem to be non-existent. Why, the man is a perfect imbecile! Only yesterday he pulled up all my sweet williams in the belief that they were weeds!'

'"He has been ill," she protested. "He has had a touch of the sun. He will improve, Mark; you will see."

'"He is certainly sickly-looking: he makes me feel ill every time I see him. But this house is not a charitable institution, Laetitia, and much as I dislike the thought of turning a man out when he has no other post to go to, he will have to go."

'I thought then that the matter was settled, and I certainly intended that it should be; but my wife begged and pleaded and cajoled, until once more, much against my better judgement, I relented. I have little doubt that I am a fool, but I could not resist the imploring look in her eyes. There the matter rested, and rests still. Do I weary you with my story, Mr Holmes?'

'Not at all,' replied my friend languidly, as he knocked his pipe out upon the hearth. 'But I fail to see in what way I can help you in these matters, Mr Pringle. I make it an invariable rule not to interfere in domestic affairs, for there is generally profit in it for no one.'

'At least hear the end of my story, Mr Holmes, before you make up your mind. On Sunday last I was so weighed down

with these problems, and, as I now realize, with the beginnings
of another bout of the fever, that I found I was quite unable to
sleep. About one in the morning I dressed quietly and slipped
out into the darkened garden, thinking that a little fresh air
would help to soothe my nerves. It had been a very hot, close
day, as you no doubt recall, and the night was heavy and black
and lowering. As I stepped down the path to the river, a single
large drop of rain landed upon my cheek, and before I had gone
another thirty yards the skies had opened, and the rain was fairly
crashing down. I ran for the shelter of an old yew tree which
I knew to be just ahead of me, although I could scarcely make
out its shape in the darkness. There I was standing, thankful for
the dense cover that the tree provided, when there came a series
of mighty flashes directly overhead, accompanied by the violent
and deafening crack and rumble of the thunder. In an instant the
veil of darkness was lifted from the garden, and all was illuminated with that strange, ghastly light. With a thrill of horror that
set my hair on end, I saw that there was someone upon the path,
not thirty feet away and looking straight at me.'

'A man or a woman?' said Holmes sharply.

'A man – so I believe; but I had only a moment in which to
judge the matter. For as abruptly as the light had come, the
darkness descended once more, just as if a black cloth had been
cast across my eyes. I shifted my position and prepared to defend
myself, though against whom, or what, I did not know. I must
have stood there in that rigid pose for several minutes, but
nothing fell upon me but a few drops of the icy rain. Then for
a second time the sky was split asunder by the zigzag strokes
of the lightning, for a second time the garden was bathed in its
eerie white light, and I saw that the path was deserted. Whoever
I had seen was no longer there. The rain was still teeming down,
but I left my shelter and dashed at the top of my speed back to
the house. To my surprise I found the garden door wide open,
the rain splashing in and forming a puddle upon the parquet
floor of the corridor. I was certain that I had closed the door
firmly as I went out, and although it was possible that the sudden

force of the storm had blown the door open – for in truth the catch is not a very secure one – I was not prepared to take a risk upon the point. I loaded my revolver and made a thorough search of every room in the house, but found nothing amiss.

'My walk had done little for my insomnia, as you will appreciate, and I spent a sleepless night with the loaded pistol at my bedside. In the morning I scoured the garden for any trace of the intruder, but discovered nothing. I had half expected to see another of those infernal hand-prints, but that at least I had been spared. At breakfast my wife announced that she would accompany me up to town, as there was a sale of oriental fabrics at Liberty's which she wished to attend, but I felt too ill and tired to go to work, so she travelled up alone, and I returned to my bed, where I slept half the day away. In sleep, at least, I could escape from the troubles which beset me; but it was a false escape, for when I awoke, these troubles seemed to weigh yet more heavily upon my mind and appear yet more insoluble and impenetrable. What power is possessed by this woman, Helen Dobson, that she can gain such an influence over my wife in so short a time? What manner of man is her brooding, taciturn husband? Why does he pretend to be a gardener – which he very evidently is not – and what does he hope to gain by such an imposture? Who is it that creeps about my garden in the night-time, and prints his freakish hand upon my wall? Does someone wish me dead? All day long, and late into the night, I cudgelled my brains with these questions and a thousand others, until I began to think that it was all a fevered nightmare, in which no answers or explanations might ever be found, but from which dawn would release me. Alas, this morning I woke up and saw the pistol beside my bed, and knew that some answer must be sought in the world of reality.

'I had heard your name, Mr Holmes, in connection with the Claygate Disappearance Case, a couple of years ago, and it seemed to me that in you might lie my only means of retaining my sanity. And yet, even as the thought of your reputation brought a flicker of hope to my reeling mind, I still was not sure that consulting you would be the right thing to do. For the matter is so dark, and in some ways so delicate and personal –'

'– And yet you have come.'

'This arrived by the morning post.'

Our visitor drew from his inside pocket a long blue envelope, from which he extracted a folded sheet of paper. This he passed across to Holmes, who unfolded it carefully and examined it upon his knee. With a quickening of the pulse and a prickling sensation in the hairs upon my neck, I saw that the paper bore but a single mark: the vivid violet print of a human hand.

'Be so good as to pass me the lens, Watson,' said my friend, an expression of intense interest upon his face. 'It is a man's hand,' he remarked after a moment; 'a coarse hand, with short, thick fingers; no stranger to physical work, I should judge, from the general development. Hello! He has a ring upon his second finger. Is this the same as the previous prints you observed?'

'So I believe.'

'There is one point upon which I can set your mind at rest at once, Mr Pringle,' said Holmes with a grim smile. 'Whoever made this print has no more fingers than you or I: the sixth digit is a fake.'

'What do you mean, Mr Holmes?'

'The anatomy is quite wrong. If you will look closely at the fingers you will see that whereas the first three and the last arise from a pad on the palm, the fourth does not, but arises from between the pads of the two adjacent fingers. Do you see, Watson? There is no indication whatever of a metacarpal. He has, it is evident, printed his third finger twice, having previously splayed out his little finger, in order to make room for the addition.'

'Why, so he has!' cried our visitor. 'I can see it clearly now! But why should anyone do such a thing?'

'Ah! That is another question! May I see the envelope which contained this remarkable communication? Hum! Common enough sort of stationery! Posted yesterday afternoon in the West End. Dear me! What a dreadful nib the pen must have –

no doubt the address was written in a post office, or the writing-room of an hotel. Well, well! Your name has been curiously mis-spelt! The remainder of the address is correct, I take it?'

Pringle nodded as Holmes passed the envelope to me, and I saw that our client's name had been rendered as 'Mr Pringel'.

'What a most interesting detail!' said Holmes slowly and quietly, apparently addressing himself. With his elbows upon his knees and his chin cupped in his hands, he sat in silence for several minutes, an expression of intense concentration upon his face.

'Do you see some clue, Mr Holmes?' cried our client at last, clearly unable to endure the silence a moment longer.

'Eh? Oh, possibly, Mr Pringle; possibly,' replied Holmes in an abstracted tone of voice. 'The mis-spelling of your name is certainly a singular thing. It is so grotesque, so un-English, you see, that it argues not simply for the hand of a stranger, who was obliged to inquire your name, but for that of an illiterate or a foreigner, who was then unable to spell correctly the name he was given. The remainder of the address is so neatly and correctly rendered, however, that the first of these alternatives seems unlikely. It also suggests –'

Holmes lapsed once more into silence.

'What is it?' Pringle inquired eagerly.

'Something I must think about,' Holmes replied at length. 'There is of course a further possibility,' he added more briskly.

'Which is?'

'That the sender of this letter is someone known to you, who wishes to disguise the fact.'

'If so, it is an absurdly crude attempt!' said Pringle with a snort.

'I quite agree; nevertheless, it is a possibility we must bear in mind. The case is at present a chaotic and confused one, and we cannot afford to dismiss any chance, however remote. Tell me, have you ever travelled in the Balkans?'

'Never!' replied Pringle in some surprise. 'I have not even been near that part of the world, unless a passage through the Suez Canal qualifies.'

'Your wife?'

'To the best of my knowledge she has only twice been away from England since she returned from Ceylon, and on both occasions it was to stay with a distant cousin who lives on the outskirts of Paris.'

'No matter,' said Holmes, shaking his head; 'you are a finger short, in any case. Is there anyone you would call an enemy – someone who might perhaps feel he had cause to persecute you?'

'None that I know of. I was once called up to act as a witness to a hanging, during my time in Ceylon, and there was some ill feeling in the area for a while afterwards, stirred up by the man's family; but it was not directed principally at me, for I had no other connection with the matter. In any case the trouble subsided fairly quickly, for the poor wretch had certainly been guilty of the most ghastly murders, as even his own family admitted.'

'You were married at Gloucester, I believe you said. Was that simply because your wife was living in that part of the country at the time?'

'Not entirely. Her family had always lived in the town. Her maternal grandfather, she told me, had at one time been dean of Gloucester Cathedral.'

'Very well,' said Holmes, leaning back in his chair and tapping the tips of his fingers together. 'The problem you have presented us with, my dear sir, is a most remarkable one, with several features which are not yet clear to me. But if you leave these papers here, I shall give the matter my consideration and let you have my opinion in due course.'

'You have hopes, then, of uncovering a solution?' cried Pringle eagerly. There was something almost pathetic about the beseeching look upon his face, which was terrible to see in so fine a figure of a man.

'There is always hope,' said Holmes shortly. 'Will you be in your office tomorrow? You will? Then I shall call in to see you if I have any news; otherwise please be so good as to call in here on Thursday, if that is convenient.'

'Certainly, Mr Holmes, certainly,' responded the other, who was evidently much cheered by Holmes's confident manner. 'But might I ask what steps you propose to take?'

'The only steps I shall take this evening, my dear sir, are to the chair in which you are now sitting, which is somewhat better appointed for prolonged meditation than this one.'

'That is all?' cried Pringle in disappointment. 'You will do nothing more?'

'I shall consume a great quantity of the strongest shag tobacco. It is quite a four- or five-pipe problem, and it would be unwise to attempt to come to any premature conclusions.'

Pringle shot a questioning glance at me, then shrugged his shoulders with an air of resignation.

'Did you show this letter to your wife?' asked Holmes, as his visitor rose to leave.

'I saw no point,' the other replied simply, with a shake of the head.

'You are probably correct – at least for the moment; and nor should you mention to anyone that you have consulted me.'

'I should not dream of doing so!'

'Nevertheless, you might let it slip without intending to. Be upon your guard at all times, Mr Pringle! One final thing –'

'Yes?'

'On no account go into the garden after dark. I cannot pretend to have fathomed yet the mystery which surrounds you, but that you walk amidst great danger I am convinced.'

'Well, Watson,' said my friend when our visitor had left us. 'What do you make of it?'

'Nothing whatsoever,' I replied with perfect honesty.

'You are a singular fellow, indeed!' cried Holmes with a chuckle. 'I sometimes think that you are quite the most remarkable man in London, Watson; for I have certainly never known another so honest! There are few, I should imagine, who would care to announce their ignorance so candidly; yet, in this case, I should not believe anyone who did not confess himself baffled, for Mr Mark Pringle has brought us quite the most *outré* little problem I have encountered these last twelve months. As he himself remarked, the incidents taken separately could almost all bear an innocent, trivial, even prosaic explanation; but place them together, and something more sinister begins to be discernible. The individual incidents are like the flourishes of the piccolo, the flute, the horn; but underlying all of these, barely perceptible save when the piece is regarded in its entirety, is a deep and continuous theme upon the 'cello and the double bass.'

'And yet,' I remarked, 'perhaps these things *are* just coincidences. Perhaps there is not, after all, any connection between them.'

'No, it cannot be,' replied Holmes, his brow furrowed with thought. 'Every nerve of intuition I possess tells me that the events are in some way connected – *must* be connected; and it is for us to find the connection. The difficulty lies in the fact that the incidents, as reported to us, are not only quite distinct, but, in some cases at least, mutually contradictory. One might, for instance, suspect a mere vulgar affair of some kind between Mrs Pringle and this man, Dobson, were it not for the extremely friendly relations which seem quite genuinely to subsist between Mrs Pringle and Dobson's wife, Helen.'

'There is certainly something suspicious about the Dobsons,' I remarked. 'They have some secret aim in view, of that I am convinced; although what it might be I cannot imagine.'

'And yet,' Holmes replied, shaking his head slowly, 'it does not quite make sense. Consider the matter, Watson: imagine for a moment that you were the one with the secret aim in view. You are not a man remarked for duplicity, not to any degree a natural schemer, yet surely even you would take great care to conduct yourself with modesty, self-effacement and propriety, and to do all that was required of you, in order to disarm any suspicions that might arise. But the Dobsons, so far from being discreet, seem to have gone out of their way to be conspicuous and irritating to their employer. There seems a want of cunning there!'

'Considered in that light, their behaviour is certainly odd,' I concurred.

'These are deep waters, Watson,' continued my friend after a moment, 'and may yet prove far deeper than we can at present imagine. I cannot help feeling that there is some factor in the case of which we are as yet unaware; some hidden strand, which, if we could but grasp it, might at once pull together all the other strands, unconnected though they now seem.'

'It is certainly a tangled skein at present,' I remarked, 'and I confess that the more I reflect upon it, the more baffling it seems to become. Whatever can be the significance, for instance, of the pail of violet liquid which Pringle found one morning by the cottage?'

'Ah, there, my dear Watson, you put your finger on what is perhaps the one point in the whole of his narrative to which no mystery attaches,' responded Holmes, breaking into a smile. 'For whoever had printed his hand upon the wall that morning – using perfectly ordinary ink, to judge from this sheet which we have examined – would, in the process, have marked his hand quite as conspicuously as he had marked the wall, as I am sure you would agree. He could of course cover his hand with a glove, but at this time of the year that would excite almost as much comment as an ink-stained hand, and, in any case, there may be other circumstances which would render such a device impossible. What does he do, then, to remove the stain and thus preserve his secret, but plunge his hand into the water and rinse off the incriminating ink? It is certainly what I should do in his position. But, come, we are beginning to circle around the problem without ever approaching any closer to it, after the style of our good friend, Inspector Athelney Jones!'

'Very well,' said I, laughing. 'I shall leave you to your solitary meditations.'

'Drop by tomorrow afternoon,' said Holmes, as I took my hat and stick, 'and we can review any progress in the case.'

At three o'clock the following afternoon I was seated by the window in my friend's rooms, reading the evening paper, when he returned. His face was drawn and tired, but the slight smile which played about his lips told me that his day had not been a fruitless one.

'Tiring weather!' said he by way of greeting, tossing his hat on to the table.

'You have made some progress with the Pringle case?' I ventured.

'More than that,' he replied. 'I have quite cleared up Mr Pringle's little mystery, and am now in a position to lay the whole of the facts before him. It was a simple affair after all. You will come with me? If we leave within the half-hour we should be in time to catch him at his office in the Crutched Friars. As to the advice I should give him, however –'

His voice tailed off, and an introspective look came into his eyes. It was clear that despite the solution of the mystery, there was something about the case which vexed him still. Without a word he threw off his coat and began slowly to fill his old black pipe with tobacco from the pewter caddy upon the mantelpiece, his eyes all the while far away. A score of questions welled up in my mind at once, but I forbore to voice them, for I knew well enough, from ten years' experience, that he would enlighten me of his own volition when he himself chose to do so, and that to question him at any other time was a profitless exercise.

I also knew that he rarely jested when his profession was the subject, and I had never once known him exaggerate his achievements, so that if he said he had solved the case, then I knew it must be so, incredible though such a claim seemed. How on earth, I wondered, had he, in less than twenty-four hours, discovered the key that would unlock the mystery which surrounded his unfortunate client? Again my mind turned over the remarkable series of events which Mark Pringle had narrated to us the previous evening, again I pondered the significance of all that he had told us – the disturbing conversation he had overheard upon his sick-bed, the mysterious and grotesque handprints, his wife's unfathomable behaviour towards both the

Dobsons and her own husband, and the dark, sinister figures that came in the night – but again I was obliged to admit utter and total defeat.

'Your client's part of the country seems to be having more than its share of mysteries at the moment,' I remarked at length.

'What is that?' said Holmes in a vague, abstracted tone, as if so far away in his thoughts that he found it difficult to refocus his mind upon the present time and place. 'What did you say?'

'There is a report in the early editions that the body of a man was found in the river early this morning, just by Chertsey Bridge. There was a knife stuck in his side.'

'What!'

'The police believe that the body had been washed down the river from the Staines area.'

He snatched the paper from my grasp and ran his eye rapidly down the column, a look of alarm upon his face. 'A short, squat man!' he cried after a moment, a note almost of relief in his voice; '"– with a swarthy complexion and curly black hair, and with a single gold ear-ring". Well, it is no one *we* know, anyhow.'

'So I judged.'

'Nevertheless, Watson, it bears upon the case.'

'You think so?'

'I know so. You remarked the contents of his pockets? – "Very little was found in the dead man's pockets by which his identity might be established, although he does not appear to have been robbed: three pound notes in a clip and a small amount of loose change, six whiffs in a pigskin case, a box of wax vestas and a bottle of ink being the sum total; in addition, the cork from a wine-bottle was discovered in the lining of his jacket." Now, why should a man carry a bottle of ink, who does not also carry a pen of any sort?'

'The purple hand!'

'Precisely! Listen: "All labels and marks appear to have been removed from his clothing, as if to prevent any discovery of his antecedents, but inside one pocket of his waistcoat was found a small tag bearing a single word – believed to be the maker's name – in the Cyrillic script in use in parts of Eastern Europe. The possibility that the murdered man was from those parts is given some support by the evidence of the knife that killed him. This is a narrow fixed-blade type, with an elaborately carved bone handle, which is stamped on the blade with the word 'Belgrade'."'

'What does it mean, Holmes?'

'It means that events have moved faster than I anticipated. If we are to prevent another death we must act at once. Will you come with me?'

'Most certainly. We are going to Crutched Friars?'

'No; to Low Meadow.'

He donned his outer clothes as quickly as he had thrown them off, and in a minute we were in a hansom and driving furiously through the traffic to Waterloo Station.

'No doubt you have by now formed an opinion upon the matter,' said Holmes as our railway carriage rattled along the viaduct and through Vauxhall station.

I shook my head. 'I should be very much interested to hear your own conclusions,' I replied.

'You will recall,' said he, after a moment, 'that my client felt confident of only two facts about his nocturnal visitor: that he had a deformed hand, and that he was unusually small in his overall figure. But in both these opinions he was mistaken. The hand, as we saw, is in reality quite unexceptional; and it seemed likely, once we had heard that the hand-print was made approximately five feet from the ground, that his figure was unexceptional, too.'

'Why so?'

'Because it would be the natural tendency of anyone making such a print to do it at shoulder height – try it for yourself some time, and you will see – and anyone who is five foot to the shoulders is obviously of a fairly normal build. So the intruder ceases to be inhuman and freakish, and becomes instead a perfectly ordinary specimen of humanity.'

'I can see that that would make the matter yet more baffling and difficult of discovery,' I remarked.

'On the contrary, it admits a tiny ray of light into the mystery for the first time.'

'I do not follow you.'

'Consider: if the intruder is not equipped by nature with six digits upon his right hand, then the fact that he prints it in that bizarre fashion is evidently a matter of deliberate choice upon his part. Clearly the print has some very definite significance for him, and he must expect that it will have the same significance for those who see it, otherwise there would be little point to the exercise. Thus the print as an unfathomable, purely personal thing quite disappears, and in its place we see an item of public communication, which is far more amenable to investigation.'

'And yet I am not convinced,' said I. 'For what possible significance could be possessed by such a grotesque daub?'

'You have not heard anyone speak of the Seven-Fingered Hand?' said Holmes in a quiet voice.

'Never!'

'I must admit that that does not surprise me; there is really no reason why you should; for its activities receive little enough publicity in this country: indeed, until today my own knowledge of it was exceedingly sketchy, and yet it almost comes within my field of speciality. It is a secret society, Watson – that most vile excrescence of civilization. It sits like a vile beast upon the Balkans, its evil tentacles stretched out to every remote corner, so that there is scarcely a town or village there where it cannot command the allegiance of at least one person; and that allegiance is rarely commanded but for terrorism and murder.'

'It sounds monstrous, Holmes! Whatever is the purpose of such an organization?'

'Ah! The answer to that question illustrates rather nicely the divergence between theory and practice in human endeavours; for the surprising thing is that the society of which I speak was originally formed of principled, high-minded men, who would never have chosen to meet in secret conclave had they not felt driven to it. Their purposes originally were quite altruistic, their only aim being to importune the authorities on behalf of those of their fellow-countrymen whose lot they considered a woeful one. But the society was soon taken over – some would say inevitably so – by those whose very delight it is to be secret, to pass unseen in the night-time with the knife beneath the cloak, to feel a sense of power in the anonymous assassination of the innocent. Soon all pretence of altruism was as good as abandoned, and the sole *raison d'être* of the society became its own continued existence, an existence which is sustained and nourished on the terror of the very people in whose name it was originally founded.

'The society's somewhat fanciful name derives partly from the fact that it was constituted originally of groups from seven different provinces, and also from an initiation ceremony in which the new recruit is obliged to make a hand-print upon a document of allegiance to the society. This hand-print, embellished with the addition of two extra fingers, eventually became the symbol of the society. It is used to strike terror into the hearts of its enemies, and this it will surely do, for the society has the deserved reputation of being both implacable and ruthless. I tell you, Watson, a man had rather be in with a cageful of tigers than have these gentlemen upon his trail.

'So much I managed to glean this morning, from long hours among the files of old newspapers – steep, steep work, Watson! I also learned a further fact there, which brings the history of this unholy gang up to date: the Eastern Roumelian section, having evidently transgressed some rule or other, was last year expelled from the society, amid considerable blood-letting. One finger was accordingly removed from the society's symbol, leaving just six – as in the letter my unfortunate client received yesterday morning at his breakfast table.'

'But why?' I cried. 'What possible business can this abominable society have in England? And why do they seek to terrorize Mark Pringle?'

Holmes did not reply at once, but leaned back in his seat and surveyed the tranquil countryside through which our train was now speeding. On either side of the track, a broad expanse of heathland and common stretched far away, all dotted over with bright patches of poppies and buttercups. It seemed to me incredible that upon such a day, and in such a spot, these desperate men from across the seas could be pursuing their evil ends.

'Mark Pringle is not their primary quarry,' said my companion at length. 'You will recall that our first surmise upon seeing the envelope with the mis-spelt name was that Pringle was not personally known to the sender. This suggests as a possibility that it was only because he had been seen in the garden on Sunday night that they had gone to the trouble of learning his name – no doubt from a neighbour – in order to send him a specific warning that he should not interfere in their business. The fact that they were evidently not previously aware of his identity further suggests, of course, that the first two handprints were not in fact made for his benefit at all.'

'I do not understand,' I interrupted. 'Does this mean that he is not, then, in danger?'

'I should not go so far as to say *that*,' replied my friend. 'Indeed, I believe that he is exceedingly fortunate still to be alive. But to answer your questions more fully, it is necessary to go back a dozen years, to when a gentleman by the name of James Green deposited a large sum of money in the vaults of the Anglo-Hellenic bank in King William Street, in the City. He was, according to his own testimony, the principal in a firm of wine-shippers, who specialized in wines from Greece and the Aegean Islands. At regular intervals after that, further sums were deposited and, from time to time, withdrawals made, either in London or at the branch office in Athens.

'It was only when the bank collapsed, amid a terrific scandal, early in '82, that in the course of attempts to locate all the creditors and settle with them as best they could – which was hardly at all – the authorities discovered that no such person as James Green existed, and no more did his supposed firm of wine-importers. The whole elaborate charade had been devised to conceal the fact that the funds were those of The Seven-Fingered Hand – money which had been extorted from the peasants of Eastern Europe, and which was employed in the furtherance of the society's own evil ends and to keep its leaders snug. This emerged at the bankruptcy hearing and the subsequent fraud trial, which created quite a sensation at the time.'

'I believe I recall it,' said I. 'The chief clerk had used his clients' money in a series of wild speculations, each of which had in turn failed. He had thus been driven further and further into desperate measures, and yet wilder schemes, in his attempt to recoup the losses, until in the end the bank had scarcely a penny to its name.'

'You recall it precisely. The chief clerk's name was Arthur Pendleton, who distinguished himself at his trial by showing not the slightest shred of remorse, and who was, as I learned from the court records this morning, sentenced to fifteen years for his troubles. A junior clerk whom he had somehow managed to embroil in his insane, criminal schemes received a shorter sentence, of ten years, in recognition of his lesser culpability and in the certain knowledge that had it not been for the strong and evil influence which the older man had had over him, he would never have become involved at all. The bank was sold off, lock, stock and barrel, but the creditors received scarcely one part in a hundred of what they were owed.'

'You have evidently had a busy day,' said I, impressed by the speed at which my remarkable friend had been able to gather information on such remote matters; 'but I still cannot grasp the pertinence of these matters to the case in hand. Are you convinced that there is a connection?'

'The matter is beyond the realm where it is appropriate to speak of conviction, and into that of certainty,' replied Holmes. 'I spent some time this afternoon at Somerset House, which was enlightening, and when I read that the man found in the river at Chertsey had carried an old wine-cork in his coat, there remained no doubt what was afoot.'

'A wine-cork?'

'He would use it to protect the point of the knife, and to prevent the blade from slitting the lining of his jacket, which is where the knife would be concealed.'

'Are you suggesting that the knife which killed him was his own?'

'Precisely. He was an assassin, Watson; that is apparent. But he whom he sought to kill has turned his own weapon upon him. You read that all labels had been removed from his clothes? That is a trade-mark of such men: anonymity is the very essence of their work. No connection must ever be traced between the assassin and the organization which commands him.'

'Such precautions would appear to suggest,' I remarked after a moment, 'that the man thought it quite likely that he might, indeed, lose his own life.'

'Well, it is an ever-present hazard for the assassin, as you will imagine. But it is not one upon which he may dwell; for he will be aware that failure to carry out his commission will result in the next such commission having his name upon it, not as agent, but as victim. But come! This is Staines, and we must make all haste.'

A short journey in the station-trap down a sun-baked country road brought us to the gates of Low Meadow, where we paid off the driver and entered on foot. Up the drive we hurried, round the corner of the house, and into the rear gardens. Not a breath of wind disturbed the leaves upon the trees, and the air was heavy with the scent of flowers.

Ahead of us on the lawn a handsome young woman in a white dress was sitting on a rug with a sewing-basket beside her. She started up when she saw us, a look of surprise upon her face.

'Mrs Pringle?' inquired my friend.

'Yes, but –'

'My name is Sherlock Holmes. Pray forgive this abrupt intrusion into your privacy, but our mission is most urgent.'

'You had best explain yourself,' said she with some sharpness, rising to her feet.

'There is no time.'

'I insist upon it.'

'Very well. I have been employed by your husband to make inquiries on his behalf into certain matters which have recently perplexed him. All I have learned convinces me that he is in mortal danger.'

'My husband?' said she in a tone of disbelief.

'No; your brother.'

At this she paused for a moment and took a sharp breath, then threw her head back with a peal of laughter.

'All you have learned has evidently been nonsense!' said she. 'I have neither brother nor sister, so whoever has a brother in mortal danger, it is not I!'

Holmes remained quite unmoved by this outburst. 'You cannot afford to play games,' said he gravely, 'when it is your brother's life which may be the forfeit.'

'I tell you I have no –'

'I understand well enough the reasons for your pretence, Mrs Pringle,' Holmes interrupted her, 'but believe me when I tell you that the time for such things is past. Perhaps if I tell you all I know, it may convince you that I speak the truth.'

She seemed about to reply, but hesitated, and Holmes hurriedly continued: 'Your brother, John Aloysius, was born upon the fifteenth of October in the year 1858, at Gloucester. In 1880 he married Helen Montgomery in Guildford. In 1882, whilst employed at the King William Street branch of the Anglo-Hellenic bank he became involved in a massive series of embezzlements, as a result of which, when the matter came to light, he was sentenced to ten years' penal servitude.'

'It is false!' she cried out passionately. 'The conviction was false! He only became involved with Arthur Pendleton in an attempt to save that wretched, ungrateful man, but soon found himself ensnared in the other's web of deceit, from which, struggle as he might, he could not extricate himself. No thought of personal gain ever crossed his mind. One word of the truth from that villain might have saved my brother from an unjust fate; but his heart was stone, his friendship hollow.'

'I do not doubt, madam, that what you say is true; however I come not to accuse your brother but to save him. A few weeks ago, having earned the maximum remission from his sentence and being seriously ill, he was released from prison. Shortly before his release, his wife, who had remained loyal and faithful to him through all the long years of his imprisonment, had been to see you to discuss the matter. Your husband, who for some reason knew nothing whatever of your brother, overheard a part of your conversation, but misconstrued it as referring to himself.'

'Dearly would I have loved to tell Mark the whole truth,' Mrs Pringle interrupted, a tear forming in her eye, 'but John begged and pleaded with me not to do so. He would not, he said, have his shame and disgrace inflicted upon his sister and her fine husband. I told him many times that Mark would welcome him like a true brother, and think none the worse of him for what had happened in the past; but he refused absolutely to presume upon Mark's generosity, and I was obliged to keep his existence a secret. I have acted according to his wishes all along.'

'I understand that,' said Holmes. 'It was therefore arranged that he would come here in the guise of a gardener, in the hope that he might recover his health in the fresh country air. Am I correct?'

'You are,' she said simply. 'How you have achieved it, I do not know, but you appear to know all.'

'Unfortunately that is *not* all. There are those whose thirst for vengeance is not satisfied by your brother's term of imprisonment.'

'Surely you are not serious, Mr Holmes!' she cried in alarm. 'My brother has more than paid for his foolishness. Can the law not restrain these people?'

'Nothing can restrain them, Mrs Pringle. They recognize no law but their own. You must get your brother away from here. There has already been one attempt upon his life, and I fear that the second may not long be delayed. You look disbelieving! Did you not read of the man found in the river this morning?'

'The police believe he came from Eastern Europe.'

'That is from where the danger comes. You recall the strange hand-print which was found upon the shed wall after your sister-in-law's visit? That was the work of these men. They were evidently watching her every movement, aware that her husband would shortly be released from prison, and left their mark to give notice of their presence. Later, when your brother and sister-in-law moved into the old cottage, they came again, and again left their mark, to announce that retribution was at hand. Last Sunday night, whilst walking in the garden, your husband surprised one of these men, so I believe, and they subsequently sent him a warning note. In the event, of course, the purple hand meant nothing whatever to him; but these men have the arrogance of all who submerge and hide their own identities in that of an anonymous organization, and clearly believe that there is no one who will not understand, and know fear, upon seeing their sign. Your husband was fortunate, I should say, to escape with his life. Only the fact that the assassin's work was not completed saved him; for human life is nothing to these men.'

'But, surely, if the assassin is now dead, we have nothing to fear,' said Mrs Pringle.

'He will not have come alone to England.'

For a minute the three of us stood in silence upon that neat and sunny lawn, and these words of Sherlock Holmes seemed like the evil and insane inventions of a madman. Laetitia Pringle shook her head from side to side, over and over again.

'You cannot simply wish these things away,' said Holmes at length, as if perceiving the poor bewildered woman's innermost thoughts; 'you must act, and act swiftly.'

'What should I do?'

'You must get your brother out of England – yes, and out of Europe, too. You must tell your husband everything –'

His sentence remained unfinished, for with a shrill cry of alarm, a sandy-haired woman burst upon our little gathering from behind the row of laurels.

'Lettie! Lettie!' she cried; 'John has vanished –'

She broke off abruptly as her eyes fell upon Holmes and myself. She stopped in her tracks and swayed from side to side with a wild look in her eye, as if she were upon the verge of fainting, but Holmes stepped forward and took her arm gently.

'Do not fear, Mrs Wadham; we come as friends.'

'It is Mr Sherlock Holmes,' said Mrs Pringle to her sister-in-law.

'Indeed?' responded the other. 'Your name is familiar to me, sir, and I have heard that there is no problem you cannot solve; but I fear that in this case your powers are of no avail. My husband seemed so dreadfully ill today that I left him in his bed. Just now I returned from tending the vegetable plot and found him gone, and this note upon the kitchen table.'

With a shaking hand she offered a slip of blue paper to my friend, which he unfolded and read aloud.

'"My dear Helen,"' he read; '"You will remember how often we strengthened each other with the hope that once I had served my sentence, our troubles would be over, and we could put the past behind us. Alas! that hope was futile. I have learned recently that some who lost money in the Anglo-Hellenic fiasco will not rest until those they regard as responsible are dead. As old Pendleton died in prison three years ago, I am the sole focus for their vengeance, unjust as you know that is. It is a turn of events I had always feared, although I prayed constantly that the threat might be lifted from me. Now hopes and fears alike ill become the moment, and I must meet my fate with my own hand. Last night, as I sat beside the river shortly before retiring, the first assassin came; but I am not one who surrenders his life without a struggle, despite the weakness of my limbs. He thrust at me with his knife, but I managed to parry the blow, and threw him to the ground. For a time we struggled together on the river-bank, then, without any conscious intention on my part, his own knife pierced his side, his hand still upon the hilt. I cast his lifeless body into the water, and determined to say nothing of the incident to you. I have brought enough trouble upon you and upon my dear sister and her husband: it is time for me to go. It is I alone these devils want; if I am not with you, you will be safe. Please forgive this silent way of leaving, but I know you would not let me go if I spoke these words to your face.

'"Your loving husband, John."'

'What am I to do?' cried Helen Wadham, her voice suffused with anguish.

'When did you last see your husband?' inquired Holmes in an urgent tone, handing back the letter to her.

'About an hour ago; but he cannot be long gone, for I was close by the cottage until this last twenty minutes.'

'He has not passed this way, so he has evidently taken the path beside the river,' cried my friend. 'Come, Watson; there may yet be time to dissuade him from this foolhardy course of action. Alone he does not stand a chance against these men.'

We ran down the path towards the river, the women following close behind. At the cottage Holmes darted in, but was out again in a trice, shaking his head in answer to my query. A little further on we emerged from the wood and came out upon the river-bank, where the bare earth of the riverside path was baked into hard ruts by the summer sun. To left and right we looked, and a grim sight met our eyes. About fifty feet upstream, the crumpled figure of a man lay athwart the path, his boots trailing in the water. Holmes hurried forward and I followed at his heels.

A swift glance told me that the man was beyond all human help. His shirt-front was dark and horrible with blood, and at the very centre of the stain protruded the carved handle of a knife. A torn sheet of paper had been forced over the knife-handle, upon which was the purple print of a human hand. I knew then that the pale, gentle face which gazed unseeing up at me was that of Mark Pringle's strange gardener and unknown brother-in-law. I pulled the knife from his chest and cast it aside, and with Holmes's help lifted the body upon a grassy bank.

'Keep the women back!' hissed Holmes, who, down on all fours, was examining the riverside path intently. But it was too late; they ran forward and would not be restrained. What a horrible thing it was for them to see, and how that horror was marked upon their faces!

I turned as a cry came from somewhere behind us. There at the foot of the garden path stood my friend's client. He hurried towards us, a puzzled look upon his face. 'The maid told me she had seen you – Why! What melancholy business is this!' he cried as he caught sight of the grief-stricken faces of the two women.

Quickly, in a very few sentences, Holmes gave him the gist of all that had passed. I have never in my life seen a man so stricken and so mortified in so short a space of time. For a long minute he gazed down at the body of his wife's brother, a deep and unfathomable expression upon his face. 'Had he lived I would have loved him,' he said softly at last. 'Come,' he continued, turning to me. 'Bear his body to the house. Though in life he rejected my hospitality, in death shall he have it.'

At the house Holmes secured a map, which he studied intently for a few moments.

'The river twists and turns here,' said he at last. 'If we take the main road we may yet be able to intercept the murderer before he can escape.'

On this occasion, however, my friend's resourcefulness proved insufficient, and no trace of the assassin could be found in the area. An abandoned skiff was later discovered upon the opposite bank of the river, and inquiries indicated that the fugitive had crossed over to the Surrey side and made his way down to Chertsey, where he had caught a train to London.

Acting upon certain information provided by Sherlock Holmes, the police later arrested a Serbian who was staying at Green's Hotel in the West End. No effective case could be made out against him, however, and when diplomatic protests threatened to make an international incident of the affair, the police were obliged to let him go. 'There goes a certain murderer!' said Holmes with bitterness, when he read in the paper one morning that the man had been put upon the Calais packet, with the formal warning that he should never again set foot in England.

As for Mark Pringle and his wife, I heard later that he had overcome his illness, and that they had returned to Ceylon, and taken with them Helen Wadham, in the hope that a new life amid fresh surroundings might help to erase from their hearts and minds the painful memory of the tragedy which had fallen so heavily upon them at Low Meadow.

XI

THE ADVENTURE OF
HILLERMAN HALL

Julian Symons

The young woman who made her way up the track leading from the country lane in the direction of Beachy Head was tall and elegant, with fair hair just visible beneath a close-fitting hat, what is sometimes called a peaches-and-cream complexion, and innocent china-blue eyes. She wore a dress of a colour that was not quite cream, and sensible walking shoes. The grassy track with its hedge on either side was not steep, but it went upwards all the way, and when she reached the end of it she was breathing a little faster than usual, perhaps because of the climb, or perhaps from excitement.

At the end of the track, and not before, the cottage was visible. It stood by itself in a field, a small thatched cottage made of flint and ragstone, with leaded windows on either side of the front door. There were low hedges around the place, giving it a pleasant air of privacy, and she glimpsed a garden beyond a wicket gate. The air up here on the Sussex downs had a tonic freshness, and she breathed it in gratefully as she walked across the field. She was about to lift the latch of the gate when she was checked by a cry of 'Don't move! Watch out!'

She stood quite still, but turned her head. Some thirty yards away, on the other side of the cottage, a veiled, gloved figure was bending over a beehive. He seemed to be pushing something into a recess of the hive using, as she could see, extreme care. For two or three minutes he remained bent over the hive, then slowly straightened up and came towards her, lifting the veil and taking off the thick gloves as he did so.

'I beg your pardon for calling out so abruptly, but it is a ticklish moment when a new queen is introduced into the hive. There is a risk of rejection, and to avoid it I have developed a cage of a new type that can be slipped between two combs in the brood chamber – but I must beg your pardon again, for of course the introduction of a queen to the hive cannot be of such momentous interest to you as it is to me. You are the young lady from the *South Eastern Gazette*?'

She nodded. He removed the hat and veil, and she recognized the aquiline features and piercing eyes of Sherlock Holmes. He was very much as he had been depicted in the *Strand Magazine*, except that the years had grizzled his hair, and lines of age were graven in his cheeks.

He opened the door of the cottage, put away the bee-keeping apparatus carefully in a cupboard, and stood aside for her to enter. She looked round with a curiosity touched with awe. It was a comfortable room, but one that showed marks of a bachelor's untidiness. There were things that she recognized from descriptions in Dr Watson's accounts, the coal scuttle, which as she could see contained some pipes and no doubt also tobacco, the violin case, the piles of papers on a chest. On the wall were sporting prints – surely they must have come from Baker Street? Was that chair beside the fireplace the one in which the Doctor had sat so often?

Sherlock Holmes offered her that very chair, sat down opposite her, filled a pipe with very dark tobacco, and fixed upon her a gaze whose keenness made her a little uncomfortable. He took the letter she had written from some dozen lying on the table, and read it with care.

'I am at a loss to know how you found my address. Since my retirement I have done my best to conceal it, even to the extent of making public a totally inaccurate description of my little home.'

'I mentioned my aunt E-Evelyn in my letter. Dr W-Watson

had been her physician and then became a family friend. He was kind enough to give my aunt your address.' She spoke with a slight, attractive hesitation.

'So it is my old friend Watson who has been careless – not for the first time, I may tell you – and it is to him that I owe your visit. I should tell you that the newspaper interviewer is one of the members of the human species that I most abominate. Their questions tend to the impertinent or the irrelevant, and the pieces they write are couched in slovenly English. Yet there was something that interested me in your letter, or I should not have replied to it. Fire away with your questions, which I shall answer only on the understanding that my little house is neither photographed nor in any way identified, and that anything you write will be submitted to me for approval.' He glanced again at the letter, and settled back in his chair as she took a reporter's note-book and pencil from a capacious bag. She seemed almost at a loss how to begin.

'Do you live here alone?'

'Entirely alone, except for a woman from the village who comes three times a week to clean, tidy up, and do some necessary washing and laundering. Otherwise I look after myself. My wants are few, simple food, and tobacco which I order by the pound. I grow my own vegetables, and keep my own hens at the back of the house. Once a week I go into Eastbourne, and I buy a batch of newspapers, although I rarely find anything to interest me in them. The world has moved on since the end of the Great War, for the most part in ways that I do not approve of or understand. So I walk the downs in all weathers and keep my bees, who sometimes give me instruction in human behaviour. The industrious life of the worker bee, the installation of the queen who has no power, although the colony's life depends on her, the massacre of the drones when the late summer honeyflow is over – there are lessons to be read in the bee's existence, if the world's statesmen would learn them.'

Her pencil had been flying over the lines. 'The most recent

collection of your cases, *His Last Bow*, was published a few years ago in 1917, and the last story was set in August 1914, the capture of the German spy Von Bork. Are there no l–later cases?'

Sherlock Holmes puffed at his pipe. Smoke rose and lost itself among the oak beams on the ceiling. 'There has been nothing since the Von Bork business. My world is not that of the motor car and the aeroplane. I am a skilful driver, but my chosen means of transport has always been the railway or the hansom cab.'

'So there will be no more records of your cases?'

'I do not say that. I am out of touch with Watson, but I have given him permission to record what stories he wishes, and have even made notes myself about a couple of matters. Watson does not always choose the cases that seem to me most interesting – I always wished that he'd written about the problem of James Phillimore's disappearance – but Watson makes his own choice. I daresay he may put together another collection in his own time, but they will all be cases from the past.' He paused. 'But I am sorry to say that my old friend has taken to the bottle recently and is frequently in a state of stupor, so that there is little likelihood of his putting a book together.'

'And you undertake n–no cases at all now?'

Holmes put down his pipe, leaned over and took the pencil from her fingers. 'Let us stop this nonsense. You do not work for the *South Eastern Gazette* or for any other paper. Tell me why you came to see me, and what it is that has agitated you so much.'

'I–I–was it so obvious that I am not a newspaper reporter?'

'To me, very obvious. Your letter was written by hand, on paper with a private address. A genuine reporter would have used the newspaper's headed stationery, and most probably a typewriter. On one of my visits to Eastbourne I telephoned the editor of the *South Eastern Gazette* and learned that nobody with your name was on the staff. It was then that I became curious about your object, and agreed to see you. When I watched you making notes, it became plain to me that you were using neither Pitman shorthand, nor the modern Gregg, nor any other of the forty-seven kinds of abbreviated writing of which I may modestly claim to have made a study. You were putting down gibberish, nothing more. When, finally, I made a revelation about Watson, a revelation so shocking that it should have made you jump out of your chair – and one, I may say, in which there is not a word of truth – you paid so little attention that you merely went on to the next question you had prepared.'

'And my agitation? I hoped I had concealed it.'

'When a young lady, otherwise impeccably dressed, comes here wearing odd stockings –'

She looked down and blushed, 'Good Heavens!'

'The difference between them is very slight, a matter of the patterning around the seam, but now that skirts have gone up at least six inches above the ankle it is possible for the trained eye to notice such matters.'

'Mr Holmes, I wanted to see you to ask your help. I thought you would pay no attention to a letter, but truly I am desperate. Please do not turn me away.'

'I should not think of doing so. Of what use are rules, if no exceptions are to be made to them? Now put away your note-book. I shall make a pot of tea – retirement encourages the domestic virtues – and while we drink it and eat a slice of the bread I baked this morning, you may tell me your story.'

'It is my f-fiancé, C-Captain Rogers, Jack Rogers. He has disappeared. I fear that he may be dead.'

The tea had a delicate fragrance, the cups and plates were Spode, the thinly sliced bread was full of flavour. Sherlock Holmes said, 'I had noticed the ring.'

'Isn't it beautiful?' She slipped it off her finger and gave it to him. The stones sparkled as he held the ring up to the light and then, with a murmured excuse, looked at it through a glass which he took from a drawer before returning it.

'And now your story,' he said. 'The best place to start, usually, is at the beginning.'

As she told her tale she spoke more freely, and her slight stammer disappeared. 'I live with my parents, Mr Holmes. We are not a rich family, but I suppose we are quite well off. Our home is outside Guildford in Surrey, a house which is said to go back to Tudor times. I have no sister, but one brother, Bertie. He is – he can do foolish things, but I love him, we all love him. Bertie was very brave in the War and has found it hard to settle down since then. Now he is in a stockbroker's, but really the only thing he enjoys is driving about in his little Ford car.'

'And your father?'

She look startled. 'I beg your pardon?'

'What is your father's occupation?'

'Oh, papa has no occupation in that way, he has no connection with business and I suppose he is awfully unbusinesslike. He goes into Guildford three days a week to the bridge club – I believe he is one of the finest players in the country – and then he is secretary of the local topographical society and president of the cricket club. All of those things take up time. Papa sometimes says he wishes there were more than twenty-four hours in the day, there is so much to do.'

'I can see that might be so,' Holmes said drily. 'And I assume that you are not in employment?'

'No. Papa sent me to a convent school. Our family has religious connections – one of my uncles is a canon of Chichester Cathedral. I have always thought that I should like to do something – something useful, like – oh, like nursing lepers. But papa and mamma were against it. I should like to have a job, there are times when I wish I truly was a reporter, but I know that papa would not think it a proper occupation for a lady. He has agreed that I should train to be a concert pianist, and I go up to London twice a week to a music school. Papa and mamma say I play beautifully but truly, Mr Holmes, I do not think I have the talent.'

'Was it in connection with the music school that you met Captain Rogers?'

'Oh no, that was through Bertie. Bertie has very convenient rooms in the West End – I think papa helps to pay for the rent – and there is a small spare bedroom where I sometimes stay.

One evening Jack, Captain Rogers, came round for a drink, and I met him. Shortly after that he asked me out to dinner, then to a dance, and I took him down to meet papa amd mamma. They liked him, nobody could help liking him. And we became engaged. Here is a photograph of Jack, taken in the garden at home. He is laughing, you see, Jack is always laughing.'

Holmes studied the photograph, which showed a tall, dark young man. A cap was perched on his head at a rakish angle, and he was indeed laughing. 'He is much older than you.'

'Ten years older, but I like that. I think a husband should always be older than his wife, so that she can look up to him and respect him.'

'I suppose Captain Rogers is an old friend of your brother? Perhaps they knew each other in the War?'

'Oh no, Bertie and Jack had known each other only a few days, and they couldn't have met in the War because Bertie was in France, and Jack was out in Palestine first of all and after that, well, he won't tell me exactly what he did, but I understood from Bertie it was awfully hush-hush.' She evidently gathered her courage for the next question, fingering the amber beads she wore round her neck. 'Mr Holmes, I have heard it said that during the War, after your capture of Von Bork, you were engaged on other work for our Secret Service. Is that true?'

A slight smile curved the detective's thin lips. 'You are even more innocent than you appear if you expect me to answer such a question.'

She flushed. 'I do not mean to be impertinent, but I thought that Jack might have been one of your colleagues, and that you would then have recognized him.'

He shook his head. 'I can assure you that, whatever I may have done in those years, it had no connection with your fiancé. But please continue your story. I take it that your parents not only liked Captain Rogers, but approved of him as your future husband.'

'Yes. Papa and mamma only want me to be happy, and I am – I was – wonderfully happy. And then Bertie is always singing

Jack's praises, saying he's a go-ahead fellow and a good sport, and has all sorts of ripping ideas for making money. He hasn't got any, you know. Money I mean. There was a sort of family conference when Jack said he wanted to marry me, papa and mamma and Bertie and me, and Jack told us about his father being an unsuccessful inventor who always hoped to make a fortune and never did. Both his parents were dead by the time he was eighteen, so that he had to make his own way in the world. Then he said: "I want to marry Jane, sir, but I must be frank and say I haven't a penny of capital to bless myself with, and I can't blame you if you turn me down." I knew what papa would say to that. He replied that if we loved each other, that was all the fortune we should need.'

'I see. Was nothing said about the way in which you would live, how your husband would support you?'

'Indeed, that was discussed. Papa said that it would be a sad thing if he could not help his only daughter to a happy start in her married life. Jack *hates* London, he wants to settle in the country and believes there is a fortune to be made by new methods of farming – oh, he has all sorts of interesting ideas, Mr Holmes, I wish you could hear him explain them. At the end of our conference papa agreed that if we found a house we liked, and that had some good farming land with it, he would buy it for us and provide the capital to give us a start. I know what you must be thinking, Mr Holmes, that it sounds like fortune-hunting, but if you met Jack you would not think that, he cares so little about money.

'So it was settled, and we began to look for houses. Jack knew I should not want to be far away from my family, so we looked in Surrey and Sussex. Those were happy days for me, we would set out each morning in Jack's Overland tourer and look at houses. Jack knew at once whether a place was suitable. No, no, he would say, this is too dark, even your bright eyes won't light it up. Or the approach was too awkward, or the outbuildings hopeless, or the ground unsuitable for the crops he wanted to grow. Then after a week we found Hillerman Hall, a mile or two into the country from Reigate, and Jack said at once that this was the place. Mr and Mrs Pringle had been farming there, but he had had a slight stroke and found the work too much for him. The Hall needs redecoration, and will be rather cold and draughty in winter, but Jack was in such ecstasies about the place that of course I said yes. Papa agreed the price with Mr Pringle, and the date of the wedding was fixed in August, three weeks from now.'

'Had you looked at other houses in the district?'

'We had seen two others near by. I liked one very much, but Jack said that the ground was quite unsuitable.'

'One would have thought it would be similar to that at Hillerman Hall, but no matter. Please continue.'

'Mr Pringle moved to a house called Maple Lodge, at a little village near Beaconsfield. I thought we might have the redecoration done, and we saw a local builder and chose the papers, but Jack said we should not bother about it until we went off on our honeymoon, so that it would be all finished when we returned. He would meet me in London after my day at the school of music, and take me to the theatre or a concert, or we would go somewhere with Bertie. It was a busy time, because I was also ordering the wedding dress, and arranging all kinds of things for the wedding. Then, just two weeks ago today, Jack told me that he had to go away. I have not seen him since.'

'Tell me exactly what happened.'

'I am not likely to forget, Mr Holmes. We were in Bertie's little sitting-room, although my brother was not there. Jack took my hands, and said, "Now Jane, you must listen carefully. You know that during the War I was in secret Government service. I cannot give you details, but with this kind of work there is no such thing as retirement. One may be called on at any time, and that is what has happened. I must not tell you who has approached me or what I have been asked to do, but I have to leave tonight, and may not return for three or four days."

'You will be back for the wedding?'

'He had been serious, but now he threw back his head and

laughed like the Jack I knew. "Oh, my lovely Jane, long before that. You'll hardly know I've been away."

'"Is there danger in what you will be doing?"

'"No more than in crossing the road," he said, and laughed again. Then Bertie came in, and Jack kissed me goodbye, and I have not seen nor heard from him since.'

'Had he said anything more to your brother?'

'Yes. Bertie was reluctant to tell me, but eventually did so. It seems there had been a message from the Foreign Secretary himself, and Jack had been sent on a mission that would take him to either France or Germany. That was all Bertie knew. He said there was no need to worry, Jack could look after himself, but I fear that he is dead. If he were still alive, I am sure he would have found a way to tell me. Then I thought of you, Mr Holmes, and wrote that foolish letter. When I got here I did not dare to put my problem to you at once, I thought you would be so angry. And now, can you give me any hope?'

Holmes had been in a blue study. Now he roused himself. 'There are other houses near Hillerman Hall, are there not? And perhaps it is near the road?'

'Why, yes. It is quite near the road, and there are houses near. All the land is at the back. But what has that to do with Jack's disappearance?'

'Nothing, perhaps.' He rose. 'It is an interesting little problem, and one that should not be difficult to solve, although I greatly fear –' He checked himself. 'But I am theorizing without facts, the grossest of errors. Let me see. Give me fifteen minutes, and I am at your service.'

'But where are we going? To see Bertie in London?'

'I doubt if he could add anything to what he has told you. No, we must visit Mr and Mrs Pringle at their place of retirement in Buckinghamshire.'

In the train up to Victoria, and on the journey out to Beaconsfield, Sherlock Holmes refused to say another word about the case. He talked of music, saying that one of the few things he regretted in his voluntary retirement was the fact that he could no longer visit Covent Garden on a Wagner night or hear a concert at St James's Hall, nor could he drop in casually to one of the Bond Street picture galleries, 'Although indeed I fear that the paintings shown in them reveal the aberrations of modern taste.' He spoke of various tales that were told about him in the district where he lived, that he was related to one of the Kings who had lost their thrones in the Great War, that he was a former monk who still preserved a vow of silence, and that he was a murderer who had been reprieved and released from prison. Then he spoke amusingly of Dr Watson, who was still in reasonable health, although too rheumaticky to venture far from home now, saying that Watson's infallible nose for the wrong solution was almost as valuable as an instinct for the right one. By the time they reached Beaconsfield, his companion found herself laughing at some of his stories, as she had felt that she would never laugh again.

Maple Lodge was a pleasant house on the outskirts of the village. Holmes had announced their forthcoming arrival by telegram, and Tom Pringle, a burly man with a firm handshake, greeted them warmly.

'It's an honour to have the famous Sherlock Holmes in our new home, although I understood you'd retired from practice. Is it something to do with the Hall that you wanted to know? And have you left Captain Rogers behind in London? Is it Mrs Rogers yet, may I ask?'

She blushed and shook her head. Holmes replied. 'One or two questions have arisen about Hillerman Hall, yes.'

'About farming the place, is it? We'd been there near on twenty years, and it's not the easiest place in the world to farm, what with most of the land being on a slope so that drainage is a problem. In the end it got too much for me after I had my stroke. Only a slight one, mind you, but Dr Thomas said, either you give it up or you'll be carried out feet first. But I thought Captain Rogers might have a few problems. He was a pleasant young fellow, but I don't reckon he knew much about farming.'

Jane's blue eyes were bewildered. 'But Jack has all sorts of new ideas. He said the land was perfect for what he had in mind.'

'Did he now, my dear? I wish him joy of it. But I don't see where you come in, Mr Sherlock Holmes.'

'It is a small problem relating to the past history of the house about which I have been consulted,' Holmes said smoothly. 'You say you were there nearly twenty years. There was no break in your occupation? No time when you left the place empty for a while?'

'Never. Running a farm is a full-time job. You don't take weekends off.'

'Nor holidays?'

'No holidays for farmers.'

Mrs Pringle had not spoken. Now she said timidly, 'There was that time, Tom, when we had the big storm and all the top floor ceilings came down.'

'Don't count that a holiday, do you? Had a new roof on, new ceilings, wallpaper, cost a fortune.'

'It wasn't a holiday, but we went away for two weeks while the work was done, don't you remember? And Mr Robinson looked after the place.'

'Bill Robinson from down the road,' Tom Pringle agreed. 'Did his best I daresay, but a fine mess he made of it.'

Holmes leaned forward, his eyes gleaming. 'This was a time when you left the Hall unoccupied? Now, can you tell me the year and the month?'

The Pringles were agreed that the month had been June, and the year 1913. They were bewildered when Holmes said that he had nothing more to ask them, and so was Jane. She asked what all this could have to do with Jack's disappearance.

'It may be that I am on the wrong track, although the signs suggest otherwise. But now, my dear young lady, I propose to put you on a train to Guildford while I pursue my researches.'

She shook her head decisively. 'I shall stay with Bertie. I have already arranged to do so, and told papa and mamma. And Bertie knows that I have consulted you, indeed, it was his idea that I should pose as a journalist. I have the feeling that a communication from Jack might come to Bertie rather than my parents, if he needs help.' To this Holmes made no reply. With a flash of the spirit she had shown when pretending to be a journalist, she said, 'Since I seem to be cast in the role of Dr Watson, and you will not tell me your thoughts, may I at least ask where your research will take you?'

'If I say nothing, it is because I have ideas but no proof, so that they may be moonshine. You ask where I shall go tomorrow. I shall spend part of my time in the newspaper library of the British Museum, and the rest at Scotland Yard. The old hands have gone, Lestrade, Athelney Jones and Gregson, but Stanley Hopkins is still there, and he remembers me well enough to know that I never ask idle questions. Then the answers to those questions may take me further afield. As soon as I have news I shall send a telegram to your brother's rooms.'

The telegram was delivered late on the following evening. It said: 'Shall arrive early tomorrow. Then be ready for short journey. Sherlock Holmes.'

Holmes was as good as his word. It was no more than a minute or two past eight when the bell rang. Bertie answered it, and ushered the detective in.

'Mr Holmes, you look tired. Would you like a whisky, or coffee and an egg? This is a bachelor flat, and my standards are not those of Mrs Hudson, but Jane and I will do our best.'

'Coffee and toast will suit me. I have been travelling much of the night, and age takes its toll.'

While Bertie made breakfast he came in and out of the room, and Holmes saw that the young man was remarkably like his sister, although there was a kind of wildness and irresponsibility about him, where she gave an impression of quiet strength. When they were at the breakfast table he said, 'Come on now, Mr Holmes, let's have it. What have you discovered?'

'The problem is solved, but the last act has still to be played. You are remarkably like your sister. I hope that you love her.'

'Why, I love Janie more than anybody in the world, she knows that.'

'I am glad to hear it. In the days ahead you may be able to comfort her, and undo some of the harm you caused when you introduced her to Jack Rogers.'

She clasped her hands tightly. 'Jack is dead. Is that what you are saying?'

'I almost wish I were saying that. You have been the victim of as cruel a trick as I remember. Laughing Jack Rogers – he has used other names, and sometimes calls himself Colonel or Commander as well as Captain – is one of the best-known confidence men in Britain. He specializes in making up to impressionable women and then robbing them of their savings. When necessary he goes through a marriage ceremony. Scotland Yard has a record on him as long as your arm, and it includes four bigamous marriages. Rogers came out of prison no more than three months ago.'

She put her head in her hands, but when she lifted it her face was composed, her eyes tearless. 'You could not have known this when I first told my story, Mr Holmes.'

'Of course not. What struck me immediately, however, was that yours is a much more than usually simple and credulous family. Here is a man known to none of you, who meets your brother casually, spins him a tale that cannot be checked about doing secret work in the War – work that no genuine agent would ever discuss – and is introduced to a young lady who knows very little indeed of the world and its wickedness. Your parents also are unworldly people, who believe every word the man says, and take it as a positive virtue when he tells them that he has no family and no capital. There is a whirlwind courtship, and he is accepted as a suitor.

'So the circumstances were suspicious. When I looked at the ring he had given you, and saw under the glass that the stones were not diamonds but almost worthless zircons, my doubts were strengthened. Of course if the fact had been noticed he would have said that he lacked the money to buy a diamond ring, and was ashamed to confess it. Was he simply a fortune-hunter? But as you told the story, it seemed that perhaps his object was not marriage, but had something to do with Hillerman Hall.'

'How do you make that out?' Bertie asked.

'Consider the position. He has been accepted, and the search for a suitable home is begun. Several houses are turned down, even though the prospective bride likes them. Hillerman Hall is seized upon, although she thinks it cold and draughty. The quality of the soil is said to be superlative, and yet it must be similar to that of nearby houses that have been rejected. And all this is seen to be nonsense when we learn from Mr Pringle that Rogers knows nothing about farming. Why then does he want the house? Why, when redecoration is suggested, does he say that it should be postponed until you are on your honeymoon?'

Holmes steepled his fingers and looked at them expectantly. 'You will forgive me for regarding this as an intellectual exercise, since seen in that light it has a certain fascination. When I asked myself that question *Why*, I could find no answer except that he wished to gain access to the Hall at a time when nobody else was there. It happens that I have been involved in two cases where an elaborate device was used to get somebody out of the premises they occupied. In the first instance it was to gain entrance to a cellar leading to a bank, in the other an attempt to recover a counterfeiter's outfit and his forged notes. I suspected that something of the same kind applied here, although the circumstances were different in the sense that the house was up for sale. When Rogers learned this he must have looked round for a dupe, somebody he could persuade to buy the place, perhaps in so-called partnership with him. He found you, and through you your sister. You need not reproach yourself too much. He is a most persuasive scoundrel.'

'That fits in with something Jack – Rogers – once said to me,' Bertie commented. 'He told me that he could make a fortune very quickly if he found a partner with some money. It was said in his usual joking way, and he soon saw that I had nothing. And then – I can never forgive myself for the sorrow I have brought on you, Jane.' She bowed her head again, in silence, as he placed his hand on hers. 'But are you saying that he had hidden something there?'

'If you will be good enough to follow my course of reasoning, I shall come to that in a moment.'

'But Mr Holmes,' said the irrepressible Bertie, 'forgive me for saying so, but shouldn't we set off now for Hillerman Hall? We could go in Elsie, she'll take us there quicker than any train.'

'We shall do so all the more quickly, if you will permit me to finish,' the detective said with a touch of asperity. 'I ascertained from Jane that the house was near the road and had neighbours, so that if a thorough search of it had to be made, some caution must be observed. When we learned from the Pringles that the only time they had left the Hall was in 1913, I was confident that a search of the newspapers for that year would bring some answer to the problem of what had been hidden, and so it proved. In June 1913, a daring raid was carried out in the early evening on the Surrey and Sussex Bank at the Reigate branch. The thieves got away with more than twenty thousand pounds in notes, but they were interrupted by the assistant manager, who was beaten about the head and left for dead. He had raised the alarm, however, and the hunt was on. The thieves were caught at New Belton, which is no more than half a mile from Hillerman Hall. There were two of them, Black Ned Silverman and a man named Pascoe, and they got long sentences. Silverman had planned the raid, and got fourteen years. The money was never recovered.'

'So Rogers was not one of the gang,' Bertie said.

'No, he had nothing to do with it. Robbery with violence was not his game.'

'Then how did he know of it?'

'He was in prison with Black Ned, and for a time shared a cell with him. Silverman let slip something about the big job he had done, and said that the money was safely stashed away at Hillerman Hall. I said that Rogers is a persuasive devil.'

'If Rogers knows where the money is, surely he must have it by now.'

'I did not say he knew its location, Black Ned was not careless enough for that. We, however, have the advantage of him.'

Bertie stared open-mouthed. His sister, who had been listening attentively, said, 'Mr Holmes, you are a magician.'

'You flatter me. I have known Black Ned for a long time. Of course I disapprove his way of life, but he is not a bad fellow except for an uncontrollable temper. He trusts me, because I once got him freed on a charge of which he was not guilty. When I learned that he was involved I journeyed down to the Isle of Wight where he is serving his time. The Governor let me see him, and when I gave Black Ned the facts he told me what happened. When he and Pascoe saw that they were bound to be caught, they found this empty house, hid the money there and ran off so that they should not be caught on the spot. Pascoe died in prison, and Ned will not be out for some years yet, so he had little to lose by telling me where the money was located. He knew that Rogers would get it somehow if he was not caught. In any case, he wanted revenge. I should not like to be in Laughing Jack's shoes when Silverman comes out of prison.'

'He has had two weeks to look for the money,' Bertie said. 'How do you know that he has not found it and gone?'

Holmes smiled. 'Because I have been in touch with Inspector Beddoes of the local force, and learned that our man is still there. He works alone, as always, for Jack Rogers trusts nobody, and that limits what he can do each day. But there is an aspect of the affair which I think you do not appreciate, and which has brought me here to tell what I know must be a painful tale. Police action is not possible, for Rogers has committed no criminal offence. The house is one that he expects to occupy himself, and a man can hardly be charged with breaking into and damaging his own property. Once the engagement is broken it is a different matter. So that if you can bear to accompany me –'

The colour on Jane's cheeks was high. 'I should like to see him again. Once, just once.'

Bertie drove Elsie the little Ford with dash, hooting merrily as he passed other cars. At Holmes's suggestion they stopped a few yards away and proceeded on foot. Hillerman Hall was gaunt and tall, a typical specimen of Victorian Gothic with something forbidding about its dull red brick. The entrance was a pointed archway, and above were steepled towers. As they approached they heard the sound of knocking, with something frantic, and even desperate about it.

The massive door opened when they turned the handle, and Jane exclaimed with astonishment as they entered. It looked as though a cyclone had gone through the large entrance hall. Floorboards had been ripped up and electric wires left trailing. A cupboard had been taken to pieces, half of the stair banisters removed and the rail taken away and left on the floor. They went into a room on the right and saw the same trail of devastation. The knocking came from upstairs. Holmes put a finger to his lips and motioned to them to follow him. The sound came from one of the upper front rooms. The door of it was open, and the man inside had levered up some floorboards and was crouched low peering beneath them. A step-ladder stood in one corner.

'You are not likely to have any success there, Rogers,' Sherlock Holmes said. 'You should have wheedled Black Ned into giving you more details.'

The man sprang up with an oath, which was checked when he saw the other visitors. He was no less handsome than his photograph, but the laughing expression in the picture was replaced by a scowl, and then by a look of bewilderment.

'Bertie, Jane, what are you doing here? And who are you?'

'My name is Sherlock Holmes. I was called on by this young lady, because she feared for your safety. You told your tale too well.'

As though by magic, the vicious scowl and the bewilderment were wiped off Rogers's face, and replaced by a charming smile.

'Jane, my dear sweet innocent Jane –'

Her voice was like steel. 'I was innocent, I am so no longer. Is this your Government service?'

He laughed easily. 'Let me explain. You would have thought me ridiculous if I had told you that a fortune might be hidden in the house we had bought. I wanted to surprise you, to be able to say that I was not coming to you empty-handed after all.'

'No use, Rogers,' Holmes said harshly. 'They know the whole story.'

Again a change came over the handsome features, so that the smile was accompanied by a look of calculation. 'I have done nothing against the law.'

'So Mr James Windibank, alias Hosmer Angel, said on another occasion. I agreed, but threatened to thrash him with a horsewhip.'

'I can't say that I see a horsewhip to hand. And I must remind you that this house belongs to my future wife.'

He broke off, because she had removed the ring and thrown it at his feet. 'No longer. There is your worthless ring.'

'It cost a pound or two, but let it lie. And since our engagement is broken, perhaps after all it would be polite to relieve you of my presence.'

'Just a moment,' Sherlock Holmes said. 'You may like to see what you have been looking for so long. When this house was empty it was in need of redecoration, and in particular the upper floor ceilings had come down. The workmen had finished for the day and left their equipment behind them. When Black Ned and Pascoe came in here, on the run, they knew they had not hours but only minutes to find a hiding place, and from what I was told they chose this very room.' Holmes was looking up at the ceiling. 'The ceiling was down, the laths exposed and a few of them loose. It was the work of five minutes to nail them back into place, after slipping the packages of notes above them. You should have thought of the ceilings, Rogers. The north-east corner, Black Ned said. This looks a likely area, where some cracks are showing.'

Holmes took the step-ladder across, got up on it and hacked

away at the cracked place with a chisel until he brought down the plaster. Then, seeing nails that looked newer than the rest, he forced the chisel between them, put his hand in the space he had made, and brought it out holding a bunch of banknotes.

'There are more where these came from and, Bertie, I think your young arm would be well employed in extracting them. I should not be surprised if the Surrey and Sussex Bank made a handsome acknowledgement of their money being returned after all these years. As for you, Rogers, you are now a trespasser on these premises, and if you want to avoid trouble I should make yourself scarce. Your fiancée has had a lucky escape.'

The letter that came to Holmes's cottage a few days later was in a delicate and spidery, yet still characterful, hand. He read:

Dear Mr Holmes,

I do not know how to thank you. You said I knew nothing of the world's wickedness, but I have seen something of it now. Bertie is very ashamed of himself, saying that but for him I should never have become entangled with Jack. He thinks that he is not cut out for stockbroking, and may try his luck in the Colonies. Papa and mamma have been kind and consoling. We are an unworldly family, as you say, and they had never encountered a really bad man before. Neither had I.

As for myself, what can I say? I know the man I loved to be worthless, yet I shall never forget him. I am not sure whether there is any meaning in speaking of a broken heart, but I know that I shall never marry.

This does not lessen my gratitude to you. I shall always remain your devoted admirer . . .

'A trivial little case, with some points of interest, but hardly one for Watson,' Sherlock Holmes said to himself. He put the letter into the thin file containing the other relevant details. The young woman had impressed him by her strength of character as well as by her youthful innocence, and he indexed the case under 'M'. He could not quite read the surname: was it perhaps Mantle or Maple . . . ?